The Honeymoon is Over

The Honeymoon is Over

Annett
HOLLIDAY

POOLBEG

This novel is entirely a work of fiction. The names, characters and incidents portrayed in it are the work of the author's imagination. Any resemblance to actual persons, living or dead, events or localities is entirely coincidental.

Published 2006
by Poolbeg Press Ltd
123 Grange Hill, Baldoyle
Dublin 13, Ireland
E-mail: poolbeg@poolbeg.com

© Annett Holliday 2006

The moral right of the author has been asserted.

Typesetting, layout, design © Poolbeg Press Ltd.

1 3 5 7 9 10 8 6 4 2

A catalogue record for this book is available from the British Library.

ISBN 1-84223-234-7
ISBN 978 1 84223 234 7 (From January 2007)

All rights reserved. No part of this publication may be reproduced or transmitted in any form or by any means, electronic or mechanical, including photography, recording, or any information storage or retrieval system, without permission in writing from the publisher. The book is sold subject to the condition that it shall not, by way of trade or otherwise, be lent, resold or otherwise circulated without the publisher's prior consent in any form of binding or cover other than that in which it is published and without a similar condition, including this condition, being imposed on the subsequent purchaser.

Typeset by Type Design in Berling 10.6/14.5
Printed by Litografia Rosés, Spain

www.poolbeg.com

Also by Annett Holliday

A Life Like Yours

Happily Ever After

Prologue

Perfection. That's what I wanted. The perfect wedding and the perfect bride, and I got it. Well, nearly. It had all gone so perfectly, almost too perfectly. And then it all went pear-shaped. I had almost expected it. It just couldn't last. I suppose I was lucky to have had the dream for as long as I did.

Shit! I don't really mean that. I deserve what everyone else does … happiness.

But anyway – I digress.

There I was … married a matter of hours and sitting in a tear-stained wedding dress wanting to die and wishing my bridegroom a slow painful death. Wishing my life was over because it certainly felt like it. Well, you would too, if your husband of what – say five hours, had his very attractive girlfriend show up and claim him for herself. I know they say marriage doesn't mean much any more, but there is a limit. I mean, you at least expect to get through the wedding day and perhaps the honeymoon before it all falls apart.

But not me!

No, when my life fucks up it just has to be monumental.

Yes – the honeymoon was over even before it had begun …

♥ ♥ ♥

My wedding day had begun so, at the risk of repeating myself, perfectly. In fact it was a flawless June day. The kind you see on television but rarely glimpse in Ireland. I know it's technically supposed to be summer time but talk to any bride who has got married in June, July or August and chances are you'll hear a horror story about hailstorms, downpours or even snow. Pick a day in March and you'll have a sporting chance at a dry day, but not June! But sometimes, some years, June can come up with a mini-heat-wave. So I had taken my chances on that – and won. My wedding day was flawless – weather-wise at least – bright blue sky with the odd fluffy white cotton-wool cloud just for effect. Not even a biting wind.

I was ecstatic, because the horse-drawn carriage depended on calm and my hair was being entwined with baby's breath and required perfect conditions – but that's another story.

The day was flawless and my flowers arrived on

time and were as beautiful as anything I had ever seen. I gave a silent thanks to God for creating such beauty before running upstairs and screaming blue murder at my sister Sandy for hogging the bathroom on the bride. My dress was a designer gown purchased from the most expensive boutique in the country, requiring a four-hour round trip and several thousand euros. How much it actually cost I'm not prepared to admit, even to myself – it's far too scary. However it looked amazing and I looked amazing in it.

By now you have probably gathered that I had turned into some sort of Bridezilla.

Yes, they even have a proper term for it now – it's a type of syndrome where perfectly nice, sane girls turn into shrill witches as soon as the date has been set.

That obviously was what happened to me.

Did I become so focused on the event of my wedding day that I disregarded the most important part: the groom, my childhood sweetheart? Or maybe I wasn't to blame and the fault lay in the fact that Gary Warren was just an absolute bastard? The latter, I believe, is somewhat closer to the truth.

You judge for yourself.

Here is my story.

Chapter 1

My name is Geri Murphy. OK, it's really Geraldine Murphy but I always detested that long, tedious name so I became Geri after the then well-known band member of a certain girl group in the nineties. Well, Geri *Warren* is technically my married name, but I still feel a fool if I ever use it.

Married for two minutes doesn't really qualify you for the title of Mrs Gary Warren. Yet it was what I had always dreamed of from the moment I met Gary in Fifth Year at St Bart's co-ed college in Sutton. He walked into science class and I was instantly in love and so was every other girl in the class. He was at least six feet tall with a long blond mane of hair and the bluest of eyes. But it was the long, slow Brad Pitt smile that was the clincher. I was instantly smitten and, for some strange reason, Gary seemed to only have eyes for me. And from that day onwards we were a couple.

I wasn't the prettiest girl in the class, or the brightest. I'm sort of average. I have ordinary straight black hair and nice brown eyes, I'm told, and a curvy figure and olive skin but when I met Gary I was at least a stone overweight and totally shy. Some people had talent or were pretty. Well, I was Miss Average until I acquired a totally hot boyfriend like Gary Warren. He became my best asset.

As part of a couple with a handsome guy like Gary, I attained a kind of coolness that had previously evaded me. Suddenly everyone wanted to be my friend. I saw people actually look at me differently – they seemed to be watching me, looking at me in a new light. As if they were trying to discover what mysteriousness I had that had attracted an obviously upmarket boyfriend …

I bloody wondered myself. There were far prettier girls in my year, particularly my best friend Amy, who suddenly sprouted from a tiny mousy-haired skinny kid to a five-foot-ten model type who then dyed her hair blonde and blossomed overnight. Amy and Gary would have been the perfect couple. Except for the fact that Amy hated Gary on sight and never changed her mind about him since. Seems like old Amy had maturity beyond her years. Though not when it came to her own choices – she preferred bookish types like Trevor Peyton who was the class nerd, but that's

Amy's story and this is mine though, granted, they do cross paths all the time.

Soon Gary and I were the most popular couple in the crowd and were asked to all the coolest parties and everyone seemed to love him (with the exception of Amy). He had an easy charm to go with the looks and he made friends quickly. The fact that he was failing almost every subject didn't seem to faze Gary or even the teachers for that matter – the mostly female staff seemed not immune to his considerable charms. Good looks get you places or so it seemed back then. It certainly worked for Gary.

And it worked on me. I loved the guy like no other girl ever loved anyone. The term "welcome mat" could have been coined for me.

Every wish or merest whim that Gary expressed became my mission in life. I made myself indispensable and literally propelled him into love with me. The fellow hadn't a chance because I was, underneath it all, a determined little fiend.

I lost my surplus stone through pure lust and love (in that order) and began to blossom myself. A bit of Gary's beauty rubbed off on me, I suppose. I know I gleamed with love because you can still see it in the photographs of that time – the ones that survived my scissor-cutting frenzy at least: but more about that later.

Right then, I was in love with Gary by the second date. He enveloped me – that's the only way I can describe it. I went from an average-looking girl who had the odd, usually nerdy admirer to being love-bombed by the new Sex God of the Fifth Year. Gary was sweet and attentive, picked me wild flowers, took me to the school disco and didn't even glance at the other prettier girls. He wore the coolest leather jacket I had seen on anyone since *Grease* and I was toast – well, who wouldn't be?

So I acquired a certain cachet and people started to notice I had a brain and a witty turn of phrase and in turn how pretty Amy was. It was so nice being finally cool, even if it was only by association. Amy and I were used to being outsiders, me always conscious of my wobbly bum and chunky thighs while Amy said she felt like a lanky giraffe because she towered over most of the boys. We weren't popular like Serena Wilson, who rumour had it put it around quite a lot in a rebellion against her three older sisters who had ended up as nuns (can't say I blame her), or beautiful like Michelle Carey who went on to model internationally. Amy and I were invisible until I met super-cool Gary.

A year later we all graduated from school. Amy and I took business courses – more to stave off the thought of having to get an actual job than to improve our chances – while Gary went to work for his father, Gary Senior, who owned a second-hand car yard. Hey, I know it's a cliché – would I buy a used car from that man and all the usual used-car salesman jokes – but I was only eighteen and in love, and him being a car salesman seemed ultra-cool at the time. Soon Gary was wearing flashy suits and driving a sports car (albeit second-hand) and eventually my parents seemed to gain a grudging acceptance of him.

My parents were straightforward, old-fashioned but loveable people I found difficult to spend any length of time with.

My dad, Eddie, a security guard, hardly ever peeks from behind his newspaper and my mum, Joanne – well, Mum cleans for Ireland, when she's not gossiping for it, that is. Mum is hardly ever spotted without a can of Mister Sheen in her hand or a look of martyrdom on her pretty face. Mum is pretty when she smiles, which isn't too often, and she's got a lovely slim figure that I, for one, envy. She's always been a slender size eight and can't quite figure out why I've never been. I don't know if they are happy, but they seem to rub along well enough. Dad just seems a little bit weary most of the time. Like something passed him by, something he still misses. I often wonder what that was.

Mum found out pretty soon that Gary Senior had a bit of a glad eye and that Gary's mum had her hands full with her errant husband all through their married life. Mum muttered darkly about apples not falling far from trees – codewords for her theory that if Gary Senior played away from home then Gary Junior might do the same. She should have tackled me about that possibility then and there – it might have saved a lot of heartache later on. However, perhaps I wouldn't have listened. The last time I took any heed of what my mother said was when I wore knee socks and played skipping-rope for kicks.

My dad had no sons, just myself and Sandy and Mum – a houseful of women – so he looked favourably upon Gary after about six months of being jealous of his flash car and worrying about his obvious attraction to his eldest daughter. Eventually they shared the odd pint and went off to local football matches together.

But Mum seemed inured to Gary's blarney and kept a frosty distance.

Sandy is my younger sister – well, her real name is Josephine actually (can you blame her wanting to change that moniker?). The only person who now calls her Josephine is my mother – even Dad calls her Sandy though he doesn't know how she got that nickname. It was garnered in her teens from her frequent sojourns on Dollymount strand with a succession of lovers and the consequent acres of sand that got into her nether regions. If Dad ever knew that, I think he'd have a heart attack on the spot. I think he believes Sandy took her name from his favourite character in *Grease* and likes to think our Sandy is just as innocent. If only he knew – Sandy is one sexy lady who knows what she's got and is not afraid to use it on whomever she fancies.

"He's a right ride," she commented on Gary at first. But after a while she seemed to think he wasn't all he seemed. "Jumped-up asshole" I think was the term she used.

But I didn't care. Sandy was legendary for her jealousy and I'd had years of her hating and then trying to steal my boyfriends. What is it about younger sisters?

So it didn't bother me too much.

But Amy's disliking Gary did matter to me.

I tried to talk to her.

"It's not for me to say," Amy said from under her blonde fringe.

"Amy, you are my best friend," I pleaded. "I honestly told you I felt Trevor was a total smug nerdo and beneath you, so why can't you do the same for me?"

Amy blushed. Despite our long friendship she was such a nice girl she couldn't bear to ever hurt my feelings. "OK. I think Gary takes you for granted, Geri. You're at his beck and call twenty-four-seven and yet he seems to do exactly what he pleases. You seem so wrapped up in him that you barely notice me any more and we only seem to go out whenever Gary is busy or Gary is too tired to take you out on a Friday night!"

"Meow! Get that girl a saucer of milk from the bar," I sniffed. "I know I told you to tell me how you really felt, but did you have to do it so effectively?"

Amy didn't even give me her customary smile that usually greeted my witty barbs. Her green eyes flashed with annoyance. I could tell she meant business.

"Well, you've almost forgotten me, and, Geri, you seem to have also forgotten that I am your best friend. I will be there when Gary breaks your heart and I will be the one who picks up the pieces."

"So I guess I'd better treat you right then," I replied kindly, touching her hand. Though deep inside I burned with hurt and anger. How could Amy ever think that Gary would hurt me? Why couldn't anyone see his good points?

Yes, OK, I'll freely admit I was a twenty-four-carat idiot. I know now that if it looks like a duck and quacks like a duck then it's probably a duck, but back then, despite all these warning signs from those most important to me, I cheerfully ignored them, preferring to believe that everyone else just simply misunderstood the gorgeous Gary. As they say: "Love is blind but the neighbours ain't."

I tried to keep my relationship with Amy onside while trying to see Gary as much as I could, which wasn't always easy. I often felt torn. It was like the great cold war between them and as I loved them both dearly I often felt stressed and pulled each way. I was so besotted by Gary and so insecure when he was anywhere outside my immediate view that I fretted and moped when I wasn't with him. Yet Amy was my dearest friend and I had a great deal of loyalty to her too, so I trudged along to all the late bars on our girlie nights out, pretending to enjoy myself but not quite managing it. Without Gary by my side, I became ordinary Geri again, the one with the rugby player's thighs and the pleasant but unremarkable face, and the truth was that Amy looked so model-girl-gorgeous I felt even plainer and somewhat envious when I was with her. I could never admit it to her, though – she'd be devastated. Amy didn't even believe she was remotely pretty and seemed oblivious to the admiring stares of every guy who came into contact with her. My secret envy was my deep shame and I felt awful for it but there it was. Perhaps that's why I loved Gary so much and loved being with him – I felt better, more self-assured, whereas when Amy and I went out she invariably got all the attention and I felt like boring old Geri again. I was the plainer friend who seemed to get the less interested buddy of the smitten one. We've all been there: you're sitting in a bar and having a few drinks and then two blokes approach and you just know that the nice one will pursue your friend and you'll be left trading polite conversation with his plainer disinterested mate. So I suppose my deep insecurity and paranoia about my dubious attractiveness made me cling to my relationship even deeper. Gary became my life … or a replacement for one.

Chapter 2

Nine years later . . .

"Mum, Mum! I've got something to tell you, Gary's popped the question. We're getting married!"

I ran through the house like a woman possessed. My mother rushed in from the back yard where she was hanging out a load of washing.

"Jesus, Mary and Joseph! Don't put the heart crossways in me, Geraldine Murphy!

"Did I hear you correctly? Gary Warren *actually* asked you to marry him? You're not pregnant, are you?" A look of alarm crossed her face, replacing the earlier look of shock and disbelief.

My heart sank. Would I be able to carry the charade off, could I convince my mother who had guessed at every lie I had ever told that my true love had proposed out of the blue on his own without eighteen months of threats promised and ultimatums issued?

I smiled broadly, brightly. "No, Mum. I'm not pregnant. Gary loves me and he wants to marry me. Aren't you happy for me?"

Mum stifled a look of incredulous disbelief. "Yes, love. If you are happy then I am. About bloody time, though." She sniffed crossly.

And it was.

She had no idea of the campaign I had to carry out to get Gary to finally ask me to be his wife. And she never would know if I had anything to do with it.

"I'll make us a nice cuppa, so," Mum said then, which was codeword for: I'll coax the truth out of you after I ply you with copious amounts of hot tea and your favourite biscuits.

I winced visibly. I knew the story would go down better if Gary had fronted up with me and braved the usual grilling, but the coward had opted to tell his own incredulous parents instead and we'd decided that we'd meet up later and exchange horror stories.

After nine and a half years together both sets of parents had long since given up on us ever getting our act together and naming the day. I almost had myself until my final ultimatum worked.

We'd had our usual pizza dinner and a movie followed by a quick fumble up on Howth Head.

"Gary!" I complained. "I am truly sick of conducting my sex life in this car, however nice it might be. Why can't we at least go for a house or get an apartment together? This is all getting a bit too tedious. I really can't go on with it any more."

Gary laughed, running his hands through his long blond hair. "I suppose you're right. Functioning in this cramped space is giving me back trouble! How about it then?"

I rolled my eyes heavenwards. "Not again, Gary, I'm knackered."

He laughed again. "No, you silly goose, I'm saying how about you and I getting into the whole house/mortgage thing? I mean, I give in, I'll marry you if you like. We may as well, we're not getting any younger – thirty is looming in another few years."

I was incredulous.

It wasn't the most romantic proposal I have ever heard of, but I was so shocked that Gary was even entertaining the idea of marriage after all the years we had been together, and all the countless times I had hinted then later threatened him, that now he had actually voiced a sort of proposal I was stunned into absolute silence.

Gary's smile evaporated, the bright-blue eyes looked forlorn and my heart did back-flips. Why did he have to always look so delicious?

"Geri, if you've gone off the idea just say so, but please just say something, will ya? You're making me nervous here."

I took his handsome face in both my hands and kissed him softly and passionately.

"Yes," I replied at last when we surfaced for air.

"Yes, Gary Warren, of course I will marry you, whenever and wherever you like."

And that was it.

It was about the most romantic Gary ever got. After that he never mentioned going to a jeweller's and buying a ring or even discussed any plans to actually save for the wedding or a mortgage.

So I had to.

I dragged him off to the jeweller's and we chose a nice ring from the not-too-expensive category and Gary kissed me sweetly when we chose it, but other than that he entered into the new world of a fiancé like a duck to, well, let's say the plum sauce – rather reluctantly.

It didn't matter, because I became more than excited enough for the both of us.

"So, where did he propose?" Mum now interrupted my thoughts as she poured out the tea.

I rallied my mind. "Up on Howth Head. It was so romantic, Mum. The sun was going down and it was a perfect evening and then Gary went down on bended knee and popped the question."

"Hmm," murmured my mother in her don't-believe-a-word-of-it tone. "And when is the big day? Have you set a date?"

"Well, we were thinking about next June," I lied. God, I was getting good at this. Lying to order and on the spot to boot. "That'll give us just under a year."

Mum pursed her lips. She was eyeing me chewing

on my third biscuit. I could see her mind thinking: She'll never fit into anything decent if she keeps stuffing herself with those fattening things!

"You'll need it! For the church booking and the reception, I mean." She then leaned forward and whispered conspiratorially. "You know that your father and myself have a bit of money put aside, for you and Josephine, for your weddings, that is. It may not be enough with the cost of getting married these days – I expect those Warrens will want a big splash – they're so flashy and all – but we have a few thousand. We'll have to get together with Gary and his parents and get their ideas on the whole planning of the wedding."

I felt a mixture of panic and excitement. Panic at the idea of my mum and Pamela Warren trading snide comments over the Mikado biscuits in our tiny living room and excitement at the idea that this was going to be my big chance to be the centre of attention – my Big Day. I couldn't wait!

Mum could have read my mind. She glanced around the living room with a look of distaste. "Jesus, I'll have to get your father to redecorate this room. I don't want that snooty Pamela Warren looking down her nose at our family."

"She's not like that, Mum." I tried one more big fat lie, as I was on a roll.

Pamela Warren was the biggest social climber and most histrionic woman I had ever met. I knew my mother and her would be absolute enemies when they finally met. Strangely enough, despite all the years Gary and I had been together, our parents had never encountered each other. I had made sure of it because I quite detested the sight of Pamela Warren, so I knew my mother would like her even less. Pamela was a nightmare of a mother. In order to retain Gary Senior's attentions, she dyed her hair a brash blonde and wore ever shorter and shorter skirts. She dressed like a tartish twenty-year-old and, despite their increasing affluence, she still shopped at the cheap end of the market.

But worst of all was her high-pitched, grating voice and her territorial attitude to her "Garys" as she termed them. "My Garys are my life/world/universe ... My Garys will only eat prime steak/caviar/lobster ... My Garys are so handsome/clever/witty ..." It was enough to make you hurl. If I hadn't loved Gary so much I would have detested him. Still, I wasn't marrying the awful Pamela and I was sure I could handle an occasional visit without throttling her – after all, I had managed so far. The idea of Pamela being my future children's doting grandmother, fronting up in a Jordan-style sexy mini to their birthday parties, was a nightmare I just didn't want to envisage. So I shut my eyes to her cellulite thighs and varicose veins and hoped that by the time we eventually had rug-rats she would have given in to making herself decent – clothes-wise at least.

So I now crossed my fingers and hoped that my mother would find some level of civility with which to encounter the awful Pamela not to mention the groping Gary – Gary Senior, that is. Back then I didn't realise that Gary Junior was so much his father's son but I couldn't believe that Gary Senior was such a sleaze. At his car yard he was nicknamed "The Octopus" for obvious reasons and I even got the odd slap on the bum in a so-called playful way. He didn't make me feel too uncomfortable, probably because I could see that he had been as handsome as Gary and still was quite attractive and he was obviously used to a lot of female attention in his day. It probably was a bit of a shock when he turned fifty and suddenly started to lose his appeal. So deep down I felt a little sad for Gary Senior, but even so I still kept my distance when we spent any time together and made sure my ample bum was never within slapping distance.

But right now I was even more horrified if possible at my mum having to encounter Gary's roaming hands than Pamela's open brashness and rumoured fake boobs.

"Er, Mum – there's plenty of time for you and Gary's parents to get together, maybe after we book the date with the church and suss out a few hotels. Anyway, I thought you wanted Dad to redecorate this room beforehand."

Mum looked disparagingly at the much-painted

woodchip walls that had been so trendy back in the seventies – a mere thirty years ago – God, had Dad ever properly decorated since I was born?

"Jesus, I'll need months to convince him to change this room. Yes, you're probably right, there's no rush. We'll get together with them after Christmas. I'll get your father to re-wallpaper the room before then."

Thus placated, Mum went back to the much nicer task of stuffing herself and me with biscuits and planning wedding dresses.

Chapter 3

Somehow, somewhere, between all the bridal magazines and the fuss and flurry of visiting hotels and scanning menus, I became obsessed with getting married. Not the *actual* marriage, you understand, no – that gained barely a gram of attention – just the detail of *getting* married. And I do mean the detail, every last detail – every last detail except noticing that my prospective bridegroom was slipping away from me.

But back then it was all shantung silk or silver service. Should it be the lamb or the beef, would the bridesmaids wear blue or silver, could I get my parents and Gary's parents to survive meeting each other without World War III breaking out – that sort of thing.

We couldn't put it off any longer: the day came

when we had to get the opposing sides together and bash out an agreement about keeping the seven tribes from coming to our wedding. It seemed that Gary Senior wanted to invite everyone who had ever bought a car from him, while Pamela invited anyone who was a client in her awful hairdressing salon. Mum had dug up old aunties that I would have sworn had been deceased for several decades and Dad had invited everyone down at the pub one night when he was jarred. It was seriously turning into a cast of thousands and myself and Gary (well, me really – Gary just went along with things while making stupid jokes about balls and chains and losing his freedom) decided we'd get the parents all together on neutral ground to crunch the numbers.

We settled on a nice middle-of-the-road restaurant that we hoped would offend no one – Eddie Wong's on the coast road halfway between Gary's nice posh house in Portmarnock and our less salubrious abode in Sutton. Everyone loved Chinese food and we were going to pay the bill, so Gary Senior wouldn't get a chance to flash his fat wallet around and make my dad feel inferior.

The evening was a disaster.

Pamela arrived in a low-cut spangled number, flashing equal amounts of cleavage and thigh, which left my sensible mother agape and fiddling with her sedate navy suit. My dad almost fell into Pamela's ample chest while Gary Senior held on to my mother for far too long in an overfriendly embrace. Gary remained equable and seemingly unaware of my mother's dismay at his own mother's Page 3 appearance and his father's Don Juan antics. My dad tried to be friendly at first with Gary Senior until Gary Senior offered to pay half the wedding costs. I could see my father literally fuming over his dim sums.

Pamela gushed at my mother that we should all have our hair done at her salon for the wedding, while she eyed my long hair scraped back into a ponytail and described her vision for a creation of Pre-Raphaelite curls.

"I could do wonders with her, Joanne – and yourself, of course – touch up that grey if you know what I mean!"

Mum gritted her teeth. "We have our own hairdresser in the family actually, thanks, Pamela – my cousin to be exact. And I prefer to age gracefully – we don't want to be mutton dressed as lamb, do we? After all, it's a day for the young ones." She then smiled a fake smile to match Pamela's frozen one.

I realised soon it would be handbags at dawn if I didn't rescue the situation.

"We saw a lovely hotel the other day," I blustered. "It might actually be the one. It's up in Cavan and it's this really traditional castle in fabulous grounds …"

"*Cavan?*" Pamela screeched incredulously, like I'd proposed Outer Mongolia. "You'll never get the

Warren crowd up to the wilds of Cavan! They think a trip past Howth is a bridge too far. All the Warrens and my family, the Sullivans, are townies. You'll just have to have it in Dublin, and that's all there's to it."

Gary tried to interrupt. "Mum, I think it's my wedding, mine and Geri's – we'll decide where we have it."

"Well, you'll be having it without me and your father!" Pamela blazed and stood up suddenly and tore off to the ladies'.

I looked at Gary and then my mum.

"Well, I'm not going after her!" my mum snapped. She had obviously had enough.

Gary Senior looked up from his chow mein. "Oh no, what's wrong with her *now*?" he whined, while turfing another forkful of food into his mouth.

"Geri, will you go get her?" Gary pleaded with me.

The words "Get stuffed!" were on my lips – in fact I almost did say it and I should have, because our wedding was none of the old hag's business, but of course I didn't. I played the loving fiancée to the hilt and reluctantly went and fetched the overgrown middle-aged child from the bathroom where she was applying yet another tonnage of mascara.

"I'm going home now," she announced calmly. "I'm too upset to stay any longer."

She didn't look in the least bit upset, I realised. In fact she looked quite in control and a little bit victorious if anything. I knew Pamela was a right pain in the arse but I had never realised before that she wasn't on my side – and it was a bit of a shock.

"I always knew you weren't good enough for my Gary," Pamela announced sweetly to me in the mirror while reapplying her lipstick. "But tonight has proved it. You and your square parents are not our types. I only hope our Gary realises it before it's too late. Don't expect any help from me with your stupid wedding – and if you mention to Gary anything of what I've said here, I'll deny it and you'll look a fool."

To say I was gobsmacked was an understatement. I pondered for a few seconds on how to react to Pamela while a cold fury filled me entirely.

I could have torn her peroxide hair from her head, but then that would have made me no better than her after all, so I decided against it. Her insults, however, would not go unpunished, but I decided I would wait for my revenge.

"You're not worth half of my parents!" I snapped. "And what you call square most people would just call fully clothed. Now you can take your underdressed carcass wherever you want because I couldn't give two stuffs! Fortunately, or maybe unfortunately for you, I am marrying your son whatever you say – and it would be that much nicer if you weren't there. But suit yourself, Pamela, you usually do!"

And with that I flounced out proudly.

Pamela meekly followed and finished her meal in

total silence – in fact we all finished our meals in an awkward quiet before Gary hurriedly paid the bill and my parents swiftly departed.

Mum didn't even bother to say goodbye to the Warrens but poor old Dad tried his best to wave to them in a friendly manner while chasing my mother down the stairs.

"That went well," Gary murmured ominously while I silently fumed, dying to tell him what his awful mother had said to me – yet I was just anxious to get out of there and go home. How was I supposed to become part of Gary's family when his mother patently disliked me and it was clear that our family wasn't welcome in the Warrens' weird little world?

I overheard Pamela hiss the word "Bitch!" to her husband as we went down the stairs onto the street. I'm sure Gary overheard too because he blushed and steered me away by the arm and led me quickly to his car. He then went back to the restaurant entrance and I saw him gesticulate wildly at his parents while his father put his hand on his arm as if to placate him. For a moment I pitied my fiancé for having to endure that awful pair of fools for parents. He really was unlucky. But I was still very angry at what had transpired and I hoped that Gary would put his foot down and make sure that the wedding remained ours and didn't become the property of bloody Pamela Warren. If he didn't there was going to be trouble ahead – that was for bloody sure.

Gary got into the car eventually and seemed to be just as angry as I was.

"My old dear is very annoyed with you and your mother," he said in an injured tone.

"What!" I exploded. "The nerve of the old bag!"

"Geri, that's my mother you're talking about. And she says that your mother insulted her hairdressing skills and practically called her mutton dressed as lamb."

I was amazed that the bold Pamela had made such a quick recovery into bitch mode – I could see I had a worthy opponent. She had managed to start the row and then turn it all around and make it appear to be my fault.

"Gary, your mother bitchily told my mother she could fix her grey hair. You saw how she told us where we were going to have *our* wedding. And she practically attacked me in the ladies' when I went to fetch her. She told me I wasn't good enough for you and she hoped our wedding would never go ahead."

Gary frowned and shook his head. "I find that hard to believe, Geri. I know my mother isn't the calmest of individuals but she's not cruel. She would never insult you like that. Are you sure you just didn't take her up wrongly? You know how ditzy you can be."

I was really angry now. How could Gary disbelieve me and on top of that call me ditzy – me, the one whose boss called her Little Miss Organised. At work I was the one everyone depended on, the lynchpin of

Oswald and Osborne Architects. In work I flourished and felt supremely confident running the office, but when I was with Gary I was undermined and made feel inadequate and now I was being termed as a ditzy chick.

"Let me out of the car, Gary." I said this in a calm voice but the tone was of steel.

Gary frowned theatrically. "For God's sake, Geri! You're not going to blow this out of all proportion, are you? All I said was –"

"*Gary!*" I shrieked. "All you said was I was some ditzy idiot that obviously couldn't comprehend when someone was insulting her – namely your awful mother. Now if that is the way that you really feel, then I would prefer to find my own way home." Gary stopped the car abruptly.

I was shocked he actually listened but I had to follow it through since I'd called his bluff, so I got out of the car and slammed the door nice and hard and he sped off like he was at Mondello racetrack and I had to go find a cab.

This wedding business wasn't all it was cracked up to be and I began to realise that getting married into the Warren family wasn't going to be a picnic either.

I had never seen Gary so hostile to me before – and it wasn't a nice feeling. All I had wanted him to do was listen to my side of the story and take me in his arms and say it was all OK, that what we planned was what mattered. But he hadn't and looking back now it was at that moment I should have heard the alarm bells about his commitment to me, but of course I didn't. I just fretted and fumed all night in my lonely bed after I eventually crawled in, freezing from walking half an hour up the coast road looking for a taxi.

I lay there and wondered how could I fix the debacle my wedding was becoming.

Chapter 4

The following day I went to work exhausted from a fitful night tossing and turning and worrying about where the wedding was going to be. Was Gary's awful mother going to have her way and were we going to have the wedding in the middle of the city centre to suit her, or was Gary going to finally see sense and take my side in things? After all, it was my father who would be footing most of the bill. I had some savings, which I had built up over the past few years for our dream home together, but of course Gary hadn't saved a penny (a fact that had also been the cause of many an argument in the past).

I got to work on the dot of nine despite my exhaustion. Dave Oswald and Connor Osborne were the two architects that were partners and owners of Oswald & Osborne in Fitzwilliam Square. I had worked for them forever, ever since I had finished my secretarial course with Amy. The company was small but frenetic and I basically ran the office, did all the bookkeeping and nagged the two busy architects almost like a surrogate wife.

So they needed me to be on top form every day and mostly I was. But today my heart was heavy as I imagined another row with Gary over his insensitivity and the wedding of my dreams that was suddenly turning into a nightmare.

Connor was already in. A workaholic, he lived for his job and he was a very good architect. As a husband, however, he wasn't so competent. His wife, April, had left him a year previously and went back to London where they had met. Connor seemed gutted at the time but never really discussed what had gone wrong. The fact that he worked sixty-hour weeks probably had something to do with it.

"Hi, Geri, how's the head?" Connor poked his head into my office, smiling. His black hair was wild and woolly as always and the amber-brown eyes mischievous.

"The head's fine," I said, forcing myself to smile. "It's the heart that's not doing so well."

"Oh dear!" Connor shook the woolly head. "Hang on two secs and I'll brew us both a coffee and you can tell me all about the old reprobate heart."

I smiled again, this time feeling it.

Connor was a good friend as well as a fine boss.

He'd been through most of my rocky romance with Gary and I had listened and spent many a drunken night crying and laughing with him nursing his broken heart when April first left him. He had heard all there was to hear about Gary and me and somehow was able to give me a male perspective while never being judgemental. He was eight years older than me but was so young in his attitude he was almost like the big brother I never had and I was extremely fond of him.

"So, what is it this time? Gary lose another comb?" Connor quipped, as he returned with two steaming cups of coffee and sat down on the corner of my desk.

I laughed. "No, I'm afraid it's the in-laws – or should I say the outlaws? We've got wedding trouble and the groom seems unaware that his mother has a whole other agenda, i.e. to prevent it happening."

Connor smiled grimly. "I never knew a wedding yet that didn't scare the bejesus out of the groom. We don't have the same attitudes and passions for it that you women do. We just want to turn up on the day and have the party with no hassles, and we couldn't give a stuff what you wear – in fact we'd probably be happiest if you drifted up the aisle wearing very little. And as for the in-laws, well, when you marry Gary unfortunately you get the whole package and that means all his family too. What way you react to them is another story."

I groaned. "Sometimes I just wish he was an

orphan. Still, you're right, I can't let them get to me. I just have to remain calm and make my own plans. I'll have to be clever with Gary, though – he has a blind spot where his mother is concerned."

"And what man doesn't?" Connor answered. "Look, Geri, even if you hate her guts and she hates yours, it's unfair to put Gary in the middle. All you have to do is be reasonable – then when *she* isn't he will realise eventually that you're the one he has to please."

I smiled widely and nodded, murmuring thanks. But deep inside I wondered did I really want a clever little propaganda war between me and my fiancé's vacuous mother for years until eventually I got the dubious honour of being in the right? I doubted if I could live that way, so I resolved not to let this momentary cold war between our families progress any further than it had to, even if that meant being civil to the awful Pamela. For a brief moment I wished fervently I had asked Gary to elope to Cuba or the Caribbean – it certainly would have been a lot simpler. But deep down I knew I *wanted* the big splashy wedding – that hadn't changed, and I would do what I had to do to get it.

Later on that morning I got a telephone call from Gary.

"Hi, are you talking to me yet?"

"All depends," I replied snippily. "What have you got to say for yourself?"

"Last night was a disaster, wasn't it? I'm sorry we had to fight. Seems like too much grief if you ask me. All this fuss over a wedding."

"Hmm," I replied, while crunching a paperclip between my gritted teeth. It helped stop me screaming at my future husband that his family were a bunch of trolls and he was their troll idiot son.

"Something good came out of it, though," Gary blathered on, oblivious to my silence, which was never a good thing. "Dad has offered us some money for a place of our own, seeing as your dad wants to pay for the wedding. Dad felt he should offer us a gift of cash for our present. It'll make getting our own apartment a lot easier."

Suddenly I was interested. Between the exorbitant house prices and Gary's reluctant saving policy I feared we'd never afford a place of our own.

"That sounds good," I replied guardedly, resisting the urge to ask how much.

"Yes," Gary breezed, sounding smug. "I knew the old man would come good eventually. He's given us twenty-five thousand euro, but it has to be used for the deposit on a house. And before you go getting all upset, I think that rule is more for my benefit than yours – Dad more or less said so."

My mind raced. Twenty-five thousand euro was more than I had ever seen or imagined in my bank account. It would make life a lot easier. We used to visit show homes and I would just drool in sheer longing and frustration at the idea of trying to get a mortgage. Now it all seemed possible. If we put our heads together and I used my savings too we just might be able to afford one of those little apartments we had seen at Kinsealy. My heart filled with a joy I hadn't felt since Gary had proposed.

"This is fantastic news, Gary, and it is extremely kind of your father to do this for us. I'll make an appointment with the bank. I am so excited last night doesn't seem so important now. God! There is so much to do and to plan, first a wedding and now a home. I can't quite believe it!"

"Well, believe it, Geri. Finally we get to have our own space. I knew that the old man was going to give me some money eventually for a pad, but I didn't know how much or when he was finally going to give in."

Something about that comment sent a little chill up my spine. The fact that Gary's father finally *gave in,* as Gary said, made it sound like Gary had been putting pressure on his dad to give him money. And I wondered why.

Gary had never mentioned anything to me about putting any pressure on his father for money towards a house – in fact, it always seemed that I was the one who wanted to get a place for us in the past. I had literally dragged Gary along to visit all the endless show homes in the past year. But perhaps I was being paranoid? Maybe Gary was looking for financial help from his dad in order to surprise me. Anyway, I decided not to look a gift horse in the mouth and I was tired of fighting. This was really wonderful news.

"Does your mother know about this?" I enquired as sweetly as I could. I just couldn't help myself – I was afraid of strings. Strings that meant Pamela would have control over my wedding, a fate worse than death.

There was a brief silence.

"You're not on about my mother again, are you?" Gary eventually said testily.

I swallowed hard. "Em, no … it's just that I really like the castle in Cavan and I don't want to have to change the wedding plans just because there is the gift of money from your parents."

There, I'd said it. I knew it was a potentially explosive comment but I just had to know what I was dealing with.

"I just don't believe you, Geri! We get this fantastic gift from my mother and father and you just have to twist it all into some conspiracy! Do you really think my mother is that interested in this wedding? People have *lives*, Geri! They don't spend every waking moment thinking about our bloody wedding day – everyone, that is, except you. Jesus, Geri, will you bloody cop on to yourself? Do you realise how you sound? Here I am, all excited with the news of the apartment, and all you can think of is negative things. Just call me when you get over yourself, will you?"

And with that Gary slammed down the phone. It was the most he had ever spoken to me over the phone in eight years and it had to be a lecture. I sat staring at the phone for a minute.

Was Gary right?

I felt awful. I probably should have kept my mouth shut at least for a few days until Gary had enjoyed the excitement of the money gift and we could have gone to see the apartments again at Kinsealy. Instead I managed to alienate him and made the wedding situation even more tenuous. Why did I always have to put my big size sevens into it and ruin everything? I'd managed to turn a wonderful moment into something sinister. How could I suspect his parents' motives? Well, quite easily actually – Pamela's at least. Gary's dad's motives were too close to his trouser legs to be of any threat. But still. I was a bit of a bitch. And making up with Gary wouldn't be easy.

As it happened, I didn't get too much time to think about the row, as the day was even more hectic than usual.

Connor and Dave were just putting the finishing touches to their biggest project yet, a huge financial building in Donnybrook called the Matheson Centre that would put them on the map and into the big time. So things were even more frantic than ever.

Things went wrong all afternoon with proof

drawings and reports and eventually I sloped out of there exhausted some time after six, depressed over that horrible row with Gary and bone tired.

Then suddenly I remembered another phone call I had earlier received from Amy, reminding me of an earlier promise to sew her a dress for a hot date she was having with her latest drippy boyfriend. I loved sewing – in fact it was a favourite hobby and had been for years – ever since my mum bought me my own sewing machine, which was a mini-version of hers. I ran up clothes like other people had hot dinners and I was good at it, but lately, since the wedding planning, I had little time to indulge in it and tonight especially I was too exhausted to do much.

But I couldn't let Amy down. I had stuffed things up with Gary so I needed my best friend Amy to sound things out with.

♥ ♥ ♥

Amy arrived at my place around eight for a fitting.

Mum and Dad were off out to see a play and Sandy was out with one of her many admirers so we had the place to ourselves. I cracked open a bottle of Merlot while I pinned my latest creation to Amy's slender model-girl frame. It was a flowing chiffon dress in a buttery cream, with long bell sleeves and a deep V-neck, which showed off Amy's perfect figure. I knew she would look fabulous in it. In fact, the dress would be entirely wonderful but wasted on Amy's latest geek – a guy called George, who was a professional student who seemed to drift from one degree to the next – when he wasn't protesting, that was. George protested against animal cruelty, university fees and even library charges. He was even weirder than Amy's usual guys and I failed to see the attraction. But somehow Amy seemed more enamoured than she usually was. I just couldn't fathom it. George didn't even seem particularly grateful that Amy was his stunning girlfriend – in fact he seemed quite casual and cool about her. It was Amy who made all the running – called him and even paid for the dates, mostly. The amazing dress was for a ball that they were attending in Amy's work. Amy had a glamorous job in PR that meant attending lots of functions and George was happy to attend those that had a free bar or any others, as long as Amy paid for his new shirt and trousers. Yet Amy blissfully plodded along, seemingly content.

Over several glasses of wine I told Amy about my row with Gary.

"Oh, Geri, you didn't!" Amy exclaimed, when I told her about my accusation that his father's gift was a Trojan horse and really a ruse by his parents to control the wedding. *My* wedding.

"Afraid so," I admitted, rolling my eyes heavenwards. I knew I had overdone it for sure when Amy reacted like that. Normally she murmured "good enough for him" whenever I gave her details about any of our rows.

Amy sipped her wine thoughtfully. "Do you not think you were a bit ... *paranoid*?"

I tried to explain myself. "You have no idea of Pamela Warren, Amy. I told you how she basically told me out straight that her Gary was too good for me and she hoped the wedding would never take place. There is nothing I would put past that woman – even pushing money at Gary to get him onside."

Amy grimaced. I could see she thought I had finally lost the plot. "But wasn't it Gary's father who offered the money? And wasn't it for your apartment – not for the wedding at all? They are entirely separate things and it was an extremely generous offer. I actually don't blame Gary for being mad at you – for once I am on his side. You're going to have to eat humble pie on this one, I'm afraid. At least if you want that gorgeous apartment out in Kinsealy, that is."

I had a brief nightmarish moment thinking of Gary buying the Kinsealy apartment alone and me sharing another forty years with the oldies, ending up a dried-up old spinster. "OK, you're probably right. I'll call him later and do that fake apology thing. That usually works."

"You'd better make it good," Amy laughed.

I wasn't looking forward to it. I opened another bottle of wine – some things were best done while a bit squiffy.

"I hope you're not going to do any more sewing later," Amy piped up, eyeing the bottle.

"I will if ye don't shut up and tell me all the latest on Redser."

Amy laughed. "He's not a redser, Geri – you know right well he's a ginge."

"He's a geek!"

"Hey, Missy, looks aren't everything as you well know!"

"I know nothing of the sort! Now tell me all about the Not So Gorgeous George."

"If you must know, I think he's going off me," she said quietly into her wineglass.

I was aghast. "You're not fucking serious!" (I tend to swear a lot when I'm aghast – sorry.)

Amy looked at me. A tear emerged from her eye. "I don't know why, Geri. I seem to bore men after a while – it's not as easy for me as you seem to think it should be."

I looked at Amy in amazement. My beautiful, gorgeous friend who for some reason never felt good enough and I couldn't for the life of me fathom why. If I looked like Amy I would swagger about like Kate Moss and be the queen of the catwalk.

"Do you want to know what I really think?" I ventured.

Amy nodded vigorously.

"I think you sell yourself too short and some types

seem to pick that up like a radar – especially smug control freaks who need someone to practise on. You just invite abuse. George should be down on his knees thanking God that any girl would look at him, never mind a fantastic looker like you. And not only that, Amy, you are a really nice person too. I think you deserve better than bloody George."

Amy looked dejected but remained silent.

"Anyway, what makes you think he's going off you?" I asked.

"He told me that my arse looked hefty in my new jeans. We were out at the student bar and I went off and danced with a friend of his. When I got back he made that comment and took me home."

I burned furiously. I knew immediately that the Ginger One was a jealous control freak with little self-esteem and only wanted Amy in order to boost it. Once there was the slightest risk of Amy losing interest he had to undermine her to make himself feel better. "Get rid of him, Amy. He deliberately hurt you to make you doubt yourself – he knows *you* are the catch in the relationship."

Amy sighed and poured another Merlot. "What are we like? I think the same about you and Gary, as you know. *You* are the catch in your relationship and Gary always tries to undermine you, Geri."

I looked at my friend. I knew how she felt but in the main she never discussed Gary because she knew I was besotted. "In what way?" I said guardedly, deciding to let her have her say.

"Well, he calls you ditzy when you are the least ditzy person I know. He hasn't said one positive thing about getting married since you've got engaged. All that stuff about balls and chains and losing his freedom – it's not very nice for his future wife to have to listen to. And he seems to resent all the wedding organising. I don't like to say this, Geri, but are you sure he's all that keen?"

I almost died of embarrassment and shame. Amy had voiced all the insecurities and fears I had lain awake with night after night but didn't dare admit to anyone, even her.

I blushed furiously, unsure of how to answer. "I love Gary and he loves me too. He's just not into all the wedding stuff – what man is? But he wouldn't have proposed if he didn't love me. Besides, I've put almost ten years into our relationship. I have invested too much in Gary and I can't just walk away because he calls me ditzy."

I tried to sound calm and unfazed but somehow I felt threatened – as if admitting something was wrong would bring about bad luck and then something *would* go wrong.

Amy tapped her long elegant fingers on her glass. "I never said I wanted you to walk away, but don't you ever wonder . . . " She paused. "Look, I don't want to upset you or make you mad at me."

"No, go on," I said. I had to know what she was

going to say – don't I ever wonder what?

"Don't you ever wonder if you're missing out on something different? I mean, you've only ever been with Gary. Don't you ever think what it might be like to make love to another man?"

I smiled widely. "Well, there is always George Clooney, I suppose."

George was my long-time fantasy – now if there ever was a guy to turn the head of a faithful girl it was he.

"I'm serious, Geri. You are going to make love to Gary Warren for the next forty years and you're never going to wonder what it's like to kiss another man or make love to someone new. You are *that* sure of your love?"

I looked her straight in the eye and replied, "Yes."

I hoped it was true.

"Right then, I'll say no more," Amy replied, but she eyed me strangely.

After she finally left it was almost midnight, but I still decided I would telephone Gary. I needed to apologise but more importantly I needed to hear his voice and be reassured. Amy's comments had unnerved me more than I cared to admit.

But his mobile phone was switched off. I wondered where he was. A little shard of insecurity pierced my heart. I had always felt insecure with Gary – it was his beauty – I had seen the way women looked at him with undisguised desire. I always felt a little bit threatened, but after Amy's comments I felt even more at sea. I resolved that I would telephone him first thing in the morning and apologise profusely and become the meekest, best fiancée a man could wish for. Nothing was going to come between me and my dream man and the dream wedding I had always wished for.

Chapter 5

The following morning I awoke with a hangover and a vague sense of unease. I still hadn't been able to shake Amy's comments. They sat about in my brain taunting me. I knew I had to talk to Gary and make everything all right again.

I called Gary's mobile from my bed, but it was still switched off, so I took a deep breath and called his parents' home.

Pamela answered. Just my luck! I swore silently. I had to talk to the old bat, something that I had managed to avoid since the row.

"Erm … hello, Pamela. I was wondering if Gary was there?"

Polite and businesslike was what I aimed for. I don't know if that's how it sounded to Pamela but she didn't seem to notice in any case.

"No, he's not actually. Never came home as a matter of fact. Hang on a minute – wasn't he out with you all night?" Her voice was sickly sweet but full of venom underneath and barely disguised glee. She damn well knew I wouldn't be calling if he had been in my bed all night.

I felt my head swim. "Oh, that's alright, Pamela. Gary probably was out with the lads – come to think of it, he did mention he'd be going out with them – he's probably crashed out at Vincent's place. I'll catch him later." I changed the subject. "By the way, thanks for the money, it was more than generous of you and Gary Senior."

"Money?" Pamela echoed dimly. "What money?"

Oh shit, I thought, she doesn't even know. "Gary told me that you and his father gave us a gift of money for our wedding, I thought you knew?"

"I would never give you a penny of mine, Geri Murphy. If Gary Senior is idiot enough to waste his money on the likes of you, well, then, more fool him!"

And with that she slammed down the phone.

I couldn't believe it. I don't know which shocked me more, the vitriol that Pamela displayed towards me – or that her darling husband hadn't shared with her the fact he had given a huge amount of their money away to their son and his future bride. It began to sink in that Pamela had tolerated me all these years because I had been just a girlfriend, but now that I was becoming Gary's wife she was jealous.

It was incredible. I felt a little apprehensive about spilling the beans about the gift but also somewhat pleased at being able to score one over Pamela. And if she was going to be that nasty about it all – well, she could go to hell.

I lay on my bed, wondering where the hell Gary was.

I had lied to Pamela. I hadn't the remotest clue where he had got to – I just hoped there was some innocent explanation. Perhaps he had gone on the tear after our row and had crashed at a mate's place. I certainly hoped so.

♥ ♥ ♥

Gary surfaced sometime after midday. Which was just as well because we had arranged to look at the groom's clothes hire shops in the city. I heard his souped-up engine roar from three streets away and heaved a huge sigh of relief. I was prepared to eat a lot of humble pie just to make things normal again between us.

I'd had lots of time during the morning to repair my blotchy face and had donned my tightest jeans and sexiest top to make myself irresistible to him.

He beeped the car impatiently outside, a habit that really infuriated my mother. She always ranted and raved when Gary did that. She felt it showed a total lack of respect for me and the family – so today

I ran like a bat out of hell out to the car before she shouted at him from the upstairs windows and made an absolute show of me.

"Hi!" I gasped as I plonked myself beside him. I flashed him a bright smile and kissed his cheek, which was rough with stubble.

"Hello, yourself," he replied, a small smile playing on his lips. "Are you back to normal yet?"

I was unsure how to take this. I certainly didn't want another row, so I squashed the urge to make a sarcastic remark and swallowed my pride. "I'm sorry, Gary. I was very unfair yesterday to accuse your parents of having ulterior motives. I think the pressure just got to me a bit, with all the wedding planning and the disastrous dinner the other night. It really is a wonderful offer and I'm really excited about it." I planted another kiss for effect.

I could see Gary's displeasure wilt and fade away.

"OK, let's forget it. So, what's the plan for today? I don't want to spend all afternoon in the shops 'cos I've got a raging hangover."

I looked at him. The bright-blue eyes were bloodshot and bleary. He seemed tired and worn out.

"What did you get up to?" I phrased the question quite innocently.

He looked alarmed.

"I mean, did you hit the town with the lads?"

"Yeah, yeah, we went into Temple Bar and had a few scoops, didn't get home till late. I'm knackered."

He yawned for effect.

I sat staring at the dashboard. One small problem with that last sentence: Gary didn't get home at all and he had just lied to me. I fumed inwardly. Yet I still didn't want to start another blazing row in case I had got it wrong. What if Pamela had lied instead of Gary? Just to make me crazy and fall out with him? I would have to box clever on this one. Somehow I would find out the truth.

I smiled. "Don't worry, honey, it shouldn't take too long. We'll just choose the styles and later on we can get the guys in for the fittings. Maybe we can grab a bite to eat later? We really haven't had much time alone lately."

Gary gave me that long, lazy look that he had copied from Brad Pitt, the one that was devastatingly sexy. "OK, sounds good, as long as I can get home by about seven. I need an early night."

And so we headed off to the groom suit-hire shop. I should have been the happiest girl alive. I had just been given a handsome deposit on my first home and I was going to choose outfits with my gorgeous future husband for our wedding. Yet I felt more insecure and confused than ever.

I watched Gary drive the car towards town, looking for some outward sign that things had changed, but he seemed as normal as ever, moaning about the traffic, listening to his favourite CD blast from his stereo. Situation normal except I had a little sliver of doubt in my brain, doubt about Gary's commitment to me and doubt about myself.

Was I this dopey idiot girlfriend who swallowed any guff and turned a blind eye to what seemed obvious to my friend? Did Gary really want to spend the rest of his life with me? Or was I just kidding myself in order to wear a very nice white frock?

I slid my arm around Gary's neck and he appeared to squirm a little bit.

"Gary?" I wheedled.

"Hmm?" he answered absently.

"Do you love me?"

He looked at me as if I'd lost whatever marbles I had left. "Of course I love you – what brought all this on? You're not getting cold feet, are you?" He grinned at me and turned back to the traffic, which came to a complete standstill as usual on Parnell Square.

"No," I said sullenly, "but are *you*?"

He swore quietly under his breath. "Yes, Geri, that's why we're spending this afternoon picking the clothes I will wear on our wedding day, because I *don't* want to marry you. That is why I am stuck this god-awful traffic jam with a thumping hangover, because I have cold feet. What brought all this on or should I say *who*? It wasn't bloody Amy in your ear again, was it? She has never liked me."

The traffic inched forward and the car behind beeped us to move on – like six inches was going to make any difference.

I sighed and wished I had never brought up the damn subject at all – it wasn't going as well as I had planned. I simply thought Gary would reassure me, give me a passionate kiss and make it all better. A little ego-massage and I'd be OK.

"No, it wasn't Amy, as a matter of fact, it was your mother. She just mentioned when I phoned looking for you this morning that you hadn't come home last night and I wondered why you didn't tell me." I said all these words carefully and in a friendly tone. I said it in the hope of reassurance – not to irritate him any further. After all, I had been irritating him a lot lately.

Gary frowned. "What the hell would she know? Mum's always three sheets to the wind by nine o'clock every night and in bed by ten! As I told you, I got home late. She may not have known about it or else she's still trying to get back at you for your mum calling her mutton dressed as lamb. Don't take any notice of her, Geri."

My heart began to beat a little slower and I began to calm down. Gary was making all the right noises. I didn't want to believe that my fiancé was a cheat – I mean who would? So I settled back down into excited bride-to-be mode.

♥ ♥ ♥

Gary and I had a nice time at the groom hire shop. Everything in the shop looked amazing on him. In fact the sales guy reckoned Gary would have made a good model, he was so tall and perfectly proportioned with wide shoulders and a narrow waist.

With his blond colouring we settled on navy blue. He seemed to get into the swing of things and tried everything on without whinging. I was almost in tears when he came out from behind the velvet curtain in his full bridegroom outfit. Even with his hungover eyes and his blond mane carelessly tied back into a ponytail, he looked so handsome I kissed him and whispered, "I love you."

"Me too," he replied softly. "Do you think I will pass muster?"

"You bet," I smiled. "You never looked better!"

We booked the suit and arranged for his two friends, Vincent and Jim, to call in for a fitting, and my dad and Gary Senior (separately) for similar but plainer suits.

Afterwards we went for a Mexican meal at Judge Roy Beans to stifle Gary's growing hangover and to talk about the Kinsealy apartment.

"I've booked an appointment to see the show house in the complex," Gary said over his nachos.

I was surprised. The last thing Gary arranged was a weekend away for himself and the gang of guys he hung around with. He never arranged anything that didn't involve copious amounts of alcohol, golf or both. This new responsible Gary was a revelation.

"When?" I asked. The show houses were open on

Sunday afternoons and we could just as well have visited with all the other hopefuls (except this time we were really confident of actually living in one).

Gary smiled. "The guy who opens the houses bought a car from Dad last week and I gave him a good deal, so he's doing us a favour and opening up at midday tomorrow, just for you and me."

I was amazed and delighted. For once Gary was showing enthusiasm and maturity about our new home. I began to think I was really too hard on him. All his reluctance was just boredom with the details of a wedding and was totally normal. But when it came to a place to live he was really enthusiastic. I felt again that he really loved me under it all and my heart lifted; the earlier suspicion and fears vanished.

"Do you really think we'll get it then?" I ventured, daring to believe we would actually get a home of our own.

"Yes, I do, largely thanks to my dad, of course. He'll want to give it the once-over too, so he's coming with us."

The smile froze on my face. I'd had lovely visions of me and Gary strolling around the pristine environment of Kinsealy Cloisters, walking through the plush carpeted rooms and imagining our rosy future together. I never envisaged Gary bloody Senior in tow. It would make us look like two teenagers out on a first date. It also made me feel like it wasn't really our place at all – but it would be more like an investment for Gary Senior and we wouldn't have the final say. Yet I couldn't complain. I was already on the way to an Olympic gold medal in moaning, so I had to grin and bear it.

Still, I couldn't help wondering if Gary's dad would be a frequent visitor to the apartment after we were married, treating the place like his own, I began to wish we hadn't needed his help but there was precious little I could do about it. But the wedding was another matter. Gary's dad wasn't going to be paying for any of it so Pamela could go jump off a very tall cliff if she thought that I was going to be swayed from my first choice of Cavan Castle.

I had a little power left and I was damned if I was going to give that up easily.

Chapter 6

The following day Gary picked me up at eleven sharp and we set off for Kinsealy Cloisters to see our dream home.

"Your dad not with you then?" I enquired meekly. I dared hope his father had changed his mind.

"He's meeting us out there. He doesn't want Mum to know about him giving us the money yet."

Uh oh! I couldn't let the moment pass. "I meant to ask you about that, Gary. Why is your mother being kept in the dark? I'm afraid I stuffed it up the other day when I thanked her for the gift."

"You *what*? Geri, never mention that money to my mother again! She is not to know how much Dad gave us. She doesn't even know he has any spare money, and he'll kill me if she ever finds out. If she ever knew he had thirty grand to spare she'd get it all for herself!"

I sat in silence for a moment. Firstly, I didn't think it was very fair of Gary and his father to keep such a big thing from Pamela, much and all as I detested her. Secondly, Gary said *thirty* grand to spare, not twenty-five as he had earlier told me. What the hell was going on? Gary and his dad were acting like true car salesmen, up to all sorts of trickery, and if Gary had learnt to be deceptive from his father, and with his own mother, then what did it mean for me in the future? I felt angry for Pamela and also for myself. Perhaps that's what made Pamela as insecure and histrionic as she was.

"Do you think that's fair?" I asked after a moment's deliberation.

Gary laughed hollowly, while screeching his sports car around the corner of my avenue. "Fair? Yes, I think it's more than fair of my father to give a substantial deposit on a home for us – after all, it's his money, he earned it. You don't really have a problem with it, do you? You're going to benefit from it too, and I doubt if you and I could ever afford a place on our own. Not the way the prices are going. And do you really want to live out in the sticks, travelling for over two hours a day just to get to work? Because that's all we could afford and I for one don't intend to do that for the next five years – do you?"

I had to admit, I didn't want to commute from darkest Cavan every day and I really wanted to live in the Cloisters, but it meant having to deceive my future mother-in-law. And perhaps deceive myself too in the process. But I decided I would go along with things for the moment.

"No," I answered slowly. "No, I don't, Gary. But please tell me that your father will tell your mother eventually and we can start our life together without any secrets within the family. I don't want to be sweating any time your mother comes over in case I blab about the money. You know I can't keep a secret."

Gary grimaced and glanced over at me before returning his attention to the road. "Yes, well, you'd better keep this one until at least after the wedding. Once we're settled into the apartment I'll get Dad to break the news to her. She'll be fine after the whole thing blows over. Just trust me, Geri. I'm doing this all for us. You'll thank me when you're living in our new home."

He was right, I needed to believe that, so I began to forget about Pamela and the big deception and instead I focused on making our new home a possibility.

We got to Kinsealy Cloisters to find Gary Senior there sitting in his Lexus and the salesman for Petty, Wright and Mason Developments sitting beside him.

They both jumped out as we got out of our car and there was much hand-pumping and back-slapping and male posturing before Joe, as he was called, opened up the show apartment. I got the impression all the deals had been done before we even got there.

Still, the apartment was beautiful, stylishly designed to maximise space – of which there was little – but it was an open-plan design with a fitted kitchen -cum-dining room, which led onto a small patio area, and a tiny front room with a huge bay window.

There was a small internal hallway between the rooms that housed a twisting stairwell that led to the two miniscule bedrooms, one of which managed to squeeze in an en suite. But I was in heaven at the thought it might be mine, mine and Gary's.

"Do you like it?" Gary Senior beamed, as we all squashed into the tiniest of the bedrooms. It might fit a cot at a stretch.

"I love it!" I gushed and I did.

"Well, if you do, I'm sure Joe here will take a cash deposit from me today and we can choose a number – one with a sunny aspect, eh Joe?"

Joe nodded vigorously and there were smiles all round. It looked like we were the new owners of a real-life apartment in Kinsealy Cloisters, bank permitting.

Gary grinned widely and hugged me. We all then went to the sales office to choose an apartment. It turned out to be number six, which had a west-facing garden. Joe placed a little red pin into the site map and Gary Senior handed over an envelope obviously stuffed with cash. Joe's eyebrows rose imperceptibly but he said nothing and pocketed the money. I was surprised that he didn't even stop to count it.

I felt a bit embarrassed and still a little weird – like it wasn't really our place at all – but Gary Senior hadn't laid down any rules or laws about the deposit so it seemed like it was a no-strings gift – I certainly hoped so.

"I hope you'll both be very happy," Gary Senior gushed while clutching me to his chest rather tightly.

"Thanks," I murmured into his shirt. His aftershave was overpowering.

"So I can crash on your couch when Pamela throws a wobbly then?"

I smiled as best I could while trying to extricate myself from his clutches.

"Only joking! Gary, you should see Geri's face! You'd better cancel that sofa-bed for the lounge."

"Don't be silly," I lied, making a mental note that sofa-beds were immediately off the list. "You'll be welcome anytime."

Gary senior released me. "OK, I'll leave you two lovebirds alone to get excited about your new home. There's a golf game in Portmarnock with my name on it. See you later, Gary." With that he walked away.

I almost had to pinch myself. We owned our own place. Gary and I weren't only going to be married in six months but we were going to have a dream home to come back from honeymoon to.

I felt overwhelmed. But I had seldom been happier.

What an idiot I was.

Chapter 7

I was out for a girlie night with my friends that evening. We were meeting up in Malahide for a crisis Chinese to work out where the hen party was going to be and to discuss our all-out assault on the bridal boutiques across the country to find *the perfect dress.*

Amy, Clodagh and Jackie were already there when Sandy and I arrived. Sandy had to be part of the plan because she was the one who worked in a travel agent's and could get us a cheapo last-minute deal to Spain for a week of hen party excess. She was also the chief bridesmaid and therefore important to the overall plans – the fact she was my irritating little sister and a complete slapper was beside the point.

Clodagh Rogers was my other close friend. She was small, feisty and fearless.

Clodagh had been in our class at school and had

more ambition in her little finger than Amy or I had in our entire bodies. She knew straight away that she was going to be successful – she had a talent for design and loved jewellery – so off she went and became a jeweller. Firstly, she created fantastic designs that sold like hotcakes to the hippy types in the Dublin markets, then she promptly became bored and fecked off to Australia for a year. She wrote and told us the most fantastic tales about who she'd met and where she'd been and made Amy and me green with envy. She then arrived back a year later with a swathe of broken hearts under her belt and a business plan. And so Celt was born – Clodagh set up her own jewellery business in partnership with her brother Steve and Celt proffered some of the most stylish Celtic- designed pieces in Ireland. Yet Clodagh hadn't changed much, except we didn't get to see as much of her as we used to – she was still the wisecracking cynical upstart she always was.

Jackie Mooney worked at Amy's office on reception and was Amy's best friend at work. She was a cool and glamorous blonde in Henson PR who really let her hair down come five thirty and was instantly a wanton mad woman who loved nothing more than to devour six vodka and cokes and any man passing in that order. She was a really fun person and ideal for hen parties. She and Sandy should have been sisters.

"About bloody time!" Clodagh yelled as we

approached. "Jackie has nearly undressed one of the waiters and we haven't even ordered yet."

"Sorry!" I replied as I plonked myself down beside Amy. "Sandy's bloody car wouldn't start. We had to get a lift from the old man and he wasn't too impressed at missing *Winning Streak* – what a saddo!"

Sandy glared at me. She hated anyone insulting Clara, her ancient car of some fourteen years that seldom started without a team of mechanics or at least ten Hail Marys.

Clodagh took charge. "Right, now we are all here we can order and get onto the serious business of organising the hen party – Jackie, no eating the servants until after the meal, OK? Sandy, did you bring the list of possibilities?"

Sandy nodded, her green eyes wide – she was a little bit afraid of Clodagh.

"OK, don't worry, Geri," Clodagh went on. "We'll have it sorted in no time, then we can get onto the other serious issue – your wedding dress. Now, girls, shots all round?"

We all nodded this time. Clodagh on form was a force to be reckoned with.

After our sumptuous Chinese banquet we had settled on a week-long trip to Majorca. Sandy and Jackie wanted Ibiza (naturally, but I didn't want to end up on a reality TV show just before I wed, so we settled on the more sedate Palma Nova). Sandy could get herself a holiday for practically nothing and the rest of us just paid cost price, so it worked out almost cheaper than a night in Temple Bar (have you seen the prices? You'd need a mortgage just to get hammered).

I didn't know how Gary would take the idea of me jetting off with a gang of girls for a week of debauchery, especially since we now almost had a house to pay for, but I was badly in need of some girly fun and a break from all the wedding organising.

I just wanted to be myself again for six nights and get a bit of a tan before signing my life away. I hadn't reckoned planning weddings could get so stressful or even make you feel like perhaps you were making the biggest mistake of your life.

Not that I really felt that about Gary. I mean, I just loved him so much – but sometimes when I was out with my friends life seemed so simple and easy. I felt so much myself and I didn't need to be always watching, watching for other women who seemed to always want to take him from me.

Amy interrupted my reverie. "Are you OK, Geri? You're a bit quiet tonight."

"I'm fine," I replied smilingly. "I have a bit of news actually. I didn't want to tell the others yet, but we put the deposit down on the apartment in Kinsealy today. I'll be off to see the bank manager on Monday. It seems like it's all really happening after all."

Amy eyed me darkly. "You don't sound as if you really want it, do you?"

I smiled brightly. "Of course I do – whatever gave you that mad idea?"

Amy leaned forward to make sure none of the others could hear. "Geri, I know you almost better than I know myself. I can tell when you are panicking. You get a little crease right in the middle of your forehead. I know you're under tremendous stress with the whole wedding thing but this is different. You seem like you're having second thoughts or something. What's the problem?"

I sighed heavily. I could never fool Amy, even when I fooled myself. I was feeling uncomfortable because I was about to get everything that I ever wanted, just like the Chinese proverb that warns to be careful what you wish for because you might actually get it – I suppose that summed up how I felt. I was afraid that if I got the apartment and Gary then I had everything I ever dreamt of and then what was next? But I couldn't explain this to Amy – she'd think I was a right mental case.

"Sorry, Amy. It's just Gary Senior. He arrived at the apartment with a bag of cash as a deposit and it made me feel uneasy. I hope he's not paying for our apartment with dodgy money."

Amy laughed. "Is that all? Geri, he's a second-hand car salesman! Wake up and smell the coffee – he lies for a living! You can't be that naïve!"

I laughed too, but deep inside I was thinking that if Gary's dad lied for a living, then so did my fiancé. Was

I so naïve that I never even put those ideas together in my head before, until my best friend pointed it out to me?

All this soul-searching was wearing me out so I decided to try and forget it all and just get completely blotto.

"Another round of shots, girls," I blustered loudly, "and we'll head for Tamango's."

Sandy and Jackie gave a little whoop of joy. Clodagh frowned, shaking her spiky head. She looked a bit like a pixie – her elfin face was set in a scowl. "I can't go clubbing, Geri. I have an early start tomorrow. We have some prospective buyers in town from the Netherlands and I'm meeting them at ten. Sorry, but I'll need a clear head. Do you mind?"

I did really. Clodagh not coming just proved what a grown-up success story she was and it was everything I wasn't. I had to try and not let jealousy get hold quite a lot where Clodagh was concerned. She just seemed so together, fearless, successful, driven. She hadn't a boyfriend and she didn't give two damns about it either. I wished I could be more like her. Still, sometimes I wished she'd let her short spiky hair down – just for us, her oldest friends.

"No, it's no problem, Clodagh – we know the empire must come first. You'd better not back out of Majorca, though – we need your expertise for that trip."

Amy laughed. "Yeah, we probably wouldn't make

it as far as Dublin Airport without you. All work and no play make Clodagh an international success story!"

Clodagh threw her eyes heavenward. She was used to the slagging, but I'm sure it must have irked her too. It wasn't easy being the successful one.

She left shortly after.

The rest of us failures headed for Tamango's. Amy and I sat sipping cocktails while the other two devoured two poor unfortunates that happened to pass their way.

I felt like married oul' wan already, sniffing disgustedly at the tonsil-hockey going on underneath our noses. I always missed Gary more when I went to these sorts of places.

The sooner I waltzed up the aisle the better.

Chapter 8

I was flicking through my newest bridal magazine. They were my latest addiction. I had every single issue of any publication that featured anything remotely weddingy.

I got excited just opening the pristine pages covered with gorgeous brides and grooms and featuring every detail from napkins to flowers and confetti. I immersed myself in every page until I was almost the bride within. It was truly addictive and I lost myself in the wonderful glossiness of it all.

Today it was raining and I'd settled in with a hot mug of drinking chocolate and a packet of cookies. (OK, so the diet had been temporarily abandoned due to a blazing row with Gary and I needed cheering up.) I was reverentially leafing through the pristine pages of *Blushing Bride* when I spotted it – the most amazing gown I had ever feasted my eyes on. It was truly magnificent. It was a vision of floaty chiffon with spaghetti straps and hand-beaded bodice. It was also a pale, pale pink and had a matching pale-pink wrap. It was truly stunning. There was just one small problem. I had just had a huge row with Gary over the spiralling cost of the wedding. And I definitely, absolutely, could never divulge the cost of this gown but I was getting it anyway. Whatever he said.

The phone then rang. It was Gary wanting to sort out the row we had had earlier.

I had discovered the extra five thousand euro that Gary had let slip as part of his father's wedding gift was just for him, or rather for the latest TV and DVD games package which was going to be in the spare room – the baby's room in my mind.

As I said, it was just big enough for a little cot and a little baby-changing unit. I assumed we'd be starting a family immediately after the wedding. Little did I know that Gary had other ideas – the spare room was to be his domain and he admitted after a bit of prodding that his father had given him an extra five grand to pay for his little playroom.

I was furious. Not only was I angry that he had kept it from me, but more shocking was the lack of intention for us to have children. In fact they didn't seem to figure at all in his plans. We seemed to be having totally different dreams for our life together.

Before we got engaged Gary had let me prattle on

about having kids. He had never corrected me and even sometimes contributed a little – maybe just to humour me. He never once told me he didn't want children until our king-sized row about the playroom.

"Well, are you talking to me yet?" This was Gary's codeword for saying sorry without actually mentioning it.

I momentarily considered slamming the phone down before I glanced at my bridal magazine and spied the perfect dress again.

"Maybe ..." I answered slowly. "If you can have five grand for your toys, can I have a few grand for mine?"

I heard a heavy sigh on the other end.

"That all depends," Gary answered in a suspicious tone. "What is it for?"

I thought about it quickly. I doubted if I said I needed several thousand euros for a wedding dress that Gary would agree.

"Well, I saw a really nice top-of-the-range silver cooker and a matching hood. It's expensive."

"OK," Gary replied in a much nicer tone. "It's a deal. I'll give you two grand out of the five. You can get whatever you want out of it. As long as I can have the playroom."

It was my turn to sigh. "How long for?" I ventured, holding my breath, dreading that he'd utter the word "forever".

"Five years? We need to get a hold on the mortgage first before you can give up work, Geri.

Then we can try to have a baby if you want."

I considered this. That would make me thirty-three before we could start a family.

That seemed like forever but it wasn't really. I supposed it was the best I could do.

"OK, but not a minute more, Gary Warren. I don't want to be having a baby in middle age. It's important to me and surely you want a little son to carry on the business with you, don't you?"

"I'd never want a boy of mine in this bloody business!" Gary retorted. That was the first time he had ever given me any indication that he was unhappy being a car salesman. It unnerved me a little.

"Well, whatever you want him to be, at least you seem to want him a little bit, a little bit more than you seemed to earlier. I suppose that's a start."

Gary laughed then. "Yeah, I suppose I do."

Everything was all right again, and I was going to get my dream dress too. Things were looking up.

I called Amy.

"I found it!" I yelled down the phone.

"What? You found what?" Amy enquired – she seemed a bit distracted.

"My dream dress. Amy, you have got to see this dress! It is the perfect gown. I saw it in *Blushing Bride*. There's just one problem: it's in a flash boutique over on the west coast of Ireland. So I need you to come with me."

"Jesus, Geri, why can't you just find one in Dublin

like everyone else? Where are we off to, then?"

"Loughrea, it's near Galway. Look, it's better than London. That's where I was originally looking. Come on, Amy! Please! I promise you I'll go out on the tear with you when we get there. I've booked a bed and breakfast in Galway city – we can make a girl's night of it – what do you say?"

Amy laughed. "Tell me Sandy's not coming."

Sandy got on Amy's nerves a lot. She got on my nerves a lot too, but she was my sister.

"She's not." I couldn't risk Sandy spilling the beans to anyone (especially my mother) about the exorbitant cost of the wedding dress. In fact I would have gone alone but I needed someone else with me who would give an honest appraisal of how it looked on me. And Amy had always been honest.

"OK, you're on, but you are doing all the driving."

I smiled. "Great, but Amy, just one thing – you are sworn to total secrecy on this. It's not a cheap dress and no one but *no one* must know how much it costs."

"Jesus! You mean we have to have Securicor accompany us?"

"Maybe, Amy, if my suitcase isn't big enough for the wodge of cash I need to bring. So we'll go Saturday – OK?"

"Done," said Amy, giggling.

I loved that girl. She was behind me, no matter what.

♥ ♥ ♥

The following Saturday we set off at the crack of dawn for Loughrea.

I wasn't the best of drivers (in fact, Gary and my Dad both agreed I was about the worst driver they had ever seen that hadn't made it on to a reality show about crap drivers), but Amy had insisted, so I lurched up what passes for a freeway in Ireland towards the west and my dream dress.

The conversation drifted onto my argument with Gary over the games/baby room.

"I hope you don't mind me saying it, Geri, but it seems that everything is geared towards Gary's wants and needs. I mean, five years to wait for children! Are you really happy with that? You'll be thirty-three then, and it may not happen straight away – it could take another two years of trying. You'd be thirty-five. What if it turned out you had fertility problems and you had waited seven years to find out?"

I laughed incredulously. "Amy, you're such a drama queen! You already have me as an infertile Stepford wife and I'm not even married yet."

Amy frowned. "I don't think that's a laughing matter, Geri. It does happen. But, anyway, it's not just that. Your relationship should be more equal – you both should have a say in what happens. But you seem to just go along with whatever Gary suggests, and that's not you. Not the Geri I know, anyway."

I was getting irritated. Amy's boyfriend told her that her miniscule bum was huge and she just took it, and yet here she was criticising my fiancé. I just felt it was a bit rich, that's all. "Pot, kettle, black arse!" I retorted and drove faster. We were over the speed limit but, when I was angry, going fast in my little Micra always helped.

"If you must know, I took your advice and dumped him. George, or 'Redser' as you call him, is no more. I decided you were right and he was just a control freak, so I dumped him. I told him me and my fat arse were going elsewhere."

I was amazed. "Good for you, Amy Byrne! I'm proud of you. Thank God you got rid of him! Really, Amy, you deserve better."

"Exactly," Amy said primly. "And so do you."

♥ ♥ ♥

We got to the boutique about twelve o'clock. It was called Heavenly Creatures and each and every gown was more beautiful and heavenly than the next. Amy and I were enthralled. Each gown was on a circular rack that slowly turned around showing its glittering pieces. I showed the shop assistant my choice and she murmured appreciatively.

"That's the *Persian Princess* – an excellent choice – it's one of our most expensive creations. The beads are hand-sewn on – it is rather beautiful."

Amy gasped in admiration. "It's amazing, Geri. Quick, try it on!"

I could barely breathe as I donned the beautiful

dress in the changing room.

It was a size fourteen and the biggest they did so I prayed it fit, cursing my earlier splurge of cookies during the week, resolving to diet furiously so I could choose a size twelve when the time came.

It looked divine, even though the zipper struggled up with a groan. The diet was a must now if I was to fit into the smaller size and look good in the photographs. A fleeting idea of liposuction passed through my mind before I dismissed it for the moment. I'd try the diet first – surgery would have to be an emergency tactic for later if necessary.

I swept out to my audience of Amy and the salesgirl.

"You look fantastic!" said Amy, gobsmacked.

"It's definitely you," the salesgirl agreed, "but it's a little snug around the hips. Don't worry though – most brides lose a few pounds before the big day. When is it exactly?"

I tore my eyes from the mirror where I was swirling around in my princess dress, imagining my saunter up the aisle to gasps of admiration from the congregation.

"Six months from now. Can I leave a deposit today?"

"Yes," she smiled. "We require ten per cent – that will be –"

"I know how much that is," I interrupted hurriedly. I didn't even want Amy to know the cost yet – she was far too sensible where money was concerned. I'd break it to her gently, preferably after she'd had six vodkas.

"Yes, well, we will order you an original of course. I'll just take your measurements and we can continue from there."

I stared at myself again. I definitely needed to lose a good stone.

"I'll be ordering a size twelve," I said emphatically.

The salesgirl eyed me with a "been through this all before" look.

"If you're sure ..." she said slowly.

"I'm one hundred per cent sure," I replied.

And I was.

♥ ♥ ♥

That night Amy and I went out on the town in Galway to celebrate. We had dinner in a charming pub, which served the best seafood chowder I had ever encountered, and then went on to a live music session. We had a fantastic time and met up with two dishy men from Glasgow who were on a stag weekend. Amy was quite taken with Stuart, who was quite a good-looking chap and very relaxed and humorous – not her usual type at all. His buddy, Charlie, was good fun too and also engaged so he and I just chatted and talked about our respective partners while the other two got mushy. But I had a really nice time with Charlie. He didn't scan the room for admirers like Gary sometimes did, which always put me on the defensive, and I felt he really listened to me and was interested in what I had to say.

Amy and I fell into bed at two, Amy all loved up and talking about visits to Scotland and me enraptured by a length of chiffon and some beads.

It was brilliant.

Chapter 9

We breezed back to Dublin, me with a deposit slip and the vision in my head of myself in my dream gown, and Amy with a clutch of text messages from the good-looking Stuart promising visits to Ireland to see her. I was in such a good mood I almost forgot that Gary and I had an appointment with the bank manager about our mortgage the following day

Banks terrified me and Gary was no better. They always make you feel like you are a sort of credit delinquent while they are trawling through your enormous overdraft (even though they've encouraged you to have it in the first place) – and I find it very weird that in order to convince them to give you a mortgage you have to prove you don't need it in the first place.

I doubted Gary Senior had any pull in our little

branch at Sutton – more's the pity, I thought. My Gary was a reluctant saver and my own meagre pittance that languished in the deposit account would doubtless not impress. But we were going to front up anyhow – our new apartment in Kinsealy Cloisters depended on it. And Gary's father's large gift would help.

The meeting went surprisingly well. Our manager turned out to be a forty-something dynamic woman called Carole Boland, with a sharp suit that exposed a slim figure and long lean legs, who took an instant shine to Gary and whose daughter was planning to buy an apartment at the same development.

Gary looked resplendent in a sharp navy suit and crisp white shirt, his blond hair tied neatly in a ponytail. He smiled winningly at the raven-haired Carole while she ushered us in and plied us with coffee.

"I know what it's like for you young people trying to get a mortgage these days. Tara, my daughter, is trying to get herself one – not easy even if you are the bank manager's daughter. But whatever I can do to help I will – although everything will need to be in order too, as you can appreciate. Gary, I believe your father is Gary Warren from Warren Motors?"

Gary smiled. "Yes, he is, why?"

Carole flicked through our file with long perfectly manicured hands. "Oh, it's just that he has switched all his business from the competition to our little branch here. He has quite a turnover. He never mentioned that you were coming in, but I thought I recognised a family resemblance." She gave me a quick knowing look and then went back to her file.

I could feel my cheeks burn even though I willed them to cool with every fibre of my being. I had been wishing Gary Senior had a bit of pull at the bank but this was hugely embarrassing – if he thought a cheap stunt like putting business the way of the bank would get us a mortgage, he was an idiot. I hoped he wasn't going to ruin it for us. I felt about seven years old at that moment and I had only felt fifteen when I'd first sat down. It was like asking for pocket money from your parents when you knew you'd been naughty.

"Now, let's see," Carole murmured, peering over her *pince nez*. She looked like the type of person who wouldn't wear glasses unless absolutely necessary in case they made her look her age. "Geri, you have been quite a good saver and you've been with your employer for quite some time and, Gary, you have a very good salary but not much savings, it would seem."

"Yes, I realise it seems that way, but I do have shares in my father's name and I have a credit union account and my father has also given us a substantial deposit."

I exhaled deeply. Gary had been well versed by someone and was playing a blinder.

"How much, may I ask?" Carole was all business –

her earlier chumminess had evaporated now that the shekels were being discussed.

"Twenty-five thousand," Gary replied easily.

So far I hadn't even said a word, except hello, and I had expected to do all the talking. Gary was a real surprise – he really wanted the apartment and it showed.

"You have a very nice dad, Gary. Yes, that will make a difference to you. Well, I can look over all your details later – you've given me your P60s and payslips. Can you leave it with me for the moment? I should have an answer for you in about forty-eight hours."

We both smiled nervously. I couldn't believe it was over and I hadn't even uttered a word to convince Carole how much we wanted and needed this loan.

"When's the big day, you lucky girl?" Carole whispered as we neared the door.

"In six months," I replied happily, before I realised that she might be trying to trap me into revealing the spiralling cost of my wedding. "But my parents are footing the bill," I added hastily.

"The sooner you get him up the aisle the better, if his father is anything to go by!" she murmured *sotto voce* and I was so amazed I just smiled like an idiot and blundered out the door in Gary's wake.

I remember thinking: "What an inappropriate comment for a bloody bank manager to make to a prospective client!" Anyone would think Carole had an intimate knowledge of the Warren menfolk. Then it hit me like the proverbial ton of bricks: maybe she did have an intimate knowledge of Gary Senior. It was that knowing smile along with the comment that had me wondering.

I told Gary what Carole had said as soon as we were clear of the building.

"Are you sure that's what she said?" He seemed surprised – there he was, doubting me again.

"Perfectly sure. There was something in the way she said it and the look – it was like we were two friends dating brothers or something. Do you know if he is playing away at the moment?"

Gary shrugged as he fired up the car. "I dunno – jeez, I hope not. Mum will kill him this time if she finds out. He has been looking smug lately – I thought it was because of the car yard doing so well. God! I hope Dad's not bonking her so we get the mortgage – that would be too sleazy even for my father."

I looked at Gary in amazement. What kind of family was I marrying into?

His bloody father was everywhere in our lives now – even, it seemed, corrupting our bank manager. It was like there was nothing private left – nothing for just us. Suddenly I felt very tired, tired and sad. If we got this mortgage I'd never know if we got it because of ourselves or him – it was a weird feeling. I wondered suddenly whether, if we had a baby, Gary Senior would stroll up with his gold medallion and gold rings and take the infant from us to raise himself? He seemed to be in every area of our lives so far – I doubted if he'd leave our offspring alone.

"Gary, is there any way you can find out if he is seeing Carole Boland?" I just had to know.

"I'll certainly try. I'll be seeing him this afternoon – he'll want to know how it went. Geri, don't worry about this, OK? I'll sort it. You just focus on the wedding, I'll handle the mortgage and the old man."

I kissed Gary then – his look of concern told me how much he loved me and was worried about me. "OK, thanks, honey. I'll see you later."

"I'll call you this evening, after work," he said, and with that he sped off, leaving me at the Sutton DART station to catch a train into work, as if I'd be able to concentrate on anything until I found out the real truth in the story.

♥ ♥ ♥

I spent a fruitless day misplacing files, snapping at my poor bosses and generally making a bloody nuisance of myself until five thirty slowly arrived and I escaped the office and eventually got off the DART at Sutton to find Gary waiting for me outside the station.

"I felt I had to tell you this in person, Geri. Not only is my Dad bonking the bloody bank manager but the silly idiot thinks he's in love with her! I confronted him this afternoon – it looks like the mortgage was in the bag even before we went in to see Carole, more or less. I feel like a right twit, I can tell you. The two of us, getting dressed up like dogs' dinners and going through all the preparation and he never said a word that he even knew her."

I was aghast. "What about your mother? What if she finds out?" I couldn't stand Pamela at the best of times, but I wouldn't wish this on her either.

Gary looked at me with those bright-blue eyes and he seemed very angry. "Well, she's going to find out soon enough, because the stupid fool wants to leave her for Carole Boland. I told him he's going to ruin our wedding if he leaves Mum now but he won't listen. What a bloody mess!"

And I had earlier thought that Pamela Warren showing up to our wedding barely clad in a miniscule mini and fake boobs was the worst of my worries! Now I had visions of a mêlée in the middle of the aisle if Gary Senior left her in the meantime and showed up on the day with his new mistress.

Gary took my hand. "I just feel like calling the whole thing off and maybe eloping to Las Vegas or something. It might prove safer and a lot more civilised."

I was crushed. I had dreamed of this day my entire life. I certainly wasn't going to tie the knot in some plastic Elvis-style chapel in the Nevada desert.

Not a hope in hell of me agreeing to that one.

What about my moment of glory? All the attention focused on me in the nicest dress in the world and the chance to walk up the aisle in front of all my snotty relatives that had thought Gary would never marry me.

"No way, Gary! I am not sneaking off to get married in Vegas because your parents can't conduct themselves. You'd better sort it out and get your father to behave himself for the next few months. Tell him he can do whatever he likes as soon as we are safely on our honeymoon. OK? Whatever you need to do, just do it, right? They are not going to ruin my wedding!"

Gary looked petulant. "*Our* wedding, Geri – remember me, I happen to be the groom."

I burst into tears. "Yes, well, Gary, you'd better sort this mess out then. I have enough on my plate to worry about, and I just can't take this latest debacle. We've just about got over the fact that your parents objected to every bloody venue that we saw and I thought that was sorted when they liked Cavan Castle in the end. I just couldn't cope with handbags at dawn if your dad leaves Pamela – please, you have do something!"

Gary put his arm around me and pulled me close to him. "OK, Geri, just stop crying, OK? I'll sort it out, I promise."

Somehow I believed he would.

I had no other choice.

Chapter 10

We got the mortgage, naturally. I tried to feel delighted and over the moon about it. The truth was I was very happy deep down that we were going to have our own place, but still the fact remained that Gary Senior had meddled in our affairs in more ways than one and had muddied the waters in so many ways that I didn't know where our lives ended and his began. Gary managed to persuade him not to act for the moment and to reconsider his decision to leave Pamela and shack up with the delectable Carole Boland, but he wasn't promising to hold off for six months until after the wedding. He said that he'd stay for another three months until Gary moved into the apartment before he did anything more. I was stunned at that announcement because it sounded very much like he might move in with Gary for a while. After all, he had a stake in the apartment already and he'd love to have a bachelor pad to entertain his new amour.

I could just imagine it. A horrible vision emerged in my head of shag-pile carpets and leather lounge easy chairs – those awful ones that men so loved and that resembled dentist chairs.

But I said little – it might look a tad ungrateful if not churlish to object. We wouldn't have the damn place if it weren't for him. It just wasn't how I had pictured my married life with my new husband – three in the marriage never seemed to work for anyone.

The proposition of a moonlight flit to Vegas began to seem more attractive by the minute – in fact, a permanent move there was very much on the cards the way things were going.

So I threw myself into the wedding preparations even more. I took Mum and Dad to see Cavan Castle and they both were impressed with the extensive grounds and the olde worlde charm of the place. After a detailed tour of the banquet room and much ado about flower arranging, Dad reached his boredom threshold and disappeared out onto the golf course for a few holes. And after a beautiful lunch of salsa salmon, Mum and I had a facial in the beauty salon.

"So how are things, Geri?" she enquired in her usual no-nonsense manner while we were both bedecked in towels and face mud.

"Absolutely fine, Mum, everything is right on track, so far," I replied in my brightest voice.

She wasn't convinced. "Geri, you can't fool your mother, so don't even try. There is something wrong with you, I can tell by the way you drove up here on two wheels, and it's more than the usual wedding stresses. Is it Gary, what's he done on you?"

"Mum! Gary has done nothing wrong, really he hasn't." I couldn't tell her about Gary Senior or his affair – she'd go off her brain.

She pressed on. "Well, you're certainly not like any excited bride I've ever seen. You're moody and miserable most of the time. Geri, you should be excited, radiant even. Are you really sure you want to spend the rest of your life with this man? You have to be very careful, because it *is* the rest of your life we're talking about."

What *was* it with people? They just couldn't accept that you were happy unless you were doing handstands or smiling like a fool all the time. I felt angry with my mother at that moment and if we hadn't been where we were I would have walked out – hence the reason she chose that venue to bring up her concerns.

But was I sure Gary was the man for me, the man *forever* for me? Or was I just comfortable after ten years, comfortable and a little bit scared. I knew I didn't want Gary to turn out like his dad and this latest behaviour didn't exactly give me a warm and fuzzy feeling. In fact, it had deeply affected me. Was Gary going to tire of me eventually, like has father had with Pamela, and move on, possibly leaving me with a few children in tow? It wasn't how I'd pictured my life going. Was Gary different from his father? Or did the apple fall dangerously close to the tree as my mother insisted?

I wasn't sure and all the stress of it was getting to me, but I would never let my mother know that – she'd be out hanging up the bunting with the mere idea of me having second thoughts. So I brazened it out.

"Mum, we have just bought a house. I'm simply worried that we won't have enough money for the wedding and the furniture and everything that we need, that's all – you know how money worries get to me."

Mum touched my hand. "I know, I'm sorry – I just worry about you, that's all. This should be the happiest time of your life and I want you to be happy. Don't worry too much about money – you know Dad and I can help if you need some extra for the apartment."

She was being so nice to me that I felt meaner than ever. "Thanks, Mum – you've been brilliant, you and Dad. I'm so lucky to have you. Gary's parents aren't nearly as supportive as you have been."

"Oh, I don't know," Mum replied. "Gary's father has been very good with the money. I'm sure his heart is in the right place."

"It's the rest of him I'm worried about!" I blurted out. I just couldn't help it. My mother would have made an excellent torturer – she'd make anyone spill the beans within the hour. The Gestapo would have loved her.

I told her the whole sorry tale. She wasn't exactly surprised – more triumphant really. She knew she had been right all along about Gary's father and now I also knew she would implicate my fiancé too and I'd never hear the end of it – but what could I do?

Me and my very large gob had landed myself in it again.

"There's only one thing for it," she said emphatically in a tone that allowed no protest. "You and Gary are going to have to get marriage guidance counselling. I'll phone Father Moynalty in the morning and I'll arrange everything. That Gary needs some education on what marriage is really about. Before he takes my daughter down the aisle he is going to have the Catholic Church and Father Moynalty to convince."

I couldn't believe I was going to have to endure Father Moynalty and his probing questions about our relationship. In fact he'd probably think Gary was a Protestant – he hadn't seen the inside of a church since his Confirmation day. But I thought better of arguing with my mother when she was so annoyed and it wouldn't do Gary any harm to suffer a little bit on my behalf. After all I was suffering enough on his, so I gave in.

"Alright, Mum, that sounds like just what we need."

Things were getting better by the minute.

♥ ♥ ♥

"You what?" Gary exploded. "Marriage *guidance*!, Geri! What, does your mother think that you and I are still at the holding-hands stage? What can a bloody priest who has never been married tell us about getting wed?"

He was taking it well.

"Gary, it does make *some* sense. They discuss attitudes to money and children. We could benefit from a bit of advice and, anyway, I'm not listening to my mother go on at me about it – and it's all due to your father's philandering that we're in this predicament. Do you realise she doesn't trust you? You need to get her onside, and to do that you have to go to marriage counselling. That's all there is to it. It won't do you any harm, Gary, not with your family track record. You never know, we might actually learn something that will help us."

Gary sighed and looked out the window. We were up on Vico Road, overlooking Dublin Bay. It was warm and sunny and we should have been enjoying the view. Yet Gary seemed bored and a little distracted. I wanted him to enjoy all the wedding preparations but he just seemed so jaded. I guess I could have pressed him to discover why he wasn't as keen as I was but I didn't want to unearth whatever it was that was bothering him. I didn't need any more grief than I already had, so I just closed my eyes to it.

But I couldn't be an ostrich forever.

Chapter 11

We felt like a couple of bold children as we turned up for our appointment with Father Moynalty for our premarriage guidance session. I had an attack of the giggles as Gary rapped on the large red door of the priest's big Georgian house. A housekeeper seriously resembling Mrs Doyle from *Father Ted* answered the door. My giggles became nervous laughter as she led us to a big old-fashioned room crammed with walls of books and mismatched armchairs. There was another couple sitting there looking as nervous as we felt.

"I wonder if she'll ask us to have a cup of tea?" I whispered to Gary and he replied with Mrs Doyle's classic "Go on, go on, go on!" We all collapsed with laughter and the ice was broken.

The couple were called Paul and Jessie and had

been forced into the premarital guidance course because Jessie was under twenty-one.

Paul was a nice but balding car mechanic and Jessie was a hairdresser and ten years younger than her fiancé. I wasn't too sure of Jessie's long-term commitment to her beau – judging by her open-mouthed admiration of my soon-to-be husband.

She was pretty in a made-up fashion and her long dyed black hair was sleek and smooth. She kept crossing and uncrossing her long, lean fake-tanned limbs and Gary smiled lasciviously at her. It seemed rather incongruous to be at a priest's house with all the open flirting going on – especially seeing why we were there in the first place.

But I didn't want to have a domestic in front of these strangers and our parish priest so I tried to distract Gary by giving him instructions about what not to say to Father Moynalty. The padre and my mother were as thick as thieves.

"Hello, hello!" Father Moynalty blustered in the door, his comb-over all askew.

"Sorry I'm late! I had to give Communion up at the old folks' home, so we'll get started as soon as Mrs O'Brien gives us all a decent cup of tea."

Laughter broke out again all round and Father Moynalty looked at us askance.

After the duly promised tea, we set about the tasks he gave us to ascertain what kind of partners we would make.

It was actually quite interesting and informative and not as wishy-washy as I had anticipated. I thought it would be all rhythm method and producing good Catholic babies, but it was more about what kind of attitudes we both had to parenting and money and conflict. The church had obviously done their homework and I discovered Gary and I had radically different attitudes to everything, from parenting ideas to money plans. We obviously had a lot of work to do.

I feared that Gary would refuse to return to the next session, though perhaps if the luscious Jessie was due to appear he might be cajoled into it.

I looked sadly upon Paul, her fiancé, and wondered if I might seem a little like him to others, seeming to have netted a real beauty but always looking over my shoulder to find another admirer willing to take him away.

"That was a load of codswallop!" Gary fumed as he strode towards his car. "Let's go to the pub – I need a fecking pint after being god-bothered for the guts of two hours." He hopped into the flashy sports number his father had recently given him. It would fit two people at a stretch and only if they weren't remotely chunky. I felt sardined into it at the best of times. Now I squashed my ample rear into its low bucket seats and decided to try to find out what bothered Gary so much about planning our marriage. I had given it little enough thought myself, to be truthful, until now. But I was warming to the idea that we needed to find out more about our wants and needs.

"Gary, it wasn't that bad. I learnt a few things, namely that we have very different ideas about what way we handle money and how we'd parent."

Gary shrugged, donning his Gucci sunglasses while I donned my Penneys ones.

"That's just it, Geri. I think we're fine as we are. I know I'm crap with money and I also know you'd make a terrific mother, so why do we need to go over all the details?" He made his point sound ever so reasonable.

I felt as if I was pushing him into things he didn't want to explore. "We have to go again if you don't want my mother on your case."

Gary laughed – he looked so beautiful when he smiled – those white, even teeth, that luscious, generous mouth. "Oh God, I forgot about your oul' wan! Promise me you'll never turn into her. Attila the Hun had better humours."

I felt like replying that I'd rather have my cleaning-crazy concerned mother than his tarty, histrionic, bitchy one, but I bit my tongue and said nothing. We sped away as Jessie and Paul strolled hand in hand towards his beat-up little Volkswagen and I felt like I was the lucky one.

I was determined to continue the counselling sessions despite what Gary said, but I fervently hoped that Jessie wouldn't be at the next session or we'd be in divorce courts before we were even married.

Chapter 12

Three months later . . .

We got through the premarital course. Gary eventually decided it was easier to give in and acquiesce to my mother's dark stares and we finished the course. I expected a little certificate to state we were suitable for marriage or something official (like a medal) but all we got was a "well done" from Father Moynalty and Gary got some more lascivious looks and fluttering eyelashes from the long-limbed Jessie. I discovered throughout the course that we had very different ideas about a lot of things. Gary wanted a single child (I really believed it was preferably *no* children, but he was too chicken to admit it) whereas I wanted at least four. Gary believed that the men should be the ones who ran the finances of the household and I believed I was the person better equipped to do it – after all, he could barely manage his own money never mind an entire family's. Still, I figured we'd managed so far and it had worked so we could solve our differences after the wedding.

Anyway, we had more important things to think about.

Gary Senior had left Pamela.

He had jettisoned Pamela three months after we had discovered his secret, coldly leaving her a short note and promptly moving in with the delectable Carole, and it seemed that he never looked back. After thirty years of marriage he simply walked away. And his timing was lousy. I know it's a tad selfish of me but I really hoped he would have waited at least till after his only son had been married.

Now he wanted to show up to the wedding with the new girlfriend attached, because he "was deeply in love" as he informed Gary. What were we supposed to do with the awful Pamela? She had already caused a scene at the garage when she rolled up drunk and keyed a few cars before the police were called and she was forcibly removed.

It upset Gary deeply but his father was unrepentant, asserting that Pamela should get over it and "move on".

Now both Gary's parents were bribing him to take sides and we still were at an impasse as to who was sitting at the top table, and if in fact Pamela was even going to attend the wedding. "Handbags at dawn" was not just a bad joke any more – it seemed now a real possibility.

Even though I detested her in general, I felt sorry for Pamela. After all, she had given her best years to Gary Senior and he'd simply discarded her like a used tissue. Gary was solicitous about his mother, which pleased me, because I felt if he treated her so nicely then the chances were he'd treat me the same.

Pamela called me and tried to get me to assure her that Carole wouldn't be invited to the wedding and I was really caught in the middle because, as Gary Senior had given us all that money, I felt if he wanted to take George W Bush to the bash we couldn't have argued.

So I told her the whole sorry tale of the twenty-five thousand.

Now that really set the cat amongst the pigeons.

Pamela hit the roof and issued several expletives that would have embarrassed a docker. She said Gary Senior had assured her that the business was doing badly and he couldn't give her a generous settlement – that she would have to go out and get herself a second job if she wanted to stay in their huge new house. It was after that she went in a fit of pique to the garage and keyed all the cars causing several thousand euros worth of damage and got arrested. I could understand her ire. Then Gary Senior seemed to come to his senses and agreed everything had gone too far. He had pushed Pamela too far and he deserved punishment. So he backed off and didn't press charges. But he still paraded Carole at the golf club and Pamela lost the social crowd that she had been used to. All their friends accepted Gary's new partner and excluded his wife. Pamela was suffering terribly and I fretted that she might explode any day, even our wedding day.

All the stress of Gary's parents' cold war and my own dieting dilemmas and worry over the perfect wedding caused me to comfort-eat. Did you ever eat despite the fact you just knew you had to diet for the most important event in your life – but you just couldn't stop yourself reaching for that biscuit tin and stuffing your face with custard creams, regardless of the consequences? Well, I did. I would start every day on a plain grapefruit for breakfast, followed by a few crisp breads – but by midday I was craving the golden arches and by seven p.m. I was diving head first into the cookie jar. I hated myself. And the abject fear of not fitting into the elusive size-twelve dream gown seemed to spur on my out-of-control raids on the kitchen instead of stopping them. In the end Mum caught me mid-munch one evening standing on a kitchen chair while raiding the bikkie tin that she had hidden on top of the cupboards and she shrieked at me wildly and after that biscuits were furthermore banned until after "the Big day".

I began to take more than a passing interest in the

cosmetic surgery pages of the magazines – liposuction was looking increasingly attractive. I kid you not. The idea of ten pounds of ugly flab being simply sucked away in minutes seemed so irresistible only my absolute fear of surgery forbade me – for the time being anyhow. If I didn't get my act together soon, I'd have to resort to the knife.

I kept putting off the fittings for my wedding gown even though Heavenly Creatures had been on so many times I think she thought that the wedding had been called off and I was just afraid to tell her. I was afraid to tell her I had blubbered out to an even larger size fourteen verging on the dreaded and always unspoken size sixteen. I told no one but just tried to overcome it – the sooner the better.

Meanwhile, Amy had been to Glasgow to see the handsome Stuart and he had been to Dublin to see her too. It was all going very well, which was unusual for Amy. Stuart was handsome in a Marty Pellow kind of way and Amy seemed to be smitten – she had that dreamy look whenever we spoke about him and her phone bill was horrendous. I was happy for Amy if she was happy, but I didn't like the idea of her migrating to Scotland so I dearly hoped that Stuart would continue his love affair with the Irish pub and decide to move over here instead. At least I didn't feel guilty for spending less time with Amy than before.

Mum and I had decided to make the bridesmaids' dresses ourselves and save some money. So far the wedding was costing the entire yearly outlay for a small African nation and was rising steadily by the day. It was probably due to the fact I simply *had* to have imported freesias that didn't come cheap and I suppose the wedding favours that I had insisted on *were* very costly, but it was the most important special day of my life and I wanted it to be – again at the risk of sounding repetitive – *perfect*.

So Mum whisked me off into town to get some wonderful fabric for our creations.

I wafted into Hickey's with a vague idea of floaty organza in a perfect shade of oyster that would complement my palest pink dress. I hadn't realised the expense of organza or the difficulty in locating the exact shade. Mum puffed and panted so much at every shade I discarded that I felt she would have blown a gasket if I hadn't whisked her off to Debenham's for an emergency cappuccino and sticky bun. I tried to explain my vision for the bridesmaids. I hadn't told her that I wanted each to have an individual style to suit their very different figures – she already thought I was going over the top. Mum's idea of nice was a cheap violent pink satiny number that was selling at a knockdown price. (Obviously you wouldn't be seen dead in it.) But I wanted my bridesmaids to look as good as me (well, almost). It was bad news that the organza fabric cost over thirty euro a metre (I didn't even dare do the sums – it was just going to be expensive) but it had to look right.

Mum's view was why was I going to all that trouble for just the bridesmaids who were only going to wear the outfit once? Well, you could say that about the bride's gown also. It was worn once for a few hours and yet it cost thousands – but my theory was that it happened to be the most important few hours of your life and I wasn't going to budge an inch or compromise on quality just to save a few euros.

So after I convinced my mum of the importance of a good quality material to flatter all the girls' figures, and reassured her that I would pay, I went back to Hickey's and I whipped out the credit card (the only one left that I hadn't already maxed out) and prayed silently while the lady whisked it through the machine. Minutes later we were laden down with acres of organza and the two of us giggled like bold schoolgirls as we headed back with our cache to the car.

"You really are incorrigible," Mum laughed. "I hope Gary knows what he's letting himself in for."

"He has no idea," I grinned in return as I stashed the myriad bags into my tiny boot. "No idea whatsoever."

"Lucky for you then," Mum quipped in a rare glimpse of humour.

And it was.

Chapter 13

Three months later . . .

It was three weeks to my wedding day.

We were off to Palma Nova for my hen week. All the girls were very excited. I had made us all shorts from old faded jeans that I customised with little rhinestones and we had matching T-shirts with diamante names on the front and *Geri's Hens* on the back. Everyone was dying for the week away, not least me. I needed a break from choosing which flower matched exactly the bridesmaids' dresses and a break from being on a starvation diet to fit into the size-twelve dream dress. It now finally fitted perfectly – in fact, I had a few pounds to play with, and I intended to eat drink and be merry for an entire seven days with my best friends.

We were having a riotous laugh even before we boarded the plane and I knew Sandy and Jackie were going to be the life and soul of the party, but Clodagh and Amy seemed to be exuberant too at the thought of a girly week away in the sun.

I was sipping my wine and smiling as Sandy and Jackie flirted with two guys barely out of their teens that were on our flight. But inside I was feeling a little bit fretful. Gary had just moved into our new apartment and was planning to have a huge stag party while I was away. I wasn't overly keen on the idea of fifteen blokes (well, I hoped it was only guys attending) spending a weekend wrecking the place before I had even moved in. Gary had suggested to me that it would be much more romantic if I didn't move in with him until after the wedding. I was a little bit disappointed, but I felt my mother (not to mention Father Moynalty) would be rather relieved that I was at least keeping up the pretence of being a good Catholic. So I reluctantly agreed. But now that meant Gary having the full run of the place while I was away. We hadn't much furniture and the floors were wooden but still I fretted. Gary's friends were animals at the best of times. And I was going to be hundreds of miles away so there was precious little I could do to control any of it.

"Earth to Geri, come in Geri! Seriously, babes, you are off on your hen, you have to stop thinking about what Gary is going to get up to and plan what you are going to get up to instead."

It was Amy, proffering another wine. She could

read me like a book.

I smiled wanly. "That obvious?"

She grinned back. "A little. But we'll soon knock this wimpy bride-to-be out of you, won't we, Clodagh?"

"Hmm?" Clodagh looked up absently from her *Financial Times*.

"Clodagh! You are supposed to be switching off too. Now turn off that mobile and ditch the boring newspaper and drink up. Look at the other pair! They've already scored before they've even left Departures. Now, I don't need you two to be acting like elderly grannies in Spain, otherwise I'll have to side with the man-eaters. Clodagh, it's your official task to make Geri enjoy herself for this week, OK? That means you've got to make an effort to have fun yourself."

"Who died and made you a Butlin's redcoat?" Clodagh retorted but she was smiling.

My heart lifted. We were going to have a great time. Gary would have to wait.

♥ ♥ ♥

Three hours later we arrived at Palma airport. The balmy air assaulted us as we disembarked. It was dark but we could still glimpse the coastline and the glittering lights of Palma Nova as the bus wound its way down the coast road.

Our apartments were basic but clean and had the most fabulous views of the bay. We could hear the waves lapping against the rocks and I would have slept in a box if it meant having that fantastic view every day. We dropped our cases and reapplied emergency lipstick before we headed for the nearest bar, which happened to be an Irish one. I felt light-headed and giddy. Even though we were all clad in T-shirts that advertised my almost married status, I felt strangely single and it made me a bit euphoric. Spain wasn't very far away from Ireland but I already felt the shackles of my love for Gary lift a little. I sincerely hoped he wasn't feeing remotely the same way I was feeling, or else we were in trouble, but still . . . the bar was thronged with strange and gorgeous men that I could easily envisage snogging and I wasn't sure if it was just the excitement and strangeness of the place but I felt I wanted to get a little ·tipsy and act inappropriately.

Jackie got a huge jug of sangria from the bar and happened to meet a large contingent of golfers from Dundalk that were in Spain for a week of chasing a tiny ball around, and she enticed five of them over to our table.

"We're here to kiss the bride!" enthused the lads and there were pecks all around before the introductions.

Adam, Barry, Con and Des and Éamonn were all builders from the same company and were a really nice bunch of lads. There was one for each of us, which made me feel exhilarated and also a little bit scared, but chatting was no harm and we all sat around the Irish bar having a laugh and a few sangrias. Adam was quiet with black hair and intense brown eyes. He smiled a lot but said little and I was drawn to him. I felt a bit guilty about it but I was having my hen after all – a girl is allowed to have one last flirty fling before she commits to her one and only. I hoped Jackie or Sandy wouldn't devour him themselves, but they seemed more interested in the louder of the guys, Des and Éamonn, who were both hilarious. Amy was chatting animatedly to Barry, who seemed besotted, and Con was trying to chat to Clodagh with little success. Clodagh was a funny one – she never seemed to want to get involved with anyone. We knew she was dedicated to her career but it was a bit strange all the same. Ever since school she had been running away from guys, breaking many hearts but never falling in love herself. We often speculated that she must be lesbian but was afraid to tell us. We even rigged up situations that would give her an opening to confess all – like starting up discussions about lesbianism and how we all thought it was cool. We even invited the few lesbians we knew for drinks over the years in the hope of making Clodagh let down her guard or start up a relationship. But we couldn't draw her out.

Lesbian or not, Clodagh intrigued me – sometimes

I wished I were more like her, a little harder and more independent. She didn't seem to need male approval, whereas one way or another both Sandy and I craved it. I wondered sometimes why we were like that – perhaps it was because my father had his head stuck in the newspaper for the past thirty years or so and his attention was very hard to get.

"Not having any fun?" It was Adam asking the question, smiling, but his eyes were serious.

"I was just thinking about my father," I replied without thinking.

Adam laughed. "I expected you to say you were maybe thinking about your fiancé – but not your dad. Are you are Daddy's girl or something?"

I wondered was I? I'd never given my dad too much thought – he was just there, like Mass on a Sunday or the armchair with the wobbly arm that was in the lounge – always a constant but not something you gave much attention to. I resolved I'd make a little bit more time to get to know him properly when I got back.

"Not really. I was just thinking I never spend any time with mine, that's all. And you?"

Adam looked at the ground. "My father is dead."

I was embarrassed. I had meant was he having fun, but now I felt like a prize eejit.

"Oh, I'm sorry. Was it long ago?"

"Last year. Heart attack. One minute he was there, telling me to clean all my crap out of the garage, and next minute he was gone. We always lie about his last words because they were not what you'd want your last words to be."

I couldn't help myself. "And what were they?"

"Like I said: 'Get that fecking crap out of my garage before I effin' kill you!'"

I stifled a guffaw, not sure of Adam's reaction to me laughing at his father's demise.

"Are you serious?"

"No, but it got you laughing. Sorry, shouldn't have done that – my old man is as alive as the next one, somewhere. I haven't laid eyes on him since I was six years old. I have this imaginary father that tells me to clean up my act and takes me to footie matches."

"Or dies while giving you a lecture! I've heard some crazy stories in my time but the one about the fictitious dying father is new to me."

Adam looked at me seriously. "I was trying to impress you. I guess I stuffed it up. You just looked so worried and unhappy that I had to try and cheer you up. Sorry."

He was a strange one, I thought. Trying to impress me – it was quite a while since anyone tried to do that. I wasn't sure why, but I liked this quirky intense guy. He was so different to Gary, I suppose. It made a refreshing change.

"And why would you be trying to impress me, and me almost a married woman?"

"Ah yes," replied Adam with those dark dancing

eyes. "But you're not married yet, are you?"

I don't know why but my heart fluttered just for a moment, and I imagined kissing him and running my hands through that black glossy hair, then I thought of Gary and felt instantly guilty. I was taking this hen thing a bit too seriously – surely most brides-to-be didn't feel at all lustful for strangers they met before their big day, did they? None of my friends were married themselves, so I couldn't find out.

"No, but I can't wait," I answered. "Now if you'll excuse me, Adam, I think I need some fresh air."

With that I jumped up and bounded out of the bar and onto the tiny winding street.

Soon Amy was behind me. "Geri, are you OK? You ran out of there pretty fast – what did Adam do? Did he insult you? You look furious."

I felt a bit ill, and I didn't know why but a feeling of dread had overtaken me.

"No, Amy, he was nice. I just feel a bit weird that's all, a bit guilty."

Amy watched me carefully. "Why would you feel guilty? Did you find Adam attractive, is that it?"

I nodded, the feeling of dread started to recede.

Amy laughed. "Is that all? Jeez, Geri, I have that problem all the time. I love Stuart and yet because we have this long-distance relationship I feel attracted to lots of people – you wouldn't be normal if you didn't – it's what you *do* about it that matters. You're getting married to Gary in two weeks and that is what you want, right?"

I nodded vigorously, Amy's reasonable voice calming my inner fears.

"Well, then, that's all that matters."

"But, Amy, I just have this awful feeling that something will go wrong, something will prevent us going ahead with the wedding – and being away from Gary, well, it's making me feel a bit scared, that's all."

Amy looked at me as if I was from another planet. I knew it sounded like I was this limp-wristed clinging limpet who was nothing without her man. A Tammy Wynette song sounded in my head – "Stand by your man".

"Jesus, you don't half talk some crap at times," Amy retorted at last. "It's one week, a week of fun with your best friends, and I for one am not going to let you feel all weepy over Gary. You know damn well he's already pissed and having a rare old time – he sure as hell isn't crying into his beer over you tonight! So come on back inside. I promise I won't make you snog anyone you don't want to."

I knew I'd never live it down if I didn't rejoin the party – after all it was my party.

But I didn't know how long I could resist the darkly handsome Adam.

Suddenly a week away from Gary seemed to be very long indeed.

Chapter 14

The following day we awoke to find a bright azure sky and matching sea – the view from our room really did resemble a postcard and it calmed me – suddenly I felt serene. I took a deep breath and decided I was going to enjoy this last week of freedom. Gary and I had been together for ten years, so what was the worst that could happen?

Well, I suppose Pamela could murder Gary Senior and boil a bunny in Carole's new kitchen in her pristine new apartment or Carole could announce she was with child – after all she was only about forty and nothing Gary Senior could do would surprise me.

Still, I wasn't going to fret over Gary's parents for an entire week in sunny Spain – all that trouble was waiting for me back in Dublin. I'd get to it soon enough. This week was going to be fun. And I was determined that I was going to make the most of it.

"Amy, get up, the weather is truly fantastic. I'm going down to the beach for a couple of hours, are you coming?"

Amy was immediately awake and alert. "Wait two minutes and I'll go with you," she said as she rose swiftly and donned a miniscule yellow bikini.

I stamped on a pang of jealousy that rose within me – how I envied her tall, rangy, skinny body that looked so good in everything. Even though I was now lighter than I had been since I was twelve (thanks to a starvation diet and some sleepless nights of worry over the dress splitting while I lumbered up the aisle) I still had a little potbelly and the ever-so-chunky thighs.

"So, where are the rest of the troops?" Amy asked.

I smiled. "Sandy and Jackie never came home – they obviously got on well with the bould men from Dundalk – and Clodagh has already gone for her power walk. Looks like you and I are the only ones who are here for the suntans and the beach."

Amy laughed. "Those two, what are we going to do with them? Sandy doesn't realise that she, as your chief bridesmaid, is responsible for you having a good time and making sure you don't get into any mischief."

"Chance would be a fine thing! We'll be lucky to get her home for the wedding at all. I'm afraid Sandy was only chosen by me because my oul' wan decided it was that or she was pulling the funds. You are my real chief bridesmaid, Amy."

Amy grimaced. "Gee, thanks. I don't feel like I want that job. Does that mean I have to make sure you don't turn into lobster woman or have peeling shoulders in your fabulous dress?"

"Yes, it does," I replied, slathering on the sunscreen in a panic. I had good skin but it had been bereft of any sun to speak of for a year – and lobster red wouldn't do with a pink wedding gown. I wanted light bronze and healthy for the perfect photos.

"It also means you can't let me fall for the delicious Adam."

"I knew it!" shrieked Amy, breaking into giggles. "I could tell he unhinged you. It's now my mission that you snog the guy and then maybe you'll run off with him and dump Blondie.'

"Too late, babes, I've already got the dress and the invites have gone out, so you're stuck with him."

"No," Amy replied deadpan. "*You're* stuck with him, but come on, let's get to the beach. I want a nice day today, so no wedding talk, deal?"

I bit my lip. I couldn't tell Amy that it hurt me so much that she criticised Gary so openly to me. I loved him – why couldn't she respect that fact? But I didn't want to fall out with her just before my wedding so I stayed quiet, grabbed my trashy novel and followed her skinny ass down to the beach. But I wasn't very happy. Not only were most of my hens missing but the one who was left was the least enthusiastic.

I felt like grabbing my mobile and giving Gary a quick call just to get some reassurance – but we had decided that we weren't going to call each other for the week and I'd feel like a weakling if I caved on the first bloody day, so I silently fumed while reading the same page over and over and Amy lay oblivious beside me on the beach snoozing.

By lunchtime I had got over my earlier annoyance and I began to look forward to having a lovely lunch and a nice siesta before getting ready for a mad night out – that's if bloody Sandy and Jackie ever reappeared. They surfaced a little after three p.m., both chronically hungover, and dived into their beds, but not before I made them both promise to be upright and coherent by the evening.

Clodagh rushed in after her afternoon power walk (she was big on power walks) and announced that she had been in a little boutique in the town that had raved over her customised shorts and had asked if I had some to sell.

I was amazed. I had been asked before about my little creations but this was the first time someone professional had offered to buy some.

"I want you to come down there with me this evening with all the shorts and we'll try to sell them to her," Clodagh enthused. I could tell she was wearing her entrepreneurial hat. Her little eyes were glazing over and I could also see the buzz of a new business was ticking in her mind.

"Do you think I really could?"

I hadn't got a scintilla of Clodagh's self-belief, but I was willing to go with her if she was going to do all the talking. Deep down I believed I could do something creative with my sewing, if I had a bit of encouragement.

"But what else are we going to wear? They're our hen-party outfits!" Sandy wailed from underneath her covers.

"Shut up, Sandy!" we all chorused.

"Bring a few of the T-shirts too," piped up Jackie from underneath her sheet, "and there's that glittery top you made last June – that's totally gorgeous."

"Right," said Clodagh emphatically. "Let's go down now – there's no time like the present and if we hang about Geri will just lose her nerve. Let me do most of the talking, OK, Geri? I'm used to the selling game."

She gathered all the items, placed them in a large carrier bag and made for the door.

"We should have Amy to model them," Clodagh then said.

Amy frowned for a second and then, seeing my disappointed face, agreed.

"It's not my fault I'm so fabulous!" she quipped as she donned a pair of skimpy glittery shorts and a white vest top that I had customised. With the beginnings of her tan already emerging and her long beachy hair she looked the part and the trio of us sauntered down the hilly streets towards the town to the boutique.

We arrived at Victim a few minutes later. It was larger and trendier than I had imagined. The owner, Rosita, was young and very savvy but expressed a lot of interest in the garments. She spoke English almost fluently and showed us the type of one-off items that she favoured – a fair smattering of eclectic styles.

She cast a critical eye over Amy and nodded approval as several teenagers in the store admired the other shorts and vesty tops that lay on the counter.

"Yes, I like these ones bery much," she purred in her sexy Spanish accent.

"Do ju have more?"

I faltered and looked askance at Clodagh.

"We have stock back in Dublin, you understand," said Clodagh. "We are just here on holiday and not intending to sell any, but they are very popular in our country. Each piece is an original and hand-sewn so they are unique and one-offs, so they are not many – you understand?"

Rosita nodded. "*Sí*. A lot of my designers are the same. I carry only several of each garment, but I like to have some of each size as ju can understand." (There was a lot of understanding going on.)

Clodagh looked at the clothes. Most of them had been worn once and I wasn't quite sure how the girls would react to their shorts being sold. The vest tops I had bought as T-shirts and customised myself so I didn't mind too much about those.

"We could have several of each size to you within six weeks," Clodagh breezed as if we ran up acres of shorts every day, conveniently forgetting also that I was getting married in two weeks and I was going on honeymoon for another fortnight afterwards. So how all this was going to happen already had my stress levels rising – it didn't seem real. But I stayed silent until I saw what the outcome was going to be. Clodagh did this sort of thing every day.

"OK," Rosita said slowly. "I take one of each size to start with and two of these tops."

She pointed to the flimsy chiffon top with the slash sleeve that I had made myself from a sarong I'd bought in Penneys for a couple of euro.

Excitement began to overtake the earlier stress. Someone wanted to *buy* my stuff! I was ecstatic. It was great having friends and family like your creations and telling you that you had talent but it was quite another to have a hard-nosed businesswoman offer to stock your creations. I was amazed and was grinning widely like an idiot and we hadn't even discussed price yet.

"Do ju have a business card and email address?" Rosita enquired.

Clodagh flashed one of her *Celt* cards. "I design jewellery and this is my card – Geri is just getting started and sells her stock from my store."

I looked at Clodagh in amazement. I couldn't

believe the lies that just fell from her lips. But it worked because within minutes we had an order and I was walking back to the apartment in a daze.

"Clodagh, I can't believe what just happened! How am I going to fill this order and plan a wedding too? I'm getting married in less than two weeks."

Clodagh shrugged. "Don't worry, Geri, you can get a bit done in a week, can't you? We'll all help. I know the wedding's important but can't you just imagine getting your own business off the ground! What a kick to have people in Spain buy your creations! You could have your own store in Dublin and maybe one in Paris too! This could be the start of something big, something you have always wanted." She looked at me earnestly.

I did have a vague pipe dream that someday I'd be ultra-successful like Clodagh was – but deep down I didn't believe that I was special enough to cut it, to follow through with my dreams. Now that it seemed like a reality I just felt scared. But I was more scared of Clodagh than anyone else so I feigned confidence.

"It is great news, I can't believe it. It's something I want to do, but it's weird timing, that's all."

"You've got to go for it, Geri," interjected Amy. "The wedding will be all over in a month and if you let this opportunity go you'll regret it forever. I will do anything to help, and so will the rest of us. Anyway, I'm sure if we tell Rosita that you're getting married she will give you a few extra weeks' grace."

They were right. I couldn't look a gift horse in the mouth – I needed to take this opportunity despite the lousy timing. Suddenly the fear dissipated and my heart began to soar. Could it be that all my dreams were finally coming true?

♥ ♥ ♥

We went out that night to celebrate. I persuaded the girls to try a different spot, as I really didn't want to meet up with Adam and the men from Dundalk again.

We had a lovely meal in a restaurant overlooking the beach and the inky sky was dotted with stars while the waves bashed against the sand. In fact, it was a really romantic location and I winced as I imagined Gary and me here together. But I couldn't spoil everyone else's time so I faked happiness and soon felt it as the sangrias went down and I was toasted by my friends about my success in the rag trade.

"Why don't we try the Irish bar on the hill for a change?" piped up Sandy. I suspected that she had prearranged a meeting with Des or Éamonn or whatever his name was.

"Irish bars?" squeaked Clodagh in disgust. "We totally get enough of them back home. I think we should try a tapas bar off the beaten track."

Jackie rolled her eyes heavenwards. "Why don't we

just run off to the nunnery and be done with it? Get real, Clodagh! I reckon a karaoke bar is where it's at for craic. We're here to have fun after all."

"Yeah," quipped Amy. "And that means having fun with the bride, not fecking off with whatever pair of trousers happens to wander past, OK?"

Sandy and Jackie looked miserable but nodded agreement anyway.

"Karaoke bar it is so," I ventured. "I bags the All Saints number."

"Bitch!" hissed Sandy. "You know that's mine! Now I'll have to sing 'I Will Always Love You".

"Screech it, y'mean!" laughed Jackie.

"Look who's talking – I've heard crows with better tones!"

Amy smiled beatifically. "Now, ladies, no fisticuffs till after the seventeenth vodka and Red Bull. None of us are Whitney Houston, so cool it – you know I'll be beltin' out 'I Will Survive' by the fifth drink, so embarrassment all round, I think – just what we need."

We made our way to the strip where all the karaoke bars were located and we set up camp in the one with the open doorway so the passersby could glimpse our talent (or lack of).

After a few drinks we were ready for action.

There was a competition for the best singer and while none of us could possibly win, it didn't matter and we gamely ploughed on, each one of us sounding even dodgier than the next. I raced up to screech out my version of "Never Ever " and was plodding through it when I spotted Adam and all the boys from Dundalk taking their seats beside the girls. I almost died from embarrassment, but I had to carry on and tolerate the poor applause that followed. I was crimson and totally sober by the time I took my seat again. Adam gave me a huge hug and told me I had done well. For some reason I felt entirely grateful for that. He had seen my embarrassment and tried to make me feel better. It endeared him to me.

As Sandy belted out her version of Whitney's hit, Adam tried to talk to me again.

"So, how's the tan coming on?"

I grinned. "Fine – everyone is on pink patrol, so the first sign of sunburn and they whisk me off the beach."

Adam eyed me lasciviously. "That must be why you're looking particularly nice tonight – your tan is coming up but you're not burnt." His finger touched my bare shoulder.

I shivered involuntarily. I moved away slightly. "And you, what did you do today?" I tried to keep my voice light and avoided looking at his lips.

"I went diving," Adam replied, surprising me. I thought he was a golf fiend like the rest of the crew.

"So no little white balls then?" I said, trying too hard to be funny and not realising the implication of that stupid comment.

Adam raised his eyebrows while gazing downward at his crotch. "Hey, that's a bit personal! I know we're discussing tans and all ..."

I pucked him in the arm, laughing.

"Sorry, no," he went on. "I hate golf. I just like coming on holidays with the lads. Two of us go diving and the rest spend hours in frustration chasing that little ball around."

He smiled, revealing even white teeth. He looked different when he smiled. Kind of impish – hey, I was getting carried away, noticing his impishness. I really needed to keep myself alert to this one – it would be too easy to slip into his arms and kiss the face off of him.

"I think I need to go to the bar," I said then and escaped into the throng. I ordered another pitcher of sangria and tried to cool down. Why was Adam so appealing to me? Was I that weak that a few days out of my fiancé's sight had me drooling at another man, no matter how attractive? Or was it simply that I wanted to snog my last attractive stranger before I settled down with the man of my dreams?

I'd settled for option two by the time my order was ready and I went back to the gang, deciding to take things as they occurred. All this thinking was making me crazy – a few sangrias and I'd be tipsy enough not to care anyway.

"Doesn't your sister like Éamonn any more?" enquired Adam.

I looked around to see Éamonn pining in the corner while Sandy hung on to every word of some tall, handsome backpacker type, who seemed to be Australian by the dead giveaway of his cork hat and Aussie cricketing shirt.

"She's got a short attention span when it comes to men, I'm afraid."

I smiled at her. She was gazing up into the Aussie's eyes like she was totally in love with him. Sandy was very attractive in a kind of wild, feral way. Her hair was short and at the moment pink (that would have to change within the next two weeks) and she had a pretty face if you ignored the piercings. The Aussie seemed besotted right back, much to Éamonn's chagrin.

"She's not like you, so," Adam said quietly and he downed his pint.

Then he kissed me. Right then and there.

I responded first from pure lust and forgetting where I was until I heard the huge roar of approval from my friends and I suddenly broke off in sheer embarrassment.

I fled.

"I'm sorry, Geri, really I am!" Adam called after me as I ran from the bar.

I didn't stop until I reached our apartment and my heart thumped for a lot longer than the sprint required.

What kind of a person was I? I had kissed another

man a few days away from my wedding. I felt so ill, literally sick to the stomach, at the idea that I had cheated on Gary and, even worse, had *enjoyed* it. I had the audacity to suspect my fiancé at every turn and yet here I was, at the first opportunity, diving on the first attractive bloke to pay me any attention in years. I felt truly awful and spent the night tossing and turning with burning shame and embarrassment.

I barely slept.

Chapter 15

I pretended to be asleep when the girls fell in the door in the early hours. I was still burning with shame over what had happened and even though they would have thought it was a bit of harmless fun, for me it was a betrayal. I was shocked at how easy it was for me to fancy someone else a scant twelve days from pledging myself for life to my soul mate and even worse kissing the face off him to boot.

The next morning Amy tried to discuss it, but I just said that I needed space so I escaped and went for a long walk on the beach just to clear my head. The big problem with kissing Adam was that I *liked* it so much.

By the time I got back to the apartment everyone had left for the beach except for Sandy, who clung to her bed like a clam to its shell.

"I don't know why you're making such a big deal of this," she murmured as I heavy-sighed myself onto my bed. "All ye did was kiss a bloke –"

"We're not all like you, Sandy. Switching from one bloke to the next in a nanosecond. I happen to feel bad because I betrayed Gary and let myself down."

Sandy laughed hollowly. "Oh, puleazze, spare me the Mother Superior act. I'm free to choose whatever and how many men I so desire, whereas you just settled for bloody Gary and now you're feeling sorry for yourself. Grow up, Geri – the world doesn't stop because you kissed a nice-looking fella! Do you seriously think that Gary has never snogged another girl in all the years you've been together?"

I didn't answer. I didn't want to think about Gary kissing other girls, especially seeing as I found it so easy to do myself. "All right, Sandy, I get the picture – let's change the subject. So, tell us about your latest conquest. Poor old Éamonn was devastated you moved on so swiftly, so who's the latest?" I left out the phrase "in a line the length of the Great Wall of China" – but things were tetchy enough between us.

Sandy sat up, suddenly animated. "Oh, Geri, he's the nicest bloke I have met in such a long time. He was a total gentleman and didn't even pounce on me."

I grinned. "I'm surprised that you found that an attractive quality, going on past experiences."

"Stop that!" Sandy retorted, all huffy. "You always make me out to be some sort of hooker, but I'm not,

Geri. I haven't slept with as many men as you seem to think. I don't like it when you put me down all the time. You are supposed to be my sister. I've got enough people knocking me without you as well!"

I resisted the urge to make a quick jab about knocking – Sandy didn't seem in the mood. "I suppose the next thing is you'll want us all to call you Josephine again and you'll start wearing floor-length skirts and going to Confession."

Sandy laughed despite herself. "Bitch!"

I sat on her bed. "Seriously, Sand, I didn't mean to hurt you, so I promise I won't joke about the revolving door to your boudoir again. You really like this dude, then?"

"Yeah, he's called Chris and he's an Aussie. I'm seeing him this afternoon, so I'll be free tonight. He's taking me into Palma for a tour of the city."

"Well, at least he sounds like he's got more than one brain cell. Do you want to borrow my spangly top?"

Sandy smiled back happily. "Yeah, that would be great – thanks, sis, and I promise I'll never call you a square old witch ever again."

And that was the longest conversation we'd had in over ten years. I was beginning to understand my little sister a bit, and even feel a little affection. It must have been sunstroke.

After much ribbing and general banter from my friends about my loose morals and worn-down lips, I was dreading going out at all in case I met Adam. He seemed to have a radar where my location was concerned so I felt like pulling a huge sickie and staying at home in bed, but I was the star of the show so I couldn't let them down – well, that was what I told myself anyway. But I still managed to wear my best, sexiest dress, a fact that didn't go unnoticed by Clodagh.

"Dressed to impress, I see," she murmured quietly as we tottered down the many stairs of the apartment on impossible heels.

"I don't know what you mean," I lied, as I teetered towards the taxi. If I was going to bump into Adam, at least I had to look good.

I didn't have to wait too long. Mid-mouthful of my paella at a tiny traditional restaurant well off the beaten track, the five lads strolled in.

Adam looked as shocked as I felt when he saw me. Any attempt I had made at glamour was lost as I had an octopus leg dangling from my lips.

Of course they joined us. We all sandwiched up and before long the sangria was flowing again and eventually Adam got close to me and, feeling seventeen again, I blushed and awaited the apology that I knew he was going to give.

"I'm really sorry about last night," he began.

"I didn't realise I was such a lousy kisser," I quipped. I had rehearsed that earlier in case of the apology. It didn't sound as funny now.

Adam smiled. "You're not. I don't regret kissing you – that was wonderful. But I regret compromising you, what with you getting married and all. I'm sorry I upset you." He looked truly contrite.

"It's OK," I replied easily. "I upset myself – there were two of us in it. Look, I'm getting married in a fortnight and I felt a bit guilty, that's all. Friends?"

"You bet," smiled Adam and we shook on it.

A frisson of disappointment rushed through me. I'd rather hoped he would put up more of a fight.

Sometimes Gary was right: I was never happy.

Adam and his golfing entourage flew home the next day.

♥ ♥ ♥

A few days later, a nice toasty brown, we flew home for the final onslaught of wedding preparations. I put the unsettling meeting and subsequent pashing of Adam behind me as the plane sped towards the dark moodiness of Ireland. We landed in torrential May rain and I prayed that even though Gary and I hadn't spoken for the entire week he'd have the brains and romance to greet me at the airport. I needed it to assuage my insecurities and to prove to my friends that Gary loved me deeply and he missed me.

For once he didn't disappoint. He was there in all his glory, all six foot three of him, grinning like an idiot in the arrivals hall. There weren't any flowers but it didn't matter. He scooped me up and kissed me passionately and I was delighted to see him.

Even Amy cracked a smile to see me so happy.

"Miss me?" he murmured into my hair as we walked to the car park. I had left the girls behind in my excitement and was now feeling rather guilty. I knew they would be irritated – after all they had gone to the wilds of Spain for me and then I couldn't even finish off the week away with a few last drinks at the airport. Yet I needed to be with Gary to convince myself the kiss in Palma Nova had just been an aberration. I needed to smell him, quiz him and check on the apartment to see if he had behaved himself and the place was still in one piece.

"Of course I missed you!" I kissed him again.

"You look fantastic," Gary then said. "I can imagine how you'll look on our wedding day judging by how you look today. I can't wait until I get you home!"

I looked at him. I couldn't wait either but I felt interminably guilty. I took out my mobile and rang Clodagh.

"Where are you guys? I got lost in the mêlée."

"We're in the bar at the arrivals hall. Sandy is taking bets that you're already halfway to Kinsealy Cloisters, but I said that you wouldn't let us down. I'll have a cocktail ready for you – do I need to get a pint for the big fella?"

I looked at Gary – he was putting my suitcases into

the sports car's tiny boot.

"I guess not," I said. I hung up.

I turned to Gary. "My hens haven't quite finished with the bridal preparations. I need to go back for a while, Gary – do you mind?"

He looked like he was going to complain for a moment, then changed his mind.

"No, go ahead, but I do expect to see you tonight – we have a few things to talk about."

I wasn't sure how I felt about that, but I was tired and just wanted to get back to the girls so I wouldn't seem like the biggest wuss.

It was difficult trying to please everybody, but I knew if I didn't join my friends they would be rightly annoyed as we had planned the drinks from earlier on the plane.

I kissed my fiancé and promised to see him later and rushed back to the bar.

The girls gave me a rousing cheer as I approached. I saw a fiver pass between Sandy and Clodagh. I was relieved that I had returned. Clodagh passed me a cocktail and I smiled brightly as Amy whispered that Sandy had told them all that I had to check out the apartment for lipstick stains on cups and even worse. Swearing I'd kill her later, I managed to convince the others I was coolly enjoying myself recounting the holiday, but inside I was already over at Kinsealy Cloisters checking the bed linen and Gary's laundry basket. Sandy knew me better than I had realised.

Why did I suspect Gary so much? Was it because I couldn't be trusted myself?

Several Manhattans later, I stumbled into a taxi and hightailed it over to Kinsealy Cloisters to get my man and my suitcases and carry out surreptitious checks on our boudoir. Gary was half asleep in front of the TV with a half-eaten pizza still lingering in its box on the new coffee table. The tiny kitchen was awash with empty beer cans competing with dirty dishes for attention. The sink had an unidentifiable liquid gunk in it and I had to count to ten in order to prevent me from scratching Gary's eyes out then and there. But I demurred. I would break out my Marigolds later. Right now I needed to know if my man had missed me but not so much that he had to find a temporary replacement, much as I had. So, after a preliminary scout around for lipstick stains and the like, I woke him up with a soft kiss and asked jokingly if it was the maid's day off.

"Hiya, hon," Gary replied sleepily, stretching out his long arms and pulling me to him. "Sorry, I had meant to clean it all up before you got back but I guess things got on top of me a bit – it's been hectic at the garage all week. But don't worry, I'll clean it up later. C'mere!" He kissed me passionately.

But for some reason Adam suddenly popped into my head – well, Adam's kiss popped into my head. Maybe it was because I felt so guilty after what I had done, but I couldn't help comparing them. Adam's kiss had been lingering, sensual and head-spinning, whereas Gary's kiss was familiar and comfortable but it didn't make my head spin and, come to think of it, it never had. But life and love weren't built on kisses, were they? Or maybe they were. Either way I couldn't shake the feeling of unease, even after Gary had scooped me up and carried me to the bedroom and made mad passionate love to me. Guilt was a horrible thing. It had rightly stuffed up my reunion with my husband-to-be.

♥ ♥ ♥

The next morning I decided to tackle the terrible appearance of the apartment and shunted Gary off to a game of golf with his dad so I could clean in peace and also do a thorough check to see if there were any tell-tale signs of female company about the place. Of course there weren't. Even if there had been, Gary wasn't so stupid that he'd leave evidence, but it still reassured me that I found seventeen beer cans concealed about the place, but no knickers.

What did disturb me though was the change that had taken place in the baby room, or the games room as Gary had termed it. Inside the room was a total gym, complete with weights, a running track and a rowing machine. There were even prints of sports cars on the wall. It was a total bloke zone and it infuriated me. I just couldn't believe that he had no thought or consideration for my feelings whatsoever.

I mean, I knew that we weren't going to have a baby for the required five years, but deep down in my heart I hadn't really believed Gary had meant a *full* five years, and I certainly hadn't expected this haven of male testosterone to be created while I was away for a mere week and Gary hadn't even bothered to tell me. It just looked *so permanent*.

So I marched into the bedroom and fetched my handbag. I took out my packet of contraceptive pills and strode angrily into the toilet and flushed them away.

Gary bloody Warren would see where his little selfish plans would get him.

I would see to that. That was for sure.

Chapter 16

I kept the pill-flushing ceremony to myself. I hugged it to me like the child I so desired and imagined myself to be already surging with fertile hormones. Maybe I was even already with child – well, perhaps that was taking things a little *too* far; it had only been a couple of hours, after all. I didn't care what Gary would say – he'd have to come around eventually and I knew he'd love any baby I presented him with. That gym of his was going to have a short and sweet existence before being replaced with bunny rabbits and teddy bears. We could all be selfish and have our own agenda. Still, I felt sort of illicit, like some fifties woman, trying to trap her man. It wasn't very honest, I admit, but I had a need too – my biological clock was just beginning to hammer out a tune that couldn't be ignored, and anyway, it might take ages and as Amy said there were no guarantees that I would fall pregnant immediately, if at all. It just made me feel good to remove some of Gary's power – it restored the balance as it were.

Anyway, I soon forgot about my duplicity after Amy's phone call.

My mobile trilled just after eleven.

"Geri, it's me!" Amy squeaked in that little-girl whisper that I hadn't heard in a while, the voice she had used when she had little confidence, when she had been treated so awfully by George and Trevor and any number of wasters over the years.

"What's wrong?" I instantly knew she was upset. I could imagine her cute pointy chin quivering and those pale-blue eyes filling with tears – I'd kill bloody Stuart if he had dumped her.

"Oh, Geri. I've had an awful shock. I telephoned Stuart just to say hello. We hadn't spoken in over a week, with me being in Spain and all. Anyway, when I rang his mobile it rang out for ages and then a girl answered."

"A girl?" I echoed. "It could have been anyone, Amy!"

"No, Geri, not anyone. She specifically said that he didn't want to speak to me any more and that she was his ex-girlfriend of two years' standing and they had just got back together. Stuart was very sorry but he couldn't see me any more and I wasn't to call back." Her voice wavered. I could tell she was more than upset.

"Look, Amy, there's more to this than meets the eye. I'm coming over. I'll be there in half an hour."

"Are you sure?" Amy replied worriedly. "I mean, I feel so awful – you've just got back to Gary and here I am ruining your Sunday."

"Nonsense," I insisted. "I banished him to the golf course. The place is a tip and I had to clean it up – I'm just about finished. Having a tiny apartment has its advantages, the housework is done in no time, so put the kettle on and don't stress, I'll be there really soon, OK?"

"OK," she replied, sounding forlorn and yet relieved.

I sighed as I grabbed my handbag and car keys and rushed to my little car. Just when things had being going so well for Amy, now this – I couldn't see how there was any kind of innocent explanation for the strange phone call, but I would try to think of something on the twenty-minute drive to Dollymount, where Amy lived.

By the time I got to Amy's apartment I had imagined all sorts of scenarios for the mystery girlfriend, none of which were plausible but were possible – unlikely but possible.

Amy rented a small but pretty apartment overlooking the sea – she had decided to escape her five younger siblings and her strict parents and had moved out almost as soon as she was twenty-one. I always felt like a stay-at-home slob because I hadn't moved out of my home and become all grown-up like Amy had. I suppose I was always waiting for Gary. Well, now I had my own apartment with Gary and I felt good about that as I skipped up the stairs after she'd buzzed me in.

Amy had the coffee bubbling and was pink with stress as she answered the door.

"Right", I said, as I plonked myself on her tiny sofa and she ushered in the coffee and cookies, our necessary accompaniment for any emergency. "Tell me all of the phone call from start to finish and don't leave anything out – it may be important."

She told me the whole sorry tale, that she had called Stuart on his usual number to no reply. Then when she called his mobile, this other biddy had answered and warned Amy off.

"Perhaps Stuart has lost his phone and it was some strange girl answering, Amy," I offered. Though I hardly believed it myself.

"I've thought of that," she replied sadly, looking out the window to the receding tide.

"But if that is the case then why hasn't he called me, and why doesn't he answer his house phone? It sounds like he is letting her dump me and is avoiding my calls. Oh, Geri, I'll go mad if this is another failure. I just can't go through all this again, I am so sick of being walked all over. I really thought Stuart was different."

So did I.

"Did she sound credible," I asked, "like she knew what she was talking about?"

"Yes, I think she did, anyway. I'm not ringing him back – he can contact me next."

"But," I said, warming to the theme of ex-girlfriend scorned, "what if she is a bunny-boiler who won't leave him alone and stole his mobile – then when you rang she warned you off?"

Amy suddenly brightened. "You know, you could have something there, but I'm still not calling again. He knows I'm back from Spain and he's due to come over for your wedding so if he doesn't call me in a few days then I'll know it's over. It probably could never have worked anyway – long-distance relationships seldom do – but he was just so cute."

Yes. I remembered his soft Scottish burr and infectious laugh – the unfaithful sod! I would have words with him if it were the case that he had been a right coward and dumped Amy by proxy. He wouldn't get away with it, but for now Amy seemed to be vacillating between seizing on my explanation of the bunny-boiler ex and believing the worst. Either way she had polished off eight cookies, which was most unlike her.

I nibbled just one, ever conscious of fitting into the dream dress.

I tried to change the subject, to distract her if possible. "I need you and Clodagh and Sandy to have one final fitting of your bridesmaids' dresses tomorrow night, if that's OK? Mum is just putting the finishing touches to them and they look fabulous apparently. You'll look terrific in it with your gorgeous tan."

Amy brightened. "Yeah, I can't wait to see it finished. Have you told Clodagh yet? She called me today, mentioned something about bringing someone called Karl to the wedding."

I was intrigued. "Karl? Who the hell is he when he's up and dressed? I've never heard her mention him before. Jeez, she's a dark horse – she's never told me about this Karl bloke. I wonder if he's someone she's met in work. About bloody time she met someone anyhow. I was wondering what was up with her – she is so serious lately. This is just what she needs."

Amy shrugged, not wanting to be reminded of budding romances when her own looked like it was floundering.

"She'll probably tell you tomorrow night – at the dress fitting, I mean."

"Right, I'll text her and Mum will tell Sandy. I have to get Mum to break it to Sandy too about the pink hair – it's got to go. It'll clash something shocking with my wedding dress."

Amy giggled while reaching for another cookie. "Yes, I can't imagine her hair a boring brown though, can you?"

"It'll have to be blonde, brown or red until after

the wedding, then she can have purple with pink stripes for all I care. It'll probably be green and gold considering she's fallen head over heels for the Aussie."

"Yeah, I thought she'd never be parted from him at the airport – they were like Love's Young Dream."

I rolled my eyes heavenwards. "Can you believe he's supposed to be coming over for the wedding? Sandy invited him to stay at our house. Can you imagine Mum when he rolls up with his cork hat and backpack two days before my big day? She'll have aunties hanging out of the rafters and then Sandy will front up with the big Aussie just to complicate things."

Amy frowned. "I'll look like a right loser if everyone else has a new boyfriend and Stuart doesn't show up. Maybe I'll give him a call tomorrow, after all."

"You do that," I replied, "because I need you to be my bright and shiny best bridesmaid – you've got to be happy and smiley for all the photographs." I squeezed her hand.

"It'll be OK, Amy, I'm sure of it. You'll see, everything will work out and you'll be up to your oxters in kilts before you know it."

Amy smiled like she half believed it or perhaps she was just humouring me, I didn't know which.

♥ ♥ ♥

The following morning I returned to work. I really should have been already on annual leave to prepare for the wedding, which was only a couple of weeks away, but as the guys were so busy with the current project and it was at such a crucial stage, I offered to go in for one more week. I was up to my eyes when Clodagh called.

"Can I prise you away for lunch, Geri? I really need to talk to you alone."

It sounded serious, but I was under a lot of pressure to finish preparing the proposal.

"Can't it wait until tonight when you come for the fitting?"

Clodagh sighed heavily. "I'm afraid not. I'll pick you up, we'll go local and I'll drop you back, if that makes a difference. I promise not to mention the Spanish order for the clothes, if that's what you're worried about."

Shit! I'd forgotten all about that. I hadn't even considered how I was going to fill that order. My head was swimming with wedding preparations, architects' drawings and now I was expected to become Superwoman designing and creating an order for the Spanish boutique! There just weren't enough hours in the day.

Anyway, I decided to forget about my one-woman empire for the moment and meet Clodagh for whatever disaster had befallen her. Jeez, it seemed like I was turning into a crisis counsellor on the side.

Hadn't anyone realised that my wedding was only around the corner?

"OK," I agreed reluctantly, eyeing with a sinking heart the burgeoning pile on my desk. I could actually feel my blood pressure rise by the minute. "Make it Scruffy Murphy's and you have yourself a deal, and by the way, you're paying."

"OK," laughed Clodagh. "Jeez, you drive a hard bargain. See ya at half twelve."

By the time twelve thirty rolled around, my neck and shoulders ached from poring over architects' drawings and the incessant photocopying and I had completely forgotten Clodagh was even meeting me for lunch until she peeked her head around the door.

I grabbed my coat gratefully and we sped off in her smart VW Polo along the few cluttered streets to our favourite watering hole.

"So, what's the big emergency?" I ventured, as she parked the car up a side lane on a double yellow line (I told you she was fearless).

"Wait until you have at least a glass of wine or two inside you," she replied unsmilingly, which worried me more than a little.

Was she going to tell me something dreadful about Gary or what? My mind refused to contemplate what that something dreadful might be.

As we settled into a booth and ordered from the bar menu, Clodagh ordered a carafe of house red and we made small talk about the wedding until the required two glasses were quaffed.

"Right, Clodagh, I can't stand the suspense any longer. Spill the beans – what is so awful that you have to get me half shot to tell me?"

Clodagh blushed profusely – something I hadn't seen her do since she was fifteen and had to ask Charlie Harris out for a bet.

"I want to take someone to the wedding, someone who has become very important to me in the past six months. But I want to have your blessing first."

I smiled in great relief. Was that all? Clodagh was so old-fashioned, really!

"Oh yes, the mysterious *Karl*. You kept him very quiet, Clodagh! What's the story? Why have you never mentioned him before?"

Clodagh knocked back the rest of her wine. "Because he is *married*. Karl is married with two children and he has no intention of leaving his wife, and furthermore I don't want him to. But I feel deeply for Karl and I'd like you and Amy, as my friends, to be part of my life – *all* of my life – and Karl is a very important part of that. But I realise you may not approve and may not want him to be there."

"So why did you never tell us about him?" I asked, trying to keep the shock out of my voice.

"I kept it quiet at first because I didn't want to fall for him. I knew he was married from the outset. It was the same for him – he fell for me without wanting to – we didn't plan it, but there it is. We love each other but there is no question of him leaving his wife, because of their two children."

"And how does his wife feel about this cosy little set-up?" I blazed, incredulous that she was telling me this just over a week away from me pledging my life to my future husband. Here she was asking me to give my blessing to her having an affair and then parading it at my wedding! I was supposed to take my vows in front of someone flouting theirs.

Clodagh looked crestfallen. "She doesn't know. Look, I know this isn't a perfect set-up. I wish to hell Karl was free. I didn't plan to fall for him, but it happened, and I kind of hoped that you could support me, even if you don't agree with it. I hardly agree with it myself, Geri …" Her voice trailed away.

"And to think we all thought you were gay!" I blurted out unnecessarily and instantly regretted it.

Clodagh glared at me. "*What*?"

"Well," I blustered, "you hardly ever had a date or even seemed interested in anyone. We just guessed that you might prefer girls and didn't want to say. Anyway, that would have been OK – a damn sight preferable to husband-stealing!"

"So I guess that's a no, then," Clodagh said huffily, the atmosphere plummeting between us.

But I just couldn't see past this one. It was too big.

"I'll have to think about it," I said finally, imagining myself short one bridesmaid if things deteriorated any further between us.

"OK," she replied quietly, fiddling with her lunch. "Can I just say that the reason I kept it so quiet is because I felt that it would fizzle out before very long and I'm not proud of myself for seeing him – but I just can't help it, I couldn't let him go."

"And where did you meet?" I asked, a little icily.

"He's in the trade – he's a jeweller actually. We met at a conference and we were just friends for ages, then one night we happened to bump into each other in Cork at a trade fair and we had a few drinks."

"And you just *fell* into his bed?"

As you can see I was taking it very well.

"No, as it happens, but I am *human* and I do make mistakes and we're not all like you, Geri, lined up for sainthood and the martyrdom of marriage!"

I stood up. "Right, that's it! I am one week out from my wedding. I have bridesmaids' dresses and arrangements up to my tits and I have two stressed-out bosses back at the office, not to mention the unmentioned Spanish order for the shorts which looks like it'll never get filled! I just don't have time for your dramas, Clodagh. Now I really have to get back before one of us says something we will regret later."

"Right," she said. All the energy seemed to have gone out of my normally feisty friend.

I knew I wasn't being supportive and it was wrong of me to judge her, but I just felt it was a bit much asking me to accept a married bloke at my wedding as her partner, making a mockery of the whole event. Clodagh had also waited until the last possible minute – she could have told me weeks ago, or even in Spain – we had plenty of opportunities for heart to hearts. Now she had left me precious little time to get used to the idea. I knew I could never tell my mother – she'd have an absolute heart attack.

I got up to leave.

"You stay and finish your lunch, Clodagh. I can walk back to the office – it'll probably be quicker."

"No, that's OK," she said feebly, wearily. "I appear to have lost my appetite. I'll drop you back. I promise I won't mention Karl or the invite again. I'll let you decide for yourself."

She rose swiftly and we walked back to the car in silence; a huge rift between us that hadn't even been considered an hour earlier. I simply couldn't even think of anything to say to her. I just felt I didn't even know Clodagh any more and yet she was one of my oldest friends. It wasn't any of my business that Clodagh was having an affair with a married man, yet she was making it my business by putting him in the middle of my most special day

We drove the odd mile back to my office in an awkward silence.

As I got out of Clodagh's car I said, "So I'll see you tonight for the final fitting for your dress?"

Clodagh looked at me with a pained expression. "If you still want me?"

"Of course I still want you, Clodagh. My wedding just wouldn't be the same without you. You are one of my oldest and best friends. I just can't get my head around this Karl thing, but look, we'll talk later, OK? I have so much on my mind – my head is swirling. Now, I really have to go. Connor and Dave need me on top form this afternoon – so I'll see you at my mum's after seven, OK?"

"OK," Clodagh shrugged and sped off quickly.

I could tell she wasn't happy.

But then again, neither was I.

Chapter 17

Later on that evening I managed to get to Amy before Clodagh arrived and I gave her a quick run down of my shocking lunch with Clodagh. Amy was so surprised it took her mind totally off her own romantic problems.

"*What?*" she screeched in my bedroom where I had sequestered her in the mortal fear that my mother would overhear. If she did, Clodagh would not only be banned from the altar but probably the entire wedding as well.

"Yep," I replied sagely, "he is twenty-four-carat married, complete with two point four children and probably a dog and pension plan as well, but it doesn't seem to bother our Clodagh. *No*, she wants us to be a '*part of her whole life*' and that includes bloody Casanova Karl. We're supposed to go through an entire charade at the wedding like he's a normal boyfriend, all the while knowing that his poor wife is at home wiping snotty noses while he lives it up in Cavan Castle canoodling with our Clodagh! I mean, *really*, Amy, it's too much to ask."

Amy bit her lip. I could see a fence-sitting sentence of *understanding how everybody felt* coming on.

"I agree," she said finally. "Normally I'm pretty easygoing with people doing what feels best for them, but I think she is being very inconsiderate of your situation and the fact that you're about to start your marriage and there she is breaking one up. I think you should tell her no, outright, Geri. After all, it is your day."

I stared at Amy – it was about the most forthright she had ever been. I liked the new rod of steel that was propping up her backbone. And I felt better because she made me realise that I wasn't being unreasonable, that Clodagh was. Yet I still had this uneasy feeling that if the cretinous Karl wasn't allowed to attend the wedding that I would be short a bridesmaid. Not to mention what would I tell my mother.

"Right," I whispered now, because I could hear my mother rustling the bridesmaids' dresses outside on the landing, "say nothing for the moment, let's just see what Clodagh is like when she arrives. I can take it from there."

Amy nodded and we quietly crept downstairs to the lounge where my mother was waiting with the fabulous gowns in the newly refurbished front room. Dad had nearly had a seizure when he saw the decorator's bill for the painting, but he had to admit the place was looking a lot more upmarket since the new leather suite had arrived.

It was just a pity after all Mum's hard work and putting up with Dad's whinging over the cost of everything that now Pamela and Gary Senior were never going to see it.

Mum preferred to pretend that Gary Senior and Pamela didn't exist at all and wouldn't even entertain the idea of mixing with Gary Senior since he ran out on his marriage – hence my worry about her reaction to Clodagh and Karl if I ever let them attend and she found out. So things had been difficult. It had required a lot of diplomatic juggling on my behalf to keep things on an even keel. The Warrens were still a dirty word in the Murphy household at the moment.

Now I smiled widely at my mother and tried not to chew with angst on my newly grown nails as I waited for Clodagh to arrive.

Mum was holding Amy's bridesmaid dress reverentially, waiting on her model girl to step into it and do her creation justice.

"Josephine," Mum said, as she helped Amy into her gown, "I mean *Sandy*, is off getting her hair coloured with the Aussie. We're in no hurry to see the pair of them back in anyway – they're like sticky plaster with each other, as if I haven't got enough to do with your Aunty Pearl coming and the wedding dresses to finish. I'm feeding the Aussie, who eats like it's going out of style, and he and Sandy keep getting under my feet, canoodling and kissing like two teenagers. Anyway, try this on, Amy."

Amy looked amazing in the Grecian-style oyster organza dress that nipped into her tiny waist and flowed freely to the floor. With her long blonde hair and light tan, she was almost too pretty – I had a hard act to top even as the bride. Still, I knew Amy would be fantastic and that was that. I only hoped Clodagh would still agree to appear and that Sandy wouldn't have her hair dyed green just to spite me.

"I love it!" Amy enthused as the doorbell trilled.

It was Clodagh. She seemed subdued but still smiled as she walked into the hallway.

"Just go through to the front room – Mum is waiting," I breezed loudly, giving her silent signals not to ask any awkward questions.

Mum fussed about, fitting Clodagh's dress on her, and made lots of small talk, so it took some pressure off. Clodagh's dress was slightly different in style to suit her petite boyish figure and it really looked great. And she seemed her pert, bouncy, wise-cracking self except for the large circles under her eyes.

Soon after, Sandy arrived home, complete with besotted Aussie and a new caramel hair colour that flattered her green eyes and made her look almost beautiful. I threw my arms around her and hugged her fiercely. I knew it had cost her a lot emotionally to let go of the mad punk hair, but somehow I knew that Chris was having a very positive effect on her. And she looked so happy and in love that it almost made me wince to see my friend Clodagh seem so different with her love. So *depressed* – it was hardly what I had hoped for her. But what could I do? She was a big girl now and as she had fallen for a married man she couldn't expect cartwheels – or even, it seemed, acceptance.

We soon all escaped down to the pub to talk the talk to Clodagh. I tried to get Sandy to come alone but she couldn't be prised from the Aussie hunk – so I persuaded her that Grainger's was way too boring for Chris and I was sure he'd prefer a traditional Irish music session at Slattery's in Capel Street, so Amy and I were alone with the formidable Clodagh.

I flicked through my mobile as Amy went to fetch the drinks and Clodagh tapped her fingers in an irritated manner. I had to tell Gary I was going to be late seeing him yet again. I had hardly seen him since I got back from Spain with one crisis and another.

"Lover boy not answering?" Clodagh issued sweetly with a sarcastic grin.

She knew my insecurities with Gary were deep, but right now it seemed like she was saying "your situation is little better than mine".

"He only said he *might* be home by now. I'll text him and we can meet up later. Anyway, Clodagh, I have told Amy about you and Karl."

"I guessed as much," Clodagh replied airily. "So what's this – you and Amy are going to ambush me?"

"Hardly," I retorted huffily. "I haven't even figured it out for myself, Clodagh. I'm still in shock with your news – it hasn't quite sunk in yet. I just felt we should talk about the whole thing, trash it out as it were."

Amy arrived back with the necessary alcohol to defuse the tension between us.

"So, Amy," Clodagh began mischievously, "how's your love life, seeing as you seem to know an awful lot about mine."

Amy frowned and I suddenly remembered I hadn't even asked her if Stuart had called. I was so wrapped up in all my own problems that I hadn't even considered hers.

"If you must know," said Amy, "it seems that Stuart has more than a passing interest in another lady, making me not quite number one in his life, but you'd know all about *that* now, wouldn't you, Clodagh?"

Clodagh stood up in a temper. I froze. This was all getting a bit out of hand.

"Now, Amy. I know you're upset, but that wasn't really necessary. Clodagh, sit down, *please*. Amy didn't really mean it – she's been upset by Stuart since she got back and he's been avoiding her calls. What's happened, Amy?"

Clodagh sat back down – it seemed she needed to hear Amy's sorry tale too.

Amy's pretty face crumpled as she almost came to tears. "Well, Stuart never did return my call. I eventually got him on his mobile and he admitted that he had been dating another girl for three years before we met, but that she had broken it off, and now she wants him back. He said they had met up again and had a few drinks too many while I was in Spain, and he ended up in bed with her. He says it only happened the once and it's over. It was right after that event I called and she answered."

"And how do you feel about that?" Clodagh asked in a gentle voice that seemed quite unlike her own.

"I feel like shit, actually, Clodagh. No matter how he dresses it up, he still cheated on me with another woman and I can't trust him any more. How do I know it's all over between them, I only have his word for that, and what is his word worth as a cheat?"

A tear escaped Clodagh's eye and rolled down her cheek. "Exactly," she said quietly, sipping on her vodka and cranberry juice.

"Is that how you feel too, Clodagh?" I asked.

"Yes," Clodagh nodded. "It feels so bad to love someone that doesn't belong to you. I feel my heart break every time Karl goes home to his wife and I am left alone."

I felt the old hackles rise. It wasn't the same at all. Amy hadn't met a married man, whereas Clodagh knew exactly what she was getting into.

"But, Clodagh, you *knew* that Karl was married – he wasn't yours to have. Amy met Stuart in Galway and he told her he was single. It's not the same at all."

"But I fell in love with him!" Clodagh wailed. "*I couldn't help it*."

I didn't know if I wanted to slap her face or hug her, but she was my friend and she was in pain so I hugged her, even though I still hated what she was doing.

"Clodagh," I said as evenly as I could. "Karl cannot come to the wedding. Apart from the fact that someone might know him, my mother would have a pink fit if she finds out and it's bad enough that she can't prevent the groom's father from attending, because believe me, she would if she could. I just can't have a married guy who is having an affair with my one of my dearest friends sit there and listen to me say my vows. Now I am sorry but I can't change my mind."

"OK," she said in a small voice. "I guess Amy and I will have to battle it out as the Desperate Bridesmaids, after all."

"Speak for yourself," smiled Amy. "I wouldn't touch any of Gary's mates with a bargepole. I'll be taking a vow of chastity for the immediate future and I'm dead off tartan too."

"What are yez like?" I smiled. "Desperate and dateless, the pair of yez!"

Clodagh gave a small wry smile that didn't reach her eyes. "Desperate is just about right."

The worst was over for the moment in my bridesmaids' crisis, but one look at my two friends told me that they still had some pain ahead. Wasn't I the really lucky one, to be marrying the man of my dreams in a little over a week?

What a romantic, deluded idiot I was.

Chapter 18

It was the final week before my wedding.

And the stress was getting to me.

Apart from my worry about the state of my best friends' love lives, my mother's considerable moodiness with entertaining Aunty Pearl and Uncle Fred, feeding a ravenous Aussie and finishing off the bridesmaids' dresses, all the while policing Sandy's bedroom door late at night in case the Aussie got any fresh ideas – I was also worried about Gary. The closer we got to the big day, the more remote he seemed to become.

I know that most bridegrooms find the preparations alien to them and it's all a bit too girly, talking about place settings and flower arrangements, but Gary seemed a bit worried or perhaps even scared. I wondered if it was cold feet or was he just concerned that there might be a scene between his mum and Carole at the wedding, yet I kept my worries to myself.

Still, all the romance seemed to have gone out of him. And I hoped deep down it was just the arrangements and not me that he was bored with.

I had heard that most married couples go through a lot of stress in the lead-up to the Big Day and have lots of fights, but that was just it: we weren't even fighting – there was no emotion at all, it seemed. And I was so caught up in all the finer details and just so exhausted with all the myriad "*things still left to do*" that I just couldn't deal with another problem. Or else I didn't want to.

On top of that, Gary had a few friends jet in from New York for the wedding and they were staying at our apartment for the week, so we weren't even getting much time alone.

So I grabbed a bottle of champers and brought him out to Howth for a drive one evening to spend a bit of time together. I was about to go up to Galway to collect my perfect wedding dress. It had been a considerable strain travelling all that way for each fitting and now I was off to finally bring my perfect dress home. But I was leaving Gary yet again and we'd had so little proper time together since I had returned from my hen week.

The sun was shining brightly and it was a beautiful clear evening. You could see the entire bay area and

Gary and I sipped our Moët while drinking in the view.

"This time next week it'll be all over bar the shouting," I smiled up at him while nestled into his chest.

"Yep, sure will," he replied, staring out into the blue. There were several white sail-boats floating on the glassy sea and the ferry was arriving into Dublin port.

"Do you still really want to go through with it?" he suddenly asked, still looking out to sea, the sun glinting onto his champagne flute.

I was incredulous, unsure of what I had actually heard.

I looked at my future husband for traces of mirth or concern, but his face was calm, peaceful even.

"Yes, of course I do! What kind of a question is *that*?"

Gary smiled and kissed me on the forehead. "I just wondered if you felt all this hassle was worth it, that's all. You just seem so stressed out by all the organising – I just …" his voice trailed away.

An icy chill ran through me. "You still want it, don't you?" I asked in a tremulous voice. I could hardly bear to listen to an answer.

"Yes, of course I do, silly. It just seems to have grown bigger than *Ben Hur*, that's all – it hardly seems as if it's about just us any more. It's like this big production number, almost a big show. I think the idea of a tiny wedding in Vegas was still the best one."

I smiled. "And stop our poor mothers from getting the chance to embarrass us with their awful hats? And what about that drunken uncle that always feels up the bridesmaids? How could we miss out on all that?"

Gary laughed, lighting up his handsome face, and my heart ached with longing for him.

"Yeah," he said, "and you forgot my friends throwing up outside the reception room after seventeen pints, and the practical jokes they'll plant in our honeymoon suite!"

I hugged him, crisis averted.

"Y'see? You'll have a great time. Now, finish up your champagne, because I have to have an early night. I'm off to the west to collect the wedding gown tomorrow."

"So who are you taking this time?"

"I think I'll take Sandy and Chris. He hasn't seen much of Ireland yet and Sandy hasn't seen the dress either. Amy and Clodagh aren't in the best of form with their romantic troubles. I'm really lucky, you know, Gary, now that's all behind me and I've got you."

Gary knocked back his champagne in one fell swoop. "Right, so," he said, brushing his jeans free of imaginary grass. "If you need your beauty sleep early, then I can take Steve and Warren to the pub tonight."

"OK, but just remember – I don't want you to look

all puffy and hung over on the day, so take it easy for the next few days, OK? I want you to look as handsome as you do right now."

Gary sighed. "You know I really can't wait until this is all over and we can get back to normal."

I tried to get myself to say "me too", but really I didn't want things to go back to normal. Despite all the stress of planning the wedding, I still thrived on all the attention and the idea of prancing around in my dream dress while everyone looked on as I wed my dream man. I couldn't say I wanted that to end because I didn't – but I did realise that Gary wouldn't feel the same way. All the same, I was a little concerned that he seemed less than excited.

"I know what you mean," I said instead. "Then you'll have me all to yourself, in our little apartment, for the rest of our lives."

Gary never replied because his mobile rang at that very moment and he strode off down the hillside to answer it.

"Who was it?" I enquired when he got back a few minutes later.

"Oh, just Mum," he groaned. "She's still not very happy that Carole is going to the wedding."

"Oh, you poor thing! No wonder you want the whole thing over – you must feel under pressure, trying to please your mum and dad. Don't worry, love, we are going to make sure that your mother gets pride of place and that Carole is placed well down the back of the room. I know it won't be easy but if we both make the effort to make sure your mum is treated well it should be tolerable."

"Yeah, you're right," he replied. "Now, I better get you back home if you want to get up early for Galway."

He strode off towards the car, leaving me to grab the champagne flutes and the empty bottle – the last of the Big Hot Romantics – no doubt rushing back to grab the lads and head down for a few pints and a footy game at the local. Within minutes he had me back to Sutton and my arse was barely out of the car when he sped away on two wheels.

I was left staring after the pall of exhaust fumes, wondering just how desperate a man could get for a pint. Still, at least Gary would have a chance to catch up with his old friends and unwind a bit. As for me, well, I was filled with excitement about bringing my wonderful wedding gown home tomorrow and showing it to my mother for the very first time. I just knew she was going to get all teary and melodramatic when she saw me in it.

And it was just a week away from me wearing it for real.

♥ ♥ ♥

The following morning we all set off for Loughrea. Chris sat in the front, all six feet four of him barely folded into my little Micra. Sandy sat glumly in the back, bereft at being apart from Chris's luscious lips for more than two minutes. Still, I wasn't going to let Sandy drive, as I planned on making it alive to my wedding day. She was bad enough on a normal day, when her eyes weren't all misted up with deluded love – today I doubted if we'd even make it onto the Naas road before we collided into another car while Sandy made sheep's eyes at her current passion.

After we made it out of Dublin and Chris was suitably amazed by the green countryside speeding by, Sandy announced that Chris and she were going back to Australia together as soon as the wedding was over and she could get her visa through.

They were in love, as Sandy explained, and couldn't be apart. Chris's year-long European holiday was nearly over and she was going to go back with him down under.

I looked at Chris for a moment, risking us all in the process by taking my eyes off the road, but was amazed to find him nodding back at Sandy with devotion and squeezing her hand tightly.

"I do love her," he then explained quietly. "And we want to be together, we *have* to be together. Sandy's the best thing that ever happened to me."

I looked in the rear-view mirror and watched Sandy's expression. She looked radiant, and prettier now than I had ever seen her. I wondered if I looked like that. I felt like checking the mirror for my own reflection, but I didn't want a disappointment staring back at me. I was happy for my little sister – she seemed to have finally cracked it.

But the look of love on her face and that of her besotted Aussie somehow made me feel discomfited. I wasn't sure if Gary and I had that same elusive quality that made couples glow with love. I tried to put it to the back of my mind and enjoy their company up in Galway, but it quite unsettled me and as I swirled about in my magical wedding gown in Heavenly Creatures to the *oohs* and *aahs* of my captive audience, I suddenly knew the meaning of cold feet and mine were feeling more than a little bit cool. In fact they were feeling very chilly indeed.

Chapter 19

After we got back from Loughrea with the fabulous wedding dress and I modelled it for my teary-eyed mother, I hung it from my wardrobe door as a kind of permanent reminder of the momentous event that was about to occur in a few days. I decided that my cold feet up in Galway were somewhat due to the fact that Gary and I had spent very little time together since my return from Spain, and because of that we were losing that close connection to each other. So I decided I'd organise a romantic meal for us both – alone and free from any interruptions.

I picked Cruzzo's in Malahide Marina, where the views of the sea were perfect and the food was second to none – besides, I knew Gary loved the place.

I texted him at five o'clock and told him to be out there *alone* for eight. I decided to wear my new little black dress that I had purchased for my honeymoon. It was dead sexy, showed off my best assets and hugged my curves in all the right places. I teamed it with my highest, thinnest heels and piled my hair high in a glamorous chignon. Gary wouldn't be able to resist, or at least that was the plan.

I arrived a little early, despite driving around the marina for several minutes, and spotted Gary's sporty car in the car park. My heart leapt to see that he was as keen as I was. I raced up the stairs to see Gary at a window seat, looking resplendent in a sharp new suit.

"This was inspired," Gary announced as I sat down.

Our waiter poured a nice glass of chilled white wine.

"I knew it would take a fabulous meal to get your attention," I replied silkily as I shimmied into my chair.

"You look amazing in that dress," Gary said admiringly.

Now this was more like it – I finally had the attention of my intended. A warm feeling came over me, and it wasn't just the wine. I felt I had Gary's full attention, something that had been seriously amiss lately.

"I wore it specially, just for you. I feel that we've been caught up in all this wedding malarkey and you and I haven't had any time just to be together. So I want us to enjoy tonight, just the two of us."

Gary smiled and then leaned over and kissed me

softly. "Well, I happen to think it was a great idea. I know I've been a bit off lately, but it hasn't been easy, with work pressure and my parents splitting up and all. I'm sorry if I've been a bit of a pain."

I smiled sweetly. I hadn't quite forgiven Gary's cavalier treatment of me before our wedding, but I wasn't about to cause more trouble at the moment. I just wanted to get him back on track first. After the wedding and honeymoon I'd tell him how hurt I had been, how scared.

But right now I was enjoying myself immensely and we had a fabulous meal and a few wines and a really lovely time together. I was reminded of why I wanted to marry this man and I hoped it was the same for Gary – he certainly seemed to be smitten again, judging by the reaction I got to the sexy dress.

After the meal we went for a long walk along the seafront. It was a balmy night for a change and it was quite romantic walking along together, holding hands as the waves were crashing onto the shore in the inky moonlight, the lights of Howth twinkling in the distance.

We didn't talk, but it was nice just being together. I held Gary's hand tightly and relished the moment, but deep down I wanted him to tell me how much he loved me and how much he was looking forward to making me his wife – but men never do that, do they? They never tell you what you need to hear at those most important moments – the moments that you want to treasure forever, but I figured that I always wanted too much, so I enjoyed the walk and shook off any wistful feelings.

Afterwards Gary took me back to our apartment. He had obviously told his buddies to stay away and I was delighted to find that he had our bedroom filled with numerous candles, which he lit while I fetched some wine.

It was so romantic I almost came to tears. The room was now ablaze with dozens of candles and Sade was playing on the CD player. Gary took the wine from me and wordlessly took my hand and slow-danced me around the bedroom.

"Gary, this is amazing. I'm so happy. I'd forgotten how happy you make me."

Gary murmured, "I'll be very happy if a certain girl can get out of that sexy dress for me. You look really amazing in it, but I'd still prefer you out of it!"

At that moment I would have done anything for my future husband. I had seldom felt more in love with him, so I smiled and wordlessly took my dress off, whereupon Gary lifted me up and carried me to the bed and we made the longest, most sensuous love that we ever had in all our years together. I thought it might have been that it was only a few days from our wedding and we were both aware of our commitment to each other, but as Gary told me over and over that he loved me, I felt the most fulfilled and contented that I had ever been.

All those earlier jitters I had felt in Galway had dissipated and fallen away – I was now dying for my much-awaited wedding day to arrive so I could finally become Mrs Gary Warren. The perfect wedding was right on track and, now that the groom seemed to be also, I was the happiest girl alive.

I crept out of bed after two, leaving my beloved snoring gently and got dressed and left. I felt a bit of a fraud but I needed to keep up the charade of being the pure and virginal bride and it wouldn't look too good for my mum in front of Aunty Pearl and Uncle Fred if I fronted up like a trollop at seven in the morning looking like I had just had rampant sex. So I drove home happy and contented and feeling all at one with the world.

♥ ♥ ♥

The following morning I actually had three hours to spare so Mum and I were going to customise some shorts for the Spanish order, more out of an abject fear of Clodagh becoming more furious than she already was with me than any great wish to fulfil my promise to the Spanish boutique owner. I was flattered and all, but the timing was awful, and really I wasn't sure that I wanted to be an entrepreneur at all, what with being married and having a full-time job and perhaps even a baby in the not too distant future. Yet something deep inside, probably the show-off in me, wanted to do it. I liked being the centre of attention (you might have already gathered that from my obsession with the wedding) so I liked the idea of my shorts being snapped up and becoming a must-have item and I had fanciful ideas of me ending up on TV 3's *Ireland A.M.* in a fashion segment.

We were in the middle of sewing on our thousandth sequin when the phone trilled.

It was Connor, my boss.

"Hiya, Ger, little bit of an emergency this end. I know it's your first week off and we're supposed to be all sorted for the project, but the Anderson file has gone mysteriously missing and we really need to find it. Could you come in this afternoon?"

I wasn't happy. I had left everything explicitly explained and detailed lists with the dozy temp and I just didn't have time for this – not right now – but Connor sounded so Little Boy Lost . . . he knew I was a sucker for his needy-little-boy routine.

"Connor, I know you're devastated without me, but really, did you have to hide the files to prove it? OK, I'll be there by two. But, Connor, you better make it worth my while, and you'd better pay for my parking."

Connor laughed, that boyish laugh that made him sound fifteen. "All right, Miss Bossy Boots, whatever you demand – just make sure you take your happy pills before you get here, OK?"

I laughed then. Connor knew he'd just have to ask

and I'd give in – even though he knew I'd make him suffer at the same time. I liked feeling indispensable in my job, and it gave me more than a modicum of satisfaction that they couldn't manage without me. I'd ask for another pay rise soon.

I just had to tell my sequin-irritated mother that I was abandoning her to an afternoon of sewing alone.

I hotfooted it into Fitzwilliam Square for about three, after extricating myself from a none-too-happy mother, up to her eyeballs in sequins and unwelcome relatives, and only after I promised her to spend the evening entertaining the terminally boring Uncle Fred and the sherry-swilling Aunty Pearl. It was lucky I was so fond of my job or I would have been really annoyed. But Dave and Connor were like the two big brothers I never had and I knew they'd be cactus without me and somehow it always gave me a warm and fuzzy feeling that they needed me so much.

I breezed into reception. Surprisingly, nothing seemed out of place: the temp was merrily typing away, albeit much slower than I did, and the much-talked-about Anderson file was sitting prettily on the top of the in basket. I was just about to roar my head off when Dave suddenly appeared around the door followed by Connor.

They yelled "Surprise!" in unison, and I almost dropped the file.

"Open it," said Dave excitedly. I didn't know whether to 1augh or cry – besides, I was much too amazed by Connor's new haircut. He had lopped off the long woolly thatch, and the new closely shorn hairstyle showed off Slavic cheekbones and made his amber-brown eyes look huge. Suddenly he resembled Antonio Banderas and actually looked rather cute.

"Open the file, Geri," he said smiling, mistaking my amazement at his appearance for surprise at the, well, surprise.

I opened the file to find a wedding card and inside the card was a cheque for a thousand euro.

I was overwhelmed. I'd figured on a nice present, perhaps a fridge even, but not this huge amount of money.

"Oh, you guys!" I blurted out through tears. "You shouldn't have. This is much too much."

"Right," quipped Dave. "We'll have it back, so. It was all *his* idea. You know I'm the stingy one!"

"It was not!" Connor replied hotly. "We both feel you deserve it, Geri – you've been terrific lately, even with the wedding and everything – you still managed to be on top form with the project. We just wanted to show our appreciation. You can put it to the honeymoon costs or maybe some new appliances."

I hugged them both. They were really nice guys and I was totally gobsmacked by their wonderful gesture.

I ruffled Connor's newly shorn hair. "So, what's this, then? Getting all spruced up for the Wedding of the Century?"

Connor blushed, something he seldom did. "No, not really, more like I need to look sharp for the media. We've got to do a presentation of the Matheson Centre design and it's going to be covered by the financial sector of *The Times* and maybe even the commercial property section of the *Indo*."

"*Oooh* – soon you'll be hanging out with the big boys! Next it'll be tailored suits from Louis Copeland and facials at the Four Seasons spa, and we'll have to banish your old duffle coat and that uni scarf to the bin."

Connor laughed. "You *know* that duffle coat came with me to the South of France in August and I ain't giving it away for no one! I'm not changing my lifestyle – all this is, is a long overdue haircut!"

I smiled at his naïveté. "Yeah, g'way outta that, Connor – that's more than a haircut. You'll be beating them off with a stick, now."

I had to admit, even I looked at him in a new light – who knew *that* face lurked under that unruly mop all these years?

Dave interrupted. "Geri, give over or you'll give him a huge loaf. Now come on, we're taking to you dinner at Roly's, after a few drinks first. You haven't anything planned, have you?"

I thought briefly about the long night of playing cards and listening to boring Uncle Fred, with his tales of army life and that trip to the Congo, and Aunty Pearl, comatose by nine with two bottles of sherry under her belt.

"Not a thing" I breezed, "lead on, Dave! Being feted by two of the handsomest bosses in Fitzwilliam Square is something I am going to enjoy."

♥ ♥ ♥

We had a great evening. The food at Roly's was, as always, sensational, and I had way too many Bacardi Breezers to even consider driving home, but we had so much fun talking about the new temp and how hopeless she was compared to me and Connor's latest cross-channel fight with April over custody of their dog Sarge.

"I mean, he's not even *hers*. He's a temperamental bitser who chews all the shoes, which she hated him for all through our marriage. Now suddenly she decides she can't live without him."

Dave grimaced. "Connor, this poor girl is about to get married. She doesn't need to hear your jaundiced views on marriage or your custody battle over a flea-bitten mongrel."

"Dave, I'm trying to educate Geri. You can't be too careful. I never thought April would ever get so mean that she'd fight me for the one thing that I ever really loved."

I giggled. "You mean you never loved April? That *Sarge* is the love of your life? I'm beginning to feel sorry for your ex-wife – competing with a dog!"

"I am resisting the urge to say that it was a fair contest as one was a bitch," piped up Dave with a grin, "and with that I must take my leave of you both, or else I'll be in divorce courts. Lulu doesn't like being left alone for too long with the tiresome two-year-olds while I have fun. Now, Connor – make sure you get this girl a cab home and don't let her drink too much more – she's getting married in a few days."

"OK, Mammy," Connor replied in mock seriousness and Dave waved and strode off purposefully towards home and his wife and the twins. Dave did everything purposefully. I guess that's why he was so successful.

"And are you? Really getting married in a few days, I mean?"

Connor was staring at me, rather seriously for someone who had six pints of Guinness on board.

"Yes, I guess I am," I replied, smiling at the thought.

Connor looked into his almost empty pint glass. "Geri . . . are you really sure Gary is what you want?"

I wasn't sure how to reply. Connor knew a lot about Gary and me, a lot of the crappy things that had occurred, and he knew that I had practically pressured Gary into proposing. He also knew I loved Gary and had done so for a long time.

"I think so, " I said honestly. "We're good together, and anyway it's too late – the faces are already on the tea towels."

Connor looked perplexed. "What the hell does that mean?"

I grinned. "When Princess Diana was going to marry Prince Charles she had a touch of the wobbles a few days beforehand about going through with it and her sisters told her that it was too late to back out of it because her face was printed on all the tea towels."

"Yeah," murmured Connor darkly, finishing off his pint. "And look how *that* turned out."

"Connor, don't go all maudlin on me now!"

"I'm not, Geri, but it's just that you deserve so much better than Gary. But I'll shut up now – you are a big girl and can make your own decisions. Just remember, though, I'm not only your boss, I'm your friend."

I looked at the newly handsome Connor with his cheekbones and his big brown drunken eyes that held concern and affection. He looked like a large puppy dog and so handsome that I realised I really had imbibed too many drinks and needed to get home pronto as I appeared to be wearing my beer goggles and he was getting more handsome by the minute.

"I know that, and thanks, Connor, for everything. Now, I've really got to go home before I fall down. So I'll go and grab a taxi and I'll see you at the wedding, OK?"

I kissed him chastely on the cheek and got up and quickly left, glancing back to see him rubbing his newly shorn head and looking so lost and alone that I almost ran back to him.

But I wasn't going to make the same mistake as I did with Adam in Spain.

I was about to go down the aisle with the man of my dreams and nothing or nobody was going to stop me.

Chapter 20

The following day, the day before my wedding, with a thumping hangover and a mother who was giving me serious daggers looks over my non-appearance at the oldies convention, I had to go and deliver the bridesmaids' dresses to Clodagh and Amy.

I decided to get the worst out of the way and do Clodagh first. We hadn't had any contact since the last fitting and I wasn't even sure that she was still going to be my bridesmaid if she was to choose the faithless Karl over me, so I took two Nurofen and carefully placed her dress and the Spanish order of sequinned shorts and tops into my little car and headed over to her place at Baldoyle. I arrived at the artisan's cottage at midday. Her smart VW Polo gleamed in the tiny driveway. She worked from home a lot in the purpose-built shed at the rear where she toiled on all her best pieces. Clodagh had bought the small artisan's cottage years ago. As always she was way ahead of the posse – in this case, the property boom – and got the small house for a song and spent a long time renovating it to a smart open-plan modern space. The shed had always been there but Clodagh smartened it up and still made her individual designs there.

I plastered a huge fake smile on my face as I held the gown and boxed creations aloft and waited on her to answer the door. I could vaguely hear Coldplay echo out in the distance and, if I was not mistaken, laughter coming from inside.

The door opened a bit and Clodagh's head appeared around it. The boxes were almost blocking my view so I had pushed my way inside before I registered that she was resisting – holding the door against me. Then I registered she was clad in a sexy negligee and not much else apart from the frozen smile on her face. I knew something was wrong and that was *before* I saw the small, wiry, balding man behind her wearing only a pair of boxers and (typically) a pair of black socks. Attractive he wasn't. I think that's what amazed me so much. Clodagh had spoke, about Karl like he was some kind of Adonis that she simply could not resist. I couldn't reconcile my mental image of a model-type hunky guy with the small, thin person who was scuttling off to the bathroom with an armful of clothes.

I smiled anyway like the village idiot while Clodagh attempted to cover her embarrassment.

She went and grabbed a dressing-gown, which she donned over her negligee.

My mouth suddenly felt watery and I felt queasy. And it wasn't just the hangover.

It was all so tawdry. Karl on his lunch hour hopping over for a quick one while the missus would never suspect. And apparently Clodagh actually seemed happy with this quare set-up.

I didn't know quite what to do. I didn't want to stay there and make polite conversation with someone of whom I didn't approve, yet I knew Clodagh would never forgive me if I went over all holier-than-thou. And I needed her and she knew it. I'd just have to grin and bear it, although I wouldn't be myself for quite some time.

"Coffee?" Clodagh breezed brightly as she passed into her kitchen, which was a vision of stainless-steel perfection.

"Love one," I smiled in return, following her and plonking myself on one of her tall steel stools. "I'm not feeling too clever. Dave and Connor took me out for a meal and a few drinks last night."

Clodagh rolled her eyes. "Jeez, you're brave, going out with that pair so close to the wedding – you could have ended up in Cork with a load of rugby players the way they carry on when they're on a bender."

"They gave me a thousand euros as a wedding

pressie, can you believe it?"

Clodagh sat down, gathering her silk dressing-gown about her pale legs. "I'd keep that quiet if I were you. You don't need to tell Gary. It can be your escape money."

"Charming, I'm sure! I'm not even wed yet and you're already planning my escape!"

Clodagh poured the coffee. "My mother always told me that a girl should have a few bob put aside for an escape, if she ever needed one. She always had a few hundred stuffed down the mattress in case of a quick getaway. Turned out she didn't need it. Dad popped his clogs long before she ever tried to leave him."

I stayed silent. Clodagh still missed her father horrendously and she seldom spoke about him at all. He had been dead for years. Her mother never looked like she was the type to have an escape plan – she was a staid, buttoned-up type of woman – but obviously Clodagh had inherited some of her preparedness.

Karl sidled into the kitchen, this time fully dressed in a business suit.

"Karl, meet Geri. Geri this is Karl."

"Didn't recognise ye with your clothes on!" I joked to a stony silence.

"Pleased to meet you," Karl said stiffly.

I really failed to see the attraction – he seemed so colourless and devoid of any humour.

"Do you want a coffee?" Clodagh enquired. I knew the way she said it that she would have killed him if he had said yes.

Karl shot her a look. "Em, no thanks, love. I can see you girls have a lot to discuss. I'll be off." He pecked her cheek. "I'll call you later. Good luck with the wedding, Geri. All the best."

He disappeared from the kitchen, closing the door quietly.

Cheeky sod, I thought. Fancy being smart enough to wish me well for my wedding when he seemed to have forgotten his own wedding vows pretty damn quickly.

Clodagh looked wistfully after him. I was amazed. I would really have to get her down to the opticians and get those sparky little eyes checked – she was obviously in need of a major overhaul on the glasses front.

"I'm sorry if I interrupted, Clodagh," I offered. "I just thought I'd better bring your dress and the designs over and see how you were feeling over the other night."

"It's OK," Clodagh smiled. "It's just that we haven't seen each other for a few days, that's all – one of his kids was ill."

She said it without even noticing that the comment she had just uttered was so sad and awful. One of Karl's children had been sick and the only way that affected Clodagh was that she had been unable to bonk her boyfriend, who happened to be their father.

"Anyway," I continued, wishing away the chasm that was growing wider by the minute between us. "I hope you can get those things posted off to Palma for me. I never got a chance to do the labels, so I just used the '*Designs by Geri*' tags you got made up for me. I hope that's OK – it's just that I have to take Amy's dress over to her and I have a ton of things to do. So I won't be staying. If you like you can try on the dress to make sure it's perfect."

"I'm sure it will be," Clodagh replied anxiously. I could see that she wanted me out of there just as much as I yearned to race for the door. "I'll try it on later, if that's OK. I can call you if there's any problems, if that's alright, and I'll post those shorts this afternoon. But you really need to get serious about getting labels and treating this as a little business, Geri. It could really take off if you give it some attention. We'll have to talk about it more after you get back from your honeymoon."

I nodded and made all the right noises, but in reality I couldn't wait to leave, so within another few awkward minutes I was out of her house and firing up my little car – wondering if the rift between one of my oldest friends and me could ever be bridged.

I drove over to Amy's in a half dream and realised when I got there that I didn't even remember the journey. I hoped she was in. She had planned a half-day from work in order to get her fake tan topped up and herself beautified for the wedding.

I was delighted when she answered the doorbell and buzzed me in. I carted her dress unceremoniously under my arm, so deflated was I by the awkward encounter with Clodagh. It disturbed me that her affair with Karl was affecting how I felt for her, one of my dearest friends, and I needed to talk to Amy about it.

Amy answered the door with a green face and curlers and still managed to look attractive. "I know I look like Shrek at the moment, but I'll be fabulous tomorrow," she joked until she took one look at my face.

"What's happened?"

"Oh, Amy, I've just met Clodagh's Karl and it was *awful*."

I practically stuffed the dress into her arms and forgot all my earlier excitement about showing my friend her gorgeous gown.

Amy led me into her bedroom and hung the dress up carefully while I tried to find a clear spot on the bed to sit down. It seemed that every item from Amy's considerable wardrobe was on the bed. She was obviously having a fashion crisis of some kind.

"Sorry about the mess, but first things first. Tell me everything about it and leave nothing out."

"Shouldn't we be at least having a horrendously fattening cake or a large whiskey to mull this over?"

Amy grimaced. "By the look of you, you have

already had enough jar in the past few days. If you don't keep off today you may forget your clear complexion for the wedding. And I don't even have to tell you about fattening cakes, Geri Murphy, so just sit there and tell me all about it and I'll make you a healthy smoothie when you're finished."

I began to unload my sorry tale about the meeting with Karl and how tawdry it all seemed.

Then I started to laugh. Amy looked comical with her green face while trying to look serious and listen to my story. "Oh, Amy, clean off that stuff – I can't talk to you when you're looking like a big kiwi fruit!"

"Charming!" Amy exclaimed and went to wash off the green gunk.

I waited, still brooding on Karl.

"Right," she said as she returned, freshly washed. "Leave nothing out."

I told her about surprising Clodagh and her married lover in their daylight tryst.

"So," said Amy gravely. "She seems to be smitten all right – to have him over for a bonk in the middle of the day. God! His poor wife, you'd have to feel sorry for her."

I frowned. That was the worst part. I never thought Clodagh was capable of doing that to another woman – she was always so highly principled. "That's the worst part, Amy. I just don't know if I can ever be the same with Clodagh again after all this – she's not the person I thought she was."

Amy looked out of the window. Her long blonde hair glinted in the sunlight. She looked like an angel. "Love makes us do the strangest things, Geri. Don't be too hard on her."

I was contrite. "Oh, Amy, I'm sorry. I haven't even asked you how you are and if you've heard from the cheatin' kilt-wearer."

Amy burst into tears. "He's not a cheat, Geri! He made a mistake and I have decided to give him another chance. You are so bloody judgemental! I hope Gary never lets you down, because you've a long way to go in life and people aren't perfect!"

I sat quietly, in amazement. I never realised that I was judgemental. I just wanted the best for my friends. But I had hurt Amy's feelings and I didn't want that.

"Oh, Amy, I'm so sorry. You do whatever you have to do. If you care about Stuart, you take him back. It's different for Clodagh. She's really headed for heartbreak."

Amy sniffed and was somewhat placated. "I know you have her best interests at heart, but you have to realise Clodagh will have to make her own mistakes. You are about to go down the aisle and live happily ever after – well, we need to find happiness somehow ourselves."

I handed her a tissue. "And is Stuart coming over

for the wedding?" I ventured carefully.

Amy nodded. "Yes, he is. I hope his invite still stands."

"Of course it does. As long as he wears the traditional kilt and no knickers!"

We both laughed.

If I made it up the aisle without any further problems it would be a miracle.

Jaysus, there was never a dull moment.

After Amy perked up, she tried on her bridesmaid's dress and, as expected, looked ethereal in it. I left her shortly afterwards and headed home.

I dearly wished I could see Gary tonight, but it was supposed to be unlucky for the bride to see the groom before the wedding, so I just texted him instead and said that I loved him and not to be late. I got a text back from him as my little car trudged towards Sutton, telling me not to have too many Bacardis before I put on my make-up and that he'd be waiting at the altar.

I got home totally exhausted, to find a huge hooley going on in the newly decorated front room. Dad and Uncle Fred had several of the local wrinklies enjoying a few whiskeys as Frank Sinatra blared out, while Mum was in the kitchen with Aunty Pearl and several of the neighbours quaffing gin and tonics and eating curried egg sandwiches. I crept quietly to my still-teenage bedroom and promptly fell asleep, after shedding a maudlin tear for my last night in my little narrow bed as a single woman – blissfully unaware of the nightmare that was shortly to unfold about me.

Chapter 21

It was my wedding day.

At last!

I awoke early. The birds that had nested the previous winter in the gabled roof above my room had been my alarm-clock call for a long time now and today was no different – they chirped merrily and matched my sunny mood. I could tell already that the day was sunny from the sunlight that streamed through the window and I could hear my mother already pottering around downstairs in the kitchen. I was so excited! This was the day I had waited for all of my life. I pulled open the curtains and saw a flawless blue expanse above me. I knew it – I had always known it would be a perfect day and it was – even God was on my side. I said a quick prayer of thanks and scrambled out of bed and ran downstairs.

Mum was happily sizzling some bacon in her dressing-gown and curlers.

"How are you, love? I'm cooking you up a mother and father of a fry – you're going to need it. It's a very long day – you don't even realise that until you go through it. Sit down there – it'll be ready in a jiffy. You and I can have our breakfast before the rest of them get down. I want to have a nice breakfast with my daughter for the last time while she lives under my roof."

A lump came to my throat. I had never thought of it like that before. I was so involved with my own aspect of the wedding I never realised that it was a loss of sorts for my mother and things would be different for her. Soon Sandy would be off to Australia too and Mum would be an empty-nester.

"What will you and Dad do with all the time together after we're gone?" I asked, smiling.

Mum shrugged, a worried look crossing her face. "Oh, I don't know – we'll probably take a world cruise – either that or we'll kill each other. I haven't been alone with him for any amount of time for over thirty years."

I fleetingly wondered if I'd still feel in love with Gary after thirty years. It scared the bejesus out of me thinking of myself in thirty years' time, never mind him, so I dismissed the idea immediately and focused on my poor mother, who had spent all these years making it her job to look after me and my sister and now she was about to be made redundant. It was a pretty thankless task being a mother.

"And would you marry him again if you could turn the clock back?" I asked.

She placed the huge breakfast before me and gave me a funny look. "I don't think if I had my time over that I'd marry anyone, Geri, but to say that would mean I might not have had you two girls, so I don't regret marrying your father, but I might not do it again."

I felt sad that she felt that way and even sadder that after all these years I realised that I didn't really know my mother well, not in any deep sense, and I resolved to change that after I was married. I'd be really grown up then and we could be friends.

"But you've been happy, haven't you? Most of the time anyway."

I dearly hoped her answer was going to be yes.

Instead she just sat quietly, her eyes misting over with a faraway look.

"Not really," she said quietly after what seemed like an age. "We just got married back then because it was the thing you did. You young ones seem to have your heads screwed on a bit better. I hope that you are happy with Gary, I really do, but if you aren't, and I don't care what the reasons are, you can always rely on me. I'll be here and I want you to know that you can come to me for anything. Don't think that you've made your bed and you have to lie in it, like my mother said to me."

I was shocked by my mother's comments. All these years I had believed that my parents were happy – perhaps not Mills and Boon happy, but contented none the less – and now I discovered on my wedding day that it had all been a bit of a sham. I was shaken by her admission, but I wanted desperately to be happy this day of all days and I knew that she was just trying to tell me that she would support me no matter what, so I focused on that instead.

"Thanks, Mum. And thanks for everything. You've been terrific helping with the wedding and making the dresses and all. I'm going to take you off for an overnight when I get back from our honeymoon, just you and me, OK? We'll take off to the Powerscourt spa for a long and luxurious beauty session, after Sandy goes to Australia."

She put her hand over mine. "That'll be lovely, love, and don't mind me, I'm all right really. I just feel a bit sorry for myself lately, what with you getting hitched and Sandy off on an adventure. I'm a bit of a sad old duck. I just worry about me and himself rattling around this house together with very little in common. But I'll be fine – maybe you'll make me a grandmother soon and I'll have something new to fuss over."

I smiled enigmatically. "Well, Gary wants to wait for a few years, but I've a feeling we might hear the patter of tiny feet a lot sooner than that, if you catch my drift."

Mum's face lit up, but before she could enquire any further, Dad blundered into the kitchen looking for a razor that wasn't blunt – Sandy had stolen his last one and was now hogging the shower.

"Honestly, that young one, she spends hours in that bathroom and I wouldn't mind if she emerged looking dramatically different. There's going to be no hot water for anyone else!" He looked at us for agreement, his face as red as a tomato and his hair askew.

"Calm down now, Eddie, or you'll have a heart attack before you get your firstborn up the aisle. Now, sit down and I'll make you a fry, and I'll get you a new razor before you're finished. Now, Geri, if you're finished your breakfast, you go up and get herself out of the bathroom. You're the bride, not her, and there's a lot of people to get a shower this morning. We should have got that second bathroom years ago."

Dad rolled his eyes heavenwards – another house extension and more expense were more likely to raise his blood pressure than Sandy's leisurely shower habits.

So I left them to it and escaped to the relative quiet of the bathroom, after screaming to oust my newly preening sister from it, and began to get myself ready.

The butterflies were beginning to multiply in my

stomach and by the time Linda, my cousin, arrived to do our hair and make-up I was beginning to get really nervous.

Sandy picked up on my pale face and stricken look.

"It's time for a little drinkie, I think," she said to me, winking, and fetched some champagne that her Aussie had bought. She mixed it with some orange juice and made us all one, except Linda, who had a job to do.

After that I began to get better and when the flowers arrived and looked so perfect I felt a sense of elation. Everything was turning out just the way I had planned it – all my hard work was paying off.

Linda began to weave the baby's breath through my hair and by the time she had finished my make-up I really looked amazing. In my bedroom it was an oasis of calm but downstairs I could hear the hectic panic and constant stream of people coming and going.

Clodagh and Amy arrived and came upstairs with their dresses. Amy seemed excited but Clodagh was red-eyed and silent. I gathered that there had been some sort of row between them and I hazarded a guess that it was because Clodagh would have discovered that Stuart was back on the scene and had arrived for the wedding. I could tell Clodagh was simmering over it and probably feeling unfairly singled out because the awful Karl was barred, but I wasn't going to have any truck with arguments today of all days so I completely ignored the heavy sighs and stony looks from Clodagh,

I fussed about instead with my dress and the shoes and all the little details. Clodagh would have to get over it, because there was no way through it.

Twenty minutes later all three girls had climbed into their dresses and looked individual and amazing, Sandy had plied Clodagh with enough champers to cheer her up and we were ready. I was about to be married. Suddenly, surrounded by my dearest friends and my only sister, the sense of occasion overwhelmed me and I came to tears.

"Now don't start blubbin'," Sandy admonished gently while she offered me a hankie.

"Linda will go mental if your make-up runs – come on, have another sip of champers and I'll go and see if the pony and trap is on the way, OK?"

I nodded while blinking tears away. Amy rubbed my back and Clodagh bit her lip nervously. I had to calm myself. I wasn't even up the aisle yet and I was a basket case. I took a deep breath.

"OK, I'm fine. I need you three girls today, OK? I need you to be there for me and help me so I don't stuff it up. Are you with me?"

"We are," Amy said fiercely and Clodagh nodded in agreement.

Sandy rushed back into the room. "The pony and trap is here and the car for the bridesmaids too! This is it, Geri! You're on!"

My heart leapt up in my chest and did a few somersaults before settling back down. My moment had arrived – I was about to really get married.

I descended the staircase with aplomb, flanked by my bridesmaids. My father was at the door looking debonair in his smart morning suit, puffing hastily on one of the cigars that Uncle Fred had widely distributed to anyone who was silly enough to take one.

"Put that out this instant, Dad!" I roared, back in full Bridezilla mode.

The poor man spat it out immediately.

"I don't want to smell of awful cigar smoke," I then said a bit more kindly when I noticed the gathered crowd of neighbours giving me awkward looks instead of admiring ones.

"You look beautiful!" my father exclaimed and other people around the door agreed.

The dress was amazing and it surprised everyone by being pale pink. And the bridesmaids' gowns of pale silver organza really set it off. Each girl had a small posy of pale pink and cream tulips and I carried a loosely tied bouquet of long cream lilies. It had all come together so well, I felt immensely proud and happy. I couldn't wait for Gary to see me.

We set off for the church after the bridesmaids and my mother had departed in their Daimler. The pony behaved impeccably and the trip to the church was delightful. People stopped to look everywhere and even waved and I just loved being the centre of attention.

"There's still time to turn back, you know," my father said gently as he held my hand.

"I know," I replied squeezing his hand. "But I really don't want to, Dad."

He looked at me lovingly. "I'm supposed to say something really wise and meaningful now, love, but I can't think of anything to say other than be happy – that's what I want most for you, OK? And if this bloke makes you happy, well then, you're a very lucky girl."

I smiled happily. "Dad, I am the luckiest girl alive."

We arrived at the church almost ten minutes late – that too was perfect, not too late to be an irritation yet not too early to look desperate either. I glided into the little church on my father's arm and noticed Gary at the top of the aisle. He was facing the altar and I could see that his blond head was shaking with nerves. The poor guy, how sweet, I thought, he is nervous about marrying me. He turned to look at me, as did most of the congregation, and he smiled widely.

"You look fantastic!" he whispered as my father gave me away to him and I almost came to tears again I was so happy.

"You don't look too bad yourself," I murmured as I

took his hand for the last time as a single woman. I clasped it tightly as the priest began …

Chapter 22

The wedding ceremony went entirely to plan. I was a bit worried when I spotted Pamela Warren looking fierce and Cruella de-Ville-like in a truly terrible black and white ensemble. I had made sure that I had placed her in the front pew and Carole, as agreed, stayed far down the back, so even though it was awkward (and I wasn't sure if Pamela would make it through the whole day without scratching Carole's eyes out) so far only her venomous looks towards her husband were any giveaway about her feelings.

Other than that it was amazing. The violinist and harpist played our favourite songs in a haunting way and Father Moynalty played a blinder, making the congregation laugh and cry at all the right junctures. As we read out our personally written pledges there was hardly a dry eye in the house, and when I said, "I do," the tears fell freely from my eyes. My dream wedding had actually come true and now I was Mrs Gary Warren and everyone in the world that was dear to me – and a few that weren't – were there to witness it.

It had all been worth it.

We sailed out of the church hand in hand as husband and wife.

I had organised pale-pink flower petals to be thrown over us instead of ordinary confetti so the family scattered them over us and the sun shone relentlessly as we gathered for the photographs.

"I have a surprise for you," Gary said, as we were being congratulated by all and sundry.

"What is it?" I was excited. I had seen a really beautiful eternity ring that he knew I had my eye on.

"Come with me," replied Gary mysteriously and led me away.

"Now close your eyes, wifey!" he said and I did so.

"Now you can open them."

I looked to see a really cool little soft-top sports car in a mad yellow colour. I was overwhelmed. Gary had bought me my very own sports car.

"This is amazing, Gary! Thank you so much!"

He blushed. "Well, it was Dad's idea too and he gave me a terrific deal on it – he thinks a lot of you, Geri." He kissed me on the nose. "We're going to drive to Cavan in it – that's if your dress will fit. And don't worry – I won't have the top down to ruin your beautiful hair."

I kissed him passionately to catcalls of "Get a room!" from our wedding guests who had spilled onto the pavement.

"I love you, Gary Warren!" I exclaimed.

Gary grinned back happily. "Right so, I think we have a wedding reception to get to."

♥ ♥ ♥

An hour and a half later, as we turned the new sports car into the long, sweeping driveway of Cavan Castle, it looked truly majestic. I was so delighted we had picked this place despite all the opposition. It was truly special and it seemed like eons ago since Pamela had her little mad outburst about the location – a lot had happened since then, her marriage going down the toilet for one. I wondered how she was feeling today. It must have been really difficult having to see Gary Senior arrive with another woman. I had to admire her courage for coming alone and enduring the humiliation, and I fully intended to tell her that when I got a minute.

The weather was holding well so we would be able to have some wonderful pictures in the lavish grounds for our hugely expansive photo album.

Amy, Sandy, Clodagh and the rest of the wedding party arrived in the specially hired tour bus – we were all staying at the hotel overnight so no one had to drive. The wedding party spilled out onto the long gravel drive and while we got our photos taken they all adjourned to the mezzanine-level outdoor bar and quaffed champagne in the sunshine. I spotted Stuart, looking incongruous and self-conscious in a tartan kilt and full regalia.

I smiled at Amy. "I wasn't really serious you know, Amy – about the kilt, I mean."

She laughed happily. "Well, he took your instructions to the letter, Geri, including going commando, so let's hope the breeze doesn't become too gusty."

"We should give him the bumps later, just for the crack," piped up Sandy, forgetting her new refined persona for a moment.

We all laughed and the photographer got the best shot of the day.

After we finally had the last picture taken and we got to the bar to join our guests, Gary disappeared to get us a drink and I mingled with all my extended family and friends, each one enthralled at the location and admiring of my dress and the wonderful job I had done on the day. I hoped that the food would live up to its earlier promise from my visit with Mum. I was so happy standing there in all my glory looking about to see my mother, so beautiful in her elegant outfit, smiling at her sisters, feeling so proud, and Dad with his brothers having a pint of the black stuff and a joke or two. It was what it was all about. Gary Senior was in a corner close to his new amour and I could see Pamela Warren sneering at him from about ten feet away. She was knocking back the whiskey so I decided to head her off at the pass and go make my peace with her.

"Pamela, you look terrific!" I breezed, hoping the comment would throw her off track. "Thanks," she said in a small dead voice, her eyes darting to and fro in agitation. "You look beautiful yourself, Geri. I hope you'll be happier than I was."

She finished off her drink in one gulp. "I meant to call you last week. I had something to tell you. Something I wasn't a hundred per cent sure of, but I needed to check with you."

I was perplexed. "What do you mean, Pamela?"

Just then, Gary arrived back with a large Bacardi for me, and then he grabbed his mother and gave her a huge kiss.

"Mum! C'mere! You're still my number one girl, you know. That won't change just because I got hitched. Doesn't she look great, Geri?"

I nodded. "Yes, I've been just telling her. What were you saying earlier, Pamela?"

Pamela looked nervously from me to Gary and back. "Oh, nothing, I'm sure it'll keep, Geri. I see my sister Dolores over there – I'd better go and say hello."

With that she walked off.

"Is she OK?" Gary asked me suspiciously.

"I think so," I murmured, not too sure that she was.

"I hope she can keep it together, at least until after the speeches."

"Me too," my new husband muttered darkly, "or there'll be hell to pay."

The reception unfolded as I had planned: the food was excellent and there was plenty to go around. Everyone seemed to enjoy the meal and the wine was flowing as the guests relaxed and unwound.

Gary made a lovely speech in which he thanked his mother profusely for all her love and support and barely mentioned his father. Pamela ran from the room in tears and there was an awkward moment where we had to retrieve her to present her with the bouquet of flowers that a traditionally given to the mothers of the bride and groom. I could tell my mother was severely embarrassed by the openly emotional Pamela, who clung to Gary like a limpet and sobbed into his shirt. We hastily cut the cake and took to the floor for our first dance as husband and wife. I'd selected my favourite song, which was U2's "All I Want Is You", and I held Gary close to me and held my breath, never wanting the moment to end.

It was truly magical – it was our wedding day and I never wanted it to be over.

Eventually though, after the meal was over and the band had begun and the whole place rocked, it was time for the bride and groom to retire to the honeymoon suite to change into their going-away clothes. We weren't off on our honeymoon for another good few days yet – but despite loving my dream gown, I felt so hot and restricted that I was dying to get it off and change into my new John Rocha cream linen suit and finally let my hair down.

I saw Gary dancing with Pamela, who looked a lot happier, and I wound my way across the floor to rescue him. I spotted Stuart doing a sort of Scottish can-can and coming dangerously close to revealing his crown jewels while Amy looked on aghast.

Connor and Dave were propping up the bar, no doubt still talking business, looking all intent and serious. Clodagh was nowhere to be seen and Sandy was stuck so fast to the Aussie it was hard to tell when she ended and he began.

I finally prised Gary from his mother and grabbed his hand and led him out of the hot rocking reception room into the cool hallway.

"We've got to get changed into our going-away clothes," I explained as I led him towards the lifts.

"God, I can't wait to get you out of that gown, Mrs Warren," he said in a slurring voice. My groom had obviously enjoyed a few too many brandies. He staggered after me, grabbing my train as I giggled and ran towards the lifts.

Once inside the room, Gary continued his attempt to divest me of my wedding dress. He fumbled with the tiny buttons at the rear while I tried to laughingly pawn him off with a promise of things to come later.

"Look at this room, Gary, you haven't even

noticed it. It's just *gorgeous*."

The honeymoon suite was large and sumptuous. It had a huge four-poster bed with lots of cushions and beautiful bed linen. There were also two fat sofas and a well-stocked mini-bar. There were cream lilies scattered on the bed and a bucket of champagne lay chilling nearby. It was hugely romantic.

"Yeah, what a bed, we'll have a lot of fun trying that out later … hey, fancy some champers?"

I fetched my crisp linen suit from the wardrobe. "I think you've had enough for the moment, Gary. If you want to have fun, as you say, later, you need to stay standing, OK? I want my groom in one piece tonight."

Gary shrugged. "OK, fine. As long as I'm on a promise!"

With that there was a sharp knock at the door.

"If that's the lads coming to dismantle the bed, just get rid of them," I joked. Some of the stunts they pulled in the honeymoon suites were legendary, usually resulting in a hefty bill for the newlyweds.

Gary opened the door.

From here everything happened in slow motion.

Or at least it seemed to.

It was *her*.

The whole lithely fake-tanned, long-legged, caked-on make-up lot of her.

"*Jessie*?" Gary screeched.

I froze, literally, *froze*.

"What are you doing here?" he managed, mouth agape.

I simply stared open-mouthed. It was Jessie, that tarty little madam from our marriage guidance course, the one batting eyes at my fiancé when she should have been making eyes at her own future husband.

Gary had made eyes at her too.

Suddenly it all fell into place.

"I am here to tell *her* that you are mine," Jessie said in a strong steely voice. A voice that spoke of ownership and the confidence of someone who knew what she was talking about – that was what scared me even more. "I am also here to tell her that you love me and I came to get you."

She smirked at me triumphantly.

"It's being going on for months, hasn't it, Gary? Right under your nose, Geri. He didn't want to marry you, you know – you *forced* him into it. He tried to tell you more than once, but you had to have your *stupid* wedding, no matter what. He is going to leave you anyway, aren't you, Gary? Because we love each other."

I just stood there, letting the awful words fall over me. Then one look at my new husband told me that she spoke the truth.

I threw up right then and there, all over my beautiful wedding gown – the dress of my dreams – but all my dreams were now shattered, much like my life.

My wedding meal spewed forth and covered

Gary's wedding shoes.

"Geri!" Gary said in a tortured voice, moving towards me.

"*Noooooooooooo*!" I wailed and ran from the room.

I was in such shock that I hadn't even realised that my dress was so badly stained or even in fact that I was running at all, until I reached the ballroom and I found that I was in the centre of the reception room in hysterics and all my family and friends were gathering around me, wondering what the hell had happened.

"What's *happened*? Jesus! Geri, are you alright?"

It was my mother, holding me by the arms.

She called my father over.

I managed to get some words of sense out, somehow. I haltingly told him that Gary was in our honeymoon suite with his other woman.

I had never seen my father in such a cold rage.

He took me by the hand and led me away, away from the crowd of shocked onlookers. People that had celebrated my wonderful day a few minutes earlier and now had witnessed its destruction.

He took me back to my now defunct honeymoon suite.

They were actually in an embrace when we walked back in.

I think that's what shocked me the most and demolished any love I had left for Gary Warren right then and there. He had just destroyed my life and then hadn't even bothered to follow me and see how I was coping. No, there he was comforting and cuddling that *bitch*, Jessie.

My father took two paces forward and landed a solid punch right on Gary's jaw.

"*Get out!*" he roared at the top of his lungs, pushing Gary for good measure. "And take that trollop with you! I knew you were a no-good bastard from the first moment I met you, and you've proved me right. I'll deal with you later, me bucko. And I'll have something to say to your father, but just get out right now. Geri has enough to deal with and I don't want you anywhere in the vicinity of my daughter!"

"I never meant to hurt you, Geri ..." Gary began but his voice trailed away.

I was sitting on our wedding bed, a bed that was supposed to be awaiting two newly married people that were totally in love. I was incredulous that this was happening to me and this slip of a girl had walked right into my wedding and ruined my life and Gary Warren had let her.

Jessie took Gary's arm and they walked to the door in silence. Jessie simply looked back at me and that sly smirk she gave me just twisted something inside me and I snapped. I leapt off the bed in one move and grabbed Jessie by her long black ponytail and pulled her down to the ground with a high-pitched scream. I shocked myself that I had done that, but the look of abject fear on her face had been worth it.

My father pulled me off her immediately. "Geri," he said kindly, "don't distress yourself. I am here now and I'm going to look after you."

I burst into tears and my father sat on the bed with me and held me tightly and soothed me, even though my dress was badly stained and I must have stunk to high heaven.

When I looked up Gary was gone and my marriage was over even before it had begun.

Chapter 23

After what seemed like forever, I finally stopped sobbing. Dad prised himself from me and told me that he was going to go down and tell the guests that the wedding was over and fetch my mother.

This sent me into a mad spin of panic.

"You *can't*! I am so ashamed. Don't tell anyone, Dad. I couldn't bear it! Not yet. Just tell them that I am ill and I can tell them all later. Please, Dad!"

My father shrugged. He looked shrunken and deflated. This wasn't just affecting me.

"But, Geri," he then said, "a lot of them heard what you said when you came down. And they'll all be here in the morning. What can we tell them if not the truth?"

It was all too awful to even contemplate. I couldn't cope with any of this. It was just too much to deal with and true to form Gary had left me to cope with the fallout and had got away scot-free.

"Get Mum," I finally replied. "She'll know what to do."

My father reluctantly left me.

I sat on the marital bed and caught sight of myself in the large mirror that was hanging over the ornate dressing-table. I looked like a bad freak show. My carefully flower-woven hair had come undone and my face was streaked with mascara, but worst of all was my beloved wedding gown – it was heavily stained and ruined with the contents of my own stomach.

This had been the best day of my life and now it was the worst. I just sat there staring at myself in horror, fresh tears streaming down my face, and I stayed like that until my mother, closely followed by Sandy and my dad, arrived.

Mum took charge.

"Sandy, run the shower. Eddie, go and fetch her a strong brandy. Come on, love, I'm going to get you cleaned up, and then we'll have a little chat. Mum is here for you now, OK? Let's get you out of that dress."

I did what she said, like a little girl.

Sandy and Mum helped me into the shower after carefully and gently undressing me.

I felt exposed in my now redundant sexy cream basque and stockings. I felt ashamed at my mother witnessing my hopeful sexiness. It seemed so crass now.

Sandy was wide-eyed and silent as she helped, but all the while my mother chatted softly to me like I was a little child and I let her cosset me – it felt very comforting.

I felt the hot shower rain down on me and it seemed to wake me from my shock a bit.

At least I felt alive. I just wished I wasn't.

After about ten minutes I emerged and my mother fluffed my hair with the towel like she did when I was small.

When we got back to the bedroom, Dad was sitting on the bed holding the brandy and, of all things, a cup of tea.

A cup of tea just sorted everything, didn't it? From a baby to an earthquake and even a rotten, heartbreaking bridegroom, yes, a cup of tea would just make you forget all your troubles.

I downed the brandy in one go and then the tea, more to placate my mother than anything else. The brandy warmed me and after the tea I suddenly felt bone tired, like I had been awake for a century. I just wanted to sleep and maybe when I awoke the nightmare would be just a bad dream and not my new reality.

"What am I going to do, Mum? What am I going to *do*? How do I tell all my family and friends that my new husband has run off with that bimbo bitch from hell and my marriage is over before the ink is even dry on the certificate? I am so ashamed. How could I be such an idiot?"

Mum smoothed my hair and started to brush it slowly. "Firstly, you don't have to explain anything to anyone. Your father and I will tell everyone when you are ready for people to know. Secondly, this is not your shame, Geri – it is his, Gary's shame. He had no business going through with the wedding considering what he was up to."

I was so glad she didn't say I told you so, that she had warned me – like father like son – and of course Gary was going to be a cheating bastard like his father and why didn't I get some sense before it was too late. She never said those words that were running through my mind like some awful audiotape, because deep down I couldn't help feeling that this was all my fault – I wanted the wedding of my dreams and had overlooked everything to get it.

Sandy came and sat beside me. "Everyone downstairs is here for you – they are all concerned about you and no one will blame you, Geri. All we have to do is tell them you are feeling a bit under the weather and in the morning you can decide what to do. But I do think you're going to need your friends. Amy and Clodagh are outside."

But I just couldn't face anyone – even Amy.

I shook my head. "I just want to go asleep, Sandy, after a few more of those brandies, that is. Will you stay, Mum?"

"Of course I will, Geri."

She took off her expensive green jacket. She had looked so beautiful for my wedding and she had been so proud of how it had all turned out. Now how could she explain to all her relatives that her daughter couldn't even keep a husband for more than a few hours.

I felt so sorry for her and my dad too – all the expense that they had gone through for this and I had let them down. It was my fault that I was such an idiot and had crap taste in men. And my poor parents had to pay the price.

There was a knock on the door to the bridal suite.

We all looked at each other, my poor, ordinary dysfunctional family. It was probably the first time we had all been in a room together for more than a few moments without a row breaking out.

"Whoever it is," said my father, *sotto voce*, "get rid of them."

Sandy went to the door.

Pamela Warren burst through into the room.

"I just have to have a word with her! Geri, I am so sorry. I tried to tell you I had suspicions but I wasn't sure and I thought that you'd think I was just trying to stop the wedding. I'm ashamed that Gary is my son. You are a good girl and don't deserve this. I wouldn't wish what I went through on anyone, least of all a bride."

I didn't know what I felt for Pamela – anger that

she had given birth to such a bastard or sympathy that she had been let down not only by her faithless husband but also her son. She seemed genuinely sorry and was close to tears.

"What suspicions did you have?" my mother asked crisply. I could tell she hated every hair on Pamela's head and was barely containing her rage against anyone with the name Warren.

"And why didn't you tell her?" accused Dad.

Pamela wrung her hands. "There wasn't anything concrete. I've just got used to looking for signs of deceit. He seemed edgy and a few times he wasn't where he said he'd be – for instance, he said he was going out with the guys but later they rang looking for him and when I asked him about it he said he'd been with Geri, but I could tell he was lying. I tried to ask you about it today, Geri." She looked pleadingly at me.

"It was a little late, wasn't it? To be asking me on my bleeding wedding day! Do you not think you might have brought this to my attention before I made a fool out of myself in front of all my family and friends?"

"I think you'd better leave," my mother said frostily. "I think your family has done us enough damage for one day, don't you?"

"I am sorry," Pamela said again. "It was very difficult to come here today and see Gary's father on the arm of another woman. I would never wish that on anyone else, least of all my new daughter-in-law. Be assured that I will have a lot to say to him, Geri." She put her hand on my arm briefly and then left.

"The nerve of that woman!" exclaimed my mother. "As if this wasn't any of her fault!"

"Now, Joanne," my father said placatingly, "now is not the time for this. Geri has had an awful shock and I think we need to attend to her for the moment – there'll be plenty of time to talk about all this later."

So we all sat in the room clutching brandies until a lot later, finally numbed with alcohol, I fell asleep on my marital bed, surrounded by my parents and sister.

The nightmare had only begun.

♥ ♥ ♥

The next morning when I awoke there was a single brief moment, a nanosecond, when I had forgotten what had transpired the day before. Then the realisation hit and fell on me like a fine mist, blotting everything else out – this was followed by an almost physical pain in my chest. I now knew what people meant when they said they had suffered a broken heart. Mine indeed felt broken inside me. I felt bereft.

I wished to go back to sleep for perhaps six months or so, at least until this awful sense of grief had receded. I just wanted it all to go away. But it wasn't going to go anywhere, unlike my new husband who had already disappeared.

My heart was hurting but it was in serious danger of being overtaken by my head, which thumped resoundingly after the copious brandies that had eventually rendered me unconscious.

My mother was lying beside me snoring gently. She looked a little bit old, I noticed, in repose. All the stress of the previous day was on her face. I almost came to tears, I just felt so sorry for her and my father. They had been totally supportive to me over what essentially was my mess and they didn't deserve that. All their lifelong savings had paid for the debacle that had become my wedding! My heart went out to them. I didn't know how I was ever going to make it up to them. The phone then trilled. It was Sandy.

"Hiya, Ger, em … I was just wondering if you or Mum wanted any breakfast? The buffet is about to close, or maybe I could get something sent to the room if you didn't want to see anyone."

I certainly didn't feel like eating or seeing anyone – in fact I was entertaining the idea of being packed into my rather large suitcase and being smuggled out of the place. I was also a bit afraid of how I would react if I saw anyone remotely connected to Gary. I wouldn't trust myself to be civil to any of them, especially his rotten father.

"No, I don't want anything to eat, but Mum might – but she's still asleep."

"Well, you could wake her up – and, Geri, I have

Amy and Clodagh here and they are really worried about you. They want to see you. I'll organise some breakfast for you and Mum and get the girls to call up to see you later, if that's OK."

It wasn't remotely OK. I didn't want to see them, my best friends, I just wasn't ready. And as for Clodagh, well, I just couldn't be the same with her since she'd gone over to the dark side. Yet I knew I would need all the friends I could get in the next few weeks.

"OK," I replied reluctantly, eventually.

"Right." She hung up.

"Jesus," I murmured as I replaced the receiver, "I need a brandy right now."

"You do not!" retorted my mother indignantly, all of a sudden wide-awake. "You don't need to become an alcoholic because that bastard doesn't realise what a terrific girl he had. You have to become successful in spite of him, Geri. It's not going to be easy for the next while – it'll be sink or swim."

I nodded vigorously. "The breakfast is on its way," I announced shrilly and fled to the shower where I dissolved into hot tears and my racking sobs were concealed by the noise of the water jets. I emerged a while later, giving what I figured was a good impression of Normal Geri, a girl who was gone forever.

Soon after breakfast my friends arrived.

"Tried marriage and decided I didn't like it much!"

I quipped before fresh tears pricked my eyes.

"Oh, Geri!" Amy wailed and began to dissolve into tears.

"He's a right bastard!" hissed Clodagh fiercely.

I could barely look at Clodagh. After all, she was doing exactly the same thing with the awful Karl to some other poor cow, ruining her life.

Yeah, you'd know all about bastards, *Married Karl's girlfriend,* I felt like shouting.

But I couldn't, so I focused on Amy instead.

"It's OK, Amy, no one died – yet, but I *am* planning his demise."

I looked at Clodagh, who was chewing her bottom lip, something she only did when extremely stressed.

"What are you going to do?" she asked tentatively, as if she didn't want to hear the answer.

"Well, I'm going to try very hard to breathe in and out until I don't have to try to do it any more, and after that who knows?"

Chapter 24

We left the hotel after five that day, like fugitives, when every last straggler of the wedding had finally left and there was no chance of me being accosted at reception by wayward guests quizzing me about my missing bridegroom.

As Dad packed my bags into his sensible Ford, I spotted my wedding present lying forlornly in the car park, and I couldn't resist going over to the sports car I had received less than twenty-four hours earlier and stroking its shiny yellow bonnet. I noticed some petals still lying on the front seat and couldn't help remembering Gary giving me this gift with so much love – how could he *do* that? How could he be so kind and loving and less than a day later just walk away from me?

Suddenly my father was there, peering over my shoulder.

"What do you want to do with it?" he asked quietly, his forehead furrowed with concern.

"Burn it!" I replied more fiercely than I had intended. "Preferably with Gary and his mistress inside! Give it a nice good flame!"

"Come on, let's get you home," Dad said gently and ushered me away. "We can get someone to pick it up later. Have you got the keys?"

I tried vaguely to remember. Oh yes, Gary drove up. I winced as I recalled the laughter we shared on that journey and the happiness – I was so content. The memory made me nauseous.

"Gary's got the keys," I said and suddenly turned on my heel and ran back towards my dream car.

"The bastard!" I screamed out to the trees and looked around for a weapon, anything to destroy the last vestige of the lie that was us – I grabbed a handful of gravel and hurled it at the windscreen – it didn't do much damage. Now, if I could only find a match and some petrol I'd feel a whole lot better.

"Geri, come on, love, he's not worth it," said my poor father, taking me by the arm and buffetting me into the car.

My mother was uncharacteristically silent. The shock of it all was finally sinking in and she was taking me, still single, back to Dublin. No doubt all the nosy neighbours would be watchful, the net curtains at the twitch, all laughing at high and mighty Geri Murphy arriving back from her fancy weddin' without her new husband.

So I got into the car like a recalcitrant teenager and we sped back towards Dublin.

Sandy and Chris had cadged a lift from Amy and Clodagh. As for poor kilt-wearing Stuart, well, the poor guy had probably hightailed it back to Glasgow in shock at the carry-on that seemed to be an Irish wedding.

As the green fields of Cavan sped by and we neared Meath I felt a rising panic inside me and I had the weirdest feeling that my head was lifting off of my body. Suddenly I grabbed the headrest in front of me before everything went black.

As I came to I saw my parents lurch over me. I was sprawled across the back seat and the car door was open. We were obviously stopped on the hard shoulder as millimetres away the cars and trucks sped by on the busy road.

My poor parents looked so worried, I felt guilty. I really had to pull myself together, at least for their sakes.

"I'm sorry, Mum and Dad, I'm really sorry about all of this."

"You fainted, Geri. Are you alright?" My mother looked flushed and up to high dudgeon.

"I've been better," I said weakly. I couldn't face the idea of going home to my childish bedroom like nothing had ever happened, yet I needed to be cosseted and protected and looked after. Besides, I had nowhere else to go.

"Just rest here for a little bit," said Dad in a kind voice, "and we'll set off as soon as you're more yourself."

I gave a little smile. More myself. I could never be more myself again: that trusting, naïve idiot that was *myself* was gone forever. A new hardened, brittle self would be the one to replace her and she was never ever going to be trod on again.

"OK, Dad. Maybe a little bit of fresh air and some water would help. I just felt so hot back there."

Mum rummaged in her bag and pulled out a small bottle of twelve-year-old whiskey that we had placed on the dining tables as a wedding favour to our guests. "Here." She proffered the drink, the woman who hours earlier was worried about me becoming an alcoholic. "This might help put a bit of colour back on those cheeks. We don't have any water. Drink it up, love, you're probably still in a bit of shock."

I took it gratefully and knocked it back in one gulp.

"How many more of those have you got stashed in there?" I said, grinning, eyeing her large handbag that held a multitude.

"Enough," my mother smiled, for once a conspirator.

And that was it. I knew that they were on my side and, knowing that, I knew that somehow I would just have to survive this, and if it was going to be one whiskey at a time, then so be it.

We got back to Sutton that evening about eight. If it had been autumn then I might have escaped the neighbours' stares under cover of darkness, but in June, the damn street was thronged with kids playing and people mowing their lawns and chatting over hedges.

I ignored any open stares and marched smartly into our house, fortified by several of mum's mini-whiskey bottles. Inside, though, it was a different story. The house was covered with reminders of the hectic mêlée that had taken place the previous day. The front room was littered with wedding gifts, leftover greenery from the flower buttonholes and numerous empty champagne bottles and glasses. Worse still, Uncle Fred and Aunty Pearl were still there – they hadn't gone back to Boston yet, so I had to endure their obtuse questioning before I fled to my room within minutes.

My mobile rang. It was Amy. I clicked it off. I couldn't talk yet, not if I didn't want to dissolve into a blob of hot tears again.

I collapsed onto my small little single bed, still covered in hair-straighteners, copious bags of make-up and myriads of sexy underwear that I had bought, just in case.

"Well, Geri Murphy, this is your life!" I said aloud to the ceiling. "Another forty years of being the sad spinster daughter living with her parents."

I felt like I was going to crawl out of my skin if I

stayed there another minute. I just needed to get away, somewhere, anywhere, to someone who understood and wouldn't ask stupid or sincere questions, who wouldn't ask *any* bleedin' questions, and I knew just the person.

I dialled his number.

"Connor? It's me. Can you come and get me right now? I'm back home in Sutton with Mum and Dad."

"I'll be there in twenty minutes," was the reply and he was.

♥ ♥ ♥

The black Saab 93 Turbo slid quietly along to the next house outside. I grabbed my bag and jacket and jumped the stairs in threes to escape Fort Knox without anyone noticing.

Soon we were speeding down the coast road in silence.

"Where to?" Connor asked eventually, eyeing me seriously.

"Dunno," I said. I knew I had to get out of my house. I just couldn't function to the level of making any conscious decisions beyond that. "Wherever."

So we just drove for a while along the coast road towards town. Connor didn't question me, as I knew he wouldn't. He had gone through all the same things when April had left him and I knew he understood the sheer uncomprehending pain and numbing shock of it all. I was still reeling and he had been too, all those months ago when April had suddenly left him without any warning.

People were strolling along the beachfront in the evening summer sunshine, enjoying the nice mild weather. They were walking their dogs, jogging and life was going on pretty much as normal, yet it all seemed slightly surreal to me as my world had stopped.

I just wished I could swap places with any of them.

Connor's car glided effortlessly through town and onto the East Link bridge until we were over to the south side, into his territory.

"I'm going to take you to my place and make you some dinner, Geri," he announced suddenly and I hadn't the energy to argue.

"OK," I mumbled and stared conscientiously out onto the coastline at Sandymount,

Connor suddenly laughed. "You're doing well, Geri. I didn't say 'yes' till about day eleven."

I smiled despite myself. "Yes, we had many a lovely quiet day at the office back then."

We drove to Connor's little artisan cottage in Dalkey village. It was small but hugely expensive due to its proximity to Dublin's famous Vico Road and its varied celebrity inhabitants, including Bono. Being an architect, Connor had lovingly restored and modernised the house so that every bit of space was utilised and its quirkiness was highlighted by the open-plan design he had implemented. He had extended the back of the house and its rear wall was made entirely of glass, which gave the illusion of space and looked out onto a tiny but well-designed courtyard. I sat there in the garden drinking red wine absently while Connor sizzled some steaks with U2 blasting out in the kitchen.

"Want another?" Connor asked, proffering another glass of Merlot.

"You bet," I smiled wanly. There wasn't enough red wine in the universe to anaesthetise me but I was going to give it a try.

"I reckon Bono can hear his album from here – are you trying to get his attention or something?"

Connor laughed. "I see you haven't lost your sense of humour anyway. You know U2 sound best at 180 decibels. And what way do you like your steak? Burnt to a crisp or still mooing?"

"Somewhere in between," I grinned and this time it was genuine. I began to feel glad I called on my dear friend. I felt safe somehow, as if anything I did was OK. Connor was unshockable and best of all he had been through it all before.

The late summer sun went down as we ate our steaks and drank more than we should have. I began to uncurl the knots that tied up my stomach and question Connor as to his take on the entire debacle.

"I can't explain why some guys are idiots, but it

always seemed to me that Gary wanted whatever he didn't have, like that red sports car, then the black one, then the apartment – it was all about acquiring things. He had you so it might have been that he wanted to then acquire someone else. It's not so much about you but about him. He's got a self-esteem problem if he needs to be defined by what he owns."

I frowned. "Well, he's pretty much fucked up any self-esteem I might have had, the bastard, and on my wedding day too!"

"Well," said Connor slowly, "*technically* that wasn't actually Gary's doing, but the other woman's."

"Yes," I insisted hotly, "but when she did show up and confronted me, he didn't even tell her to bugger off and try to sort it out. He didn't *choose* me, a mere few hours after he had promised himself to me forever – that is what has destroyed me, Connor!"

I burst into tears again. Was there no end to my river of soggy sadness? I seemed to have cried forever and yet there were ever more reservoirs of tears.

"Oh, Geri, I am so sorry!" Connor touched my hand, then wiped away my tears.

Then, sometime after he stroked my hair something strange happened.

He was holding me close and I somehow found his lips and kissed him. I don't know to this day why I did that. I think I just needed to be held, to be cherished – to feel something other than destroyed and discarded.

He looked at me questioningly before kissing me back. Before I knew it we were overtaken by something beyond us, a passion that was born of sadness and longing, and we ended up in Connor's wide and trendy leather bed making passionate and sensual love. I didn't know how I felt about it even as it was happening. I just didn't want to feel any more desperate than I had felt the past twenty-four hours and being in someone else's arms, someone who cared about me, definitely helped.

I fell asleep in Connor's arms feeling like I was falling, falling from a huge height, and I had just been caught and I was holding on for dear life.

♥ ♥ ♥

The next morning when I awoke, I realised that I had been sleeping on my hand, my left hand, and the imprint from my engagement ring was stamped into my cheek. It seemed like some kind of payback, a reminder that I was still married and I had just slept with someone else. I felt inexplicably guilty, like I had betrayed my wedding vows, when I knew deep down I had betrayed nothing. I still felt weird, and so embarrassed.

I looked out of Connor's bedroom window onto a sunny day. The birds were chirping and I could see the spire of the village church in the distance. My head hurt and my heart did too, but now I was worried about how Connor was going to be with me. I feared that we wouldn't be able to remain friends and, even worse, boss and employee. It was hardly the best of situations – but I had to tread carefully too. Connor had been hurt so badly by April, I wasn't going to do anything that would hurt him further.

"Morning, Geri, here's some juice. I've got some bacon and toast on the go. How are you feeling?"

It was Connor, bright and breezy, obviously not in the least bit perturbed or embarrassed by our night of illicit passion. He didn't even have the decency to be hungover, or look remotely dishevelled. He still looked as shockingly handsome as he had since he'd had his unruly mop chopped off and the Antonio Banderas cheekbones and sultry brown eyes had emerged from under their thatch.

"Thanks, Connor, that'll be lovely. Oh, jeez, I just remembered. My mum and dad don't even know that I left the house last night. I'd better give them a ring."

"OK," he smiled easily. "Well, the en suite shower is through there. I don't have any girly stuff, I'm afraid. I chucked it out a while back, when I had my ceremonial bonfire of April's things. So it's all blokey stuff. I'll be slaving away in the kitchen – breakfast will be ready in about ten minutes."

With that he disappeared.

I quickly phoned my dazed mother, who had just awoken and was somewhat stunned that I had even managed to resurrect a sort of social life within a day of being dumped, never mind becoming a dirty stop-out.

"And when will you be home, love?" she enquired, as if I was fifteen, which I was in danger of becoming if I stayed at home much longer.

"Oh, I suppose later on in the day. When are Uncle Fred and Aunty Pearl leaving for their flight?"

"It's OK," Mum said quietly into the phone. "They're packing now and your father is taking them to the airport within the hour – they'll be well gone by the time you get back. Is that why you went to Connor's?"

"Um … yes, Mum," I replied, glad she couldn't see my crimson face. "I just needed to get away. I'll see you later, OK?"

We had a leisurely breakfast on the patio. Connor had cleared away any evidence of our copious alcohol consumption from the night before and we managed to stay away from the issue of us madly bonking each other a scant few hours earlier. Isn't it amazing that you can be as intimate as it is possible to be with another human being and then afterwards return to polite conversation as if it had never happened, embarrassed by the talking about it, yet not embarrassed enough to prevent its occurrence!

"Where's the mutt?" I enquired idly, wondering why I hadn't noticed earlier that the love of Connor's life was missing.

"Sarge is staying at my brother's. I couldn't leave him alone while I gallivanted off to the countryside to your wed– God! I'm sorry, Geri, I mentioned the W word."

I smiled. "It's OK, Connor. I'm not that delicate that the very word sends me into tears, not at this precise moment anyhow, but that may change. I'm not sure the madness has really set in yet."

Connor cleared away the dirty dishes – I had never known how domesticated he was before – obviously a man of deep and hidden talents.

"I'm going to fetch Sarge soon – would you like to come to Seán's? He only lives a mile or so away. I can't do without my main buddy for too long."

"Yes, why not?" I agreed. "I'm hardly likely to be bounding off on honeymoon, am I?"

Connor stopped his dish collecting. "You know, I was just thinking about that, Geri. The honeymoon, I mean. Did you keep that money we gave you or has it been spent on the honeymoon already? I think you may be able to cancel the original tickets and change them. You do have them, don't you?"

I searched my frazzled mind for any recollection of my life before two days ago.

"Yes, I do, somewhere. I was going to surprise Gary with the upgraded honeymoon I had booked. Do you really think I can change them at this late stage?"

"I'm not sure," said Connor, grinning. "But wouldn't it be nice if you could cash in that ticket for somewhere truly fantastic for yourself? It would give you some breathing space. It would be just the thing to help you cope."

"Yes, it just might, Connor. I'll check it out later

with the travel agent's. Sandy works there so if strings can be pulled perhaps there's a way she can do it. I'd love to get out of Dublin for a while."

As we left Connor's smart little cottage to fetch his dog, I began to glimpse the merest chink of light through the dark cloud of my situation – perhaps there was a chance I could get away from all the fallout of my wasted wedding and put some distance between me and the whole horrible episode. I hadn't forgotten that I had yet to deal with Gary and his little harlot, but that was something I wasn't yet strong enough to cope with, but I knew in time I would be, and he hadn't escaped my wrath, not by a long shot.

Chapter 25

We walked the two miles to Connor's brother Seán's house to collect Sarge.

Seán lived in nearby Killiney in a large rambling house with his wife and five children. He looked just like Connor except instead of an unruly mop of black hair, he had an equally untidy crop of blond curls.

He opened the large door and let out a bounding Sarge and several running children, all bouncing and jumping on their uncle who seemed to be a favourite.

"Hi, come in, come in!" Seán roared above the mêlée and ushered us into the big hallway, which was scattered with myriads of toys and varied debris.

We stepped gingerly over all the toys and followed Seán to the large sunny kitchen, which was just as cluttered but still stylish and well appointed – what you could see of it, that was.

"Coffee?" he asked above the din of kids and dogs clattering along the wooden-floored hallway.

We nodded, smiling.

"This is Geri, my friend and colleague," Connor said carefully.

I smiled ruefully. He had handled it well, considering the night before.

"Ah, the famous *Geri*! I have heard all about you. Aren't you getting hitched soon?" Seán said cheerily as he poured us both a cup of industrial strength Java from his percolator.

I looked at Connor's horrified expression and rescued him. "Yes, I got hitched, and instantly unhitched just as quick. Now what have you heard about me from this fella here?"

Seán just stared for a moment, unsure of how to proceed.

"Don't tell her she's indispensable or it could cost me a humungous pay-rise, Seán," warned Connor sagely and we all laughed.

Just then the riot of kids bundled into the kitchen demanding cookies and milk and Sarge decided his owner needed a fresh bout of affection so the awkward moment was gone, but I realised there would be a lot more awkwardness to come, and it really hadn't even begun yet. And much as I liked being in a cocoon at Connor's, I couldn't stay there forever and I would have to return home and face the music. Suddenly the idea that I might be able to change the honeymoon tickets and escape for a while seemed like the answer to my prayers.

So after a nice chat and a terrible coffee with Seán, I asked Connor to take me home to Sutton. It was time to talk to Sandy.

"Seán's really nice," I ventured as Connor sped me northwards.

"Yes, he and Mary are really happy with each other and their brood. I envy him you know, Geri. He has everything I have ever wanted. A happy marriage and a load of kids."

I looked over at Connor and he seemed really sad. I realised that he was far from over April and their big split. I never realised that he felt that strongly about children or family. He had always seemed so driven by his career – in fact I was sure that was what caused the breakdown of the marriage.

"Didn't April want kids?" I asked, my natural nosiness getting the better of me.

"No," frowned Connor, glancing in my direction. "Why do you think I buried myself in my work? She told me in no uncertain terms that she wasn't ruining her modelling career or her size-eight figure for kids. I thought when the modelling work dried up she would change her mind, but as the modelling assignments tapered off she got more insistent about keeping her looks, not less."

"Is that why she decamped to London?" I ventured.

"Yes, she figured it was a bigger pond and she had more chances of work. It's my own fault, Geri – she never promised me that she'd have kids. I just foolishly believed she would get the longing I had eventually. So no wonder it all fell apart. I married April knowing exactly what she was like, more fool me."

"Me too!" I replied giggling. Suddenly my predicament seemed hilarious. I had known what a shit Gary was – yet I still blundered towards the altar like a mad woman. "I was so dead keen on gallivanting up the aisle I conveniently discarded the evidence before my very eyes. The fact that my bridegroom, apart from being a king-size shit, was such a reluctant partner. Why, I practically forced the guy to propose every year for the past five years. I think he just did it to shut me up!"

We both roared with laughter at the absurdity of our situations.

"What a pair of eejits!" Connor roared as we both laughed longer than we needed. There was a touch of hysteria to it all but for the moment it helped.

But by the time we got to Curlew Drive in Sutton, a frisson of awkwardness had grown up between us. It was almost like we had had a hot passionate date and one or both of us expected some sort of follow-up.

I leapt out of the car like my arse was on fire to a parting shot of Connor saying, "I'll call you later."

I waved briefly before fleeing indoors.

Once there, I wondered what my hurry was. Mum emerged from the kitchen red-eyed and watchful, while Dad was simmering in the newly decorated lounge. I gathered that they had "had words" over my wedding and about "what to do next". Dad seemed to think this involved some sort of decapitation of Gary's cranium (which, incidentally, was something that I would have quite enjoyed) while Mum's attitude was to suffer in silent dignity and pretend we weren't all destroyed by the event. But really we *were*. But I could see Mum's point too – she had had enough for the moment. I think we all had.

"I was thinking about going away for a while," I said to them in a bright voice.

"Connor tells me I can change the ticket name for the honeymoon and I can take Sandy or Amy with me instead of ... well, you know. It'll mean Sandy might have to call in a few favours. I'll call her now." Mum's face lit up like a Christmas tree. I could see the prospect of getting rid of Sandy and me for a number of weeks as a real bargain. I couldn't blame her really.

"That's a great idea, love. You could do with some cheering up."

"The phone's been off the hook for the past four hours," Dad piped up waspishly. "We got sick of answering calls from all the family and your friends wondering what the hell was going on. If I get my hands on that bowsie I'll rip his head off."

"Now, Eddie, calm down – you'll do your blood pressure no good at all. Don't mind him, Geri, there weren't that many calls – give Sandy a ring there and see what she can do. She managed to tear herself away from the Aussie for a few hours and go to work."

I realised with a start it was the first time I had spoken to my sister since we had been at the hotel. Or for that matter, I hadn't spoken to my friends either. I resolved to talk to them later. I was feeling a bit stronger, though I wasn't sure for how long.

Sandy wasn't so sure about the possibility of changing my honeymoon tickets.

"Ooh, it's not going to be easy, Ger. Not at this late stage. Now if Gary had a serious illness, that would make it easy to get a refund."

"That can be arranged!" I muttered darkly. "So what can we do, Sandy? This honeymoon cost me a lot of money and I need to get away."

There were a lot of heavy sighs and multi-clicking going on at the other end.

"You're supposed to be going in three days' time. It may be too late to do anything at all, but leave it with me. I'll have to talk to Barry the manager. Maybe I can call in a few favours."

That was the best she could do, so I had to just sit and wait.

So I called Amy.

"Geri!" her voice said in reedy whisper.

"Don't cry, Amy!" I said fiercely. "I am just about

holding this all together and I need you to be strong. Can you come over after work? I'm at my mum's."

"I'll be there," she replied in her strongest voice.

I then lifted the receiver and dialled Clodagh's mobile. But then I put the phone back down. I couldn't face Clodagh right now. I loved my friend but somehow she had gone over to the other side and I just couldn't talk to her about how crushed I was when I was feeling such animosity towards her for being part of Karl's sordid little world.

But my number must have shown on Clodagh's phone because she called straight back.

"Geri? You called me, are you OK?"

I took a deep breath and closed my eyes. Hearing her voice, I just couldn't be as cruel as I felt towards her, so I chickened out. "Not really, Clodagh. I'm staying at my parents' for the moment ... You hardly thought I was moved into the apartment with Gary and his mistress, did you?"

"No, I guess not," came the reply – a reply laden with guilt. Suddenly I even felt sorry for her, just a little bit.

"Can I come over and see you?" she asked, and I knew that was difficult for her – she must have been feeling terrible, knowing that she too was the other woman.

"I just want to be there for you, Geri. Amy does too – we want to help in any way we can."

"I don't think anyone can help me," I said sadly.

"Have you seen him?" Clodagh asked bravely.

"No, I haven't."

I suddenly thought of my night of passion with Connor and blushed profusely – glad my friend couldn't see me. I really wasn't any better than she was for all my moralising.

"Sandy is trying to get my honeymoon tickets changed so I can go away for a while. I need to be somewhere else so I can get my head together."

There was a small silence.

"Geri, I am so sorry about everything that has happened to you – it's just too awful. I have been thinking about you constantly the past two days."

"Yes, well," I replied before I could help myself, "maybe you can spare a few minutes to think of Karl's wife, because she is going to feel as devastated as I am when she finds out about you and her husband."

I could hear Clodagh gasp audibly. "I suppose I deserve that, Geri. I'm not proud of what I have done, but it's hardly the same situation. Karl and his wife lead separate lives and have done for quite some time. It's entirely different from what Gary did on you, Geri." She sounded the slightest bit indignant, like she held some sort of higher ground than my cheating husband and the awful Jessie.

My temper rose. "Really, Clodagh, is that right? Well, maybe you should go over and visit with Karl's life partner and see if she agrees with that theory. Maybe then I will see your side of the story, when you've heard hers!"

With that I slammed the phone down.

Damn. I already wished I hadn't lost my temper.

Right now I needed all the friends I could get and it looked like I had just lost one.

The phone trilled again.

I was almost afraid to answer it in case it was Clodagh again.

But thankfully it was Sandy.

"Good news, Geri, I managed to rescue something from this whole debacle, though it's cost me enormously. You can still fly to Cairns, but it'll cost another five hundred euro for a name change at this late stage if you want to take someone else. They weren't very happy about it happening at all but Barry's brother happens to be the manager at Qantas so he pulled a few strings."

My trampled spirits lifted. "Oh, Sandy, you don't know how much that means to me. I feel like I'll crack up if I don't get away from all the reminders of Gary and this awful situation."

"No worries," my sister replied happily. She was glad to help. And she had been brilliant so far. "I just need a name, Geri, and I need it now. The name of the person on the ticket to accompany you."

I thought hard for a moment. My brain wasn't at all rational but for some reason Connor flashed into my mind.

But common sense won out.

"Amy," I replied eventually. "I'll be taking Amy. Maybe you, me, Amy and the Aussie can all meet up for dinner when you get out there."

Sandy laughed. "Yeah, maybe. I'll see you tonight, OK?"

"Yes," I replied feeling brighter. "And Sandy, thanks, thanks so much for being my best sister during all of this."

"It's the least I could do. You would do the same for me if I were in your position."

"I hope I never have to do anything like this for you, Sandy. And judging by the smitten look of Chris, I'll never have to."

"Hmm ... If I've learnt anything from your situation, Geri, it's that you can never take anyone or anything for granted. But I'm having fun at the minute. You better call Amy and see if she can get holiday leave at such short notice."

I hadn't even considered that Amy might not be able to come with me. I knew she had some time due to her, but her boss was very exacting and by the book and it was far from a foregone conclusion that he would let her go at short notice. I began to panic again.

I decided to call her and give her some notice.

"Oh, Geri, Pierce is on holiday at the moment and I'm sure he wouldn't let me go at such short notice. I don't know who else to ask, though Sadie Kelly is technically in charge. I could try her. She's a bit frosty but I'm told she's a real feminist so I'll do my best. Say a few prayers for me and I'll call over straight from work, OK?"

"Fine, Amy." I put the phone down.

I knew I had one more thing to do.

I had to go over to the apartment at Kinsealy Cloisters and fetch my suitcase, which held my honeymoon clothes and all the hopefully purchased items for my holiday of a lifetime. There was a chance that I might bump into Gary or the awful Jessie. And I wasn't sure I was ready for that. But I knew I had to go, sooner or later.

I didn't know if I was brave enough.

But soon I would find out.

Chapter 26

I seemed to be holding my breath as I drove the few miles over to the apartment. Our apartment. I had been so happy as we had decorated it and I imagined myself waking up there every morning beside Gary – happy, secure, looking forward to making handsome little babies with him. My stomach churned when I even thought about him. I could not imagine actually meeting him. In fact I was actually losing memory of what he looked like, despite the fact it had only been two days. Had it only been forty-eight hours since my life was torn asunder? It seemed like eons ago.

As I got near to Kinsealy Cloisters I almost turned back several times. But something drove me on (apart from my faithful little Micra, that was) – it was anger and desperation and the inner feeling that I must go there, partly to see if he was shagging her on our bed at that very moment. I was even running a video in my tortured mind of coming upon them both *en flagrante* and then me calmly bashing their heads in with that heavy expensive clay pot that we'd bought in Habitat.

When I got there my hands were shaking so much I could barely get the key in the door, even though Gary's car was not in the driveway and I knew I was alone.

Inside everything looked eerily the same. Dirty dishes in the sink, the carpet not vacuumed, Gary's clothes strewn here and there. I ventured into the bedroom. The bed was neatly made and there were candles on every available surface. Obviously a night of romance had ensued and as far as I recalled Gary had never made the bed in all the time I had known him, so it dawned on me that Jessie had made it. My temper rose considerably. I spotted two suitcases in the corner, Gary's and mine, both unopened. When I noticed Gary's wedding ring lying on the bedside table, I was thrown into a deeper shock. There was something so final and deeply cruel about that, seeing the ring so casually discarded. I realised that the ten years I had loved Gary were in ruins. It was over and I really knew it was over. Suddenly I felt bile rise in my throat and rushed into the en suite and violently threw up. My legs went from under me and I sank to the floor helplessly. I sat there immobile, my head resting on the cool tiles, breathing deeply until the dizziness and nausea passed. I eventually got up and splashed water on my face – it was then I noticed a strange toothbrush on the washbasin. It was pink and distinctly feminine and I knew it was *hers.* I took it up and then impulsively brushed it rapidly along the inner rim of the toilet. Then I placed it back where I found it.

I then went back to the bedroom, still feeling weak, and I fetched my suitcase. I stared for a few minutes at the wedding ring and the bed that my replacement had made. Something snapped. I was in such a rage I had to stop myself from putting a match to the bed itself. But I knew deep down that I couldn't do that, not legally anyway. So I went to the kitchen and looked into the fridge and found the small red chilli that I had bought a week earlier. I rushed back into the bedroom and rubbed the chilli along the fresh sheets and then also into the crotch of Gary's entire collection of Calvin Klein undies. I then took Gary's shiny wedding band and put it into the toilet, where it shone up at me. It was where it belonged.

Then I took my suitcase and passed the baby room that Gary had transformed into his macho gym room and I realised that Gary had never intended to stay with me long-term or ever have a family with me. The gym room stated that more eloquently than all the vague statements that Gary, made about waiting to start a family. The tears flowed down my face unabashed as I left the apartment and drove away. It didn't feel any better to wreak some revenge – not yet anyhow. All I felt was emptier than I had ever been and so tired that I felt I could sleep for a month.

But I couldn't sleep. I had to make sure Amy was able to come away with me first, so I could breathe easy again, and yet I still felt that I wanted to see Gary, to slap his face and demand to know why he had hurt me in the worst way possible. Perhaps I could drive over to the garage and plough Mavis (my car) in through the expensive plate-glass window of Warren Motors – that would certainly grab Gary's attention but maybe that was a bit too *Starsky and Hutch*. I now understood why Pamela Warren had been desperate enough to go down there to the garage and key all the cars. She needed some justice. But there was none, so I meekly drove home and awaited my friend Amy, whom I prayed was going to say yes, she would come with me to Port Douglas and the Great Barrier Reef and do all the wonderful things that I was going to do with my new husband just a few short days ago. Because right then I really felt if I didn't get on that plane I wouldn't be responsible for my actions. I really needed to put some distance between me and Gary Warren and I needed it soon.

♥ ♥ ♥

Amy came over that evening straight from work. I

could tell by her bright eyes and jaunty demeanour as she entered the house that it was good news and I cheered up immediately.

"Please tell me you got it!" I demanded impatiently as I pulled her into my room where I had barricaded myself since I had got back home.

"Yes!" she smiled widely. "I was lucky that Pierce was away – you know what a bastard he is about annual leave. Once I told Sadie your story she was more than helpful."

I wasn't too sure about my tragic story being the talk of Pender PR but I bit my lip and remained quiet.

"So, that's a relief," said Amy. "I've got the passport ready and all I have to do is pack. Are you sure you want to do this, Geri, go ahead with the honeymoon, I mean? It might make you feel worse."

I explained to her that I couldn't feel any worse than I had done when I went over to the apartment earlier, and gave her the full story.

"That's really horrible. He ought to be strung up by the balls, Geri!" Amy said fiercely.

I was touched by my friend's concern for me.

But I hadn't told her yet about my row with Clodagh or my out-of-character slutty behaviour with my boss, of all people. I was just working up the courage to tell her all when my father shouted up the stairs to tell me that Connor was on the phone.

Amy looked at me quizzically.

"Tell him I'll call him back in a few minutes," I

yelled. I could feel my face rising rapidly to deep magenta.

"What's going on?" Amy enquired archly. She knew I only blushed for one or two reasons and the main one was to do with men. She could always tell when I was up to something, like back in Spain when I fancied Adam.

"Amy, you are going to think I am the worst bitch ever. I did *two* awful things. First I got drunk at Connor's and made a pass at him, and we sort of ended up in bed together."

Hugely raised eyebrows followed this admission so I carried on.

"Then, I had a big row with Clodagh today on the phone and I basically called her a home-wrecking floozie. I am proud of neither and I'm not sure of how to get past either thing. I feel awful, Amy. Connor doesn't need to be messed around after what he has been through with April, yet I need another relationship like a hole in the head – and as for Clodagh, well, I know I'm taking her relationship with Karl personally because of what's happened to me. But I can't help feeling this way about it."

Amy gave me a hug. "I think you're being too hard on yourself, Geri. Connor is a big boy and he knew what he was doing. In fact he took advantage of your fragile state, not the other way round – and as for Clodagh, well, she knows what she and Karl are doing is not right so she should expect some kind of criticism. Of course you are going to feel strongly about adultery as it has just *happened* to you. The sooner we get you away from here for a nice break, the better. Now, let's go out for a pizza and you can give me all the juicy details, like how was it finally being with someone other than Gary? And is Connor a good kisser? We need to get you out of this bedroom and keep you out of other people's, Geri Murphy!"

"Speak for yourself!" I quipped, surprising myself with an attempt at humour and a lift in my mood. I could pack a suitcase tomorrow evening and get out of Dublin and away from my life for two weeks. Gary I could sort when I got back. Things couldn't look as bleak on a sun-saturated sandy beach, could they?

After Amy and I had been for a pizza and numerous cocktails at *Sosume,* I checked my mobile to find three brief messages from Connor and one from Clodagh. Being tipsy, I regained some of my earlier bravado and called Connor back in the cab on the way home, with Amy giggling away in the background.

"Geri, at *last,* I was really getting worried about you. Are you OK?"

"Never better," I chirped merrily. "I've just been busy, Connor, arranging a honeymoon for one, no, sorry – that's just me feeling sorry for myself – I mean an exciting trip for me and my best friend Amy who are going together. Sandy managed to call in a few favours, so I didn't lose the honeymoon after all.

Thanks for your help, Connor. So I'm off down under tomorrow, and you … how are you … um … after what happened? You don't feel weird or anything, do you, Connor?"

He laughed nervously. "Me? No, well … maybe a little bit. I think we had way too many shots. I just wanted to make sure you are OK and to tell you that I'll be thinking about you while you're gone. I care about you, Geri – I just wanted you to know that."

"I know that. Thanks, Connor – for everything."

"Right, er … well, you just enjoy yourself, Geri, I … we'll miss you."

I laughed a bit nervously. "Sure one look at the disaster zone that replaced the office since I left on leave will remind you of what you're missing. I'll see you in a few weeks . . . and, Connor?"

"Yes?"

He sounded a little crestfallen, though it was difficult to tell.

"Thanks, thanks for being there for me, I do appreciate it."

"Any time, Geri. Any time. Have a great time and I'll see you when you get back."

I rang off, grateful that I wouldn't have the awful embarrassment of seeing him over coffee on Monday morning, imagining our night of passion in blushing daylight. At least this way I could defer embarrassment from everything – for a while.

Amy broke through my thoughts. "What about

Clodagh? Are you going to ring her back, Geri? I think you should. I'm sure she'll understand why you lost your cool with her. It would be nice to let her know we're off tomorrow."

Amy was always like my little conscience – I could never get away with much: she was too damn principled.

"OK, OK, I will. It's just as well I had that Harvey Wallbanger last – it's made me quite fearless."

I quick dialled Clodagh's mobile, but it just went to messaging. I left a brief, terse message telling her that I was sorry for yelling at her and I was under a lot of stress and that Amy and I were off to Cairns for a couple of weeks and hopefully I would be more amenable upon my return. (I doubted it.)

Amy dropped me off at my avenue with excited cries of "Tomorrow we fly!" and I fell in the door inebriated, climbed up the stairs on all fours and barely managed to fall into my bed before passing out. I didn't even have time for a crying-to-sleep jag, so I didn't have to think any more that day of my hopeless situation and tomorrow I could get away. Right then I felt as if my life and sanity depended on it.

Chapter 27

The following morning I awoke in a lighter mood. At least I now had a distraction, a different place to focus on, and some new surroundings to prevent me from descending into the depths of depression. I also wanted to have some time alone to talk to Amy, to find out her take on the whole affair, to ask her if she had suspected anything, and to enquire as to her relationship with Stuart. I hadn't even asked how they had got on at the wedding. We would have plenty of time to chat on the long flight. The hot sun and all the attractions of Queensland might take my mind off of my troubles at least for a while.

I couldn't help wondering, however, if Gary had given any thoughts whatsoever to me today. He knew we were due to fly out for our honeymoon – was he that much of a heartless bastard that it didn't even cost him a thought? I tried to crowd out my mind with the idea of the flight and the excitement of flying halfway across the world so I wouldn't sink back down into despair again. Thinking of Gary wasn't doing my health any good.

I packed and repacked my suitcase with a vengeance, taking care to remove any of the sexy lingerie that I had secreted before my wedding day, deliberately replacing the black lacy numbers with sensible white cotton briefs. I wanted no reminders of my earlier, more promising life.

Then I had a nice breakfast with my mother and father, who were both glad for something else to chat about – something cheerful for a change.

My parents had really been so kind to me through out this whole affair that I felt quite in awe of their stoicism in the face of such ignominy. I had grown closer to them because despite everything they never once judged me – unlike the way I had always judged them. Someday, I vowed, I'd make it up to them.

The doorbell rang as I chomped through my third slice of toast – I had rediscovered my legendary appetite at last.

"I'll go," my father sighed listlessly as he padded into the hallway still clad in his dressing-gown and slippers.

I then heard a commotion and the sound of raised voices.

My mother and I looked at each other and ran out

to the doorway.

We both gasped at what was before us.

My dad had Gary in some sort of a headlock and was dragging him around the hallway, aiming him hither and thither and trying to hit him at the same time.

I didn't know if I was more shocked to see my errant husband or more surprised to see my father behave like Mike Tyson in our tiny hallway.

"Get him off me, please!" Gary roared through a darkening purple face.

"The nerve of ye, ye bowsie!" yelled my dad. "I'll teach ye not to shame my daughter!"

Dad danced around with Gary's head some more and then ploughed it through the lounge door. It was then that Mum and I decided to rescue Gary, even though he didn't deserve it.

"Eddie, stop it now! He's not worth it, Eddie, remember your blood pressure!" Mum wailed. "Get off him!" She prised him off Gary with my help and shunted Dad off towards the kitchen but not before he shot me a triumphant look and I couldn't blame him. It felt a bit better to see Gary suffer. I had quite enjoyed it myself – momentarily.

Now I was faced with the man I had spent the past ten years with, the man I hadn't seen since I'd walked up the aisle, and he looked like a complete stranger, so much so that I found it hard to think of a single thing to say to him.

He looked at me with those piercing blue eyes and my treacherous heart did a little somersault. I shot down that emotion quickly and sat down, suddenly aware that I was wearing my sad bunny flannelette pyjamas and I hadn't yet washed my hair. I feigned cool indifference.

"Well, why are *you* here?" I managed with a glacial stare.

Gary ran his hands through his hair manically. "Geri, I just had to see you before you left. I just wanted to say I am so sorry. I never planned to hurt you that way. I tried to tell you so many times that I wasn't into getting married … but I was going to go through with it. I had finished with Jessie before the wedding, but she never could take no for an answer. I never thought she would show up like that…"

I could hardly believe my ears. Somehow it was now all Jessie's fault. He was wangling his way out of it again, poor little innocent bystander Gary, just fell into another woman's bed and forgot he was about to pledge his life to someone else.

And then when he tried to dump her and go back to playing happy families it didn't work according to plan.

"After ten years that is the best you can do?" I asked incredulously.

Gary opened his mouth and closed it again.

He knew sweet lies weren't going to cut it this time, his legendary charm for once deserting him.

That must have been a nice bang on the head Dad gave him.

"You ruined our *wedding day*, Gary Warren! And you cheated on me with a woman that you met at our *marriage guidance* course! How low can one person get? All the years of preparation and the expense that my parents went to – do you not think you could have given me the courtesy of calling the whole thing off beforehand? The lack of respect you showed towards me and my family made the whole thing much worse!"

"That was why I couldn't call it off, Geri! Because of all the preparations and the whole huge affair it turned into. I tried so many times to tell you I didn't want to go through with it, but it was your big dream, *your* big day, it had very little to do with me!"

I sat back down, deflated at those words. I had suspected that Gary had got lost in all the wedding preparations and I had become immersed in my wedding fantasy but that was hardly an excuse, not one big enough to cover what he did.

"So now it's poor ignored Gary who had to find some attention – he couldn't be the centre of the universe for every living moment during the wedding preparations so he had to go elsewhere. Look, I don't need this shit right now – what did you really come here for?"

He looked at the floor forlornly. "I just needed to explain what happened. I feel terrible about it all and

I never intended to hurt you, Geri – you *must* believe that."

"So why propose, Gary, why ask me to marry you at all?"

"You won't be too happy with the answer," he announced shortly.

Suddenly my heart gave another lurch, this time one downwards towards my naff bunny slippers.

"OK, I kinda proposed because I knew you wanted it and expected it and because my father promised me the twenty-five grand but only if we bought the apartment together. And it seemed like a good idea at the time."

I couldn't believe what I was hearing.

My lovely romantic proposal was nothing more than a business deal – Gary knew that he couldn't afford the apartment alone and even with his father's offer of twenty-five thousand euros he still needed me financially. I knew Gary was reluctant to tie the knot, but I had never even guessed that his intentions had been so clinical and detached. If I had been shocked and hurt before, now I was furious and so ashamed. I had never been so enraged or felt so *used*.

If I had physically flinched I hoped it hadn't showed. The last thing I had to hold onto was my dignity and I wasn't going to go to pieces right now in front of Gary Warren. I could collapse later if necessary.

"Well, you didn't do me any favours, Gary. But as

you have moved on I have decided to do likewise. In fact I already have, so if you have quite finished I have a honeymoon to go on and Connor will be here soon to go to the airport."

"*Connor*? Connor who?" Gary exploded, enraged. "Not Connor Osborne, I hope!"

I gave an icy smile – he didn't like it when the shoe was on the other foot. "None of your business as it happens, not any more. Oh, and I think an annulment is in order, as the marriage wasn't consummated. Please leave now, Gary, you'll be hearing from my solicitor in the near future."

I walked to the door and opened it widely.

"Go on, Gary, get out, before I let my father loose on you again. I'm sure he'd enjoy finishing you off."

He rose slowly and walked out the door. I resisted the urge to push him down the steps.

"And don't come back!" I yelled before slamming the front door and collapsing into hot, furious tears.

"What happened, what did he say?" My mother was beside me, crouching down on the floor by my side.

I told her what Gary had said, that my proposal had simply been a financial deal between him and his father so he could get on the property ladder and get ahead.

"The rotten bastard!" my mother exclaimed. "And to think I pulled your father off of him! I should have bloody joined in. What a prize shit! Having the audacity to front up here and actually admit to that."

My tears suddenly dried up. My mum was so cross and annoyed for me it cheered me up. I smiled to think of her climbing onto Gary's back to give him a few pucks.

"Dad was great, wasn't he? I reckon he would have done some damage if we'd have let him."

Mum smiled too. "Wait till he hears this latest episode – I don't think I could hold him back, Geri. Maybe we'll wait until you get back from your holiday before we say anything about it – I don't think I can cope with any more Arnold Schwarzenegger moves for the moment. Now, come on, there's a love, dry your eyes and I'll make you another cup of tea. Then I'll get your father to run you and Amy to the airport – what time is she coming over?"

I thought briefly of Connor, and Gary's face when he thought that Connor was going to be coming on honeymoon with me. At least I had hurt him a bit back, but not nearly enough. Connor had been so good to me. I decided to text him before I left for the airport.

"She should be here any minute now, Mum. Come on, let's have the cup that cheers – but it would want to be good to work its magic on me after that shock."

And she led me back to the kitchen by the arm as if I was a fragile doll.

I had wanted so badly to see Gary, I realised that

now. Up to a few minutes ago I desperately hoped somewhere deep down in my subconscious mind that he would come and rescue me, he'd win me back and pledge undying love with some wild and wonderful tale about how it had all been an awful mistake – but now he had come and that hadn't happened. In fact he had rubbed salt in the wound and made my intolerable situation even more bleak. I thanked God above that in a few hours I would be out of there and on a plane to the other side of the world – even that wasn't far enough away from Gary bloody Warren.

Chapter 28

The plane banked to the left as it made its descent into Cairns International Airport. Amy squealed as she glimpsed the breathtaking sight of the Great Barrier Reef. It was a swirl of the bluest blue ocean and living coral with the golden ribbon of sand on the coastline. It was truly the most awesome sight we had both ever seen.

"Ohmigod! I can't believe we are actually here!" I exclaimed, excitement getting the better of my severe tiredness. The flight had been endless, and I was totally squashed since Kuala Lumpur on one side by a rather large gentleman that stank of garlic and Amy on the other, who was all elbows and angles and could sleep on broken bottles and snoozed away for eleven hours straight. Eleven hours that I had fretted alone over my insane situation. What else could I do but quaff free champagne and watch *Love Actually* sixteen times – I cried every time, especially the bit where Emma Thompson's shit of a husband buys some floozy a flash gold chain for Christmas and she finds out about it when she discovers it in his pocket and she thinks it's for her, but he gets her a lousy CD instead, and she is so heartbroken that she sobs in the bedroom. He has destroyed her belief in her marriage. Well that's what happened to me. Gary destroyed my belief in everything.

Anyway, we were here, the destination that I had always dreamt of, and from the air at least it was every bit as spectacular as it appeared to be in the brochures, so I was genuinely excited to be there, despite the circumstances.

"It's so sunny and bright," Amy said excitedly, looking out the window to a lushly green Cairns as we bumped onto the tarmac. "I can't wait to get out there onto the reef, can you?"

"No, but I have to admit I'm knackered and I could do with a few hours' sleep first."

I was developing a king-size hangover from all the champagne. And I was surely dehydrated from all the crying too.

We were amazed by the hot air that blasted our faces when we disembarked.

It wasn't just warm like Spain was in summer: this was like a hairdryer that you held too close to your cheek – it almost burned us to a cinder and we were perspiring heavily by the time we gratefully got into the Arrivals hall.

After we were given the once-over by a towering hunk at passport control and had been severely sniffed by the sniffer dog in rather an intimate fashion, we were through to collect our bags and embark on our adventure. We ventured out into the stifling heat and were there met by another tall handsome Aussie, this time in a khaki outfit and a pith helmet, who had arrived to take us to our hotel, the famous Cairns Colonial Club. I had chosen it with great care for Gary and me and it had looked fabulous on the Internet, so it gave me a momentary stab of pain thinking about it – before the glorious sight of Bruce's (no kidding) tanned and muscular thighs absorbed my attention.

"I think I'm in love!" muttered Amy as Bruce carried our heavy bags easily towards his large open-topped jeep. He was certainly easy on the eye, and we joined another three Japanese tourists who smiled at us widely and took endless photos as we sped towards the hotel. Cairns looked tropical and luscious as we glimpsed it go by and I couldn't wait to explore it. We got to the hotel in minutes and it definitely lived up to the promise.

The hotel was a long low-slung colonial-style complex with a myriad individual bungalows, some of which, like ours, were luxurious honeymoon suites. All the staff wore khakis and pith helmets and the overhead fans fluttered gently in the elegant reception area that was reminiscent of the Colonial Raj. We were taken by golf-cart to our bungalow and we gasped in wide-mouthed surprise as the suite was unveiled to us. It was very large and had dark wooden floors and a big floor-length window that overlooked the freestyle swimming pool, which had a softly cascading waterfall. There were voile floor-length curtains that gave the room a soft feel, and the bed was enormous and deep, with a large voile canopy. It was perfect for a honeymoon couple, complete with red rose petals scattered on the crisp bed-linen. Obviously the word hadn't completely got through to all the staff that the bridegroom was a no-show and this bride was a poor sad cow that had to take her best friend along instead.

Amy spotted me biting my bottom lip anxiously and tipped the bellboy and slammed the door shut in seconds.

"Sit down," she ordered as she swept the bed free of rose petals.

I did as she said.

"Now, we both know that what happened to you was a crock of shite and it's terrible that you're not on your honeymoon, but, Geri, we *are* here and we're not going to let that bollocks win by being miserable, are we?"

I stared blankly at her, close to tears.

She grabbed my arms and looked at me earnestly.

"*Are we?*"

"Er, no, we're not. Sorry, Amy, it didn't seem so *honeymoonish* until I got into this room. I mean an enormous double bed and fecking rose petals – there's probably champagne on ice in the bathroom, and the staff think we're a couple of lezzers who got married in Thailand or something! It just feels weird."

Amy was resolute. "If the room feels weird we can change it. Nothing about this situation is normal, you know, Geri – but I came here with you so you could put some distance between you and that creep and so we could have a few laughs and make you feel a little bit like yourself again. We are going to go out on the Barrier Reef, take a few tours, get golden tans and get drunk every night, and by the time you leave here you are going to feel a bit better, or maybe even a whole lot better, OK?"

I was afraid to tell her that it wouldn't work – nothing would apart from a frontal lobotomy – but as she was so fired up I demurred.

"OK," I lied. And smiled for effect too. It was exhausting trying to pretend that I was going to snap out of this but I had to at least humour her – the poor thing was trying so hard.

"Right!" she said, appeased. "Now, we're going to have a few hours' sleep and then we are going to have a huge meal and copious cocktails, and after that we're going to explore this town and see what it's got to offer. Are you with me, Geri?"

I stared at this new bossy Amy. I wasn't sure if I liked her or not but she seemed to be in charge and I was too exhausted to argue.

"I am," I replied, and I had to be. My own judgement wasn't up to much so I decided right then and there that I would listen to Amy and do what she said, because only one of us knew what the hell they were doing and it certainly wasn't me.

So we both crawled into bed right then and there and went to sleep. I did so in silent stifled tears and with the smell of rose petals in my nostrils. Amy couldn't know how destroyed I felt to be here on what was supposed to be the most romantic time of my life without Gary, who despite every rotten thing he had done to me was still lingering malevolently in my heart.

When we awoke disoriented some hours later, it was nightfall. I looked out of our huge patio window to see the waterfall all lit up with a myriad lights in the big swimming pool. It looked so inviting I felt like just running from the room and leaping into it, so I woke Amy and that's exactly what we did, giggling like a couple of schoolgirls. After that we had blistering hot showers and got all glammed up for our big night out in Cairns.

There was an enormous seafood buffet in the fine dining room at the hotel so we feasted on lobster, crab and the biggest prawns I had ever laid eyes on. There also happened to be a cricket team staying there and they were in the dining room having dinner too and looking rather dashing in their official uniforms. There was little doubt that Australian guys were truly gorgeous, with their even white teeth and long bronzed limbs. Even though I was seriously off men, I wasn't dead yet, and there was still red blood coursing through my veins. I cheered up markedly as Amy and I scored them all out of ten.

After we had stuffed ourselves silly and smiled flirtatiously at the cricket team, we headed off in a cab downtown into Cairns to sample the nightlife. After the air-conditioning of the Cairns Colonial Club, the heat, even at night, was incredible. Our make-up began to melt from our faces almost immediately and our carefully straightened locks began to dampen and curl into wispy tendrils. Within minutes we had abandoned all attempts at glamour and piled our hair up high and began to resent our hot clothes.

"Quick, find somewhere that's air-conditioned, pronto!" urged Amy as we struggled along in the deep humidity.

We fell into the nearest bar, which had a dress code that specified "*no thongs, no stubbies, no vests.*"

"Fancy barring thongs!" laughed an incredulous Amy, "It's lucky we're big-knicker girls!"

"Speak for yourself," I replied archly. "I've got a collection of those cheese-cutters in my drawer, and that's where they're likely to stay – anyway 'thongs' over here means flip-flops, but I don't know what the hell 'stubbies' are – maybe it means the men have to be closely shaven or something. Anyway, the men in here look like the cast from the Village People. I've never seen so many check shirts and huge biceps in all my life. And that's just the women!"

Amy guffawed as we sidled up to the bar, somewhat overdressed compared to the locals in our John Rocha linens. It seemed that the skimpiest clothes (or check shirts) were the order of the day. Cairns was casual.

"I feel like a right eejit in this get-up!" I moaned to Amy as we got another startled glance from a bunch of girls looking tanned and toned in flimsy sarong skirts and bikini tops.

"Spot the Europeans!" Amy replied as our schooners of beer arrived.

"I'm sweatin' too." I tried to fan myself with a beer mat as trays of free cocktail sausages were passed around. "What are we like? A pair of whinging Paddies!"

"Tell you what," Amy whispered. "After these, how about you and me ditching this idea for the night and we catch a cab to our cool air-conditioned room and watch some Aussie TV in our underwear and empty the contents of the mini-bar instead?"

"That's the best idea I've heard all day," I said gratefully. "These clothes are sticking to me and I'm not sure I'm up to a big night right now. Do you mind, Amy? I feel like I'm cramping your style a bit."

Amy gave me a hug. "Hey, it's my idea! It'll give us a chance to catch up. I haven't told you the latest about Stuart or found out what Gary said before he went three rounds with your father. So come on, drink up and let's get out of here."

An hour later we were sipping champagne in our underwear watching *Burke's Backyard* and eating chocolate in the blissful coolness of our palatial bedroom.

"Well, aren't you going to tell me what Gary called over to say to you?" Amy ventured after what seemed a decent interval.

"I haven't quite figured it out myself, though I've thought of little else all the way over on the plane. It's made me look at myself a bit closer – and my own motives. I hate to admit it but it mightn't be all Gary's fault, after all. I mean, he's still a total shit for the way he did it, but I pushed the whole thing."

"So what did he say?"

I looked at her. Amy seemed confused, amazed even, that I should find any pity for Gary. "Well, he more or less said that he'd tried many times to tell me he didn't want to get married, but I was so caught up in the whole wedding thing that I wouldn't listen. He only proposed because I had practically forced him into it with all my ultimatums. He never wanted to marry me, Amy – it was a business move."

"*What?*" Amy was incredulous.

"His father promised him the twenty-five grand for the apartment if he proposed, so Gary figured he'd never get onto the property ladder unless he had me along. I doubt if he thought the whole thing coldheartedly through, though – as he said himself, it just seemed like a good idea at the time."

"The bastard!" Amy was furious. "I can't believe that you are defending him, Geri! This makes him even more of a prize shit than before, not less. What a cold, heartless thing to do!"

I shook my head. "Yes, but that's not the whole story. I didn't think of anything else but that wedding for almost a year. I never gave *being* married any thought. I knew Gary didn't want kids and he was a selfish sod, but I overlooked all of that because I needed to be Mrs Gary Warren more than anything. So what was so wrong with being single Geri Murphy? I have wasted my entire twenties on that man and I am only beginning to learn why. I don't even know who I am, Amy – because I defined myself by being Gary's girlfriend, then Gary's fiancée and finally his wife. I've got a lot of thinking to do, but this I am sure of: I was part of it, I colluded in the deception, so I bear at least some of the responsibility."

Amy poured us another glass of champagne. "I think you are being way too hard on yourself, Geri. You loved the guy. You gave him ten years of your life. Of course you wanted to marry him and have kids –

that's what most people want. If he didn't want to marry you he should have said it at any point up to the wedding, not steal off and cheat on you. He was a coward, and as for using you to get the apartment – what a total bollocks! You should sue the arse off of him, get your half."

I smiled slowly. "I'm not a total idiot – I might still do that. In fact, revenge is very much on my mind, but I have to examine what kind of a dream world I was existing in that I wasn't even aware of my future husband's feelings or attitudes."

Amy was still in shock. "I don't get it, Geri. You're not yourself."

"No," I allowed, "I am not myself, Amy, and I'm not likely to be that girl ever again. But I'll be taking no prisoners – that's for sure! And remember, by the way, I did sleep with Connor. That's not something the old Geri would do, is it?"

"No," replied Amy, eyeing me darkly. "And I'm not sure this Geri has all her marbles yet. You'd better be careful, you know, because this could all come down like a pack of cards."

I stared right back with a venomous look of my own. "It couldn't be much worse than the pack of cards I built myself over the past ten years."

Little did I know how wrong I could be . . .

Chapter 29

The following day we arose early and had a long buffet breakfast before we set off for our day-long adventure on the Great Barrier Reef. This time we dressed more appropriately for the weather, in shorts, bikini tops and wide-brimmed hats, and brought gallons of sun cream for the hot Aussie sunshine.

A coach took us to Port Douglas, which was a stunningly pretty port that looked like the Australian version of Marbella with its large swathe of big yachts and impressive speed-boats.

Ours was a huge catamaran with an enormous deck area and we scurried aboard to get coveted spots on it, so we could have sea views. It was a perfectly calm and sunny day, much to my relief, as I wasn't the best of seafarers. We soon set off for the reef and enjoyed the cool breezes and sea spray, which cooled us down in the relentless sun. The boat was pretty full and I couldn't help noticing how many beautiful people there were – both men and woman, all with perfectly tanned and lean limbs, hair under control. Amy and I were pasty by comparison and my hair looked like rats' tails. I marvelled at these specimens of human perfection and wished I could be more like them. But by the time we reached the reef, the beauty of the natural wonder had overtaken them in my interest and both Amy and I were enthralled at what we could see. The boat docked at a huge steel structure, which seemed to be anchored onto the sea-bed. There were several ladders and dive-off points. We were given a pep talk about safety and then issued with lifebelts and snorkels so we could see the reef from the water. Amy and I leapt into the water gratefully and were stunned by the colourful array of coral and amazing fish. It was a riot of colour and quite overwhelming. I had never seen anything so beautiful and I actually felt my heart lift. I was very glad to be alive and it made all my problems seem very small and insignificant.

After we spent an hour diving and watching the sea life, we had to get back on the catamaran for a buffet lunch. We then got into a mini-submarine, which took us further down underwater to see more unusual coral and fish. It was like the brightest most colourful movie you could ever see, and I didn't want it to end. But eventually it had to and we sped back to port, all of us exhausted and happy, sunburnt and suitably amazed by what we had witnessed. It was simply the best day of my life. I had always thought my wedding day would be and I was cheered up by the fact that today had been instead. That meant that my life wasn't over – I would have happy days again and I would survive and get over what had happened to me, eventually. My heart felt lighter as we tiredly clambered onto the coach that took us back to our hotel. I didn't tell Amy anything of what I felt. I had to digest it myself first. I would tell her later, but for the first time since my wedding day I had a glimpse of hope, and for the moment that would have to do.

After our day on the reef, I began to relax a little bit more and enjoy myself. We spent our days sunbathing or taking off to explore North Queensland. Amy and I turned a lovely golden brown and we became indolent and chilled out. The idea of putting some distance between Gary and myself had been an inspired one and I owed Connor thanks for that. I had been thinking about Connor a fair bit since I had arrived in Australia. I hadn't dared to even think of our night of passion since it had occurred, mainly due to extreme embarrassment. I tried to put it out of my mind completely – it had been just an aberration. But now, looking back, it had been a tender, wonderful moment. I didn't trust myself to feel anything for him, I was far too numb of emotion for that, but I did look upon him with fondness, insofar as I could feel anything for any male, apart from my dad. I did worry, though, about how Connor would be when we were both working together in close proximity again.

As for Gary, well, boiling in oil was too good for him, but I decided I was going to extract my revenge from him financially. If I couldn't hurt him emotionally, well, then I sure as hell could hurt him in the pocket. I was going to see a solicitor as soon as I got back to Ireland.

Australia was a revelation to me. It was so laid-back, sunny and beautiful. I could have stayed forever. Everything seemed so far away and you could forget yourself completely for a while as you strolled on the white sandy beaches or dozed in the sun.

Amy too felt completely relaxed and came to a decision about Stuart.

She had confided in me that Stuart had told her that he loved her and he'd asked her to move to Glasgow to be with him.

I tried my best to be encouraging. "Erm, so how do you feel about that? It's a big move, Amy."

She smiled beatifically. "Yes, but, Geri, I love him, I love being with him and one of us has to move. It just so happens that he has the better job and I would love to get out of Dublin. I decided this while you were getting married and Clodagh was happy with Karl. I felt I could move on. But now I feel horrible and guilty. I feel like I'm leaving you in the lurch."

I frowned. Partly due to that loved-up tone Amy used. I had an allergy to anything lovey-dovey at the minute and I couldn't abide people being deluded by the early flush of ardour in a relationship. But who was I to talk? I had been deluded for almost a decade. So I faked it.

"Don't be silly, sure what is Ryanair for? I'll be up to Glasgow every few weeks. I just worry that you're making the right decision. It's a big wrench for you, yet Stuart isn't making many changes. Just be absolutely sure it's what you want. Don't be an idiot like I was, putting Gary before everything else – including myself – and look where that got me. You have got to do what is best for Amy."

Amy beamed back at me. "Exactly, and I am, believe me. I know I was an idiot with George and Trevor and Gerard – God, there's been a lot of them, hasn't there? But I have learnt from that and I know enough to know that Stuart is different."

I hoped she was right, but I didn't believe it for a moment. All I knew was that not only was my only sister going away but also my best friend was leaving me and my partner of ten years had already gone and right now I was feeling more alone than ever. But it was time that I stood on my own two feet and sorted out a new life just for myself. I could only depend on one person and that was me and I was about to find out for the first time in my life what that was really like.

♥ ♥ ♥

The following week sped by in a series of daytime tours and long boozy nights by the pool with the cricket team, who were visiting from Western Australia on tour and happened to be the nicest bunch of blokes that we ever encountered. Amy had a few snogs with one of them called Barry and I got friendly with another called Owen but only on a strictly platonic basis. He made me laugh and entertained me with tales of his own sad love life. It made our holiday a lot more fun to spend time with them and we couldn't believe it when the fortnight was almost over and we were due to fly back to Ireland.

I dreaded my return. Over in Australia I could suspend reality because I was away from all the normal day-to-day little things that would remind me of what I had been through and had yet to endure. My dad had phoned to say he had collected my little sports car from the hotel in Cavan and it was now languishing outside the front door, like a permanent little reminder of what a sick joke had been played on me. I had yet to face all of my neighbours and friends and colleagues from work. And Connor. How was I going to be normal with Connor after what had happened between us? Even my job was going to be awkward. I decided I couldn't even contemplate that yet. I had to get home and just take things one day at a time. My life was going to have to change dramatically. And in some ways it had altered already – in more ways than I had yet discovered.

♥ ♥ ♥

We were six hours out of Dublin, over southern Turkey, when Amy woke me up.

"Sorry, Geri, you looked so peaceful there I hated to wake you – but I need some Tampax, my period has come on. Do you have any?"

I looked at her blearily, trying to focus on what she had said. I had just managed to get to sleep after more than fourteen hours of desperately tossing and turning. I just couldn't sleep on planes no matter how exhausted I became, but sheer tiredness had finally overcome me – and now bloody Amy was waking me up and asking for tampons.

"Yes, I have some in my backpack in the overhead locker. Just get them yourself, will you? It's a new packet." I heard myself say the words and something in my foggy brain clicked and suddenly I was wide awake.

I had bought that packet of Tampax before we left for Cairns. *Way before*. And I hadn't had a period in several weeks. But how many? I searched my addled mind for the information.

Then in slow motion I saw in my mind's eye a vision of me angrily flushing my pills down the loo that night I had discovered Gary's gym room.

That night, weeks and weeks ago …

Oh no! I couldn't be, could I? I couldn't actually be pregnant. Life just couldn't be that cruel? *Oh my God,* what was I going to do if that was true?

"Are you alright, Geri? You look awfully pale."

I tried to recover my equilibrium. "Emm, yeah, I just can't remember when I last had a period myself, Amy. I bought that packet weeks ago."

Amy looked unconcerned. "Don't worry, Geri. First of all long-haul travel can interfere with your cycle – I'm actually a few days early. And not only that, you've been through a major trauma – that can stop them too. So don't worry – when you get home you'll get back to normal and it'll come along, probably on your first day back at work when you won't want it."

I smiled with faint relief. Amy was probably right. I had been through a lot, and it could be the reason why I was late. I certainly hoped so. But a niggling thought deep down told me that I had more to worry about.

A cold, icy knot began to form in the pit of my stomach.

Married, jilted and pregnant wasn't anything I had ever aspired to and it just didn't bear even thinking about, so I put the fear to the back of my mind and willed the jet ever forward back home, where I could weep in my room and pull the blankets over my head and wish it all away. And after that I'd go and get the pregnancy kit while Mum called Jerry Springer.

The nightmare had just got bigger.

Chapter 30

Two days later I steeled myself to buy a pregnancy kit.

In between staring out the window at my sad-looking little sports car, my shiny, but now defunct, wedding ring and my fading Australian tan, that was. Every time I looked at my poor hopeful mother who had hugged me so fiercely at the airport and had said she couldn't believe how healthy and happy I looked, I felt a complete fraud. Yet I had to find out one way or another. It was just that I couldn't contemplate the future with me being a single mother, tethered emotionally to Gary for the next twenty years – knowing full well that I was raising a child he never wanted and, worst of all, it was entirely my fault. Then there was the second, even scarier option. The indisputable fact that *Connor* could be the baby's father – try to picture me explaining that to the relatives! I was so terrified I could not face the trip to the chemist alone, so I roped in my poor sister Sandy to come with me.

"I don't think I can do it!" I whined as we stomped off to the chemist in buckets of torrential rain and covered in SAS-style rain clothes so no one would recognise us or spot our dead giveaway purchase.

"Yes, you can," Sandy insisted. "You're driving me nuts with your wailing and worrying. Besides, you need to know. Mum is already becoming suspicious. And if you *are* pregnant, would it really be the end of the world? By the time the baby arrives you'll be almost thirty, hardly a spring chicken – time you got to reproducing if you ask me, and lots of girls go it alone these days. Anyway, it might be Connor's, and he's loaded so you'll be OK financially and the baby will be so cute if it gets his looks!" Sandy always looked on the bright side.

I managed a weak laugh. "OK, I'll get the damn thing – anything to shut you up. You already have me turned into an over-the-hill lone parent who sucks men dry financially for me and my brat. You're scaring me, Sandy – anyway, why do you think mum is getting suspicious?"

"Could be the twelve pounds you put on over in Oz? But you're looking a bit, well, *large* in the tummy area, Geri. And your boobs have got even bigger. Mum hasn't actually said anything as such but she keeps watching you."

"Great, thanks, Sandy, I'm a fat sad lump after two weeks down under – you're doing my confidence the world of good. I'm half wishing I am pregnant now just to give me an excuse for my huge stomach!"

I bought three pregnancy kits just to make sure and vowed on the way home to go on a strict diet the next day if I wasn't pregnant – I couldn't promise *what* I would do if I was!

So we slunk home and fled to our rooms to avoid detection. Dad had gone to the pub with Ned, his buddy of twenty years, and Mum was cleaning something or other that didn't need it.

"Are you going to do it now?" Sandy whispered on the landing.

"Maybe ..." I wavered. "I need some time. It's not easy, you know."

"If you want I'll help you." She touched my shoulder. My kid sister who a few weeks earlier I had considered a total idiot was now being more of a grown-up than I was.

"Thanks, Sandy, but I think I need to do this alone."

Just then the phone rang downstairs.

Sandy's face lit up. "It's probably Chris. He should be in Donegal today."

Chris had taken off to the wilds for a week alone because Sandy couldn't take any more time off work without getting the sack.

She took the stairs in threes.

"It's Connor!" she yelled up, looking a bit disappointed.

My stomach churned, did several back-flips and then sank.

Calm down, I told myself – he's probably checking about work. I was due back the following day and I wasn't looking forward to it.

It was just the thought of having to go back to my normal life when it was anything but normal.

"Geri! How are you?" His voice sounded velvety and a little shy. "Was it as great as you hoped down under?"

"Yes," I said, warmed by the sound of his voice. "Connor, it was fantastic, just what I needed – I feel quite a bit better actually."

"Well enough to come back to work?" he ventured.

"Yes, I'll be back tomorrow." Suddenly, for some reason I felt a little deflated.

It must have been something in the tone of my voice that made him say, "Eh, Geri, that wasn't why I called actually – or not *just* why, anyway. I wanted to see how you were. I thought about you a lot while you were away. I could have texted you, but I didn't want to hound you. So you've been feeling OK since you got back?"

I forgot he knew all about the pain I was suffering. "Well, it's been a bit difficult – the sports car is smirking at me outside the door for starters."

Connor laughed, that warm infectious laugh that

was so catching. "Sell it! Or else call Gary Warren Senior and tell him you want it replaced with something entirely different at no extra cost – it's the least he should do."

I brightened up considerably. "You know, that's not a bad idea. I think I might do that. So, how are you? And how are things at the office?"

A heavy exaggerated sigh followed. "Well, you were right about the temp. She's stuffed up all the filing and spends most of the day on the phone to her mates – and, dare you even *look* like you might be considering asking for a coffee, she gives you this evil glare that would kill a horse. Dave is terrified of her. We can't wait to give her the marching orders. Otherwise situation normal – EFU!"

I laughed – that was our office code for "Everything Fucked Up". "OK, you've convinced me, I'll be in tomorrow! But try to keep your hands off my super-tanned body, though I know that'll be difficult." I had said it as a joke without thinking.

A slightly embarrassed laugh followed. "I'll look forward to seeing you," he replied, and we said goodbye.

I wasn't sure if that was a nice and polite boss saying that or an interested man whom I had been intimate with saying it – and furthermore I wasn't sure how I wanted it to be either. This was all getting too complicated.

Jaysus! Maybe my hormones were playing up,

making me fancy the father of my hypothetical child more. This was getting *way* too weird. I had to "take the test" as they say on Ricki and find out for sure if I was pregnant at all – and then I could get to the complicated bit of who the father was.

I had no sooner put the phone down when my mobile rang.

"Hi, it's me, Clodagh. How are you, Geri?"

I bit my lip. "Clodagh! I'm fine, still a bit jetlagged but other than that I'm OK. Had a great time down under – I'd thoroughly recommend taking a honeymoon alone. And yourself?"

"I'm not bad," she replied a bit quietly. "I've broken up with Karl, you'll be happy to know. I just thought I'd tell you that – it might make things right between us again."

I felt contrite. "Clodagh, I'd hope a man would never come between us, but I have been through such a lot. And I'm sorry, I just couldn't stand by and see you become unhappy and settle for a married man without saying something. But I am sorry if I was too hard on you."

There was a small silence.

"Well, my reason for dumping him wasn't so noble. His wife got pregnant again and I realised I was just his bit on the side ..." Her voice trailed away. "Listen, Geri, I'd love to come over. I need to see you about the Spanish order as well – can I come over for a while? I need to talk."

I hadn't the heart to say no. I had been hard on Clodagh and now that she needed me I couldn't just tell her I wasn't up to company. The pregnancy test would have to wait.

"Sure, Clodagh, come right over. I'll get the coffee on."

♥ ♥ ♥

Half an hour later Clodagh was sitting in my kitchen looking red-eyed and miserable and suspiciously like she'd been hitting the Jack Daniels since I had left.

"Right, sit down there and spare me no details," I said as I placed a coffee and a large plate of fattening biscuits in front of her.

"Have you nothing stronger, a glass of wine even?" Clodagh asked.

"You look like you've had a few last night. Let's start with coffee and see how we go, OK?"

She nodded. God, she really looked miserable! I didn't think that the weedy Karl would have this much effect, but the heart was a curious thing. I felt bad for being so cruel to her.

"So tell me, when did it all kick off?"

She sipped her coffee thoughtfully. "Well, I knew Karl would never leave her – he told me as much and I never expected him to – but he did say that the sparkle had gone out of the marriage and they were great friends and good parents, but they were more like –"

"Brother and sister!" I interrupted triumphantly but seeing her dark look of disgust I shut up immediately. She didn't need me to tell her the whole affair had been one big cliché.

"*Anyway,*" she continued pointedly. "Then, just after you and Amy went off to Australia, he started to act funny, kind of cold and withdrawn, kept making excuses not to see me. It was only when I pressed him that he admitted that his wife was pregnant and that they were over the moon and were trying again as a couple. Of course I knew it was all bullshit – I could see it written all over his face. There had never been any problems in the marriage at all and I was just a gullible idiot who wanted to believe all his crap – so I ended it, then and there. But I have been gutted by it all, Geri, and what made it all worse was you tried to warn me and I wouldn't listen – and I also wasn't really there for you when you were going through your trouble. I was a selfish cow and I'm sorry about that, Geri."

I looked at her, pale and red-eyed, shoulders hunched, all the fight gone out of her, and I felt angry that we did this to ourselves – we women who put too much into our relationships with men and precious little into developing and loving ourselves. We expected and *got* so little.

"Don't be sorry, Clodagh, just do me a huge favour. Don't waste one more minute fretting over that idiot Karl or anything that has happened. It's all in the past. Let nothing come between us again and, while I'm being honest, I wasn't as clued up when it came to my own relationship with Gary, was I? Ten whole years of deluding myself has got to be some sort of record, but I'm trying real hard not to delude myself any more. Now . . ."

I almost said, *I have a pregnancy kit here and are you going to help me find out if I'm up the duff?* But somehow I didn't. I wasn't ready. So I said instead, "Is there any good news among all this bad?"

She blinked rapidly as if to rouse some sort of enthusiasm she didn't feel. "Yes, actually, we had great reports from your sample shipment of clothes to Spain. They sold out and we have a further, more substantial order. This could really take off, Geri, if you decide to go for it in a bigger way. There's a real demand for your stuff. Those labels I had printed for the shorts and tops last time – remember, you weren't in the mood to think up a name so I just got ones printed up with *Designs by Geri* on them? I think you should get a better name, something cooler, more fashionable."

A chink of faint, bright hope began to light up in my mind. "Do you think I'd really have a chance of making a go of it like you did with Celt?"

Clodagh looked pensive. "Maybe. But you'd have to give it a lot more thought and attention – you leave a lot to be desired in the ambition stakes, Geri."

I shot her a dark look. "I *did* leave a lot to be desired in the ambition stakes, Clodagh. That's because my only bloody ambition was to be Mrs bleeding Gary Warren. Things have changed a great deal since then. I need something to focus on, something to get my teeth into, something to forget myself with, and this could be just the thing. Yeah, this could be just what I need."

Clodagh eyed me dubiously. I knew she thought this was only a nine-day wonder until I drifted on to something else.

"And," I continued, "I have just the name too."

"Oh yeah?" asked Clodagh, all ears. "So what's it to be?"

A slow smile crept across my face. I could see the funny side of the whole sorry tale for once. "Ditzy," I replied. "The name of the Geri Murphy fashion label will be Ditzy. That was what Gary called me. I want it to remind me on a daily basis of everything I am not going to be: dependent, clinging, ditzy. I have something to prove and with your help and expertise, Clodagh, I intend to do it."

Clodagh smiled for the first time since she had arrived. "I do love a challenge, and it's not like I have anyone bashing down the door for my illuminating company at the moment. Of course I'd love to help you, and of course I'd expect to get first dibs on showcasing Ditzy in my Celt stores. Yes, I'd love to help you. Ditzy … it kind of grows on you – it's a cute name."

And so, unceremoniously in my kitchen, between two women with not much else to do, Ditzy was born.

There was still the small matter of a pregnancy test to do, but I had enough excitement for one day. First thing in the morning I would find out if I was with child or not, before I went to work and saw Connor. Yes, first thing in the morning I was about to discover if my world was about to get turned upside down again.

♥ ♥ ♥

There was a faint blue line in the second window if you held it up to the light, which indicated I was a little bit pregnant. I burst into shocked tears at first – I just never believed I could be pregnant, not *really*. But it seemed I was. Test One had been inconclusive but Test Two had this palest of blue lines and Test Three was a little more definite, so I pretty much realised that it was really true. I had just complicated my life by another one thousand per cent. I ran and aroused Sandy, who wasn't too impressed at being poked from her slumber at six a.m.

"Sandy, look at this!" I thrust the applicator under her nose.

"Wha'? Does that mean it's positive? It's not very definite."

I showed her the other two. "Oh God, Geri, number three looks pretty conclusive – what are you going to do?"

I sat down glumly. "You don't know the half of it, Sandy. There's a bit of a complication …"

Sandy sat bolt upright. "What, Geri, could be more complicated than being pregnant by your new husband when he has run off with a sleazy tart?"

"The fact that he may not be the actual father?"

I glanced at her sidewards. Her look of total shock was exactly what I feared, because Sandy was usually unshockable – she was the most laid back of all my family and my friends so I guessed that the reactions from the rest of them would be far, far worse.

Sandy opened her mouth but nothing came out.

"I slept with Connor, *once*. It was after the wedding and I was so low and feeling so bereft and Connor and I got drunk and one thing led to –"

"The absolute shit!" Sandy raged, now indignant. "He took advantage of you, Geri! You were in no fit state to make a judgement call on anything after what happened to you! Connor should have known better. Even if you threw yourself at him he should have put you off. And Jesus, Geri – when the hell did you come off the pill? I thought you and Gary were going to wait for a few years?"

"It's all my fault!" I wailed. "I threw my contraceptive pills down the toilet to get back at Gary before the wedding because he built that stupid gym in the baby room and I thought I'd take matters into my own hands."

"Well, you've certainly done that," Sandy replied archly. "So what are you going to do now?"

"I'm going to go to work. I can't even think about it at the moment or I'll go nuts – please promise me you won't tell anyone about this until I get my head together, OK? No one must know. Not even Chris." I looked at her pleadingly.

"OK," she replied reluctantly – secrets were never her forte. "But you'll have to sort it out sooner rather than later, Geri. It's not going to go away."

As I hopped into the shower for work I pondered over my sister's words.

She was right: this wasn't going to go away and it was a stuff-up I had brought upon myself and it was going to have to be dealt with by myself soon.

Just when I thought things were so complicated it couldn't get any worse, they just had.

Chapter 31

My heart leapt when I saw Connor – a real sparky jumpstart. I just felt my knees go weak and I became suddenly tongue-tied and I instantly felt that he suspected my new dark secret.

But how could he? He just gave me a brotherly hug and made me my usual coffee and then quickly retreated into his office. Dave wasn't even there and my desk literally groaned with weeks of unfinished work, so by ten my mood had darkened and my earlier girlish skittishness had evaporated.

I called Amy. I needed reinforcements.

"Amy, meet me for lunch," I half growled. "I have something to tell you."

"Are you alright?" Amy whispered in her breathless way.

"No, I'm not and being treated like a total skivvy

minutes after I've got back from my holiday hasn't helped either," I moaned loudly, hoping that Connor would overhear from his office, where he seemed to be hiding.

Hadn't he noticed my rosy glow of expectant motherhood? OK, so it had been only ten minutes since I'd found out I was with child, but I hadn't too much patience where men were concerned at the moment.

"I'll see you in Milano's on Dawson at one fifteen, then," Amy replied quietly and hung up.

Connor slunk out of his office sometime after eleven. "Em, Geri, we need to talk."

About bloody time, I thought. He has realised what a cold bloody fish he has been all morning and is about to say how glowing I look.

"Yes, Connor." I smiled my best Julia Roberts megawatt grin.

"It's a bit embarrassing, actually," he said. "I know we had just the one brilliant night together and you are so far from being ready to see anyone else so soon after Gary, but I still feel I need to tell you that … well … April was over while you were away and we were sorting out her visitation with Sarge and we had a long conversation and the upshot of it all was that she's decided that she'd like to make another go of it and … well, I have agreed to take her back and give it another try."

The room seemed to be whirling.

Had he just said "April" and "back" and "another try" all in the one sentence? April, the woman he wept buckets over, detested with a passion so much that he couldn't bear to even be in the same room as anyone who wore her perfume without feeling ill, the woman he had wished eternal fungal infections on – *he was taking her back*?

I tried to breathe deep and evenly. I could not, would not, let Connor see this announcement had affected me in any way. "That's very nice, Connor. If you are sure then I'm very happy for you both – it sure beats sawing poor old Sarge in half anyway."

Connor laughed, showing those white even teeth, his amber eyes crinkling up at the corners. I felt like leaping onto his hairy chest and begging him not to go back with her.

"So you're OK with it? I'm so stupid, but, Geri, I was really worried about telling you – that's why I was avoiding you all morning. After all the things I said about her and everything that's gone on with you and me and everything ..."

"Don't stress it, Connor," I interrupted him. "It's fine. Your private life is your own affair, and you don't need to explain it to me." I smiled but my voice sounded a little bit histrionic. I hoped he wouldn't notice – I would die if Connor suspected how shattered I felt. But no one would ever again get to me as much as Gary had. Even though I was reeling, I wouldn't show any weakness in front of any man.

Not ever.

He gave me a chaste kiss on the cheek, his subtle aftershave stirring my nostrils and his rough stubble brushing my chin. My heart lurched and plummeted. It looked like me and my new passenger were a solo project. I was never going to tell him now and make him choose me by default and I was never going to tell Gary Warren either, so that left me up one shit creek without any kind of paddling device.

♥ ♥ ♥

Amy looked positively green over her pepperoni pizza. I had just landed her with all my news and she was in shock – *hell,* I hadn't even got used to the idea of me having a baby yet, never mind all the complications that were getting more tricky and convoluted by the minute.

"What are you going to do, Geri? You have to tell them, both of them. Otherwise things will get really a lot worse down the line. It seems terrible now but what happens years down the track when the child asks who its father is?"

That was some recovery from her shocked silence. I didn't need a conscience right now – I needed someone in my corner who wouldn't offer advice that I wasn't ready to hear, not yet anyhow.

"Amy, please don't lecture me. At the moment I am just trying to deal with the fact I am pregnant. All the other stuff will have to wait. I need you to just listen to me and be there."

Amy's face darkened and she lowered her eyes. "That's going to be a bit of a problem a little bit sooner than we think," she said half jokingly but the smile didn't reach her eyes; she just seemed sad.

"Why?" I asked, afraid of what other shocks were to come. It had been that kind of day.

"Well, today I handed in my notice at Pender PR. Stuart has found us a place in Glasgow and I'm moving up there in four weeks to live with him."

I knew that this was coming and it was going to be happening sooner or later. I was going to lose Amy to the gorgeous tartan-wearer, but not now, not this soon – I was really going to need her. It also felt odd that Amy had been there for me through all my traumas and she had suppressed her great happiness about falling in love with Stuart. I felt like a really selfish bitch. It had been all about me lately, but Amy needed me to be her friend also. It couldn't be a one-way street. So I gritted my teeth and acted all happy.

"Amy, that's really great news. I am sorry I've been so self-obsessed. What's the story? Is it an apartment or a flat?"

"It's an apartment in the city. And Stuart has lined up some agencies for me to see for temp work. I'm really looking forward to going, but now I feel awful leaving you in the lurch – but when Stuart and I were planning all this you were going to be happily married to Gary. I never would have done this otherwise."

I touched her hand, my dearest friend whose kind heart and pure nature I would truly miss.

"It's OK. I'll have a load of dirty nappies and a new business to keep me busy. And as I said before, Ryanair will keep us together. By the way, Clodagh and myself have patched things up – she dumped that cretin Karl and is dead off men so we can be two poisonous spinsters together. We'll take up knitting and grow our leg-hair long – it'll be a blast!"

Amy laughed and seemed relieved, but inside I was almost crying out: Don't leave me – everyone I love or care about is moving away from me! First Gary, then Sandy, now Connor and Amy. I wouldn't be able to take much more.

I subconsciously rubbed my stomach and the new inhabitant that lay within. Somehow I felt comforted, as I knew deep down that my child would be someone who would love me and need me and wouldn't be leaving anytime soon.

After lunch, where I could barely get any food down, I slowly walked back to work with a heavy heart. I had made one serious decision en route: that I was going to give up my beloved job at Osborne & Oswald. I couldn't work with Connor any more – not now, not with him back with April, her parading into the office with her simpering superiority, looking down her pert little condescending nose at me, blowsily pregnant and deserted. She had never liked me and I just couldn't watch him make a huge fool of himself again. I just couldn't do that, not now after everything – especially if he was the father of our child.

I needed change and it meant radical decisions. I would throw myself into my new venture. Clodagh said she would help me and I was sure that there was some kind of grant that I would get for starting a new business or something. It didn't matter – I would survive and succeed and I would do it alone for me and my baby and I didn't need anyone else to be my partner. No one else would get the opportunity to hurt me like that again. I was going to go it alone – just me and my little baby.

And no one else.

Chapter 32

I knew telling my parents I was pregnant was going to be traumatic. Dad would typically want to run off and find Gary to physically remove his head, while Mum would instantly begin knitting booties and redecorate my bedroom into a nursery and plan the next thirty years of me and grandchild ensconced within, without any remote chance of freedom – she'd be in her element – and I wasn't sure which scared me more.

So I took them out to neutral ground to The Yacht for Sunday lunch to break the news.

"Mum and Dad, there is something I need to tell you. Now I want you to remain calm and listen until I have finished talking. It's something that you won't be overjoyed with, Dad, but nonetheless ..."

Dad glanced up from his seafood chowder. "Geri, you are prattling on – now what could be so terrible?

You're not getting back with that bowsie Gary Warren, are you?" He instantly turned a funny purple colour at the mere mention of my husband.

"No," I replied slowly, fearing the worst, "but it's like a little bit of that, kinda sorta."

"You are scaring me, Geraldine, what the hell are you trying to say?" my mother exclaimed.

"I'm pregnant!" I blurted out. "I am pregnant and it might be Gary's."

"Jesus, Mary and Joseph!" My mother swore and crossed herself.

My father just held his spoon aloft, soup spilling over it, like he was in some sort of weird trance.

They were taking it well.

"What do you mean, it *might* be Gary's? Who the hell else's could it be?"

I felt so ashamed, even after all I had been through, and I didn't want my parents to think of me as a slapper.

"Mum, remember the night we got back to Dublin after the wedding when I was so upset and I went over to Connor's for the night? Well, we both got very drunk and he began comforting me …"

"Some comforting!" my father spluttered.

"Leave her alone, Eddie, she's been through enough! Though really, Geri, this is hardly the best situation to be in."

I put my head in my hands. "Don't you think I know that? But I am doing my best to deal with it all and I would appreciate if you guys would give me your support. I am going to keep this baby and make the best life I can. "

"And what about the fathers?" my father said. "Jesus, I can't believe I'm saying that. *Fathers.* I might have expected this of Sandy –"

"That's not fair!" I exploded. "Leave Sandy out of this. It's something that just happened! If Gary hadn't left me half insane with grief it never would have! I mean, the business of two fathers. Now can we please all calm down?"

My mother touched my father's arm like you would a toddler and he seemed to sink back into his chair, defeated.

I took a deep breath and then went on. "I haven't told either person of the possibility of their fatherhood for personal reasons. I will, in time, but for one reason or another neither of them will be involved. And I'm going to leave my job before you say anything else, because I can't work close to Connor any more for obvious reasons. I am going to pursue my sewing designs, which are really doing well out in Spain, and Clodagh is going to help me. I need you guys just to be there and support me for the moment. But I fully intend to earn enough to financially support both me and the baby within the next eighteen months – allowing me time to have the baby and all. It's not perfect, in fact it's far from it, and it's not what I intended my life to be like. I thought I'd be having a baby within a loving marriage. But I am happy that I am having this baby, Mum and Dad, really I am."

Mum was close to tears and gave me a huge hug. "Of course you are, Geri, and so are we! Well, we *will* be when we get used to the idea, and it'll be really nice to have our first grandchild, won't it, Eddie?"

Eddie looked seriously doubtful but nodded anyhow. "The father needs to be financially responsible regardless," he then insisted.

"Yes, Dad, and he will be, but I'd like to address that a little bit later. I need to get my own head together and have a plan before I involve the potential fathers, OK?"

My father's eyes softened at last. "OK, love, we're right behind you." He touched my hand and I knew everything was going to be all right.

That was until the unlucky bad timing that occurred next.

The door opened and who should stroll in at that very moment but Gary, in all his blond glory, accompanied by his father, the luscious over-tanned Jessie and his father's new girlfriend, Carole.

There was no way of avoiding them as we were seated facing the door, and as soon as they entered my father spotted Gary and instantly decided to re-enact the head-wrestling episode from our hallway. He barged towards Gary with a bloodcurdling cry worthy of a part in *Braveheart*.

"You bastard!" my father roared as he swung Gary around the room to the astonishment of onlookers.

"My daughter is pregnant, you know, pregnant and alone, and you waltz in here as cool as you like!" He stopped talking while he tried to connect his fist to Gary's shocked face.

Gary Senior pulled Dad off this time, but half-heartedly, as if he understood my father's rage. He then tried to reason with him. "Eddie, *Eddie,* please calm down, this is getting you nowhere. Now, what was it you said? Geri is pregnant?"

They looked at me quizzically, all except for Jessie who looked gobsmacked, and a part of me registered that fact and felt triumphant. And I was determined I wasn't going to act histrionically in front of Gary and especially *her.*

"Yes, I am as a matter of fact," I said confidently, rising.

Gary was still half in a headlock with my father. He looked amazed and Gary Warren Senior looked pleased, no doubt counting on a grandson to continue on with his empire – how it came about was obviously inconsequential.

"But Gary lost all rights to this baby when he walked away from us, didn't you, Gary? I don't want anything from you and I have moved on from you. So if you don't mind, all this aggression is not good for *my* baby, so, Dad, please let him go and take me home."

My mother rose silently and we gathered our things. Then she took my arm and we headed for the door.

"You can't do this!" Gary wailed after me. "You can't take my baby away from me, I won't let you!"

I walked back slowly and whispered into his ear so no one else could hear. "Chances are, it's probably not even yours, Gary, so I shouldn't worry too much."

Then I walked away.

Gary roared after me. "What do you mean? Geri, come back here! You can't leave it like this! *Geri!*"

I glanced back to see Gary's contorted face yelling after me, while Jessie was trying to grab his attention but failing miserably.

When I got outside, my legs nearly buckled beneath me.

It hadn't been how I had planned to tell Gary, in fact it had been a disaster, but at least I had managed to inform his sorry butt and upset him at the same time with the news that he might not be the baby's father. The look on his face was priceless. But none the less the encounter still shook me. I was far from over him judging by the stampede my heart was doing in my chest. I hadn't reckoned on that really.

I smiled at my brave but silly father for being the hero. "Dad, you really should take up another career as a bouncer or a boxer. This is becoming a bit of a habit, coming to the rescue of your wronged daughter."

My father frowned. "I'm sorry, Geri. It's just the

sight of him makes me so angry I can't help myself. And just then when he walked in the pub as casual as you like and you only after telling us your news, well, I just saw bloody red, didn't I? But I promise to hold my temper in future, considering your condition, and all."

I almost came to tears for this man who couldn't tell me he loved me but tried to show me in the only way he knew how, by trying to knock Gary Warren's block off.

"Come on then, you can take me and your future grandchild home." And that was that.

I wondered if I could ever have an encounter with Gary that didn't involve fisticuffs with all of my family or that bloody clinging limpet hanging off his arm – she seemed to be surgically attached to the guy. It killed me that their relationship seemed to be thriving while I was the one suffering and stuffing up to beat the band to boot.

Why couldn't Gary look distraught and haggard?

Probably because he dumped you for a younger, slimmer model, came the reply from my brain, which was never the kindest ally I had. Why should he look haggard? Well, I'd just have to change that. My earlier revenge with the chilli in the underwear was far too tame. It seemed the way to get to Gary would be through the baby he always didn't want. Well, I'd make sure he would suffer, at least as much as I did. I thought that was only fair.

I just wished I didn't still love him – that was all.

Chapter 33

Six months later . . .

I had a pain. Not any kind of pain, but a deep pain that twinged and ached to such a degree I began to fear it might be actual labour pain.

Not now, please God, not yet. It would mean I would never get the huge Spanish order out on time and also that bloody Gary was the father going by my dates and I *definitely* didn't want that to be the case. It was a bit early. Three weeks to be exact. If I was later there was more chance of Connor being the father.

I considered calling Clodagh, who was my birthing partner. Clodagh and I had become a lot closer in recent months with the abdication of Amy from Best Friend role and her subsequent decampment to Glasgow and domestic bliss with sexy Stuart.

I missed Amy so much. I had been up to Glasgow

several times to visit and we had great fun, but the day-to-day girly gossiping and closeness just wasn't there any more.

And Sandy had moved down under to be with Chris. They just couldn't be separated and theirs truly was a match made in heaven. It almost made me wince to see how happy they were together. It was a joy to witness but also hard to watch. It made me realise I had never had anything remotely like that with Gary, ever. It made me want more and not settle for anything less than true equal love, one that made you feel the most special person in the world. And I had never felt that.

I'd had a lot of time to analyse my relationship with Gary over the past few months, when the acid pain of his leaving had waned and a familiar, lesser hurt had taken its place.

I saw that I had based a whole ten-year relationship on a lie and on the fact that I was grateful that Gary, who was considered a nine in those days of schoolgirl infatuation, had fallen for me (a half-decent six on a good day) and I had wasted all of my twenties trying to hang on to the catch of the century (as I had believed) regardless of what it cost me. Our relationship had long run its course before I cajoled and prodded Gary into making that proposal. I had thought the world would end if I turned thirty without an engagement ring on my left hand. That no one would ever want me. I was so busy running to stand still just to keep him that I never even realised or focused on what I wanted myself.

Gary was a bastard and had treated me terribly but I had let him and I had to accept responsibility for my part in that.

Still, I now needed to look forward.

I had grown more in the past six months than the entire past ten years – and in more ways than one.

I realised what I didn't want and I didn't want to be anyone's welcome mat any more.

That was part of the reason I left my job and put so much distance between Connor and myself. I wasn't going to hang around waiting on Connor to come to his senses and realise that I was better for him than that airhead April. In fact I wasn't even sure if I wanted Connor to fall in love with me at all. I didn't want some dithering wuss who couldn't decide. I wanted someone to passionately want and desire me, just like Chris did Sandy. I wanted *real love*, not *"I can't believe it's not real love"*!

Anyway, I wasn't taking any prisoners these days and was ruthless with my decisions.

It seemed that the baby gave me an inner strength, a core of steel that carried me through. I walked away from a job that I loved for an uncertain future, with a scrappy bit of an idea for sewing spangly shorts and tops and a borrowed business plan from my brainier friend. I was scared that my business venture wouldn't pass muster and I'd be, of all things, a deserted mother on the dole. But I had to try and make it alone; I had to try to get myself together and make a life for both me and the baby. It was a scary time and an uncertain one – but the scariest part of the whole affair was going to be finding out who the father was.

I had left Oswald & Osborne before I began showing and had very little contact with either of the guys since so I didn't even know if Connor was aware that I was pregnant at all.

Gary had been up to see me a few times after that fateful day in The Yacht.

He texted me and managed to call over when he knew my father, aka Rambo, would be out and he wouldn't have his neck dislocated.

I tried to feel sorry for him, really I did, but I couldn't find it in my heart to forgive him and focus on our (maybe) child together. I just watched his handsome blond face yet didn't hear the babble he spewed forth. I just went into some little world of my own until he had finished and then watched him walk away, wondering at how much of a stranger he had become. Did I really know every inch of that strong face? Had I really kissed every inch of his lovely profile and marvelled at the fact that he wanted me? All I remembered after he left was that he just didn't look like mine any more – and he wasn't.

Pamela came to see me too. In the mistaken idea that somehow we could forge an alliance against Gary

Senior and Gary and use the baby to make them suffer. Well I had long since dispelled that idea as wrong – I wasn't going to use a poor innocent child for my own pathetic revenge. I wasn't going to be a doormat either and make things too easy for Gary, but I had to do right by my baby at the same time. Pamela didn't even figure in my plans except as a distant grandma, if she even was. She would have to fight her own battles.

But right now I had the annoying and more intrusive pain to deal with.

So I gave in and called Clodagh.

Clodagh instantly went into commando mode.

"I've got my kit all ready in the car – I'll be over in twenty minutes!" she barked and I hoped I really was in labour then – in case I got her mad.

But by the time she got there the pain had receded.

"That doesn't mean anything," Clodagh asserted, running her hands maniacally through the little bit of copper thatch she did have. "I read in *What to Expect When You're Expecting* that that's quite normal – especially on your first. We need to go down to the hospital just in case. I'd feel safer ..."

I wasn't sure if I felt safer in the car with Clodagh – she was almost hyperventilating.

"Well, calm down then, Clodagh. I don't want you to have a heart attack before we get there. I'll just get my weekend bag and leave a note for my parents."

"OK," Clodagh said breathlessly.

For a brief moment I wished that I had let anyone else be my birth partner.

I went and fetched my hastily packed backpack that I had thrown together while I was waiting on Clodagh to come over. I could never admit that I hadn't had it packed for six weeks already like Clodagh would have. I took a minute in my room to shed a silent tear that I hadn't got Connor or even, God help us, Gary for this experience, but it was just a weak moment and I grabbed my backpack, wiped my face and went to face Clodagh and the rally drive into town.

Of course it was a false alarm. I started to notice that when I began to scan the clothes shops along the coast road and wonder if I could ever fit into any of their slinky numbers again. No one in labour would do that. Also, Clodagh was really getting on my nerves with her incessant breathing instructions and her well-meaning advice. By the time we got to the Rotunda Hospital I almost 'fessed up and asked her to turn back but I didn't dare, so we went through the whole charade in the admissions ward before I was examined and sent on my way with sardonic smiles all round.

"Sorry," I admitted to Clodagh as she drove me home.

"That's no problem," Clodagh breezed, now exhilarated that she had fulfilled her brief. "It's no harm to have a trial run. I reckon I won't even be nervous by the real event, and we know what it's like to get into the city on Friday afternoons now, specially as it gets busier nearer rush-hour."

I knew one thing: Clodagh and I would have a serious falling out before I ever delivered the baby, if she didn't stop running the whole thing like a military exercise.

When I got home I called Adam. Yes, *that* Adam, the handsome builder that I had snogged on my hen week in Palma Nova. I had met up with him again when I was about five months pregnant. I literally bumped into him in the Jervis Centre coming out of Boots. We crashed into each other and I mumbled sorry until I looked into the brown smouldering eyes and recognised him, as large as life and far from Dundalk.

"Wow, you've been busy!" Adam exclaimed as he spotted my emerging bump.

He caught me at a weak and hormonal moment and I had instantly burst into tears – whereupon he whisked me into a nearby coffee shop and I unloaded my whole sorry tale.

"*Wow!*" he exclaimed when I had finished. "What a prize shit you married. I reckon you had a lucky escape, Geri. But even so, I still feel you need to tell the real father about the baby sooner or later. You know about my dad and the fact that I haven't seen him since I was six years old – well, I have spent all of my life so far trying to get over that and get beyond it. There's always something missing, you know –

especially if it's a boy. They need a male role model. So, Geri, please think carefully about this going-it-alone thing. You'll have to do the best for the baby even if it isn't the best thing for you."

I knew he made absolute sense, and I knew that God had sent him to me that day to tell me that. I needed to hear it from someone who had the right objective outlook.

And I took it all on board. I was just taking my time about sorting it all out.

Since then Adam and I had been fast friends. He was now working in Dublin and, while there was no actual hope of me getting involved with him on a romantic level, he took the rebuff in his stride and we met up for lunch regularly and he kept me up to speed with his rampant love life and his deep longing to go back to Dundalk and settle down and buy the elusive house when he had made enough money.

So now I called him and arranged to meet him in Dawson Street the following day. He was revamping a government building on Nassau Street and I needed to get into the city for a huge batch of sequins, and I needed to talk to someone about my scare.

"Sure," he laughed. "God! The thought of that redhead driving me into hospital would have definitely put me into labour if I were you. You should have asked me to be your birthing partner. I have three nieces and four nephews – sure I'm an old hand at this baby lark."

"I hadn't met up with you by the time I asked Clodagh. Anyway, she's very focused."

"Is that what you call it? Control freak would be more the term I'd use. "

The clang of hammers in the background prevented me from replying and we said goodbye. I could do worse than Adam, I mused as I put down the phone. He was nice, steady, he fancied me rotten and he'd be a good provider. Head over heels in love hadn't worked last time – maybe I should try another way. But I also knew my hormones were raging and I couldn't really make that kind of decision at the minute, and perhaps even a year from now that still might be the case after all I had been through. I'd settle for Adam being a good friend for the moment – and I needed all the friends I could get, as they were rather thin on the ground.

The following day I lumbered up to Dawson Street, taking the Temple Bar route and then instantly regretting that decision. I had forgotten how cumbersome long walks had become and my bump, which had now taken on the dimensions of two rather large bowling balls, made me walk like a penguin – I had to stop every ten yards with a stitch in my side. I was also roasting hot by the time I got to College Green and people stared openly as they wrapped themselves up against the biting February winds, while I strolled along (well, limped really), my coat flung wide open to reveal a flimsy linen top and my cheeks red with heat. By the time I got to Milano's to meet Adam, I was ready to collapse. Ever the gentleman, Adam was waiting outside and grabbed me by the arm.

"Geri! You poor thing, *look* at you, you should have drove up this side of town or at least I could have met you in Henry Street! You're an awful silly girl!"

I huffed and puffed. "I'll be grand in a few minutes when I have a little rest – just get me a large order of garlic bread and I'll be as right as rain."

Adam laughed heartily – he seemed to find me very funny most of the time.

He put his arm around me solicitously as he led me indoors. The restaurant was very busy and we got a small table near the window.

As the waitress took our order I heard someone call my name.

"Geri! Geri! It *is* you! I thought it was – how are you?"

It was Connor – of all people – he who hated Italian food. Here he was in an Italian restaurant standing there in front of me, looking more handsome than ever, spruced up in an expensive Italian suit with a beatific smile and those amber eyes glinting at me.

"Connor, I ... how are you?"

Then he noticed it, my huge enormous bump – after all, who could miss it? My stomach was peeking out of my overstretched, oversized linen summer shirt that had been almost roomy a few weeks ago.

He looked first at me, then more quizzically at Adam.

"Sorry," I blurted out. "This is Adam. Adam meet Connor, my … old boss."

Connor looked shocked but recovered quickly. "Less of the *old* there, Geri! I see congratulations are in order – when are you due?" There was a slight edge to his voice.

"Soon," I replied vaguely, avoiding his eyes, but it wasn't the time or the place.

Adam looked distinctly uncomfortable.

"You haven't been in touch at all, Geri! And the place just hasn't been the same without you. She was the best worker we ever had, Adam." And he smiled.

"Oh, you know how it is. I meant to – I was kind of busy," I said awkwardly, looking at the table napkin.

Adam gave me a funny look.

"Obviously. Well, I'm with a bunch of clients who insisted on eating Italian, so I'd better get back to them, but it was great to see you, Geri, and I'd really like to catch up – nice to meet you, Adam. Call me, Geri." His eyes were pleading at me over Adam's head as he left.

Then it dawned on me. Connor thought obviously that Adam was my new boyfriend; and I wasn't sure if I was happy or not about that. If Connor was still with April I would be delighted that he thought I'd actually got my life together. However, if he wasn't – well, I wasn't sure how I felt, except that my heart was beating a mile a minute.

Adam noticed. "I'm jealous, Geri – you never give me looks like that."

"Will ye g'way out of that! I never gave him any sort of looks!"

"Oh yes, you did," replied Adam sagely. He fluttered his eyelashes over a downward gaze theatrically, "Like this. Anyway, I think he thinks we're an item. He must be guessing over the baby, though. I know I would be. Why didn't you say something?"

"Like what? Guess what, Connor, you might be the daddy, just take your place in the queue?"

"You know what I mean, Geri – you really have got to sort this out."

I grimaced as I pulled on a bit of garlic bread that had arrived. "I know you're right and I will sort it out, as soon as possible."

"Call him. He needs to know before this baby arrives. It'll be a whole lot worse if you leave it till afterwards and it turns out Connor is the father. It'll create a lot of ill feeling. I know, I'm a bloke."

"No kidding!" I replied irritably.

The surprise meeting with Connor had unhinged me. I'd just wanted to leap into his arms and spill the whole sorry tale and ask him to be the father of my baby, but I feared that he and April were deliriously happy making babies of their own and Connor would simply pity me and I couldn't bear that. Anyway, it was just my hormones making me feel this way. I knew after the baby arrived I would feel stronger.

Adam looked contrite. "Sorry, Geri – I know it's not easy. None of this has been, has it? It's just that I feel very strongly about the whole issue of fatherhood. At least Gary wants to be a part of the baby's life if it is his and Connor seems like a decent enough bloke too, so it could be a lot worse. I think it might be more that you fear who the actual father is – and that's what's making you so undecided about telling Connor, is that it?"

I burst into hot salt tears – these bubbling hormones were hard graft, I can tell you.

I nodded, mid-sob.

"Either way, it's not going to be easy," I managed after I had calmed down. "Connor has just got back with his wife whom he adores and who doesn't want children even though he loves them – and Gary, well, between him and his father, they just want another Warren to carry on their little empire. Gary never wanted children at all – I had to practically beg him to agree to have kids after a five-year wait. Now he's trying to be really nice to me just so he can enjoy a son and heir without the trouble of a wife. It's just not how I envisaged my life going, that's all."

Adam touched my hand and looked at me kindly. "It's going to all work out in the end. Just you see, you've got me and Miss Control Freak in your corner and when this little baby is born you'll get the DNA testing sorted out and take things one step at a time from there."

I had an instant horrible vision of the three of us on *Trisha* tearing strips off each other while we waited on the DNA results – it just all seemed so tacky. Maybe when the baby was born it would have black curly hair and brown eyes and I would instantly know who was the father was – either way I wasn't going to have to wait much longer to find out.

Chapter 34

Connor called that night. I hadn't even had time to recover from our earlier meeting and had just got over my four hours of heartburn from the three portions of garlic bread I had stuffed myself with, after the stress of bumping into him.

"Hi," I said, more cheerfully than I felt. "I wondered how long it was going to take for you to call."

"Geri, I can't help being a little concerned. You look almost ready to have that baby and by my maths I could be in the picture. We did have that wonderful night together, remember?"

I was furious!

He could be *in the picture*? How jolly! I didn't care for his tone, all jokey and friendly. It wasn't a funny matter. In fact nothing seemed remotely funny any more and hadn't for some time. I had suffered a humour bypass with advancing pregnancy, along with my newly acquired stretch-marks and the varicose veins that tracked my poor inflated legs.

"Well, Connor, I also happened to excel at maths at school and if I had thought you were *in the picture*, as you say, don't you think I would have been in touch?"

My voice dripped with sweet sarcasm.

I know! I don't know what I was thinking. Now I can see it was a stupid and very unfair thing to say, but I had just had enough of men and emotions at that moment and I felt Connor was being disingenuous. I was tired enough of Gary just wanting my baby for his empire – what if Connor would now claim it because his wife didn't want to spoil her figure getting pregnant? I couldn't say I blamed her any more, come to think of it.

"OK," Connor replied in a flat voice. "Point taken. I was just concerned when I saw you today, Geri, that's all. I thought we were closer than that, you know. You just walked away from the job after all those years, but I never thought we'd lose our friendship as well. You just seemed to disappear from my life."

I felt sorry for him at that moment. He seemed genuinely hurt – maybe I had been a bit mean to him after all.

"I'm sorry, Connor, it's just been so difficult. I

needed to change my life after what happened, a whole fresh start. Anyway, speaking of fresh starts, how is April?"

He sighed. "Well, she's in London at the moment, shooting a catalogue."

Oh, so he just felt a bit lonely for his fabulous wife and he thought he'd call me up to see if I was having his baby on the off chance and maybe I'd be hard up enough to give him some company or even a little bit more! I was furious again (believe me your mood can change in a nanosecond when you're expecting – it used to even scare me).

"Oh, that's *nice* for her, Connor. Listen, I have to go – Adam and I are off out to a late movie, so take care, OK? Bye."

I slammed down the phone before he could even get a goodbye out of his mouth.

The nerve of the guy! I was an idiot to think he was ever any different from any other guy. He was just as bad as Gary, it seemed. Let him get stuffed! Perhaps it was time to really make the adorable Adam my boyfriend and just get on with life. At least I knew Adam genuinely cared about me and would never hurt me, but was it fair to him?

I know what Sandy would say: stuff fairness. I wished she was here. I missed her so much and Amy too. It was a time I needed them both so much.

Amy was due back a week or so after the baby was born, but I could hardly expect Sandy to jet back from Brisbane to be at my side for the delivery. She was having the time of her life Down Under and I felt that she and Chris would just get hitched and stay out there forever. Maybe if she did I would go and follow her. There certainly didn't seem to be much to keep me in Ireland any more. It was something I would have to think about – later when I had a clearer head. Nothing made any sense at the moment – except that I was lonelier than at any other time in my life.

I should have been ensconced in that little apartment in Kinsealy Cloisters, putting the finishing touches to the beautiful baby nursery that Gary and I had carefully decorated together – and *he* should have been rubbing my feet at night instead of my poor put-upon father. Large fat tears streamed down my face as I thought about all I had lost. And worst of all, this little one inside me had lost even more – a happy two-parent family that I had grown up with. Already he or she was at a huge disadvantage, being born into this. I cried for a long time that night, quietly in my still teenaged bedroom. I cried for all the dreams and hopes that had died on me one by one, and the one remaining fantasy I had left – that Connor would be the one who was the baby's father and would rescue me – had just disappeared into dust. It wasn't going to happen. And after I had finished crying, I rubbed my stomach and made a promise to my unborn child that I was going to be the best possible parent he or she could have and that, despite its poor start, my baby would have a very happy life.

♥ ♥ ♥

The following day Clodagh called in a mad panic.

"Geri, you're not going to believe this, but I've just had the owner of Naked in the shop and she absolutely loves your designs. She has already placed a huge order for the beaded halter-neck tops and the new sheer bohemian blouses for all of her stores and she said she regularly showcases a lot of her styles on *The Afternoon Show* and wondered if you'd mind her featuring some in the near future. Isn't it amazing? What do you think?"

It truly was amazing.

Naked was a chain of high-class, upmarket boutiques that catered for the well-heeled socialites around Dublin. There were twelve stores dotted all along the coastline in Malahide, Clontarf, Sandymount, Dalkey and other pockets of affluent society.

I couldn't believe Marina Carson would ever even look at my simple little designs. Most of her stock came from Milan or Paris, but she did like offbeat little numbers as well, especially smaller items like camisoles and the flimsy tops I specialised in.

"I can't believe it, Clodagh!"

"She only wants the finest materials, like the pale organza or the silk. But the really good news is she is prepared to pay substantially over the odds because that's what her clients expect, or so she told me. It was the design that caught her eye. You know, Geri, if Marina Carson thinks you have a good eye for design you really should pursue that course I told you about. I know you have talent but if you get the diploma in design it could take you a lot further."

I knew Clodagh was right. We had been suffering for some time, overstretching ourselves to fill orders and being late for deliveries – I needed to get the business on a more sure footing with perhaps a bank loan to finance me to find premises and hire trained machinists and staff. This might be my only chance for making a success of my life, and I had to take it seriously. There was the small matter, however, of having a baby in a few weeks. My timing since the business first took off had been terrible to say the least, but I really didn't have the luxury of sitting down and putting my feet up when an opportunity like this arose – I was about to be a single parent and I needed all the income I could get. I also needed a huge distraction from my current broken heart. And I began to get excited at the idea of my designs being worn by the elite of Dublin and being showcased on TV as well. My heart lifted higher than at any time since my ill-fated wedding day. Nothing was going to stop me. I had been given a lifeline when I needed it most and I was going to take it

"Right, Clodagh. We need a brainstorming meeting

and for once I'm going to listen to every single thing you tell me. I need to make this business a success and I'm going to need all the help I can get to make it. Do you think, with the right advice and some capital behind me, I can really make a go of this?"

Clodagh laughed heartily. "I know you can. You just need self-belief and a lot of hard work. If I did it, then so can you. And I'll do everything I can to help, you know that."

I almost came to tears. My stalwart friend that I had so nearly dumped over her poor choice in men had never once failed me. I felt truly ashamed of myself.

"Thanks, Clodagh, you really are a true friend," was all I could manage to get out.

"I try to be," was the quiet reply and I knew I had hurt her deeply but that she still had been there. I had a lot of making up to do.

"OK, so," I said. "Tell me when you can get here and I'll have a lovely lunch or dinner ready for you – it's the least I can do."

Clodagh laughed. "Just what I've always needed – a wife. I'll see you sometime after six."

I ran to tell my mother.

"That's great news, love! Do you think that this means you might let me loose from the sweatshop you're running and let me get back to my normal easygoing life?"

I looked at her in alarm, but her huge wide grin

allayed my fears.

"Not on your nellie, Mummy dearest, you're in it for life. Though I'll be able to at least give you a decent wage and maybe even the odd lunch hour. Won't it be great, though. If this business succeeds I'll be able to give me and the baby a decent enough life – maybe even, with the settlement from Gary for my share of the apartment, I can get somewhere for us to live."

I saw a shadow of panic cross my mother's face. I knew she never wanted me to leave. But she recovered quickly enough.

"Yes, love, though you know me and your father always have a place for you both here. It's no trouble, you know, we could always have the attic converted."

I smiled at her and then went to fill the kettle. "Mum, I don't know why you'd want your grown-up daughter and her baby here. Surely you and Dad would want to spread your wings and do things together, like you haven't been able to do for the past thirty years or so?"

"That's a scary prospect to be quite honest with you," she suddenly said, sitting down slowly. "It's been so long since we had anything in common except you and Josephine, I mean Sandy, that it scares me that there might not be anything left when you do leave."

That statement alarmed me a bit. Mum wasn't big on confessions. But I realised she was still suffering from empty-nest syndrome and was panicking a little.

"It'll be alright, Mum, you'll see – it just takes some adjusting to there just being two of you again. A few nice holidays should give you both a chance to get things back on track."

"That's just it, Geri, I don't know if I want it to get back on track, as you put it. The truth is Eddie and I have been just rubbing along for years. He had an affair, you know. Fifteen years ago, when you and Sandy were only teenagers. It had been going on for two years and he was in love with her."

I couldn't believe what I was hearing – my ordinary, plain father, whose idea of excitement was the crossword in the *Evening Herald*, had an affair! I couldn't quite comprehend it.

"So what did you do?"

"I begged him to end it, and eventually he did, more for you girls than me, I suspect, but things have never been the same between us. I just don't have the same trust in him and it still hurts that he fell in love with someone else and preferred her to me."

"I know exactly how you feel," I replied sadly and I did. I had felt the same pain as she had. But, more worryingly, if my mother hadn't fully recovered from her heartbreak, could I ever get over mine?

"Where did he meet her?" I asked, nosiness getting the better of me.

"In work. She was the manageress of one of the boutiques when he was the security man at Donaghmede shopping centre. I never suspected because he was seldom late home, but he eventually just withdrew from me and I knew something was wrong. The trouble is, when he did give her up he was miserable for about a year. I think that was worse than if we had actually broken up. To this day I'm not sure I made the right decision."

I thought about my father and the faraway wistful looks he often had, like life had dealt him a bad blow, and it all fell into place. But I still felt sorry for my mum and her brittle nature and obsessive cleaning began to explain themselves.

"I'm really sorry, Mum. But it still isn't too late, you know. He hasn't strayed since, has he?"

Her shake of the head told me he hadn't.

"Then perhaps there is still some love there. I can see that he loves you anyway. You've been together for over thirty years – you can't just throw it all away because we've grown up. You could get counselling or even just talk to each other – maybe it's time to give it some attention."

She looked at me with such weariness and defeat, as if I hadn't a clue what I was talking about. People of her generation didn't go to counselling or talk about their feelings – that's why they ended up in so much grief.

"I don't know, Geri, that sort of thing isn't something I could picture your father agreeing to."

I gave her a steely glare. "Don't give him any bloody choice. If you tell him the marriage is on the line, then you'll see his commitment."

She looked a little more hopeful. "Perhaps you're right, I'll talk to him tonight. Maybe we could go out for a quiet drink."

We sipped our tea in silence and I suddenly wondered if we ever knew anyone at all. Even my father cheated on my mother and had cheated us too. I felt really angry for a few minutes thinking about it and remembered how mad he had been with Gary, all the male posturing and head locks – had he been also angry with himself? And my mother, holding it all together for all those years, controlling her little domain as much as she could because she couldn't control her husband's philandering. And me, had I craved male attention so much because I hadn't ever got it from my distant father? The pedestal I had my father on was well and truly smashed to smithereens.

What a mess infidelity made! Right then, I was glad I had escaped from Gary and I was determined I would go it alone with my baby rather than settle for some kind of halfway love. It hadn't done much for my mother and it certainly wasn't enough for me.

I was going to throw myself wholeheartedly into my business venture and let love go to hell. It was time to focus on Geri and the baby I was about to deliver.

The honeymoon was over and reality had well and truly set in.

Chapter 35

Four weeks later and almost two weeks overdue, little Charlie arrived into the harsh, cold late-February snows. It was hilarious but also scary as Clodagh slipped and slid her smart Golf along the icy roads on half speed to the hospital while I puffed and panted in pain. It was midday on a Saturday and Mum and Dad had gone for a walk in the snow as part of their new relationship strategy and I was in the house alone. I had suffered an increasing period-like ache for about three hours but was reluctant to tell anyone in case it was another phantom pain, but when my waters broke I panicked and called my birthing partner, who swore like a docker at the idea of having to travel into town in the snow and ice.

"It's got to be a boy," Clodagh exclaimed as she slowly folded me into the car. "Only a man could have such lousy timing!"

I tried to laugh between contractions, but it was becoming increasingly difficult because the pains were coming thick and fast.

We eventually arrived at the Rotunda hospital just in time and Charlie was born within another forty minutes, which was a relief as Clodagh's cheering squad/sergeant major style was quite irritating to say the least, and I couldn't even slap her like you might a husband, because it wasn't her fault I was there.

I cried as I held my new baby and it felt bittersweet having no father present. I looked at my new infant son and scanned his face to see whom he most resembled. He had dark eyes and not a blade of hair so it was hard to say – as a matter of fact he most looked like my Aunty Pearl to be honest. But I was devastated by the fierce love I instantly felt towards this tiny little bundle of humanity. I would scale mountains and fight tigers with my bare hands for this little baby. So even though I felt a little sad that Gary wasn't there, or Connor for that matter, it receded to the back of my mind because I was more totally in love with this baby than I ever had been with either of them, so I was more happy than I had ever been.

Clodagh rang my parents and told them to get to the hospital as I had given birth to their first grandchild. I could tell by the screams at the other end that they were overexcited. I hoped that

Charlie's birth would bring me closer to my father, as things just hadn't been the same between him and me since I had discovered he had cheated on my mother. I just couldn't get past it. I felt he wasn't the man I thought he was. He hadn't just cheated on Mum, he had cheated on Sandy and me also, and it could have destroyed our family entirely. As it was, it had altered my mother permanently. Dad hadn't discussed it with me but he knew Mum had told me because it had all come out in their counselling sessions. Now I realised that my baby needed his grandfather, as he hadn't got a dad in his life as such, so I had to relent a little and let my dad back in. But it would take a long time before I would ever be the same with him, if ever.

An hour later they arrived with balloons, blue teddy bears and armfuls of flowers. They both shed a tear as they held their first grandchild and it was a very lovely moment.

"He's the image of Pearl," my dad quipped to a filthy stare from my mother. "He's a Murphy and no doubt about it. Any update on his blood group yet?"

"Eddie Murphy, have you no consideration whatsoever? Leave the girl alone – that is none of your business!" my mum exploded.

Clodagh made an excuse and fled the room, sensing a row.

"It's OK, Mum. The baby is O positive. I don't know either Connor or Gary's blood group but I intend to find out. I just want one day with him on my own before I talk to the doctors. Then I am going to telephone both of the guys and find out their blood type and we'll take it from there. OK, Dad?"

My father nodded silently, afraid any further queries might enrage Mum or me or both of us.

A small silence followed.

"It doesn't really matter, though, does it?" my father said quietly after a time. "He's here now, he's our grandson and we love him. The rest is not that important."

My mother smiled brightly at me. "Yes, your father's right. You're fine and the baby is healthy and we'll all pull together." Then she said directly to Charlie, who was sleeping peacefully: "Whoever is the father will just have to take their place in the queue, won't they, honey bunny? Because you are all *ours*!"

A small chill gripped my heart. I could envision years and years ahead of my well-meaning but clutching parents, who would run my life and that of my son's if I stayed with them, and I could see me being relegated to the role of older sister as they took over, filling their empty nest, and me being a sad old spinster with no life of her own. I decided then and there that I would have to make good my escape as soon as was practicable for my sanity and for my baby son.

After about an hour I finally prised my parents from my baby and they left with happy promises of a long phone call to Sandy and many digital photos emailed to Australia so my sister could see her new nephew. I was just drifting off to sleep beside a snoozing Charlie when I heard a familiar voice call out my name.

"Geri!"

I looked up blearily.

It was him, looking thin and worried. His face still so handsome but a bit world weary, the trademark long hair now clipped very short and darker – he looked so familiar but, dressed in clothes that I had never seen before, still different.

"Gary! What are you doing here?"

He stood about three feet from the bed, as if terrified if he moved an inch further I would scream the hospital down. He spoke quietly as if I had an Uzi submachine gun pointed at him, but you never have large arms weaponry when you need them, so I fixed him with a steely glare instead. It would just have to do.

"I got a phone call from someone. It doesn't matter who really. I just had to come. Please don't get upset. I need to be here to see … you and the baby. The past few months have been awful. I feel so bad for what I put you through and now, all of this. I need to see my baby and I …" His voice trailed away. Tears trickled from his eyes.

I had never seen him cry before except maybe when Beckham deserted Man Utd. This was a whole new departure: emotion.

I almost felt sorry for him.

Almost.

But I was too weary to argue and there were three other nursing mothers in the room with Charlie and me so a screaming match was somehow inappropriate.

"Sit down!" I hissed as quietly as I could. "Pull the curtains around," I motioned, trying to get a little bit of privacy.

He did as I said, then sat down and slumped into the chair, as if defeated. All the air seemed to go out of him. He wiped his eyes and looked over me towards the cot.

"It's a little boy, Charlie."

"Charlie?" Gary echoed, no doubt wondering why not Gary the Third. (Over my dead body.)

"Yes, I picked Charlie because no one I knew possessed the name or even knew anyone with the name, so there he is. I think it suits him."

"Can I hold him?" he ventured.

"In a moment – he's sleeping right now. I need to talk to you, Gary, about the baby. We need to set some rules down. I have had a long time to think about this and you are going to have to listen to me. Otherwise it will be a whole lot worse, believe you me."

"OK," he replied in a small voice.

I suddenly realised I didn't feel any rage at that

moment. It might have been because my sleeping infant was only feet away and I didn't want to start his little life in anger, and anyway if Gary was Charlie's father then he was going to be part of his life, something I wasn't overly crazy about but there it was. It needed to be addressed.

"I wasn't just trying to be cruel when I told you that Charlie might not be yours, Gary – that was true."

He looked like I had slapped him. I then realised he hadn't believed for a moment that I had been serious that day in the pub. I wasn't sure if I was annoyed at his arrogance or pleased that he believed I was so pure and devoted.

"But who? And when?"

"Gary, it really isn't any of your business, actually. You dumped me on my wedding day and sauntered off with your bit on the side, so after that all bets were off and I was a free agent from that day onwards. It just happened that a caring friend of mine, who also happened to be a man, became a lot more to me after you had left me. And he might be the father."

Gary tried to digest the news. "About that day, Geri, I never would have left with Jessie. I had told her it was all over days before. I was marrying you and that was that. I was still going through with it all, but when she turned up and the shit hit the fan I knew it was all over. But I wasn't going to leave you for her. I swear."

I was amazed that he thought that explanation would make me feel any better. Funny how he could gloss over the whole fact that he was cheating on me in the first place weeks before our wedding with someone whom he had met at our premarital course!

I was sure this new benign, contrite Gary was emerging because he had a vested interest in bringing me around so I would let him see his son. I began to get very tired of him and longed to get him out of there so I could get some rest. I could feel my blood pressure rising again. Suddenly I dreaded that this man would be my baby's role model. At least Connor was an honourable man with morals and ethics.

How had I ever loved this creep?

"Tell me, Gary, what is your blood group if you don't mind me asking?"

I held my breath.

"Don't you remember me telling you before? Remember that time that rescue show was on the box and that guy who fell off the mountain had the same blood type as me? AB – and only ten per cent of the population has it. And I told you then that if I ever had an accident you'd need to get me to a hospital quick or I'd die 'cos they never have enough of my blood type."

He droned on but his words washed over me I didn't care what he now said because, unless all those weeks of studying blood in Fifth Year biology had gone amiss, I was sure now of who the father of my newborn son was.

Chapter 36

I couldn't quite believe it. I hugged the secret knowledge to myself and tried not to get too overexcited. I needed to clarify my knowledge of blood groups with a qualified doctor, but by my reckoning I could now finally close off on my toxic relationship with the husband who jilted me and focus on the other guy who I wasn't too sure how I felt about but who had reunited with his wife anyhow. It looked like Connor was Charlie's father and I was infinitely happier about that. I just needed to confirm it.

I didn't let on to Gary – let him suffer on a little bit longer. He had surprised me, though – for someone who had no desire whatsoever to have a child, he sure had changed his mind quickly. Maybe the lithe Jessie would provide him with a son and heir, I thought mirthlessly as I saw him depart the ward, his shoulders slumped. It was only after he had left that I realised he hadn't even brought a cheap bouquet of garage flowers or a box of chocolates. Gary was a cheapskate to the last. Good riddance, I thought. As soon as the settlement came through from the apartment buy-out, I was going to close the chapter on that unfortunate piece of my life. I began to wonder then who in my clan had blabbed to Gary and told him about the baby.

I finally drifted off to sleep with a warm, fuzzy feeling that everything was going to be all right and work out the way I wanted it to.

Later on that evening Adam came in, festooned in balloons and baby clothes. What a contrast to Gary's empty-handed self-obsessed visit earlier on! Adam cooed and clucked over Charlie as if he was his own and I felt a real pang of remorse that I had been so emphatic to Adam that I was beyond him. Right then in that hospital room I had to stop myself from telling him I had changed my mind and asking him to take me and Charlie on, lock stock and barrel. But I knew I was being unfair and selfish, so I didn't. Why didn't we women ever fall for the Adams of this world? Why did we prefer the bad guys who broke our hearts and trampled all over our feelings, yet the dependable true-hearted men we passed over? I wondered if I could grow to love Adam – after all, I had fancied the pants off of him eons ago before Gary had destroyed my world. But my heart was so confused I wasn't sure if I could ever love anyone again. I couldn't be sure of it because it had let me down so badly before. No, I decided, stick to your guns, Geri, it's going to be just Charlie and you. Make the best of it.

I told Adam about my earlier visitor.

"How did *he* find out?" Adam replied angrily.

"I dunno, but my money is on Clodagh. She was in tears before she left because I was 'going it alone and so brave' or so she told me, so I think the birth must have had a profound effect on her. Anyhow, it wasn't too bad – at least I found out his blood group."

I waited for Adam to realise what I had just said.

"And? Geri, don't make me wait. Is he the father?"

I smiled. "Unlikely. I'm ninety-nine per cent sure it's Connor. So at least I can put Gary behind me."

Adam frowned. "And what about Connor? So far he knows nothing. I told you, Geri, I told you to tell him."

Adam was right, but what was I so scared of? Deep inside I think I was more afraid of telling Connor because he would want the baby more, and what if Connor decided he wanted the baby full time and fought me for custody? He and April had pots of money, Connor badly wanted a child of his own and April didn't want to disturb her perfect size-ten figure, so I feared being ousted gradually from Charlie's life by the wealth and perfection of Connor's world. Connor could offer Charlie everything, whereas I had precious little. I just needed a little more time – more time to develop a backbone that seemed to be sadly lacking.

That night as I lay in bed all sore and achy with the painkillers wearing off, I suddenly found myself dissolving into big racking sobs of tears. The whole situation was overwhelming me and I felt hugely sorry for both Charlie and me, facing life alone – and as Charlie woke screaming for his three a.m. feed, I cried along with him and wondered if I would ever feel normal again. I had been good at fooling myself for the past six months, deeply involving myself with the pregnancy and being bright and cheerful to get myself through, but now a sharp, hard reality had set in. I was a single mother with a newborn, about to be divorced and without a proper job, who would soon be in her thirties – or *well into her thirties* as Sandy would insist. Who would want anyone like that? *Adam would*, said a little voice in my mind and I fell asleep eventually, videos of Adam, Gary and Connor swirling about my head. I had never felt so desperate or alone.

What seemed like an hour later, Charlie awoke again and was ravenous. I was exhausted, but as I was breastfeeding I had little choice but to focus. There seemed to be no let-up in babies crying all night and the general pace in the semi-private ward was more hectic than O'Connell Street on a busy Saturday afternoon. I couldn't wait to get home to my interfering parents after all. Suddenly all their butting in would be a welcome prospect – I might actually get a rest. My moods were on a roller-coaster and I realised I could not make a decision while my mind was in such turmoil. I was going to get myself back to something approaching normality before contacting Connor.

Later on that morning – which almost seemed like an entirely different day when you had been awake since five – the doctor who delivered my baby came to see me.

"Well, how is Mum?" Dr Rosemary Stamford asked briskly. She could only have been a little older than me – middle thirties – but her thick horn-rimmed glasses and matronly bedside manner made her seem years older to me. She was an excellent gynaecologist and she really understood women, so I had enjoyed being her patient.

"I am totally cream-crackered but thanks for everything you did, Doctor Stamford – they tell me your stitching is something to behold."

Dr Stamford laughed heartily. "You haven't lost your sense of humour anyway, Geri. Can I have a look at you?"

She pulled the curtain around to inspect my poor wrecked bottom half. I felt like half of the entire hospital had seen me in a compromising condition by now and there was no dignity left. Childbirth certainly removed any that was left after nine months of prodding by aloof doctors in draughty wards, but I seemed to pass muster and she was happy with my recovery. I didn't dare look down at myself – it had been scary enough from my end during the birth and Clodagh had looked in severe shock as she left (she must have been since she called Gary!). So I closed my eyes and waited on her to finish.

"Can I ask you something, Dr Stamford?" I ventured after she had straightened my blankets.

"Sure," she said, while writing something on my chart with her ballpoint.

"Can a person with AB blood type have an O positive child with another O positive person?"

Dr Stamford sat down on the bed. A crease marked her forehead and she regarded me seriously.

"No, it's not possible, in a nutshell. Does that answer your question, or do you need to talk to me about it some more? I could give you the clinical explanation in haematology terms. "

I blushed profusely. "No, thanks, Dr Stamford – that will be fine."

She took my hand and smiled gently. "Don't worry, Geri. You'd be surprised how many times I am asked a question of that nature. Look, you have a lovely little fellow there, that's all that matters. Both you and himself are fine and in the pink of health. A good outcome by all accounts."

She stood up and pulled the curtain back and strode off to her other patients.

But she was right. I needed to get a grip. It wasn't the end of the world, but just the beginning of another one.

♥ ♥ ♥

I gladly fled the hospital with my precious bundle a few days later. I couldn't wait to get home and get a proper sleep – even in between Charlie's seven nightly feeds. At least it was quiet and dark at night at home and the baby might settle.

Mum and Dad collected me and I was unusually quiet on the way home. I was trying to suppress ever-emerging tears – the baby blues had really got me in their clutches. I couldn't help feeling so low. It was ridiculous – there I was in the bosom of my over-caring parents going to a warm and comfortable household. I wasn't some Victorian scullery maid thrown into the workhouse with her baby – yet a mist of depression hung over me.

And to make it worse I missed Sandy so much and also Amy. They had always managed to lift me up when I was down in a way that Clodagh just could never do in her no-nonsense way – so I looked listlessly onto the moody Irish Sea in the biting February winds and felt truly sorry for myself.

We got home eventually and Mum had blue balloons waving in the wind on the bushes in the front garden. I felt so proud of her – she did it to announce how proud she was of her grandson despite the twitching curtain brigade that had made several veiled comments about my failed marriage and very sudden pregnancy.

I got out of the car gingerly and was ceremoniously helped indoors by a solicitous mother and father.

"Come on into the kitchen and I'll make us all a nice cup of tea," said my father cheerfully, as Mum carted the loads of baby gifts and paraphernalia into the hallway.

"It's already made!" yelled a voice from the kitchen.

I couldn't believe it! I knew that unmistakeable voice – I rushed in to find Sandy and Amy in the kitchen.

"I can't believe you're really here!" I sobbed, first into Sandy's new beach-blonde hair and then into my best friend Amy's.

"I couldn't miss it," replied Sandy in a choked-up voice. "I had to be here for my big sister and my new nephew – besides I was so homesick I just couldn't bear being away from you all a minute longer."

I couldn't believe Sandy was actually standing in front of me. She looked so beautiful, tanned and fit, her hair longer and now blonde.

"But you were having such a ball over there! And Chris?"

Sandy smiled. "Don't worry, we're still in love and practically joined at the hip. He's applied for a work visa. Chris will be here in a matter of weeks – that'll give me time to spend on you and the little prince. Now where is he?"

Mum passed a squirming Charlie over as I caught up with Amy. I was so overwhelmed by the sudden appearance of both of them and my heart was truly gladdened to have them both back.

Amy looked beautiful as ever, but a lot thinner and a little tired looking.

"I'm only here for a week, Geri – but I have missed you so much! How was it?"

"Tougher than I thought, but I'll tell you more later. How's the man in the kilt?"

Amy smiled, but the smile never reached her eyes. "Oh, he's great – working hard, you know – otherwise he'd have come over too. It's so good to see you, Geri – you look fantastic for someone who has just given birth."

I grinned. "You should see the stretch marks – like Heuston Station, I kid you not. Motherhood is not for the fainthearted."

"Guess that counts me out, so," quipped Sandy as she passed Charlie over to my dad like an unwelcome rugby ball.

We all sat down and had Mum's special chocolate-chip muffins and copious cups of tea. I could see Mum smiling contentedly, happy to have her brood back together, and I knew she was happy because she loved us so much. I finally understood that bond, now I was a mother myself. I knew she would do everything to keep us with her for that very simple reason – because she cared so much.

"Can I come back tonight? I need to talk to you," Amy whispered in her breathy voice as she left to go home a couple of hours later.

My heart sank a little. I was feeling increasingly exhausted and despite all the excitement craved a nice long sleep. And Sandy was tired too, no doubt suffering from jet lag.

"Sure, anytime after seven. I should have his nibs sorted for bedtime by then," I said hopefully, not being sure of any such thing. I was intrigued. I didn't think Amy was going to tell me anything good, judging by her demeanour, and it was just like the old days when she would be like a rabbit in the headlights when things were going bad – particularly when she was being bullied by one of her boyfriends. I certainly hoped she wasn't being bullied this time. She had seemed so happy and in love when she had left to be with Stuart.

After I fed Charlie, Mum took over and I fell gratefully onto my bed and slept soundly for hours and didn't wake until Dad came to tell me that Amy was back and Charlie needed another feed.

Amy then arrived in the room with a squalling Charlie and I fed one while I listened to the other.

"So, Amy, what's the problem?"

She gave a small laugh. "No fooling you, I see."

"No more than I could ever fool you! We've been

friends since before we had boobs so I guess we know each other pretty well by now, so spit it out."

She fiddled some more with Charlie's chunky little feet as she tried to formulate her thoughts. "The truth is, Geri, I am miserable. I am so lonely and depressed over there I can't function. It's not Stuart: he has been kindness itself, he dotes on me and that seems to make it worse. I feel stifled all the time. It's just him and me, or him and me and his friends. We seldom see his family and I feel so isolated it's beginning to affect how I feel for him. I'm not sure I love him enough to stick it out."

I felt so sorry for her. What a dilemma! It would be almost easier if he was a bastard, then she could just pack her bag, flounce out and come back to Dublin, highly disgusted and self-righteous. But if she walked away now, it was just, well, like throwing it all away, everything she had looked for all these years.

"Is there any chance he might come back here to live?"

She frowned. "Nope. His job is so highpowered and his career is everything. He spends a couple of nights away each week, which even makes it worse. I never thought I'd miss all my bratty brothers, but I do. I miss the smell of the Liffey, for God's sake, and I detest that. I just can't stay there. I just can't. What am I going to do?"

I put my arm around her and gave her a quick hug. I had to tell her what she needed me to say.

"You've already made the decision, love. You just want me to tell you its OK. You are coming home."

And that was that. Love couldn't overcome all it seemed.

♥ ♥ ♥

I decided after my conversation with Amy that I was going to bite the bullet and call Connor. You never got anywhere in life without taking risks and, besides, he had a right to know he was a father. I just wasn't sure what kind of can of worms I was about to open and once it was opened there was no going back and my life and Charlie's would never be the same. There would no longer be just the two of us.

And I found that a bit scary.

I rose early the next morning and hesitantly called Connor on his mobile. I hoped he hadn't abandoned his lifelong habit of being at his desk every morning at eight. I didn't want to disturb him at home with the lissom April, looking like a lingerie commercial lying beside him in the large leather bed where we had created Charlie. It felt too weird even to think of that. Connor and April I mean, obviously not the night of loving passion in which we had conceived our little son.

I crept downstairs and sat on the stairs in the quiet house trying to pluck up the courage. Mum and Dad were still in bed and Charlie had gone back for his morning rest after his early feed. I prayed I could go through with it and manage to talk to him before anyone came downstairs, otherwise I'd lose my nerve.

After five minutes of biting my nails and looking at the telephone I finally dialled the number.

"Connor," I blurted out quickly, "it's Geri. Look, I really need to see you urgently. I can't talk over the phone but if we can arrange to meet –"

"You little *bitch*!" shrieked April's voice down the phone line. "You stay away from my husband, do you hear? Stay away from him or you'll regret it!"

With that the phone went dead.

I sat there as if carved in stone.

What the hell was April talking about? Had she found out about Connor and me spending that night together when they had broken up?

Or did Connor already suspect that Charlie was his son and had confessed it to his wife?

I hadn't a clue what was going on, but April had Connor's mobile and I wasn't going to be able to call the house again.

But it sounded like I was causing problems in Connor's marriage and, while I detested April, I hated to hurt her. After all, that cow Jessie had ruthlessly disregarded my feelings when she predatorily snatched Gary. I could never do that to anyone, including April, so I decided then and there I was going to leave well enough alone for the moment, and it really was going to be Charlie and me going it alone, at least for the near future.

There was still the matter of calling Gary and informing him that he was not the baby's father. I rang his mobile and it just rang out, so I called Gary Senior and told him instead. I could hear a genuine gasp and a real strain in his voice as he thanked me and promised to pass on the message to Gary.

Afterwards I didn't feel at all victorious as I thought I would, just sad and world-weary, as my son still didn't really have a father.

There were no real winners after all.

Chapter 37

A few weeks passed and Gary called to say he wanted to meet me to sort out the financial details of our separation. The idea of seeing him again was not very pleasant, but I needed to sort out my financial situation and I felt Gary owed me.

We arranged to meet at a neutral location, i.e. somewhere we had never been together and somewhere that no one would bump into us and think that we were reconciling.

So I chose The Pavilions in Swords and I got there fashionably late due to Charlie throwing up all over my one good outfit. None of my old clothes went even close to fitting over my still jellylike abdomen – honestly it felt like an alien had inhabited my lower body – well, I suppose it had really. It was just too depressing to try to squeeze into jeans or normal trousers, yet I felt like I wanted to look fabulous to make Gary regret leaving me. Who was I kidding? He hadn't regretted dumping me when I was at my most sylph-like before the wedding – what the hell chance did a moment of regret have when I looked like a small whale encased in black lycra?

"You do look fabulous!" insisted Sandy fiercely. "You spent almost a year growing that baby and it's going to take at least that long to get over it. Your skin and hair are glowing and you look radiant, so walk in there full of confidence. Remember, Geri, he is the loser, not you, and don't you forget it. And be strong: don't let him kid you out of anything, or don't agree to anything until you've run it by your solicitor."

Sandy was a fan of *Desperate Housewives* and it showed.

"OK," I had replied unconvincingly.

So I had arrived late clad in head-to-toe slimming black with a lot of hair straightened and lips glossed to find Gary looking dejected and forlorn by a window in the Coffee Dock. My heart still gave a small lurch when I saw him. I remember wondering when that would stop and if in fact it ever would.

He looked bleary-eyed and tired, but even though he obviously hadn't had much sleep, it would take more than bags under his baby-blue eyes to make him anything less than devilishly handsome.

"Hi, Geri," he said unsmilingly.

"Hello," I managed in a regal voice and I perched

down haughtily trying to hold my stomach in.

"You look very well. How is the baby?" he asked, a small hurt look crossing his face.

"Charlie is fine. I am fine. How is Jessie?" I couldn't help the sniping. Not very mature but I just couldn't stop myself.

"Oh, she is fine too. We're moving in together – I just thought you should know."

I tried not to react. "That is of no importance to me, Gary. What we both do with our private lives now is a matter for ourselves, isn't it? I have moved on and I am so happy with my life at the moment. I just want to get everything finally sorted financially so we can put it all behind us." I almost believed myself, I sounded so convincing.

"Right so, shall we get started?" Gary said forlornly. "After we order of course. Would you like a coffee and a slice of cheesecake – that was always your favourite."

I smiled with a lot of painful effort – the last thing I needed was him being all nice to me. "Not really, thanks. I'll just have a cappuccino – I'm trying to get back in shape after the baby."

After we ordered, he opened a plain manila folder that he had been fingering since I had sat down.

"OK, I've jotted down some figures, costed the move into the apartment and the valuation I had done recently. It's all there, and I figure you are owed something in the region of fifteen thousand euro."

I couldn't believe what I was hearing. I had expected well in excess of thirty thousand when I factored in how much the apartment had appreciated since the time we had bought it over a year earlier. But I tried to remain calm, because all of this was going to be scanned and assessed by my solicitor anyway.

I spotted something down the page. Gary had deducted the cost of my wedding-present sports car from the money, plus any out-of-pocket expenses he had for the wedding. I saw the cost of the flowers for our mothers on the list (divided by two of course) and all the furniture in the apartment that we had bought together had been depreciated before being listed.

I was furious. "Why have you deducted the wedding present from the money we put into the apartment? One has absolutely nothing to do with the other. The car was a gift to me from you."

"Based on the premise that we were going to spend the rest of our lives together," he retorted testily.

"And who's fucking fault is that?" I hissed as quietly as I could without frightening the other diners.

"You know, Jessie said you'd be just like this –" Gary began.

"What would she know? She's only twenty," I sneered.

"She knows how to turn me on anyhow, unlike some" Gary replied nastily.

"Trust you never to lift your expectations above your trousers," I snapped, rising, snatching the folder. I could see I needed to take the evidence with me.

I tossed him a fiver. "Here, you obviously need the money more than I do, and any further dealings regarding this will be through my solicitor. Don't ever call me again."

With that I stormed off.

As I got into the vivid yellow car Gary had bought me and was now trying to charge me for, I burst into hot, angry tears.

After sitting there for a full five minutes in that car park, tears cascading down my made-up face, it finally dawned on me that Gary was never the man I had envisioned him to be and I had been grieving the man I wanted Gary to become, not the man Gary actually *was*. I realised I had averted a lifetime of married misery just like Pamela Warren had endured with Gary Senior only to be tossed aside in the end anyhow.

It was as if a mist had cleared from in front of my eyes. I wasn't going to waste another minute grieving for what never had been in the first place. Gary was what he appeared to be, a two-timing cheat who lied constantly and only ever considered himself. I was well rid of him – Jessie could have him. Suddenly I even felt a little bit sorry for her.

At last I was finally free and it was time to move on.

I sped off home, deciding on a whim en route to call into Gary Warren Motors to see Gary Senior. I couldn't stand this yellow monstrosity of a car reminding me every day of that horrible day I had received it – my wedding day – and now this horrible day when he tried to charge me for it.

I marched smartly into Warren Motors. I must have felt a little bit mad to acquire this bravery all of a sudden.

The receptionist, Jane, who knew me, looked stunned as she saw me approach.

"Gary Senior, please, Jane, and don't bother to tell me he's in a meeting because I know he's not and it's a matter of urgency."

"Certainly," Jane replied meekly and fled into Gary Senior's office.

Gary Senior emerged a moment later, looking pink with embarrassment and buttoning up his suit hurriedly. "Geri, it's so nice to see you." He kissed my cheek somewhat awkwardly.

"Gary, I need to talk to you in private. It's urgent and rather delicate."

He took me into his black, sleek office.

"I'll come straight to the point. I'm not sure how much you know but Gary Junior has offered me only fifteen grand for my share of the apartment and decided to deduct the cost of the sports car too. And other items like the flowers for my mother on the wedding day. It's all in this folder. Now, I think you'll agree that is outrageous. The apartment has appreciated a lot more than that over the past year and I need a lot more money if I am to move on and provide for my baby. I am not asking for a handout, just what I am due, and I also want to trade in the sports car – it's got too many bad memories for me to keep it any longer."

Gary Senior looked shocked. "Oh, Geri, I can't believe he would do such a thing! I gave him a huge discount on that motor! How much did he deduct as a matter of interest?"

I told him and his eyes widened some more before his forehead furrowed and the vein in his temple started to show.

"Well, Geri, I will have something to say to him when he gets back. And don't you worry – there will be a lot more than fifteen thousand as your share. I don't know where I went wrong with that boy of mine. I know I haven't been the best example of a father, but I never left his mother short of money."

I had to bite my lip in order to stop myself blurting out that it was comments like those that made him exactly the kind of failed father that he was. But it was beyond me now and I wanted him on my side. He would have to sort Gary's character out himself.

"Right, give me a few days to sort the old finances out, but in the meantime we can fix you up with a new motor. Now, come out into the yard and let's see if we can sort you out a car more suitable for a young mother."

I smiled brightly for the first time that day.

As he led me outside into the courtyard, he enquired about Charlie. "So how is the little fella? Is he doing OK? It's a real shame that he's not my grandson – I really would have loved him to have been, Geri, and Gary would too. He was really excited at the prospect of becoming a dad."

I sniffed at that comment. "Funny that, Gary, because he insisted on turning the nursery into a gym room and told me in no uncertain terms that we had to wait five years before we even thought of having one!"

Gary Senior laughed. "But you had other ideas, eh? You're a clever girl and you would have been really good for him in the long run, if only the idiot had realised it. Still, it can't be helped now. All I can do is to be as fair as I can to you and make Gary do the same. Right so, seen anything you like?"

Twenty minutes later I was driving away in a nearly new silver Yaris, with a promise of a realistic financial settlement in a few weeks' time.

Gary Senior held me tightly as I left, but in a father-in-law type of way, and I really did feel he had a lot of regrets. Suddenly I felt stronger than I had done in a very long time.

I was on a roll – and it was time for the ceremonial burning.

After I got home, kissed Charlie profusely and waited until everyone *oohed* and *aahed* over my new flash car, I finally asked my mother the sixty-five-million-dollar question.

"OK, mother, where is it? Where is the dress? I know you've kept it somewhere and I also want the wedding album"

My mum blanched visibly. "Are you sure, love? Are you really sure you are up to it? What's happened to you today? You went out of here like Minnie Mouse and you have come back like Wonder Woman."

I laughed at the notion of me actually fitting into Wonder Woman's scanty tights.

"No, Mum, I'm not Wonder Woman, just a woman who has discovered she has been fooling herself for years. Today is the day I take my life back and to do that I need to destroy the last remnants of anything to do with Gary Warren and that includes my wedding dress and any photos with his ugly mug in it. Now excuse me, I need to go out to the shed and get the paraffin – we're gonna have ourselves a bonfire!"

Mum fetched my stained wedding dress from whatever secret hidey-hole she had stored it in. I don't know why she ever kept it, like some grisly reminder of her worst nightmare. I tried not to wince as I spied the intricate beading and the swathes of tulle and organza. It had been such a dream dress. Then I reminded myself it had all been a fake fantasy and was never based in any reality. I had fooled myself long enough – now wasn't the time to get sentimental. I took the heavily embossed wedding album that had arrived when I had been on my singular honeymoon in Australia and I had never even laid eyes on. I flicked quickly through the pages of glossy pictures of that idiot girl and laughed hollowly. What a fool! I would never be that stupid again – ever.

Sandy arrived with all the teddies and various cuddly toys that Gary had bought me over the years.

"May as well go the whole hog," she smiled and squeezed my shoulder affectionately.

I blinked away tears and smiled brightly as I put all of my past into Dad's leaf-burning barrel and poured the paraffin oil over it. I then lit a match and watched it all burn away.

"It's done," I said simply as I came back indoors as the flames died down. "Now let's have a cup of tea."

I would never again look back.

It was time to go forward.

It was time for me to discover who Geri Murphy really was.

Chapter 38

Time moved on. I threw myself into the design aspect of the business and Clodagh cosseted and cajoled me into acquiring some sort of business head. It wasn't easy, as we were sewing sweatshop style in our tiny little garage, while Mum and Sandy and I all took turns to mind Charlie. It couldn't continue, but we had to get the order for Marina Carson and the Naked boutiques out and we had to get it out on time so our good name would become known and a reputable history established. Also, Clodagh reasoned, when the money Gary Senior promised had arrived, we could take the business plan to the bank with some money behind us and then could rent proper premises and hire good staff and get better sewing machines. I began to believe in myself that I could actually do this. A little bit of Clodagh's fearless self-belief began to rub off and I knew if I gave it one hundred per cent I could make a success of my life and be proud of myself for me and what I had achieved, not for being just an accessory on someone else's arm, which had been the sum of my earlier ambition.

The fine work of hand-sewing sequins on was time-consuming and exhausting, and soon I was seeing sequins and thread in my sleep, so Clodagh raised all the prices on the hand-sewn items because they were so labour-intensive. I baulked at some of the prices, which seemed a bit steep, but, as Clodagh said, if you don't put a value on yourself how do you expect anyone else to?

The word was that Marina was very excited and that she definitely wanted to showcase several of the tops with her range on the upcoming summer fashion segment on *The Afternoon Show* so we were very excited at the prospect. It kept me going at times at night when I got scared and began to think I had taken on more than I could deal with. But I had something to prove too, to the likes of Gary and Connor. I was going to be a success despite what had happened to me, and the thought of going out to RTÉ with my little creations and people all over the country seeing them would mean I had really arrived. Already people in Spain were walking around in my little vest tops and that was terrific enough, but to think of my creations hanging in the rarefied air of a Naked boutique was mind-boggling. I had already signed up for a design course in the autumn so I could hone my skills and keep diversifying, as Clodagh kept drumming into my head. It was new and all-consuming and I knew I had a lot to learn. But with the help of my family and close friends I would be fine – I realised how lucky I was to have such people in my life and I would do anything not to let them down. My self-esteem at last began to climb out of the bottomless pit it had fallen into and I began to have a feeling of hope and excitement – something that had been sadly missing for quite a while.

Then out of the blue one day Gary Senior called.

"I have something for you, Geri," he said, beaming, as I ushered him into our hallway.

It struck me right then that he had never made it into our front room that my father had specifically decorated for the high and mighty Warrens. How different everything had been back then – then we had collectively felt so inferior to the moneyed Warrens and now, well, now they seemed kind of pitiful.

"Do you want a cup of tea?" I asked, hoping he would say no.

"Not really, thanks anyway, Geri. I just wanted to give you this in person. I'm sure you've already guessed that it's your settlement. I had some sharp words with that boy of mine, then we had another, let's say, more fruitful discussion and another valuation done, this time a proper one. Plus I've put a little extra in there myself. Money isn't any problem to me and, well, I feel our family treated you shamefully – and you need to be compensated for that. I suppose I feel it's partially my fault because I raised him and he is the man I made him be."

I sat silently, fingering the brown envelope he had passed me. It meant a lot to hear him say that, even before I opened the envelope, but when I did open it, it meant even more. I couldn't believe what I was seeing – it was a cheque for fifty thousand euro – more money than I had ever seen or envisaged in my life.

I looked at Gary Warren Senior.

He was grinning widely from ear to ear. "It's nice to know I can still surprise people," he said at last. "Now don't even say it's too much or you can't accept it, because you can and you will: you've earned it. But I will ask you for one thing in return ..."

"Name it," I replied, delirious with my handsome cheque.

"I'd like to see your baby, just once."

I fleetingly wondered if somewhere deep inside him he thought that maybe there was a chance Charlie was his grandchild.

"No problem – come and see him in the nursery.He is just having his morning nap."

I took him upstairs to the bright lemon room where Charlie was sleeping among bunny rabbits and teddy bears in his cot.

Gary Senior gazed at my son, taking in the dark brown curls and the sallow skin. Charlie stirred and opened one amber-brown eye – right on cue.

Gary touched my son's little finger. "He's a beauty and no mistake. This is what it's all about. It seems a shame that my son never realised it until it was too late. He's just like you, Geri – the baby, I mean, isn't he?"

"He really isn't Gary's, you know," I said softly, in case there was any doubt.

"I know – I always did. I suppose I just kind of hoped, you know? There's no harm in dreaming. Right so, I'll be off now, Geri. Thanks for letting me see your son – he's a little beauty – good luck with him."

As I led him back downstairs I felt a bit sorry for Gary Senior. He seemed to have it all on the outside but yet deep down he had very little. I realised that Gary must be a real worry to his parents and they would have preferred if he had settled down into marriage to me and had children, so I understood Gary Senior's bribery in getting Gary to buy the apartment with me. He hoped he could buy a future with grandchildren and happy families and it hadn't worked. But I finally believed that his heart was in the right place and he had made Gary treat me fairly, so I would always be grateful for that.

After he drove away I raced into the garage to show my team the huge cheque that would change my business forever.

"That's great, Geri," said my mum, trying to sew sequins on while listening to me.

"But it's no more than you deserve." Time hadn't tempered her distaste for the Warrens.

"Too right," agreed Sandy. "So, what are you going to do with it?"

"I'm going to invest it in the business, get you both real machines and a premises where we've got some space, but tonight I am going to go out and have a great night – that's if Mum will baby-sit!" Her quick nod told me she would. She was probably amazed that I had actually suggested a night out. I had been living like a Trappist monk for the past age and I'm sure she fretted that I would never go out again. I just hadn't been ready. Despite Amy, Adam, Clodagh and Sandy all insisting they needed me vitally on their nights out, I had steadfastly refused. Now, I felt somehow released and lighter than I had been since well before my ill-fated wedding day.

"Right," I went on, "I'm going to round up the troops. Are you free tonight, Sandy?"

"Yeah, Chris is working the nightshift again in the garage. Honestly, I can't wait until he gets a proper job and we can have a social life again. We're like ships passing in the night and never have any time for each other."

Mum rolled her eyes heavenwards to indicate that they seemed to have plenty of time for each other. Sandy's bedroom was next to our parents' and they had relented and allowed Chris to share a bed with her when he arrived back from Oz with a huge rock of an engagement ring. The fact that Sandy had at last roped in a nice and likeable fellow motivated them to overcome their scruples. I knew Mum wasn't happy about the situation, but she, unlike Dad, had been painfully aware of Sandy's sordid past and was relieved that she was now focusing on one man.

Things had certainly changed in the Murphy household. Mum and Dad actually spent time together for a start. They went out for meals and to see plays and Mum actually smiled more and cleaned a bit less. They were both head over heels in love with Charlie and he had indeed given them both a new lease on life. We seemed to be more of a family than we had been in the past and even poor old Chris got roped into trips down to the local GAA pitch to watch the team get hammered in the driving rain. I felt that when Sandy and I moved on, Mum and Dad would be OK.

"Don't worry, Sandy," I said now. "Chris will get a 'proper' job, as you put it, sooner than you think. In the meantime the garage job pays well and every cent will count when you get round to looking for a place of your own."

"I guess," my sister sighed.

"Rents are so expensive, to say nothing of mortgages. Even with this huge cheque I still couldn't afford a place of my own for Charlie and me. That's why I'm putting all of this into the business. I need to make a success of that first. A house will come later."

"Yeah," laughed Sandy, pulling a sequinned top against her chest and sashaying down the narrow space between the sewing machines. "When your creations make it onto the Paris fashion shows, you'll be able to afford a huge place up beside Bono."

I smiled and told her "as if" and hurried inside on the premise that I was going to call Clodagh with the good news. But I went inside to the hallway and sat on the stairs, looking at the telephone. That mention of Bono's place brought me instantly back to Connor's place and that night we had made Charlie. I missed Connor and I would dearly love to just ring him and tell him how wonderfully perfect his son was, how much like him he was getting with his dark amber eyes, winning smile and sunny disposition. All it would take was one phone call – one phone call that might just destroy his marriage. I couldn't forget how histrionic April had been the last time I had telephoned. How could I destroy her marriage like someone else had totalled mine? I just couldn't do it.

So I sat on the stairs and had a little cry, partially for Charlie and partially for myself.

Then I took a deep breath and called Clodagh and all my other friends. I needed a big hooley to celebrate my good fortune and they were the very ones to help me do it.

♥ ♥ ♥

That night we all met up in Break for the Border for a few drinks. I was in an ebullient mood after my big windfall, as was Clodagh, but Adam and Amy were uncharacteristically silent and sat poles apart from every one else and, more noticeably, each other. After I got the round in and we had all had a couple of drinks, I persuaded Amy to come to the loo with me so I could find out what the hell was going on and I felt I already knew what it was. I reckoned that Adam had made a pass and Amy had refused, hence the arctic air between them.

Amy was still a little bit low after her less than victorious return from Glasgow. I knew also that the family she had missed so much while away were now grating on her nerves and she needed to fly the coop but wasn't having any luck getting a permanent job and temp work wasn't quite enough to get an apartment with.

"Right, Missy, spill the beans. You've a face on you like Anne Robinson on *The Weakest Link*. What's the drill between you and 'Andsome Adam?"

Amy turned a bright pink. "I really would rather not say, Geri, if that's OK with you."

I was perplexed. Amy wasn't in the habit of hiding things from me. "Amy, whatever it is, it can't be that bad that you can't tell a girl that was forsaken on her wedding day and puked all over her wedding dress. Nothing is as bad as that, is it?"

She nodded in agreement. "It is Adam. I think I

fancy him, no, more than fancy him. I care about him and I think he may feel the same." She looked at me furtively for a reaction.

I smiled. "Amy, that is what I've been hoping for! I care about Adam but we are never going to be anything more than friends. I know I snogged him endlessly in Spain, but a lot has happened since then, and if anything were to develop between us, it would have by now."

Amy breathed out hard, relief spreading across her pink face. "Oh, thank God! I had a horrible feeling I was going to hurt you and it was going to be history repeating itself. I never told you this before, but the reason I always hated Gary so much was because just after you got together with him he told me that he fancied me rotten. I have carried that for years and I could never tell you, because you'd have hated me for it and I knew you cared for him so much that he'd have wheedled out of it and you and I would have fallen out."

I stood at the mirror mascara-replenishing and tried to absorb the information that had just emerged. I couldn't believe it. Just when I thought there were no more surprises from Gary Warren there was another stab at my shaky self-esteem. The bastard had cracked on to my best friend after he and I got together. But I understood why Amy hadn't told me – no one ever could. I always thought I knew best where Gary was concerned and time had proved how wrong I was. I wasn't going to let this late admission spoil our relationship.

I gave Amy a hug. "It doesn't matter any more, Amy. You always tried to warn me about the sly creep. In future I will listen. So, back to Adam – you can go out there and stop ignoring him and start enjoying yourself."

I gave her my biggest, brightest smile and we went back outside, but deep down I was feeling a little bit sorry for myself. Adam was always my back-up guy – or had been for the past six months. My self-esteem had been so shattered after Gary he had slowly brought me back to feeling remotely human and somewhat attractive again. It was totally selfish but I had got used to being adored from afar by Adam, and the fact that he had finally moved on to the infinitely more attractive and sexier Amy had come as a bit of a blow. But I had to be the bigger person in this. Both of them deserved happiness and who was I to stop them? I cared about them both enough to pretend to be happy for them. Yet it seemed there really was a future of me and Clodagh being the old crones of the gang, set for our middle years in the *Ballroom of Romance* and those dreaded singles dinner-dates that true saddos went to. But now wasn't the time for a pity party – so I went back out to my gathering of friends and sister and partied like it was going out of style. But when I eventually got home drunk and emotional to my little bed, I let myself cry a few tears of indulgent sadness, for what might have been and what never would be.

Chapter 39

Adam called me the next morning.

"So, I gather Amy told you the news. God, that sounds awful, like we were having a secret seedy affair. We weren't, Geri, in fact we haven't so much as kissed, but I've been feeling drawn to her since she got back and, well, you made your feelings plain, and I would like to date her, if it's OK with you."

I sighed, half from self-pity, half from my raging hangover. Hangovers and babies who woke at four a.m. for a feed just didn't mix.

"Adam, it's fine, really it is. I'm a selfish cow and I confess I'm feeling just a little bit sorry for myself. I got used to you being my fake boyfriend whenever we bumped into Connor and having you for movie nights – and I wanted to have you playing football with Charlie when he's old enough. I had you lined up as a sort of surrogate dad, if you will. Stupid, I know – but you've been such a big part of my life for the past few months, when I needed someone most. It's been really great, and you do mean a lot to me even though I never show it. I just want us always to stay close."

Adam laughed a little. "Geri, you silly, lovely creature! Of course I will still be in your life for all those things – except as a fake boyfriend, of course. But, Geri, Charlie doesn't need a surrogate dad, does he? You know he has a real dad who I am sure would love to be in his life. You need to think about what you're doing. It's all very well, being noble and wanting to protect Connor's marriage, but is he really going to thank you for it later? Why don't you let him decided that for himself? Connor and April's marriage is a matter for them to sort out and anyway some day you're going to have to explain it to someone else: you're going to have to tell Charlie eventually. What do you think his take will be on it all? I mean, look what it's done to me."

I wasn't sure what to say. My head hurt. I couldn't make a decision in my right mind never mind an addled one. But Adam was always big on honesty and always talked bluntly. He made a lot of sense, but today I just didn't want to hear it.

"You're right," I replied after a small silence. "I have a lot of thinking to do, but not today, OK? My feeble mind can't think of anything beyond making it to lunchtime without throwing up – it's not very mummy-like, is it?"

"No, it's not. But you are still young and you do have a life of your own too. We were delighted that you came out last night – we were beginning to think that you were going into an enclosed order. We had fun, didn't we?"

"Fun? Yeah, I seem to remember fun vaguely. It was something I enjoyed between 1997 and 1998 when my arse fit into a size twelve. Only kidding. Yes, Adam, it was fun, but never let me have shots when I am out again. I feel like death! Look, I'm going back to bed for an hour – I can't face those bloody sequins, not yet anyhow."

"Ooh, the joys of being your own boss! I've been on the job since seven – have you heard that jackhammer behind me?"

"Oh, is that what that is? I thought that was inside my head. When are you seeing Amy?"

Adam sounded a bit flustered. "Oh, nothing has been sorted yet, but I thought we might do something at the weekend."

"Oh." Cast aside already. (I really was dramatic – I still blame my hormones.)

"Right so, I better get back to work. Don't forget, I'm still taking you and Charlie out on Sunday. We can take him to Malahide Castle for a picnic, if it's fine."

Yeah and Amy can come too, I thought

ungraciously, then quashed that horrible jealous thought. I needed to seriously get a grip. I was happy for both of my great friends to find happiness together, wasn't I? Deep down I knew I was. It was just that the more of our gang that found eternal joy, the more I was reminded of the fact that I had failed miserably at finding that elusive happiness myself and I felt such a failure.

"That'll be great. I'll talk to you soon," I said in a bright airline-stewardess voice that would convince Adam that I wasn't the poisonous crone that I knew I was.

"OK," he replied happily and rang off.

I had never felt so low in all my life.

I went back to bed and cried until there were no more tears. It seemed that this getting over Gary and moving on was going to be a little more difficult than I had earlier imagined.

Chapter 40

By the time that spring had emerged into a watery summer, I had come to respect the pairing of Adam and Amy and realised that the fact they were a couple didn't detract from our friendship but enhanced it. I got over my jealousy and Adam made sure he spent time with me too.

But then Clodagh met someone. He was called Myles. Amy used to quip that he was well named – she'd run miles if he ever came near her – until I reminded her of her own dubious choices in the past. Myles was a Hairy Scientist and a bit of a muppet really, but he wasn't married and seemed very enamoured of Clodagh, so we were all happy for her – except me since we were supposed to be old and embittered hags together. However, I wouldn't have wanted him myself, but it did seem like everyone had taken their lovey-dovey pills except me and I became a bit reclusive again. In fact, they had to force me out socially with a pliers at times. I just felt like a giant gooseberry among all the couples and even if we did go out on our own, the girls always seemed to end up talking about their men or getting secret text messages all night long while my mobile remained resolutely silent.

So I threw myself into the business even more.

I had been avoiding the bank because of my lifelong fear as earlier mentioned and the now extra pressure of having Gary Senior's new woman, Carole Boland, as my bank manager made it even more difficult to face. I wasn't sure what kind of reception she would give me. I had never given her much attention after Gary Senior had left Pamela. Even though I detested Pamela, I still had felt a bit of kinship with her when Carole had smugly taken her man and wrecked her life. I wondered if Carole would take the issue of herself being seated at the back of the church and reception at our wedding and use it to reject my business plan.

I explained all this to Clodagh as we got ready for our interview.

"Nonsense," Clodagh retorted smartly. "Carole Boland is above all a businesswoman and I have been over your business plan to make sure it's watertight. You have the predicted sales for the next year and we've even factored in depreciation of assets. It's very thorough. Plus, don't forget that you also have fifty thousand other good reasons. No bank is going to pass that kind of money up. Anyhow, she's bound to know Gary Senior gave you the money and was probably even expecting you months ago. Come on, Geri, we'll be late!"

I sped there on two wheels in the Yaris from the nerves. Poor Clodagh was so shaken by the time she got out she had to have a cigarette before we went in.

We were ushered into Carole's sleek domain, her corner office. She looked as glossy as ever – obviously her life with Gary Senior hadn't diminished her in any way, unlike poor Pamela. My own mother had always joked that the second wife always got all the cream while the first wife got all the pain and the stretch-marks. It certainly seemed so with Carole.

"Right, Geri, it's about time. I have been expecting you for quite a while. Now, if we can get down to the nitty-gritty, you show me your business plan, give me a brief outline of the prospectus and we can discuss any pitfalls. Obviously I can't give you a final answer today, but I have been made aware already of your promising clothing designs by Clodagh so it sounds like a valid concept at least from the outside. You are lucky to have such a cool-headed and practical businesswoman in your corner, especially as she has been through all this before, and I am sure she has informed you how difficult it can be going out on your own. But I am all for encouraging young women to become entrepreneurs, so I will do all I can to help you. And having money to back you always helps."

I breathed a huge sigh of relief. Clodagh had been right, after all. Carole was a consummate businesswoman and it seemed she was enthusiastic about my business idea.

After Clodagh and I gave her the spiel, Clodagh filling in my obvious gaps in knowledge about cash flow and predicted forecasts, Carole began to tell me that I should not invest all of the fifty thousand into the business.

"I'd advise you to keep twenty thousand back for yourself. If the business fails, which by the way a lot do in the first four years, you will have something left at least for a deposit on a house for yourself and the baby. You can make up the shortfall as part of the business loan and pay it off that way. We can find a way of investing it so you can't have easy access if you're worried about it whittling away."

I had never thought of it like that before. I had no intention of my business failing, but investing all the money was risky. Carole obviously had my best interests at heart.

The thought of having some money to eventually get me on the elusive property ladder was terrific. I began to get excited about carving out, not only a career, but also in time a place of my own for Charlie and me. It was getting difficult staying at home with my parents. Much as I loved them, I was feeling a bit hemmed in to tell the truth.

I still think no matter how old you are, even if you have grey hair and a Zimmer frame, your parents still think you're twelve and act accordingly. Mum and Dad were still very much Mum and Dad and, especially where Charlie was concerned, I felt dim and careless. There was always a warm vest or hat missing that brought disapproving looks, and wind that I couldn't get up but my mother could, or Dad could get him off to sleep whereas I couldn't. I felt inept and twelve and always would, I supposed, in their house. Until I upped sticks and went it alone, I couldn't become a real bona fide parent.

So the hope of my own place lifted my spirits higher than they had been in a long time. All I had to do was get the business up and running and eventually the rest would follow.

We left the bank in buoyant spirits and went for a celebratory cappuccino before Clodagh had to rush back to her own empire.

"I think you'll be OK, you know," Clodagh smiled as we sat down. "There shouldn't be any hitches if that meeting was anything to go by. Are you excited? I know I was when I got my first bank loan. To see my jewellery being bought by people and admired by strangers was the biggest kick I ever got. Much better than anything else. I guess that's why I never worried about romance too much – it was all-encompassing, my business. But now it's nice to have someone to share it with. I still get a buzz from seeing my creations sell but I'm ready now to have a whole life, not just a career."

I smiled. "I suppose I'm at the stage you were years ago, Clodagh. I've got Charlie and now this fantastic opportunity. I don't need anything more."

Clodagh looked at me incredulously. "Who are you trying to convince, me or yourself? Geri, we all know you're still suffering over Gary and that you feel like two left feet because we all have someone. But it's time to get back out there and mingle, even if only to have some fun. You are still young and need to have a life of your own. Gary wasn't the end of your romantic life – he was just a chapter, a chapter that has been closed."

I stared out the window at the passers-by. They all seemed to be in a hurry to get to their busy lives. "Yeah, I know, but it's easier said than done, Clodagh. I still feel really raw and exposed. I can't just get back out there and start dating again. I don't trust my judgement any more – look where it got me the last time!"

Clodagh stirred her frothy coffee. "Yes but, Geri, you have learned heaps from that experience. You are not the teenager you were when you met Gary and, believe you me, your radar will be very well tuned in now to any losers that might cross your path. But you mustn't let Gary win here – he seems to be getting on nicely with his life, doesn't he? Living well and being successful is the best revenge. You've done part of it with your plan for a career, but that's not the be-all and the end-all, Geri, believe me, I know. That's how I ended up with a married creep like Karl – it was sheer loneliness. Don't let fear take hold of you and make you let opportunities pass you by."

"OK, OK, I give up, Clodagh! Really, you should be in interrogation, you've missed your vocation. I will promise to try harder and I will endeavour to get out more. It's just not going to be easy, that's all."

Clodagh smiled widely, her mission accomplished.

But she hadn't a clue how I felt inside. I just felt like the hole that was a mile wide inside my soul could never be filled, no matter how many nightclubs I went to or how many guys I kissed. Nothing was going to fill the dark sadness that enveloped me and I feared nothing ever would. That's why I focused on my career and my infant son, because I was afraid of what would happen if I sat still for long enough and let myself think.

I didn't ever think I could trust or love again, and even the embers of affection I felt for Connor couldn't be trusted or relied upon, so I damped them down and kept going. If I kept going for long enough I might just get away from this sinking feeling of dread that I carried around with me since that awful day in June when my dreams had died forever.

Chapter 41

A few days later the call came through that the bank was enthusiastic about my business plan and would sanction the loan. I was over the moon and also a little bit terrified.

"Be careful what you wish for," Aunty Pearl used to say and now I knew what she meant. I was plagued by "what ifs?". What if the business dramatically failed and I lost everything? Or even worse, what if it succeeded and I hated it? What if everyone detested my designs and I was a laughing stock? I had sleepless nights over that one.

It seemed such a tall order, to find cheap premises to rent and new industrial sewing machines and yet still churn out the orders without delay for Marina and the Naked boutiques. I couldn't keep relying on Clodagh for much longer either – I was sure she had let her own business suffer recently by spending so much time with me. It worried me too that she had balls of steel and a razor-sharp business brain, while I wasn't sure I had what it took.

So I just pretended. I decided if I bought a sensible pinstriped work suit and a couple of sharp shirts I could pretend I was a consummate professional businesswoman.

It worked for about five minutes until Sandy cracked up laughing and Charlie threw up all over my corporate business jacket. I then decided to be honest and tell everyone how terrified I felt about it all and rally the troops for help.

So I called on my dad, Clodagh and Adam and we trawled through various industrial estates sussing out properties. Most were a sad and sorry lot within our price range, even with Adam's offer to redecorate and carry out cosmetic changes for cost price. I had almost given up hope when we found a small premises out at the airport. It had good access to the M50 and the city and all the major routes. It wasn't too far from Sutton either. We all agreed it was the best we had seen, so we agreed the lease terms with the real estate agents, and I began to get butterflies that my dream was actually becoming a reality.

I took Mum, Sandy and Adam with me when we went to buy the sewing machines. It was an unfortunate fact but a true one that manufacturers took men more seriously than women and tended to give men a better deal, so we pretended that Adam was the buyer. He managed to bargain the burly salesman down and get us a fantastic deal on four of the latest Singer machines with all the whistles and bells. It looked like we were in business. The most difficult part however would be sourcing wonderful fabrics that no one else had, and that meant trips to London and Paris in the future and (fantasy time!) even further afield to the Far East. But in the meantime, with the budget we had, I would have to stay close to home.

But it looked like we were in business.

At last.

♥ ♥ ♥

Next item on the programme, Amy asked me to go apartment hunting with her and also asked me to move in with her.

I was surprised to say the least.

"Me? Are you insane? You do realise I come fully stocked with a pooey, windy male who isn't even capable of making any conversation?"

Amy laughed heartily. "He sounds like half the men I've dated, Geri! Look, I love Charlie to death, and you know I have always wanted you and me to share a place together. If we pooled our money we could get a much nicer and bigger place, maybe even with a sea view. Come on, Geri, I know you want to get out of your oldies' place as much as I do out of mine."

I pondered the idea more seriously. It would be great to have my own place and be a proper mum to Charlie, but how would my single friend cope with a baby twenty-four-seven – and how would it fit in with her love life with Adam?

"Actually, Amy, I'm wondering why you wouldn't want to move in with Adam instead of me. I would have thought you would ask him first."

Amy blushed. "Don't get this wrong, Geri. I am very fond of Adam and I really enjoy his company and I hope it'll last, but I won't live with another guy again after being with Stuart, not until after I marry – if I ever do. I'll never put all my eggs in one basket ever again. I'm going to live my life and enjoy it and that means being with you, my closest friend. Besides, if ever Adam and I decided to elope, you'd have a fabulous apartment to yourself! Come on, at least come and view with me!"

I began to think how wise my friend had become and how independent. I should take a leaf from her new book and decide to take life a day at a time, vowing to enjoy it and to appreciate friends and loved ones instead on focusing on what was missing. I should focus on what I had.

"Right," I smiled, "but I bags a bedroom with an en suite if possible – you can have the sea view, OK?"

"Deal!" she grinned and that was that.

My life was about to take another turn.

The apartment hunting wasn't nearly as traumatic

as I had envisaged. Compared to the lengthy search for an industrial premises it was surprisingly easy. With all the new developments in the city, it wasn't as hard now as Amy had had it when she'd first moved out of home. Back then, finding something decent was nigh on impossible.

The second place we looked at, on the coast road near Clontarf Castle, was a development that was about twenty years old but had held its appeal. One thing about older apartments was their larger bedrooms and living space and this one didn't disappoint. There was a nice airy bedroom to the rear of the building that had an en suite – it suited me because it was quieter and darker so it would be perfect for Charlie, whereas Amy had the desired sea view from the second bedroom, which had a small patio also. The lounge was long and bright and it had French doors overlooking the Irish Sea and, although it needed a fresh coat of paint and the kitchen was a bit dated, we both fell in love with the place.

"This is it!" Amy said breathlessly and I readily agreed.

"Let's pressure the agent to let us paint the place," I said, "and we'll tell him we have a deal. We can rope in your lovely boyfriend to help paint it a nice fresh neutral colour and we can buy some nice throws and things and it'll look more like home."

"Yes!" exclaimed Amy in delight. She must have feared I'd back out when it actually came to it. "We are going to be so happy here!"

I really believed we would be too. It would be so nice to move into my own place at last.

I pushed memories of my excitement of eighteen months ago at moving into Kinsealy Cloisters from my mind and avoided looking across the hooked coastline to the south side of the city where Connor was somewhere going about his life. Nothing was going to spoil this moment, not the ghosts of the past or the fears for the future. I was going to be like the new Amy – I was going to take it a day at a time and enjoy my life as best I could.

♥ ♥ ♥

Two weeks later we moved in.

I didn't think it would be as traumatic moving from my parent's house as it turned out to be. There were long silences and floods of tears – anyone would think someone had died. I suppose I should have expected it. Mum and Dad had become fiercely attached to little Charlie by now. He had lit up the whole Murphy household with his presence and I could understand how upset they were – but I had half-imagined they would be glad to have some peace and quiet back.

But it hadn't happened quite like that. Dad even offered to build an attic extension if I would stay on, which in turn had me in tears. I felt so guilty about taking their only grandchild away from them. But deep down I knew I was doing the right thing for all of us. It was time for me to go it alone as a parent and live my own life, independent of everyone.

After the lengthy and tearful goodbyes and promises of frequent visits (I wouldn't mind but we'd both be seeing them the following day for Ditzy work), Adam took Charlie and me and all our worldly goods (which were mostly Charlie's – I'd never realised tiny babies travelled so heavy) a few miles down the road to Clontarf. I felt thrilled and also a bit teary myself. It was exciting and a bit scary too. Now it was all down to me, the midnight crying that had me almost rushing to the hospital even though it was only a bit of wind, the settling Charlie down at night, a task my father loved so much – it was going to be different and a challenge, but I was ready, at least I thought I was.

Amy was already there when I arrived and had things pretty much finished when I got there. She and Adam had a surprise for me – Adam had got the keys early from the landlord and had spent the entire week painting the place so that Charlie and I could arrive to a freshly painted home without the strong smells. The apartment looked great even with the myriad boxes still in the lounge. Adam had painted it a warm cream with an accent wall of dark caramel. While the kitchen was a pale primrose, my room had been painted a soft pale apple, which Amy knew to be my favourite colour. Adam set about reconstructing Charlie's cot and Sandy and Chris arrived to help unpack everything else. Everyone took turns looking after Charlie while we got the place looking a little more lived-in – it was an exhausting process and by the time we got most of it finished we were all ravenous.

"I think it's time to discover the local Chinese," said Adam, putting the last picture up on the wall.

"You said it," enthused Chris, whose legendary appetite was never far from his mind.

"Right so, we'll take your orders and go get a nice meal. I think I spotted Amy bring in her wine collection so we can have a drink. Maybe Chris and me will buy a few cans and we can have a little housewarming party. What do you think, Charlie?"

Charlie gurgled happily in reply – he loved Adam.

"Charlie agrees," Sandy said.

"I knew this was a good idea," I said to Amy and Sandy when the boys left. I felt light-hearted and young again for the first time since Charlie was born. All the earlier doubts and guilt just fell away. I knew I had made the right decision and my life had taken a turn for the better.

"You bet," replied Sandy, lifting Charlie up and giving him a cuddle. "It's nice at Mum and Dad's but Chris and I can't wait to get a place of our own. It's just so right that you moved out now, Geri – at our age we need our own space. You just can't be who you really are when you still have Mum sugaring your cornflakes!"

We all laughed. How Sandy had changed over the past year and a bit! She had really grown and matured so much, and I genuinely loved her company these days.

When the lads got back with the steaming brown bags of curry, we all sat around the coffee table in the lounge and ate with gusto and had a few glasses of wine. Charlie sat in his bouncer contentedly rattling his toy and I realised I was genuinely happier than I had been in a very long time, surrounded by friends and just enjoying myself.

"I think we should have a toast," Amy said, raising her glass.

We all followed and looked at her expectantly.

"We all know that it's been a tough year all round, except for Sandy and Chris, of course, who appear to have had their best yet, but I would like to raise a toast to Geri and myself and new beginnings."

"New beginnings!" we all chorused and clinked our glasses.

A new beginning is exactly what it was.

Brilliant.

Chapter 42

Mum threw a spanner in the works.

"When are you going to have this poor child christened? I know you're busy, what with your new business and moving into your lovely apartment and all, but I think your child's soul is something that should be very high on your list of priorities. And after all, we don't want the poor child racing up the church steps before his first Holy Communion to get himself baptised, do you?"

I put on the kettle in Mum's kitchen. I had barely got in the door when she landed this bombshell on me.

"Jeez, Mum, you don't mince your words, do you? Please give us a chance to have a coffee before you bombard me with all of this. Of course I want to get Charlie christened, it's important for me too, but I have been so busy lately and I probably have put it on the long finger. But I promise I will contact Father Moynalty this evening and sort out a date for as soon as we can organise it."

She wasn't really placated. Mum was on a mission and Joanne Murphy determined was a sight to behold.

"Yes, well, make sure you do. There's a celebration to be organised as well, you know. We have to book a hotel or we could even have it here if I get enough notice. I just don't want you dragging your feet because there's no father present."

"Not at all!" I insisted brightly. "Of course that's not the reason. Don't worry, Mum, I will sort it out. Now chill and have your cuppa – we've a lot of work on today."

Mum frowned. "That's another thing, Geri. When you get sorted in the factory and the business properly set up, I don't want to come and work for you. I'm just too old to do that close-up work all day – all those sequins, my eyes just aren't up to it any more. But don't worry, I have a great idea, one which will suit us all a lot better."

I wasn't sure I wanted to hear her plan. I would sorely miss my mother's considerable talent – she was the real expert and a perfectionist in sewing. I wasn't sure I could pull this off without her.

"Go on," I said nervously.

"Well, I know you are considering placing Charlie

in a crèche, but I think it would be better for all of us if I looked after him here. It would be wonderful having him here every day and you could make it a professional arrangement by paying me. Obviously I would be a lot cheaper than an impersonal crèche, where he could catch God knows what, and being with family is always better. Your dad would be chuffed too."

I considered the idea. Losing her in the business was going to be difficult, but gaining her as the principal carer for my most precious possession, Charlie, was fantastic.

I had lain awake at night worrying about what to do when we moved onto a more business-like footing – Charlie couldn't be carted around a factory all day long. So this was a great solution.

"It's a great idea, Mum. There's no one better to look after my son than you, but I will sorely miss you in the business – my skill isn't anywhere near as good as yours."

Mum smiled and placed her careworn hand over mine. "It comes with time, Geri love, and anyhow, you'll get better when you don't have to rely on me so much. Besides, there are lots of good machinists out there. You could hire a few women going back to work after being at home looking after their families – they'll be no strangers to hard work. If it helps I can interview them with you."

And so it was settled. At least Charlie's care was.

The christening was another matter however. Deep down I knew I was hesitating about having Charlie baptised. I didn't want to face the fact that he was going to be fatherless.

I cast my mind back to the hospital when I had to sign the birth certificate form and I had come to the space where it said "*Father*". I wanted to write "*Connor Osborne*" but of course I couldn't without his consent. I felt so desolate after I had completed that form.

Adam was right. Connor needed to be told before Charlie was very much older. Now here I was all these months later and nothing had been resolved. I was just like a bloody ostrich with my head resolutely stuck in the sand, and now my son's christening was looming and I hadn't done anything about Connor.

But I couldn't just pick up the phone and call him, could I?

"Hey, Connor, are you free a week on Friday? There's the small matter of your son, who you know nothing about, getting baptised. Why did I wait almost five months to tell you and why did I lie in the first place? Well, I am a bloody idiot, I suppose, and there is also the other matter of your lovely wife who hates my guts and doesn't want a child to clutter up her perfect existence."

Somehow I doubted the conversation would just flow with bonhomie from there. The truth was, the longer it went on the harder it got. I was a coward and

I was getting more yellow by the minute.

I confessed to Amy later on that night, when Charlie was tucked up into his cot, oblivious that he was a fatherless infant condemned to a life of deprivation because his mother was a bloody wuss.

Amy tucked her feet up under her and flicked back her long blonde tresses – she always did this when she was about to give sound advice or else listen carefully.

"Would it be so difficult to let Connor know, Geri? Perhaps you could write him a carefully worded letter explaining everything. You can't be sure that April won't answer again if you call his home or his mobile and it'll make things worse. Or maybe you could go see him at work."

My look of shock told her that just wasn't an option.

"The longer this goes on the more angry and hurt Connor will be," she went on. "You know he's a good person and would make a great dad – and you need to give him the choice to be one or not. Besides, it's not all about you – it's about Charlie."

That comment hit me like a ton of bricks.

I was just trying not to damage Connor's marriage and hurt April, wasn't I? Or was I trying to keep Charlie all to myself, so afraid was I to feel again, to let anybody in? Because if I did let anyone in they could hurt me again, and I couldn't bear that.

I needed to examine my true motives.

Amy was telling the truth: it wasn't all about me.

"You're right, Amy, I will have to do something. But first I'm going to telephone Father Moynalty and try and organise the christening date at least, because you'll be organising my funeral instead of a christening if I front up to my mum's tomorrow without giving her at least a tentative date. She reckons Charlie's soul is in deepest peril if I don't get him dunked into the holy water soon."

And so we sat companionably on the tired old sofa that we had covered with luxury chenille throws, drinking a glass of Chardonnay while I telephoned my old parish priest to organise my son's special day. Whether his father was going to be part of it still remained an issue, but I decided to take it one thing at a time. At least my head was now above the sand and I knew I had to act soon, for Charlie's sake, if nothing else.

Father Moynalty was surprisingly upbeat. Even though he hadn't seen me since that fateful day, he was fully aware my marriage had been a goner before it had even begun, as I had tearfully telephoned him afterwards to get advice on an annulment.

He had been shocked to discover my groom had been having an affair with another of his pre-marriage guidance pupils. It was *very vexing*, as he put it ("I knew that young lady was far too immature for marriage"). He was still working on the annulment – there had been no news in months. Annulment was a long process, I was told – but a christening wasn't, it seemed. Father Moynalty never asked about the father of my son, but I knew my mother had been in close contact with him since the wedding so he pretty much knew all of my secrets, I guessed.

"I'm sure we'll have no problem fitting little …"

"Charlie," I offered

"*Charlie* in. Two to three weeks, if that's alright?"

"Make it three weeks to give us enough time to organise. That'll be great, Father, thanks so much. You've been very good. No word, I guess, from Rome about the annulment?"

"Afraid not, my dear, the wheels turn very slowly in such matters. But just as soon as I hear anything I will let you know. Bye, bye, dear."

I could almost hear the unspoken, "Hope to see you at Mass on Sunday!" But he at least had the grace not to push it.

"We're in!" I informed Amy, relieved at least for my mother's sake.

"You're halfway there," she replied. "But before you get busy on the invitations you know what must happen."

"I know," I replied.

Time was running out.

And I needed to face it.

♥ ♥ ♥

The following day was bright and sunny. Glimpses of a nice, warm summer day were emerging and the bright sunlight glinted through my wooden blinds in the bedroom. I felt strangely light, like things were going to sort themselves out somehow. I think finally setting a date for Charlie's christening had made a difference – I wasn't trying to hide it any more, the fact that Charlie wasn't from a regular family. If the worst came to the worst and I didn't gather enough courage to tell Connor, or even if I did and he decided not to be a part of Charlie's life, it was still going to be OK. Charlie would be well loved by all those around him and that would carry us through. He wouldn't be the first little boy who came from a single-parent family and he wouldn't be the last.

I decided to get up early and go for a walk with my baby out in the fresh air, along the coast road. I seriously needed to attend to my jelly belly, which had fallen into an even more blancmange-like state in the past five months when it should have been improving. My penchant for late-night curries and the odd glass of vino, not to mention taking the car all of five yards to the corner shop, hadn't done my post-partum figure any favours. I was looking decidedly portly and now that I had a date for the christening, it gave me the impetus to do something about it. I had three weeks to lose half a stone and look somewhat better.

So I leapt out of bed, donned my crimson tracksuit

– the only one that didn't make me look like the Michelin man – and dressed a gurgling Charlie, who had already breakfasted, so we could have a nice brisk walk together. The fresh air would do the baby good and would make me walk faster too.

The sun was quite hot even this early and it looked like we were in for a scorcher. Within ten minutes I was roasting hot and too self-conscious to remove my track top.

I didn't want to force the poor early-morning motorists to endure my jiggly belly and wobbly bum, so I soldiered on, getting hotter by the minute – joggers and cyclists flying by, taut and sleek in their well-fitting lycra. I could see this was going to be more difficult than I thought. I was hopelessly unfit and doughy. How come I hadn't noticed I was so far removed from anything near normal? I suppose when you give birth to an eight-pound baby and instantly lose a couple of stone overnight, you begin to think you're doing pretty well. I hadn't been out a lot since Charlie was born either and, when I had, I had carefully donned my stretch-to-any-size bootleg black trousers that hid a multitude of sins. But there was very little hiding going on in an overstuffed crimson tracksuit in July. I needed to sort myself out. I desperately wanted to be a Yummy Mummy and make Charlie proud of me. I had been so wrapped up in my troubles I hadn't focused on how to make myself feel better – and that was by taking control of my fitness and weight. If I was going to be a famous designer too, I needed to look good so I could fit into all the skimpy tops and shorts and wear my own creations.

So I decided, as I puffed and panted my way back to the apartment, that I was going to go out and pound the pavement every day with Charlie in tow, morning and evening, until I shifted the flab. It would help me lift my mood too – all those feel-good hormones floating around your body, or so the story went.

I looked like a big red tomato by the time I got back home. I was sure I saw Amy stifle a giggle as she spotted my big red butt bend over and lift Charlie from his pram. My face was having a competition with my outfit for crimsonness and my face was winning.

"Good on you, Geri, that's a great idea – exercise for you and baby. How was it?"

I frowned and desperately tried to gather breath. "You know how it was by the colour of my big red face, Amy. It was bloody hard. I am so unfit! I've decided that I really need to walk the coast road twice a day to get in shape for Charlie's christening. I just hadn't realised how woolly legged I'd become since becoming this little fellow's mum. I plan on making myself something really special for the baptism and it's not going to be in a size 16 – I plan to be a size 14 by then."

Amy smiled indulgently. "Good for you, Geri. But don't be too hard on yourself. And now you've decided to go on a health kick, well, I'll join you. I've been feeling lethargic lately, not eating right, so I'll get in a load of salads and fruit and we can get healthy together. Since I've been dating Adam it's been take-away food almost every night, not to mention way too much wine. My system needs a rest."

I smiled at my slim, clear-skinned friend, who needed no help whatsoever in the health or beauty department and who was obviously only doing this to help me regain my former curves.

"Thanks, Amy, that'll be great. Look, I need a shower – can you look after his nibs for ten minutes? I can't go to work this sweaty."

"Sure," Amy grinned as she took Charlie and cooed over him. "We're going to ring Uncle Adam, aren't we, Charlie, and we're going to tell him not to bring around any more of that nasty chocolate. He's just going to have to get used to a couple of health freaks for the next few weeks, isn't he?"

She went to her room to make the call while I headed gratefully to the shower, thrilled about the possibility of ten whole minutes of hot water alone. Oh, how glamorous my life had become, when a hot shower became the highlight of the day!

Chapter 43

As the week went on I began to feel a bit better. I still got hot and sweaty as I had on the first day, but I chucked in the tracksuit (too cruel to my lumps and bumps) in favour of some light linen Capri pants that I had made myself and teamed them with a cream light cheesecloth top. I stayed cooler and didn't look like a Deliberate Dieter – more like a new mum just out for a casual stroll. At least I didn't feel as exhausted as I had on that first day, and after a few days of sunshine and salad, I was getting a bit of a tan and already feeling lighter.

On Friday I set off as usual, although I noticed some dark, foreboding clouds drifting in from the Irish Sea. You really can never depend on the weather in Ireland – even going to the beach necessitates bikini, wellingtons and Aran jumpers, just in case.

I grabbed Charlie's plastic cover for his pram and a jumper for me and set off. I needed to be back for eight to get a headstart on the day and it was already seven fifteen.

Charlie gurgled happily and chewed on his fingers as we got outside. He loved our morning sessions and I really felt we bonded more, as when I wasn't hopelessly out of breath I talked to him and pointed out small dogs and boats, both of which he appeared fascinated with.

Not too far from the apartment the sky darkened considerably and I could feel the dampness in the air and knew that it was going to rain at any moment.

Damn! I thought as I put Charlie's cover on. I am going to have to dash back and cut my walk short, and I'm not even going to make it.

I turned the pram around quickly and careered straight into a man who was bent down attaching a leash to his dog.

"Oh, I'm sorry, I didn't see you!" I yelled, then a moment later froze.

He stood up. All six foot two of him. The dog leapt up onto his thighs and he ruffled the woolly mop.

"Geri?" he said.

"Connor?"

I couldn't quite believe it. He was wearing a long trench coat and his hair had grown a little bit – he looked more like Colin Firth than Antonio Banderas – but the amber eyes were burning into me like hot coals.

"What are you doing here?" I asked inanely, conscious that it was patently obvious that he was walking his bloody dog.

"Sarge happens to like the north side," he replied, smiling at his little joke. He looked down at Charlie's pram. "And who might this little fellow be?"

Before I could even consider an insufficient reply, the heavens opened and the heavy rain teemed forth liberally. In seconds we were drenched as we ran towards my apartment, which was two hundred metres away.

"Quick! Follow me!" I shouted as I ran, drenched to the core, my light cheesecloth top sticking to me like a second skin.

Connor followed and Sarge barked excitedly as he scampered after the speeding pram.

We reached the canopy of trees outside the apartment complex in minutes but by then it was far too late. We were both completely wet like we had fallen into a bath fully clothed and Sarge completed the saturation by shaking himself dry all over us.

Only Charlie was snug and dry under his waterproof blanket, laughing happily. Mum didn't usually travel so fast and being male he had thoroughly enjoyed the speedy run.

"Look, Connor, come upstairs and dry off, you're soaked," I offered and pushed the door inwards.

It seemed like an age until the lift arrived. I prayed while Connor attached Sarge's leash to the staircase inside the door and bade him to stay.

Please God, don't let him ask me yet if he is Charlie's father! I implored skywards – although I knew the likeness was quite striking and one long look into Charlie's amber eyes would tell Connor straight away what he needed to know. I just needed a minute to gather my thoughts.

As we got into the lift and I spotted the mirror, my heart sank. My hair was stuck to my head like rats' tails, my top, flattering while dry, now clung to all my abundant curves exposing all my extra baby flab. I was mortified. I tried to lift my hair from my face and undo some of the damage, but it was useless so I gave up. I looked a complete mess, so I just had to accept it.

"It is so good to see you," Connor said quietly.

"You too," I replied, and in the mirror I could see a crimson tide spreading from my neck upwards.

Connor got down suddenly on his hunkers. "He's mine, isn't he?" he then said in a strangled voice as he took Charlie's hand gently between his own thumb and index finger.

I just started to cry, softly at first but then harder. I just couldn't speak. The tears flowed from my eyes, and my throat hurt so much with emotion I just couldn't say anything. All the pain and confusion of the past year erupted. I felt lots of things: shame, relief, sadness and, most strange of all, pride.

The lift opened and we got out mechanically.

"I am so sorry," I said, when I could trust my voice to make a sound. We stood at my hall door just looking at each other.

"It's OK, Geri. Everything's OK. I'm not mad. I can imagine how difficult it all has been for you. Now, aren't you going to let me in? We'll catch our deaths if we stay in these wet clothes."

Once inside, my heart thudding, I lifted Charlie from his cocoon of warmth and placed him into Connor's arms.

"This is your son, Connor. I have tried every day to pluck up the courage to tell you that you were his father, but every day my courage deserted me. I did call a few days after I found out he was yours, but April answered and she made it clear I was ruining your marriage, so I decided to wait. Then as time went on it became more and more difficult."

"April answered? How . . . ?" He broke off and then said, "Geri, there's a lot I must explain to you. April and I are well and truly over – permanently. But please," he grinned, shivering, "can I have a towel to dry off?"

I grinned back. "The main bathroom is through there. Have a hot shower if you like. I'll take Charlie in with me to the en suite and I'll have a shower too."

He grinned again – that megawatt grin that lit up his handsome face. "OK, meet you back here in ten minutes, all towelled up."

As I showered I felt I was having a surreal

moment. Was Connor actually only fifty feet away having a shower in Amy's bathroom? And how come the moment I had been dreading for so long wasn't half as bad as I thought it might be?

I used my best shampoo and shower gel, and then as speedily as possible blow-dried my hair and donned my most flattering long, floaty skirt, one I had designed, and a long white cotton pullover. By the time Charlie and I made it back to the open-plan living room, Connor had the coffee pot steaming and two mugs waiting and all he had on was a barely fitting lilac towel of Amy's. I tried not to stare lustfully but failed miserably.

"Hope you don't mind me rooting through your kitchen, Geri, but I thought we'd need this to warm us up."

I gently placed Charlie in his favourite little bouncer by the sofa and took the mug of coffee gratefully. I knew Connor would want to look at him for as long as he could and get to know his son.

Yet we needed to talk too. I had a lot of fences to mend.

"OK," I began, taking a deep breath and a sip of hot coffee. "I found out I was pregnant just after I came back from my so-called honeymoon. I stopped taking the pill before the wedding and I wasn't sure if it was you or Gary who was the father. It came as a real shock, as I was still reeling from what happened. Then before I could tell you anything about it, you told me you and April had got back together – and, well, I wasn't about to spill the beans and spoil it all for you, was I? That's why I stopped working for you. I just needed to get away from everything and I didn't think that me fronting up there every day to work pregnant would be the best idea – considering you had just got back with your wife and you couldn't agree on having children. I didn't find out until after Charlie was born that Gary couldn't be the father. Then as soon as I got home from the hospital I called your mobile, but April answered and she screamed at me down the phone and told me I was to stay away from her husband or else. She was so upset I guessed that you had told her about us, and I didn't want to ruin your marriage like someone else had ruined mine."

"But April and I had already split up by then," said Connor. "I had left her months earlier. Things went badly wrong almost as soon as we got back together. I was a fool to think it ever could work. She fooled me into thinking she still loved me, but it soon became clear that things hadn't worked out for her in London and she just wanted a meal-ticket back in Ireland. But I was a prize idiot and believed she really wanted me back for myself. Then she began to stay out all night again and we were rowing constantly. And meanwhile I was slowly realising that I was truly in love with you. In the end I told her, told her our marriage was dead in the water and that I was in love with you. So she flung me out that very moment, just in what I was dressed in. I didn't even have my mobile – that's how she had it. Then she had the locks changed and I had to go stay with Seán. It took months to get her to leave – that must have been when you phoned."

I was aghast at how the reality was so different from what I had imagined. I'd been such a fool!

"But what about the day," Connor went on, "the day in the restaurant when you were with Adam? You led me to believe he was your boyfriend and the father of the baby, and then when I phoned you to ask if it was possible that I was –"

"*In the picture?*" I interrupted acidly, still irked by that glib phone call. "It sounded so much like you were just making a courtesy call – being Mr Nice Guy, all so jolly and friendly –"

"*Courtesy call!* Geri, if you had any idea how wrong you are! I was so thrilled at the idea, the mere possibility that I could be the father! Geri, I have wanted you so much since that very night we made this little boy. I guess I've been a little bit in love with you for years, but I never dreamt we could ever be together, what with your enormous devotion to Gary. And even after that all went so disastrously wrong and we eventually got together, I still didn't think I had a chance – you were so destroyed by it all, by what Gary had done to you."

"I was, Connor. I think I was a little crazy with grief all those months. I couldn't think straight. I'm still not thinking straight."

"But you should have been clear about one thing, Geri," he said with a smile. "About Charlie. You know how much I have always wanted children – how could you think I wouldn't want this gorgeous baby?"

Suddenly all kinds of hidden thoughts and feelings rose to the surface and ambushed me.

I hadn't really doubted it – I knew deep down he would want the baby, our son. But I was afraid – it seemed such an enormous thing to thrust into someone's life. How could I estimate the after-effects of such an announcement? It would be like pitching a bomb into his marriage and waiting to see if anything remained when the dust settled. And I was afraid, afraid I would be hurt – that he would deny it, tell me I was lying, that he would run a mile, that he would beg me never to approach him, never to tell Charlie . . . and so on and so on. Connor wasn't the kind of man who would do any of these things but . . . I was afraid.

And I was jealous. I had to admit it, in my heart I was jealous. *And* spiteful. He had deserted me for the Awful April. So why should I bless him and *her* with my precious son? They had each other; I had only Charlie.

And deep down I feared he might hijack Charlie, that he might insist on sharing him fifty fifty – fifty for me, fifty for him and April. That April would become my Charlie's second mummy, one who would have the money to spoil him in a way I couldn't afford. That Charlie might end up preferring his cool dad and yummy second mum to stodgy old me.

The list of horrific possibilities went on and on.

The truth was, I hadn't been sure until the moment I bumped into Connor if I wanted to share my Charlie. But I was sure now.

I took a deep breath. Connor was looking at me, silently waiting for my response, a concerned expression on his face. Now was not the time to go into all the whys and wherefores. That would be for later.

"I know – I was silly," I said, keeping it light. "My pride was hurt, I suppose, that you were so happy with April and you had forgotten about me. I knew you'd love a baby, but I thought it was going to happen with her, Miss Perfect Knickers, not me!"

Connor smiled. "April is not a patch on you, Geri Murphy, and never has been. Do you realise I have been walking myself sore for hours all this week along that coast road in a vain attempt to meet you – eh, accidentally? If poor Sarge could speak he would report me to the RSPCA – I have the paws walked off of him! Adam called me on Monday and told me that you wanted to talk to me but were reluctant to ring because you were afraid to break up my marriage. When I told him that it was ancient history, he told me to go see you at once. He never actually said that

Charlie was mine, but I guessed by his hinting about the serious issues we needed to discuss. So I said OK but later got cold feet. After all, I remembered how you had shut me up in that 'in the picture' conversation. Maybe Adam was all wrong and you didn't want to tell me at all? Then I remembered he said that you had taken up walking, and I got the idea that if I bumped into you 'accidentally' I could play it by ear – leave it up to you to tell me or not. But at the very least, I would be able to re-establish our friendship and start up a little relationship with my son. So Sarge and me have been tramping up and down the coast road twice a day ever since. I was giving up hope of ever bumping into you until today. As soon as I saw Charlie any notion of playing it by ear or pretending I didn't know flew out of my head. I couldn't quite believe we made something so beautiful. I just regret not being there to help you from the start, Geri. It must have been really difficult."

I tried to remember. It had been difficult at the time but now it was all a fuzzy blur, and I was feeling something fizzing up that I hadn't felt for quite some time.

And after a moment I realised it was happiness.

Happiness. Who'd have thought!

"It wasn't so bad," I said. "I had all the family to help. I was just so glad that Charlie belonged to you. I knew you'd make a wonderful father, if only I hadn't been so afraid to tell you." Tears welled up again in my eyes but I managed to hold them back. "I have something to show you, Connor." I went to the mantelpiece and fetched the piece of paper that was there propped up behind the clock for the past week.

I handed him Charlie's birth certificate.

He handled it reverently by the edges and I saw tears well up in his eyes as he saw the blank space where his name should be.

"Charlie and I would be delighted if you agreed to put your name on that. I suppose it can be done even now . . . eh, a late entry like?"

"I'd be honoured, Geri," he said on a little sob.

"Good. And there's just one more thing. Wait . . ." I went over, unbuckled Charlie from his baby bouncer and carried him over to where Connor was sitting. "Charlie has something else to say." Charlie grinned at Connor on cue. "He wants to invite you to his christening in three weeks' time. Do you accept?"

Connor looked up at me, pure joy written all over his face. "Yes, I accept," he said. He stood up and took Charlie into his arms while tears spilled freely from his eyes and flowed down his face. "Hello, little fella, I'm your daddy."

And there it was.

A family.

Chapter 44

And that should have been my happy ending. But it wasn't. Not quite.

We spent the rest of the day together. I called my mother and told her I wasn't going to be coming in to work that day, that something important had cropped up and Charlie and I would be staying home.

Mum was a bit suspicious, but I just assured her the "something important" was something good and that I would reveal all later.

I hung up, smiling, on her protests.

So after the storm clouds cleared away, the rain abated and Charlie had another feed then promptly fell asleep. I only then remembered poor Sarge still "staying" downstairs so I told Connor to bring him up. But Connor said no, he would take him home as he needed to feed him and come back alone so we could have a long talk without any distractions. That in itself was a bit of a revelation – Sarge was always top of Connor's priority list when he wasn't in work and he seldom left him behind unless it was a matter of importance.

While Connor was gone I phoned Amy and told her that her little plan with Adam to reunite me with Connor had worked.

"I'll kill you both!" I berated her laughingly. "Tell that fecking Adam he has a lot to answer for! But I love him for it too," I added, and I did. Adam knew better than I did what was best for me and had the bravery to act upon it.

So I told her all about the "coincidental" meeting on the seafront.

Amy was thrilled. "Oh, Geri! I can't believe it. This is great news. I'll make sure we'll give you plenty of time alone this evening. I'll get Adam to collect me from work and we'll go out for a pizza – you won't see us before nine, that'll give you plenty of time –"

"Steady on," I remonstrated. "We are only *talking,* you know – I don't even know where we're going from here! I'm not sure I'm even ready for one of those nasty things – a *relationship*. Once burned, twice shy!"

"I know, Geri," Amy said, her voice rising. "But are you going to let Gary Warren rule the rest of your life and have a say in every decision you make? Because that is giving him *way* too much power. Connor is about as far removed from Gary Warren as you could ever get. Please promise me you'll give Connor a decent chance. He deserves that much. Don't make him pay for Gary's sins and more importantly don't make Charlie pay either."

As I put down the phone I knew Amy was speaking the truth. The real truth a dear friend would speak whether you wanted them to or not.

By the time Connor had come back, I felt relaxed and happy. My baby's father was in his life and that alone was quite an achievement. Whatever happened between Connor and me, I was sure we would be excellent parents to our son.

When he knocked on the door, I opened it to find him clutching the biggest bouquet of white roses I had ever seen.

"Oh, they're beautiful!" I gasped. "But what are they for?"

"What are they *for*?" Connor grinned and pulled a huge blue teddy from behind his back. "Well, I never got a chance to do this five months ago, so I'm making up for lost time."

I busied myself with the flowers and made a fresh pot of coffee, while Connor paced the living-room floor in a state of high excitement.

I tried to imagine what it must be like for him, to have all of this information thrust upon him. I was amazed that he wasn't more angry about me keeping Charlie from him. I felt the urge to say sorry.

"Come and have some coffee," I said and he joined me at the coffee table.

"What's the matter?" he asked then, noticing my tense expression.

"Connor," I began gingerly, "I'm so sorry about those five lost months. I should have made certain that you knew about Charlie. I guess I was a selfish cow. But I felt so afraid. I had no idea how you would react. I *thought* you'd be pleased – the 'in the picture' phone call was a fair indication of that if I was honest with myself – and I know I reacted badly and stupidly to that but –"

"Geri, stop! Wait!" He laid a hand on my arm and then regarded me seriously, silent, a fleet of expressions crossing his face. He seemed to be trying to choose his words carefully. "There's no need to say sorry. I'm not even wondering why you didn't tell me. I'd be an insensitive idiot if I couldn't imagine how difficult it all has been for you. And today I found out that I am father to the most incredible little person I have ever seen. How could I be angry? I've no room in my heart or mind for anger. You have given me so much. And I don't deserve it. I was an idiot to allow myself to be fooled by April *twice* and I was an idiot to let you slip through my fingers. So I know about loss and I know about trust, but we both have a wonderful opportunity here to start something new, something different and clean – something that involves all three of us: you, Charlie and me. Let's forget about the past – well, at least the bad parts."

My heart melted at those marmalade eyes pleading with me. "OK, you've won me over. Let's give it a go –

one day at a time, mind. But," and I grinned, "don't expect me to move in with you or become a dependent limpet, Connor – I'm a hardnosed businesswoman now, I'll have you know, and I need my space."

Connor smiled and touched my cheek gently. "I promise I will never hurt you, Geri. You have my word."

I looked at him straight in the eye. "I don't know if you can keep a promise like that, Connor. People change and fall out of love and there are no guarantees in life. The best we can do is to give it our best effort and to always put our son first." I smiled then to take the sting out of my words.

Connor looked at me sadly. "What the hell did he do to you, Geri?"

I took his hand from my cheek and kissed his palm. "He made me grow up."

Then he kissed me. Slowly and gently at first until my head swam, then more urgently and passionately – suddenly there was nothing else that mattered but that moment and I was lost in another world until a familiar cry awoke me from my passion: it was Charlie, letting us know with his powerful lungs that he was very much awake.

"Just in time!" I joked as I went to fetch our son. Connor padded down the hallway behind me to my bedroom where Charlie was gurgling away in his cot, his chubby little arms swiping away at his yellow duck mobile.

"It's his job to interrupt us, you know," I informed Connor as I lifted Charlie up and passed him to his father.

"So there won't be another one?" Connor asked, smiling.

"Yeah, something like that," I grinned. "Speaking of which, I had forgotten how well you kissed, Connor Osborne. It could certainly turn a girl's head."

Connor smiled and kissed Charlie affectionately at the base of his neck. "There's plenty more where that came from! But now, how about I take you and Charlie out to lunch and then we can break the news to my brother Seán – I am just bursting to tell someone in my family the great news."

It felt a little strange, the fact that a whole other side to Charlie's lineage existed, including a myriad cousins and aunts and uncles, not to mention grandparents – a large and loving family for him to be a part of. Seán wasn't a problem but I wondered how Connor's parents would accept my suddenly emerging after all this time. They only knew me as his PA!

Connor took us up the Dublin Mountains to Johnny Fox's pub. The clouds had cleared and it was now warm and sunny; the fresh mountain air was balm to us all and did Charlie a world of good. He lazily snoozed in the sunshine while we feasted on homemade soda bread and smoked salmon salad and cool glasses of Guinness. I truly began to relax again in Connor's company – the earlier awkwardness had evaporated. I had become a prickly porcupine over the past few months. Now I began to uncurl my fists, which these days were always furled into tight little knots.

I loved the way Connor laughed loud and melodiously, showing those white even teeth, and the way his eyes crinkled when he was telling a funny story, or the way he always watched me when he thought I wasn't looking. He had always laughed at my stupid jokes and valued my opinion, he had always respected me over the years and I knew that afternoon as we laughed and joked in the sunshine on that mountain that Connor would make me happy, if I let him.

Three weeks later we baptised Charlie at Sutton Chapel, on a bright and sunny August afternoon. It was a wonderful day and everyone was there, including Connor's large and boisterous family that my mum and dad took to their hearts immediately. Valerie and Gerard Osborne were well-to-do professionals, so down-to-earth and vibrant they were instantly likeable. Gerard was a retired architect and Valerie had been head midwife at Holles Street Hospital for over twenty years, while also raising six children. They were silver haired and in their sixties, but so full of life they put my younger parents to shame.

I needn't have worried that they would find it difficult to accept me. I was relieved to find they took me under their wing immediately and promptly fell in love with the adorable Charlie.

Dad had booked the Marine Hotel in Sutton for the do, which had grown by gargantuan proportions by the time we factored in the huge Osborne clan, including the five of Connor's siblings, associated partners and lots and lots of children. Everyone I loved came along and I have to admit there were several scary moments when I was horribly reminded of the last big event we gathered for, but Connor was there to hold my hand through the panic that emerged every now and then and of course Amy and Adam were perfect godparents – after all, they had got us back together. I promised Sandy and Chris that they would be our choice for next godparents and Sandy said yes on one condition – that the names of any future children were less Royal Windsor sounding. Of course I agreed. Clodagh arrived with the muppet – sorry, Myles – and looked radiantly happy.

We had selected a running buffet of roast beef and crisp salads and we'd booked the large room with the huge French doors overlooking the Irish Sea. It was warm and sunny and the sunlight streamed through as the children ran out to the palm-tree-laden garden.

"It's a lovely spread, Geri," Valerie said warmly as she took her latest grandson from me for a cuddle. Charlie was looking resplendent in his cream linen christening outfit and, as Mum said, wasn't far from crawling up the aisle to his own baptism. "Your parents have done you proud."

I looked over at my father who was in deep football conversation with Chris and Connor. He looked really relaxed and happy. Mum was talking animatedly to Seán and his wife Mary, while their brood ran around their feet.

"Thanks, Valerie – I know they have. It was a terrible year for them last year and I'm just relieved to see them happier."

"From what Connor has told me, you had quite a traumatic year yourself, Geri. I'm sorry for bringing up the subject, but he told us what happened to you on your wedding day. It must be very difficult for you to trust again."

I looked into her eyes and saw only kindness – she didn't have any ulterior motive.

"It was awful, to be honest, Valerie, and that is why I didn't want to interfere between Connor and April. I didn't want to ruin their marriage, like mine was spoiled. That's why I waited – I hope you understand."

She patted Charlie's back softly as he lay in the crook of her shoulder. "Don't worry yourself about it, Geri. We're just glad to see our son happy at last. He was miserable since he and April reunited – we all wondered how it had happened – they were never a good match. And then he told me about you – it was when you quit your job after you came back from Australia. He came in for his usual Monday lunch and then cried all over my lasagne. It was then he admitted to me that he was in love with you and not April and he was worried he had ruined everything. He'd kill me if he knew I was even talking to you about this but I felt I had to tell you, Geri. I know, if I were you, I'd need to know for sure he was sincere, and I can tell you that he is. We are all delighted to be here with your family and share in Charlie's special day, but we're so happy for Connor too."

I looked over at Connor and he did look happy. He looked relaxed and content and that in turn made me feel safe and wanted.

I smiled at Valerie, her concern touching me. "I think we're going to be just fine, Valerie, just fine."

Her features softened and she smiled at me in return. "I'm very glad to hear that. You never do get past worrying about children, you know, no matter how old they are!"

"Oh dear," I replied. "I thought it would get a bit easier when they reached twenty-one. I think I'll be grey by the time Charlie is two."

Valerie patted her silvery bun. "I earned every hair of this! But it is so worth it, you know. I've had so much joy from all of mine as well as a few heartaches along the way. You want so much for them but in the end you just really want them to be happy. And I think you can do that for my son – you can help him to be happy."

I certainly hoped so.

I wound my way through the crowd, all happily up dancing to the DJ who was belting out all the best hits from the seventies and the eighties. I checked that everyone had enough to drink and that the champagne was still flowing and then I took Charlie outside for a bit of air. The sun was hot and warm despite the stiff breeze and I sat on the grass with Charlie, ignoring my delicate Chinese silk sarong-skirt. Charlie took to the grass with gusto.

Suddenly Connor was flopping down beside me. "Geri, are you OK? I noticed you come outside and I was wondering if you were alright?"

I looked out at the seldom-blue sea, which was blue and glittery today. "I'm thankful, Connor, more than anything – grateful that we have got as far as here at all. I wouldn't have given us a hope a few months ago. I just feel really lucky that I have arrived at this place, to have Charlie and now you, and all of my family and now yours. My business is taking off and I feel incredibly lucky – I'm just a little bit afraid to breathe in case it all falls apart. I suppose my belief in things is a little shaken and I don't know when it's going to come back."

I looked at him questioningly.

Connor regarded me seriously and then looked out to sea himself as if searching for an answer. "There's no time limit on trust, I suppose, Geri. It takes as long as it takes. All I can say to you is that I'm not going anywhere, and one day you'll wake up to realise that we are fifty and I'm still there, growing fat and grey beside you, and you'll probably wish I would bugger off and give you a bit of peace!"

I laughed despite myself. I really had to learn to take my own advice and take life and all it had to throw at me one day at a time, one minute at a time. There were no certainties – except death and taxes, as my dad would say.

I kissed him softly on the lips and he looked up surprised.

"Right so," I said, taking his hand, "I do believe you haven't yet done your John Travolta thing – and your public is waiting. And you owe me the first slow dance officially as a couple. Aunty Maude and Aunty Bridie expect to be outraged, so I think a scene from *Dirty Dancing* should do it."

Connor laughed and leapt to his feet, scooping up a squirming Charlie.

"Right, you're on," and he whisked us indoors to our waiting guests.

Chapter 45

It's hard to believe that a whole year has passed since then.

I am still officially Mrs Gary Warren, but I do believe that any day now a nice little white envelope should arrive from the Papal Nuncio relinquishing me from that appendage.

I am still working hard to get my business up and running. It has been an expensive year, with the outlay for new sewing machines and setting up the new factory. But the order book is nice and healthy and the TV exposure on *The Afternoon Show* was a huge boost. So on paper we look good, but every cent still goes back into the business. However, we can all see at this point that Ditzy is going to make it. The very thought gives me a warm glow.

♥ ♥ ♥

I stubbornly stayed on in the apartment with Amy – even though it was getting a little more difficult for Charlie as a boisterous eighteen-month-old, who craved space.

Connor periodically tried to get me to admit that apartment living wasn't great since Charlie had become a whirlwind toddler. Yet I still resisted. And I knew it had precious little to do with Connor and everything to do with me, me and my fear of trusting again, of letting go, of letting someone in close enough to be able to hurt me. Connor was endlessly patient, but I often wondered when the patience would run out.

Everyone tried to talk to me. First Mum with her no-nonsense approach. She told me she loved Connor to bits. Didn't I know and feel it in my bones that he would never hurt me and shouldn't I move on?

Then it was Sandy. She chose the "*ye fecking eejit*" tack. i.e. "*Ye fecking eejit!* You're going to lose that guy with all the hoops and tangles you make the poor fellow go through – it's a wonder he hasn't shot through long ago."

Amy tried to jolly me along into committing myself, with endless pep talks and reasons why she knew he truly loved me.

But Clodagh never pushed me. She had managed to resist two proposals from muppet-faced Myles and cheered me on, a one-woman cheering squad, saluting my independence.

But I knew deep down it was not glorious independence but only my abject fear – I wondered sometimes what Clodagh's excuse was.

But I knew it couldn't go on. I was pushing Connor away, subtly and gently but pushing him away all the same. I wanted desperately for everything to stay exactly the same, keeping Connor at arm's length, me living this semi-single life – dedicating my life to my son and my business, but never entertaining the idea of moving into Connor's larger townhouse in Dalkey – perish the thought. Yet I still wanted him desperately. I knew I was still mixed up and caught in the rut of fear I had built for myself. A paralysing fear had gripped me and I didn't want to address it.

So it was luck, really, that I happened to bump into Gary Warren last week. I had been into town to the wholesaler's for an order of sequins and diamante and at the last minute I decided to duck into the Jervis Centre for some lunch. I was starving and was bone-tired, what with running about so much and ignoring lunch hour. I craved a decent cappuccino and a nice hot panini and today I was going to get it.

I had just sat down with my delicious and much-anticipated lunch when I spotted Gary Warren sitting a few tables away. My heart lurched at first – it was just so shocking to suddenly see him after all this time.

Now he sat mere feet away, his hair cropped extremely short, clad in a fifties-style leather jacket and jeans. He was side-on from me and was talking animatedly to a girl that I couldn't quite see, as he was blocking my view of her, but I could tell that she was holding a small baby – a girl by the plethora of pink blankets and teddies that littered the pram alongside.

I watched them for a moment. Gary seemed solicitous, fetching bottles of baby formula and stirring sugar into his partner's coffee, laughing and then holding the baby while his partner drank it. He leaned over, as I sat transfixed, to put the infant back into her hi-tech pram, and I saw that it was as I had suspected. It was Jessie, looking as long-limbed and svelte as ever, even though it was quite obvious that she had recently given birth.

It was then that Jessie spotted me and instantly bright pink flooded her face. I hadn't time to turn away and I was so taken aback by the scene I was still drawn to openly stare at the little family before me. They looked happy and complete – and I found that shocking. So after a moment I stood up, pushed back my chair and walked quickly over before I changed my mind.

"Hi, Gary, how are you?" I somehow said, acting "normally". I smiled for effect, politely acknowledging a still-blushing Jessie with a nod. Up close he looked older, more settled, late-night bags under his eyes and stubble on his chin, but he still looked handsome. Some things never changed and his movie-star looks were one of them.

His eyes lit up. "Geri! How *are* you? You're looking well – look, we've just had a baby. Here she is – this is Amelia!" He lifted the tiny mite from her pram. She must have been very new, muffled in copious blankets and matinée jackets that only newborns fit into. "Isn't she adorable? Jessie just came out of hospital a week ago – this is our first time out into town and she's a little nervous."

Jessie smiled, embarrassed. This wasn't remotely easy for her either.

Gary placed Amelia gently back down into her cocoon. "And your little fella?" he continued unabated. "He must be walking and all by now, is he? I can't wait for Amelia to get to that age. Listen, I heard you're doing really well in the rag trade? Good for you, Geri. It looks like you're really getting on with your life and I'm really happy for you, although I had a bit of a cringe-factor moment when Mum told me what you called your fashion label – Ditzy, eh? Like I used to call you. I'm so sorry, Geri. I was a real asshole then – but I've grown up a lot since. Are you still with Connor?"

I nodded mutely. Words just wouldn't form themselves. I wasn't sure if I was angry with him or them any more. I was just stunned that they had so simply moved on with their lives. Our past didn't seem to have affected Gary at all, yet it had almost destroyed me back then and, to a lesser effect, it still was ruining my life.

"She's lovely," I finally said, finding my voice, and she was, a beautiful delicate, little girl, so unlike my Charlie who had never been delicate from day one. "You must be very proud," I then said, addressing Jessie for the first time. It must have been shared motherhood or something, but I didn't even feel like scratching her eyes out. Though it could have been that she had the decency to look thoroughly ashamed and uncomfortable.

"Look, Geri," she began, "I always wanted to tell you how sorry I was about everything ..." Her voice drained away.

"That's not necessary," I replied. "Look, Gary, I'd better get back to my lunch – I have a busy day ahead. Congratulations to you both on the birth of your daughter." But I couldn't resist it. "A father at last, eh?" I added, shooting Gary a quizzical look.

His happy smile told me that he was no reluctant father – in fact, he had never seemed more real or more focused, that bored, jaded man I had been besotted with for so long.

I walked away slowly, straight past my eagerly awaited lunch and out of the entire centre. I kept walking until I got to my car and I sat in it in silence for a full fifteen minutes before I realised where I was.

All that kept running through my mind was: *What a waste! What a waste!* I had been trailing sackcloth and ashes ever since my wedding day – *all this time*. Oh, I told myself I had moved on but I hadn't really –

not moved on to the level that Gary had – and I just felt so foolish. So stupid!

Why should I hold onto my grief for another minute?

Meeting Gary had shocked me into realising that life had indeed moved on and so had he. Leaving me clinging to my fear and loathing like an old friend. It was time to let it go. I wasn't going to let it control me a minute longer.

So I fired up my little Yaris and headed for Fitzwillliam Square. I needed to get to Osborne Oswald immediately.

Connor was in his corner office, poring over his easel, the tail of his shirt sticking out slightly from the top of his trousers. He was immersed in whatever design he was working on.

I put my arms around his waist and pressed my face into his back. "Hey, you, watcha doing?"

Connor jumped. "Geri, you frightened the life out of me!" He closed the large sketchpad quickly and turned around, kissing me. "What brings you here?" he asked, surprised. My new cool, aloof persona hardly ever darkened the door of Oswald & Osborne – too *girlfriend like.*

"Oh, I've just come to take you away from all of this, for perhaps an hour if you can spare it. Something quite wonderful has just happened and I want to share it with you."

He looked at me quizzically, head to one side.

"What?"

"I'll tell you over a coffee or a pint."

"Don't tease. Give me a hint."

"OK." I paused. "The nutshell version: at last I'm ready to start living the rest of my life."

The meaning of my words slowly sank in and a smile crept across his face. "Welcome to the rest of your life, Geri," he said and he kissed me. "Speaking of which, I've got something to show you."

He looked a little nervous as he opened the large sketchpad again to reveal a huge set of architect's drawings of a fantastic house, a dream home. It had lots of gabled roofing, an attic master bedroom and oodles of living space.

At the top of the page, he had written in fancy lettering:

~Connor & Geri's Place~

I was amazed. "How long have you been working on this?"

"A very long time," he replied, eyeing his work objectively. "It's not quite ready yet, though – quite a bit of tweaking needed – and of course," he kissed me, "I shall need Madame's input. I didn't want you to see it until you were ready."

How lucky was I to have a man like this in my life?

"Is there a block of land to go with this fabulous house design?" I ventured. Connor was nothing if not thorough.

"You know me so well!" he laughed. "Come on – let

me take you out to see it."

As we drove I told him about my meeting with Gary and how something had shifted in my mind that day. He didn't say much, just reached out and took my hand and kissed it.

I was surprised as the car drew northwards across the Liffey, along the quays and then north towards Swords until we passed the airport and turned onto windy country back roads that made me feel relaxed and serene, with all the rolling hills and greenery. We eventually reached a small hamlet called Ballyroughan, halfway between Swords and Ashbourne. It was high up on a hill near a big golf course, less than ten minutes' drive from the airport and close to my business, but green and quiet and a perfect place to raise a family.

"It's here," Connor said, strolling around the long grass of the land he had bought. "We'd have to level a garden off for Charlie, of course, but there's almost an acre, so there's plenty of room."

I stood and imagined our little boy playing happily in the garden that Connor envisaged. And I could imagine it too, because at last I had decided to take the risk and open my heart completely again.

Epilogue

And so that was a week ago.

There hasn't been a bended-knee request for my hand in marriage yet and I am in no rush to go back into planning any sort of wedding.

But who knows? Connor has decided to take me off to Barcelona for a weekend (just the two of us) so it's anyone's guess. All I know is if and whenever Connor gathers the courage to propose, I am going to take a deep breath, cross my fingers and say yes.

But don't worry, dear reader, there won't ever be another wedding dress or even wedding reception. If we do wed it'll be just the three of us somewhere on a sandy sun-soaked beach in our swimwear.

I don't much care.

Why?

Because I have finally grown up and realise that it's not about the acres of satin or tulle or whether the bridesmaids look good in pink or if you have the salmon or the beef. It's about the content of your heart and whether the person you are pledging your life to looks at you with love and kindness when you least deserve it and could survive life without you but would prefer not to.

And because I've survived the worst life could throw at me, I believe that this honeymoon isn't even close to being over, not by a long shot.

THE END

Dedication

Our sons lost their beloved mother, and I my adored wife Annett, last July to cancer. Myself and our two sons, Alex and Finn, still struggle with the fact that she isn't going to walk through the door again. Every day we face a new and ever changed reality.

We are comforted by the fact that Annett was able to fulfil her ambition of writing not one but three novels, which are a constant reminder of her determination and courage.

This book is a tribute to our family, Alex, Finn, Annett and myself, which she dedicated herself to for so many happy years.

I would like to thank those family, friends and medical people who have helped and supported us over the last year and will into the future.

To those of you who bought and enjoyed her work, it gave Annett great inspiration and encouragement.

Annett, we love you and miss you, may God bless you, rest in peace.

Alex, Finn and Peter Leo Holliday.

Published by Poolbeg.com

A Life Like Yours

ANNETT HOLLIDAY

With handsome hubby Des, an impressive home in Co Meath, two beautiful daughters, a designer wardrobe and perfect figure, Kate Heathcoat has it all. No one who meets Kate could fail to envy her seemingly perfect life – least of all her neighbour Grace Kelly.

Grace is discontented with her ample figure, tiny house and hectic life. And commuting to Dublin every day to her boring job and pervy boss certainly doesn't help. To top it all, Grace has always envied her successful sister Olivia, the golden child of the family. But in fact, Olivia's life is not a bed of roses, and she has to take drastic steps to find herself.

Grace is so focused on what she doesn't have that she can't see that her best friend Dymphna Coffey would kill for a life like hers. Dymphna is a bright career girl but a walking disaster with men, and she envies Grace her husband who plainly adores her.

As each of the women's lives unfold into unforeseen challenges they discover a real bond of friendship, and realise that you should be careful what you wish for.

ISBN 1-84223-198-7

Published by Poolbeg.com

Happily Ever After

ANNETT HOLLIDAY

It's the 1970s in Dublin, and Ali O'Neill and Trisha Costello – best friends since forever – want nothing more than to dance the night away at the Grove disco. But soon both girls are falling in love for the first time, changing their lives dramatically.

As they approach their twenties, family tragedy and class snobbery threaten to overwhelm Ali, while Trisha struggles to break the mould and have fun. Desperate to escape, the best friends book their tickets and set off on an Australian adventure. But Trisha doesn't expect to have to return home suddenly, and Ali finds herself stranded thousands of miles from home with a pressing problem.

But is there a chance the girls will live happily ever after?

Sometimes you have to go halfway round the world before you realise that the best things are on your doorstep.

ISBN 1-84223-118-9

Direct to your home!

If you enjoyed this book why not visit our website:

www.poolbeg.com

and get another book delivered straight to your home or to a friend's home!

All orders are despatched within 24 hours.